ADJACENT LAND

ADJACENTLAND

RABINDRANATH MAHARAJ

Buckrider Books is an imprint of Wolsak and Wynn Publishers.

Cover design: Ingrid Paulson
Interior design: Mary Bowness
Author photograph: Vicky Maharaj
Typeset in Adobe Devanagari
Printed by Ball Media, Brantford, Canada

Buckrider Books
280 James Street North
Hamilton, ON
Canada L8R 2L3

Library and Archives Canada Cataloguing in Publication

Maharaj, Rabindranath, author
    Adjacentland / Rabindranath Maharaj.

ISBN 978-1-928088-56-1 (softcover)
    I. Title.
PS8576.A42A65 2018 C813'.54 C2018-901439-3

The publisher gratefully acknowledges the support of the Canada Council for the Arts, the Ontario Arts Council and the Government of Canada.

In memory of my parents

*We can make no distinction between the man who
eats little and sees heaven and the man
who drinks much and sees snakes.*
– Bertrand Russell

STAGE ONE

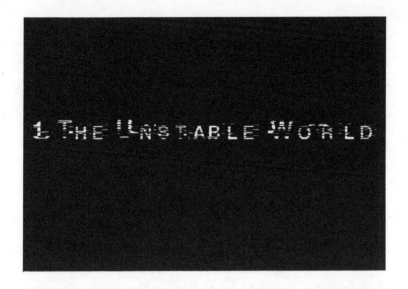

1 THE UNSTABLE WORLD

Nine days ago, I awoke with a hum in my left ear that sounded like the steady strum of a bass guitar. I must have lain still for half an hour, fearfully watching the door and the jalousie, trying to establish some familiarity with my environment, passing my fingers along the two tiny bumps at the base of my skull, wondering at my situation. My neck and limbs felt as if I had been pressed into a tiny box. When I got up, I immediately fell to the floor and it was another half an hour before I was stable enough to fully appraise my surroundings. I noticed an unevenly stained closet stocked with clothes and a sum of money in the slim drawer of an escritoire with teeth marks on the right corner. Beneath the escritoire, I discovered two wicker baskets, one with an assortment of fountain pens, well-used pencils and some sort of boomerang-shaped bamboo totem nestling in a circle of incomplete illustrations and the other stacked with spiral notebooks and hard-bound sketchbooks with oilcloth covers. Between the books were three envelopes, each stuffed with onion-skin pages.

When I first opened the envelopes, I saw that the pages were filled with scratchy charcoal drawings of men and women frozen in a moment of action or just standing with their arms folded over their muscular chests and gazing heroically at the silhouettes of devastated cities. On one of the sketches I saw the word *Adjacentland*. I cannot say if this is a real place and if, in fact, these illustrations are representative of actual cities. Nor have I been able to confirm their authenticity from the inked versions of these sketches, some of them framed, on each wall. Beneath every illustration was the same phrase: *Today is a new day but yesterday was the same day.* On one of the odder drawings situated above a locked cast-iron safe with a sturdy knuckle-shaped handle in the middle of a spiral of fingers was the declaration: *Nothing exists until we deliver our verdict.* This sketch, in watercolour, seemed out of place in that it depicted a scene that, on the surface, appeared serene and normal. A mother is holding a child in her arms. The child, a girl of around three or four, is frightened and the mother, well, her expression – and her gaze – changes from day to day. I have tried to understand what is so terrifying in the foreground but all I can see are fallen leaves that are so detailed I can count all the nested loops. Each day I have returned to the vaguely familiar patterns on the leaves before I turn to the scribbles at the bottom of the sketches. So far, I have been able to distinguish just one; this, attached to a watercolour painting of a child, her back turned, gazing at the air. At either side of the drawing, which seems to be cropped, are two pairs of feet and beneath, a scribbled line that is also cut off: *The child –*

I will add here that although there is some familiarity about the drawings and their subjects, I can feel no real connection with either. Nor, initially, with the clutch of letters I discovered hidden in a jacket hanging in the closet. They all instruct me to record my impressions and "my range of emotions" but there was one that described a relationship characterized by manipulation, bullying, jealousy and, not surprisingly, betrayal. The tenuous relationship, I worked out, was between a writer and an artist. It took a full week before I worked out the identity of the artist and that of the writer and decided to record what I have learned. This may sound desperate but a man with little to remember is forced to remember everything.

But you, my friend, already know all of this.

Are you disappointed that I am, here, referring to you? If so, you will be even more distraught to know that I have determined – from your manner of evoking accusations in an abstract and indirect way – that you are secretive and sly. Here is this sentence from one of your letters, for instance: "Once we shared the same thoughts and beliefs, complimented each other's views, made fractions whole but all of that was ripped in half. We each went our separate ways, walking away from ourselves, never looking back." In another letter torn into six pieces and scattered within the inner lining of my jacket were these cryptic instructions. "Look to the drawings. I have disguised my writing and it is my hope that by the time you determine my identity you would have understood enough to forgive me. We are the only ones left. Trust no one. Least of all yourself."

I have gone over that last injunction several times, trying to understand your meaning. Did you leave me here? Will you soon return and explain everything, elongating my recollections beyond the nine days since I have found myself in this place; beyond my only memory of the unstable world outside? Or maybe it's the memory that is unstable. I am in a single-carriage train. Or perhaps it's a bus with a high, sloping roof, I can't be certain. In this reconstruction, I am gazing through the oval window of the vehicle. The clouds are lower than usual, forming a latticed ceiling that resembles a drooping cobweb. I feel I can touch it if I stick my hand outside. The vehicle comes upon a row of derelict buildings – theatres, casinos and an abattoir – with billboards turned the wrong way. A flock of iridescent birds with scabbed wings have perched on all the eaves and they seem to follow us into the night, which falls suddenly. The moonlit night sky is a mellow greyish-brown and this tint, repeated in the fields beneath, makes it look as if the melting sky is rippling downward. We pass a child standing alone and when she shrinks from the vehicle I hear a shuffling behind me and realize there is another passenger.

Now there is a town ahead. In the front yards of the stuccoed mansions are alabaster statues haloed with rings of dull light. The hands of the figures are raised to the sky and from the bus, the scene looks like a conjuration of frozen ghosts. There is an odd intimacy to the positions of the statues and I think of a city destroyed so swiftly its residents were preserved in their last acts. The trees seem to be afflicted with an infestation that renders the leaves cottony and pale. In the distance, the headlights illuminate a black speck. We get closer and I see it is a child, dressed in dark green, standing alone. She is holding a bow-shaped toy with which she swings as if to strike the vehicle.

I hear a low, melodious chuckle at the back that eases into words I only decipher as we enter a tunnel, its sides glistening like freshly cut tissue. "Let it be known, brethren, that the unknown is simply a place not yet visited." The walls of the tunnel seem to be closing in. The other passenger does not appear concerned. I hear him singing, "You cannot hide it any longer. We know what you have and we shall pluck it out one fibre at a time. And yea, we shall hold it up to the morning light and when a newborn witnesses it, mysteries shall live and die in the span of a single tingle. You have brought this upon yourself, brethren. You have taken the fire with you and there's no stopping it now. A great turbulence is before us." The voice gets closer and I am seized with panic. "They know what they are searching for but cannot recognize it. Advantage is yours."

I have used the word *reconstruction* because this retrieval has the quality of a vivid dream. I am recording all of this with the hope that, as I write, I will eventually come to some greater understanding of the man I once was and will understand my condition not from disconnected episodes, but will grasp eventually a complete life. Perhaps this is what everyone wants at the end. A quiet understanding. But there are more immediate concerns.

The room I now occupy is devoid of mirrors – or any type of glass – so I cannot describe any new disfigurements that may have altered my appearance. The wrinkles and spots on my mustard-coloured limbs and my shallow breathing suggest I have passed the point of middle age, though I cannot tell how far along. It's not simple vanity that causes me, each morning, to examine the visible parts of my body but rather a curiosity about the extent of the shrouded years that have slipped by and the portion remaining. Since I cannot see you, too, I am unaware if you are surprised or simply amused by this ignorance, this darkness about my prior life. But here's something that might surprise you; it's more than darkness because each time I recall an event, another, of equal importance, is lost. My mind is a leaking crucible and sometimes this image is so stark I instinctively feel my forehead and the back of my neck for some discharge. I awoke nine days ago, as I mentioned, so I am certain that my memories are relatively stable for this duration, at the least. The flashes of non-sequential events and pliant faces from the preceding period might as well be interpretations of overheard conversations because I can feel no connection with them. Furthermore, these random, recurring retrievals are puzzling because they cannot be placed into any context and, more significantly, because the emotions associated with these memories constantly vary. The slices of déjà vu are confounding, too, because I often get the sense that I can affect the outcomes; as if my memory is one aspect of a reality waiting for completion. Perhaps this is a form of overcompensation and all those who share my condition might assume they possess this odd power. My condition. Forgive me for using this word but I can think of no other that is so vague and all encompassing.

In spite of what I have mentioned so far, I would like to assure you that I am not completely without resources. My loss of personal memory has not affected my ability to think, plan and write. Moreover, the retrievals to which I referred show glimpses of a shy but imaginative man. *Imaginative*: the word brings an unease, or rather, a bubbling fear that is puzzling to me. In any event, I would like to believe I am this man.

To preserve my sanity, I have tried to establish a routine. In the mornings, I spend an hour looking at the sketches on the walls, another hour gazing out from my jalousie, memorizing my observations of the Compound, a sprawling structure with three or four dozen wretched people roaming about. There may be fewer or many more, I can't recall counting. In spite of everything, the Compound is an intriguing place. Consider the view with which I am presented each morning.

It never varies. There are two groups marching until they are alongside each other. Sometimes I imagine they are marching to the tune of Vivaldi's *Four Seasons*. It's odd that I should remember something so obscure but nothing of myself. The group assembled by the sage sandbush is dressed in military blue and the other, coming from the direction of the sentry box, is orange-clad. They could be going to a parade but once they are alongside each other, they stop to engage in an odd choreograph of imaginative salutes and little pirouettes that give the sense of taunting buffoonery. Both groups seem oblivious to either the jeers or the encouragement of the loiterers. They keep this up for an hour or more and when my eyes begin to burn from the glare, I shut my slit jalousie. When I reopen the slats a few moments later, I notice the teams seemed to have exchanged some of their players and a couple of the loiterers are now leading the charge with mops and brooms. Sometimes I feel the marchers are doing this only for my amusement, like auditioning actors. At other times, I imagine that some of them are familiar, particularly a tall man whose height and heft is disguised by his slouch and another jumpy man in a long overcoat, but I have concluded that my faulty memory is stringing along arbitrary addendums, elongating details and events and faces to fill in the gaps. Maybe the mind creates meaningless distractions to fill the gaps and breaches. Or perhaps it's like the intricate nested loops I observed on the painting of leaves.

In the late afternoons when I am watching from the same spot, I notice the gaps between the ivy-covered single-room cabins and the wobbling lanes leading to the cemetery on a hill collapsing into implausible angles and the light scrambling around the glutinous trees appearing alive and combative. Perhaps I should add that the old men and women on the pathways are always losing their mooring and caroming forward and backward like rubbery toys. This disorienting vision, thankfully, recedes with each passing day. As do my bouts of dizziness.

I will mention here that I have not yet convinced myself that it is prudent to reveal all of this to you. You, my imprisoner. Faceless and nameless. And curt, too, judging from the letters I found in the jacket and from these two sentences, more clearly visible, written in block letters and left on the escritoire: *You are in possession of your notebooks and letters and the drawing implements. You need nothing further.* I have wondered during every one of the last nine days why you chose not to go beyond this. Nothing about your reason for doing so and more worrying, no clues as to why I acquiesced. Why did you leave the hidden warning I should trust no one, not even myself?

Perhaps I am relating this also with the hope that you will suddenly show yourself and accompany me during one of my surreptitious evening strolls. And as we walk together, avoiding the main areas of congregation (along the barrack-like enclosure that houses a canteen, a dispensary, a launderette and a stockroom), you will explain why you left me here. We will walk side by side to the cluster of single-cell buildings that serves as living quarters and just beyond, the derelict pavilion dotted with rusted spears and iron balls and at each building you will remind me of something I have forgotten. A date, a name, a place, an event. When we arrive at the chapel built like a capsized boat and decorated with copper snakes on the stern, you will pause to reassure me that my stay here is temporary. You will reassure me that I am not crazy and as my memories become more stable, I will understand everything and I will no longer worry that I am in a prison or a madhouse or an unwilling participant in some horrible experiment. But I know you will do none of this; your cryptic instructions left on the escritoire do not suggest a lingering friendship.

And so, I walk alone. I have seen the congregants milling about and a few standing reverentially before the Compound's massive front gate, designed to imitate the outstretched wings of a ridiculously stylized albatross clutching a leaking hourglass in its claws. From a distance, the worshippers resemble crustaceans gazing from beneath their carapaces at the town outside. These gazers or acolytes, I have noticed, soon get bored and shift their attention to one of the many billboards, empty but for the signs of age: mildew, rust, frayed paint and a few tantalizing letters hanging like lopped-off limbs. The gazers stand apart from each other, making no attempt at cooperation; nothing to communicate what the missing words might signify. For my part, I try to avoid any eye contact and whenever I slip up, I see dullness, hostility or a flickering curiosity that is so brief it barely registers. Once, I spotted an old man, immaculately dressed, holding a suitcase as if he planned to leave and another day a little man afflicted with blepharism who pointed to me and muttered, "It's your fault we are struck here. You made us do it. Over and over."

Another day, a stutterer, dressed in the clothes of an unemployed auctioneer, told me, "There are-are…"

"There are what?" I prompted him.

"Two of-of every-every…" I could see his frustration both at his difficulty in completing his sentence and at my inability to help. "L-look." He pointed to the sky and I saw a circling bird, its revolutions remarkably unvarying.

"I can see just a single bird," I told him. "It seems stuck in a particular orbit."

He seemed excited with my observation but unfortunately this did not help his stammering. When I eventually walked away he was still grunting.

In the evenings, I resume my observations before I head to the huge library that is different from every other part of the Compound I have seen so far. Its sorting room smells of blue cheese coated with rat dropping and dusted with magnolias. Perhaps for this reason, the library is always empty, although this could also be because someone had taken the time to pluck random chapters from a variety of novels, memoirs and manuals and glue these between bogus covers.

For instance, there was this paragraph in one of the fantasy novels, *The Model Monkey*. "It was in the year 2075 when it was first observed that the fusion of man and machine into a unified consciousness, a singularity, had gradually eroded the ability to speculate. Patterns and coincidences had been decoded, mysteries solved, enigmas demystified, puzzles resolved. There was no need to dream or reflect because everything could be predicted through algorithmic interpolations. And because there were no mysteries, the imagination was seen as a vestigial reflex. In time, it was viewed as worse."

Yet in the same novel I saw this segment that had been plucked out, I suspect, from a romance novel and placed in *The Model Monkey*. "She sat on the bed, packing photographs and sewing needles and pieces of fabric on which were stitched a variety of insignias. 'So you are really leaving?' he asked her and when she did not reply, he added, 'If you really intend to go to *that* place I should warn you that it's pure madness. You will be surrounded by rogues and vagabonds.' She zipped her bag and got up. 'They celebrate craziness and worship tricksters. What do you expect to find there?'

"'Chaos,' she replied sweetly as if it were a special brand of chocolate. 'It's the gift we all have been looking for. Haven't you?' She blew away a tuft of hair above her almond eye, spread her arms and sang, 'I cannot live like this anymore. I want tohubohu and bedlam. I want freedom.'

"'Please. We can –'

"'You believe memory is a tattered thing that can be stitched and joined but what's gone is gone. Wouldn't you say?' He remained silent, wondering what exactly she was talking about and she repeated her question, watching around as if she was addressing a hidden audience."

Book after book followed this pattern. Overblown romance novels shifted in my hands to manuals detailing the diseases of farm animals and handbooks on brain surgeries diverted to fairy tales fluttering with genies and swooning princesses. Religious tracts, consuetudinals, devolved into advice on fashion accessories. Who, I wondered, would take the time to rearrange these books and for what purpose? The violations were even more confusing when chapters from the same books were rearranged because there was no sense of time advancing.

Three days ago, I was forced to adjourn my visits to the library. In a reading room, I saw a tiny, naked man squatting on a stool. He was shivering but there was a celebratory grin on his blubbery baby face when he looked up from his knitting. He seemed crazy with his bamboo needles in one hand and a mess of yarn in the other. I was certain of this when he leaned forward and said, "Lolo still want a cuddle."

"What are you doing here?" I managed to ask.

"Waiting all the time. When are we leaving? I must finish this." He held up his knitting that looked like serpents looping into each other. As I hurried away, he shouted after me in a topsy-turvy voice that sounded like a litany of crazy names. His appearance there was unfortunate. Every night, before I departed the library, I would tiptoe on the same stool on which his aged testicles had been dangling and stare through the lancet window at the town outside the Compound's towering wall.

I have to tell you that I used to look forward to the view of the shingled housetops that all seemed to be slanting at odd angles as if the ground had curled beneath the foundations and the walls were balanced on roller bearings. Later and alone in my modest room, I would try to picture this old town outside the gate but could only come up with scenes from the illustrations on my wall: dungeons with spike traps that led to perfectly furnished kitchens with wide-eyed women sitting around a table and not seeing the toddler wandering into the garden, mauve with poison. Beyond the garden, I pictured lopsided streetlamps swaying in the breeze intermittently casting their aureoles around capsized lorries frozen in steely blue ice. The trucks were always decorated with bright stickers and decals and there were stiff tufts of fur embedded in their carriages and wheels. At first, I imagined the town to be a facade with nothing beyond the front walls, but in the nights, I heard a choppy wailing as if the wind was fretting against the gables and alcoves and once, I saw beams of lights that appeared to be gambolling across the sky. I can think of no other verb.

Here is a confession: I believe a man who does not know if he is a prisoner is worse off than someone whose status is less ambiguous. The prisoner becomes habituated to his limited space as his glances retract while the deluded man or woman, inventiveness fuelled by threadbare hope, constantly gazes outwards; constantly adds to his horizon. And so, locked in my room, the noise outside withering to a single and prolonged squall, I envision the slow passing of winter bringing ribbons of mist that obscure the supple hills behind the town, giving the place a liquid appearance. It always ends as an underwater scene, and when I awake in the early mornings and fall into the realization that I am in a place not of shimmering and indolent sea creatures but of deformed and slouching brutes with lips of unacceptable angles and eyes that shift from blank to hostile; men and women given a last gasp of life by their inquisitiveness, I wish I could hightail it to a region a thousand miles away. But where? Where, I ask you? What else is out there? And what if the world of which the might-be-prisoner dreams is just as malformed and incomplete as the one in which he is trapped?

I know I sound hysterical and my excuse is that one of my retrievals unspooled a universe in distress. I glimpsed, ever so briefly, men who resembled each other attempting to erase this resemblance with every type of weapon. Maces, clubs, hammers and glistening armours that shot firebolts that resembled sprigs of marigold. I saw other men with flowing beards heaving out roaring machines they claimed would stop the flow of time and children scurrying into caves to escape the flashes in the sky and young women lying on brown, flattened fields. I saw transparent walls being built, rising higher and higher as if they were ladders to heaven and beyond the walls, ragged women throwing their screaming babies in the air. I saw a flood that was replenished not from the storm above but from the water surging from every vent and rathole on the ground. I saw gods cavorting among their creations and forgetting they were gods.

I saw the beginning of time and its end.

I have to tell you that I have struggled with these visions or dreams or whatever they may be. One of the books in the library had advised, before its transposition into a diary of a widowed farmer's account of his mutated livestock and tractors rejigged into weapons, that what is gone is gone forever and it was just as pointless to peer into the probable future as to glance backwards. We favour our memories like a wayward uncle, long dead and of no use to us, was one overwrought description. It was utter nonsense, of course, this early section, but this is how I measure my retentiveness. Moments, instalments and episodes, boxed-in sequences that spring from nowhere and lead to nowhere. Think of tracks that are pulled away the instant the carriages roll over them. I have determined that for me, there is no simple return voyage. I say this because I cannot determine a starting point.

As silly as this sounds, there are moments when I wonder if I am as real as the people shuffling about. Sometimes I have to touch things, to feel pain, grate my fingers along a rusted iron railing or the nail dents on a wall to assure myself that I am not trapped in a dream. I listen to the snuffling on the roof at nights and in the mornings, I inhale the acrid aroma of vitriol and dead trees. I must admit that I have not entirely convinced myself. This, I believe, is why I have recorded the beginning of each day with the phrase I saw on the day of my awakening. *Today is a new day but yesterday was the same day.* Beneath, I affix the phrase *Day One* and *Day Two* and so on. My last entry, earlier this morning, was Day Nine.

In assessing my condition, *limbo* is the most charitable word that comes up. *Limbo*, a word that suggests flexible tunnels, interlocked caves and vast empty spaces that lead to nowhere. I know it's not an exact definition, but this is how I measure my life, or the little that I remember of it. You may wonder why I do not stop here; why I am recording and relating an account that does not promise a resolution. No one wants to hear of jumbled memories and capricious experiences. What is the significance of recording my misery, you may well ask? It's a valid question and I will use an analogy you might remember. "My thoughts seem to take their cues from my visions; they are like moths circling a gloomy room. It is only when I record that I can trace their arcs and glimpse their trajectories. I record so I might stumble upon some connection." I have no idea when you mentioned this to me and if your face was thickened by some shared distress or if there had been a mischievous smile when you noticed my confusion. I even wonder sometimes if we spoke in English because, in recording this, I feel as if I am translating my thoughts from another language. I cannot recall – or I can recall only fragments of – colloquialisms and slangs and farcical expressions and nips of tart humour and I am aware that this formal account might be stilted and whinging to you as it is to me. I feel that I was once gifted with a humorous manner of transcribing events, but unfortunately that is gone now and I can only describe my situation with the tools left to me.

This evening I decided I would not avoid the library because of a naked old man so I placed the boomerang totem into my jacket and headed in that direction. Midway there, I discovered the same craziness that had led to the creation of the hybrid books in the library had also incited the recent placement of contrary signs and directions along the pathway. I ended up in a room that was, in a manner of speaking, new to me. This room, tilting to the left and smelling vaguely of brine and camphor, does not belong here, I thought at the exact moment I stumbled through the canting doorway.

"Come in, come in, come in." The voices, though different in pitch, seemed to harmonize with each other and the blended effect was not unlike the throbbing purr of a damp and dangerous cat.

2. THE THREE HEADS

There were three old men wedged around a grey pedestal table. The table was undersized and for a moment, it seemed as if their heads possessed a single stalk. They glanced up all at once and I noticed that the light reflecting on their ripened faces came not from the humming bulb on the ceiling but from its reflection on the tabletop. The light was dull and fat and it softened the cobwebs on the rafters and made the walls seem flabby and viscous. It also gave the table the illusion of rotating. "I am sorry," I told them. "It was not my intention to interrupt." I should have added that they might have properly locked this room for their conference or whatever was going on, as it was indistinguishable from the line of abandoned office cells that seemed to be lined with a prefabricated corklike material.

And I now saw how these three old men, curious about my intrusion, were also calculating if I might be trusted to apologize for my mistake and simply walk away. "Have a seat," one of the heads said and all three gazed at me while I was deciding how to frame my refusal. Then their gaze shifted to the wall on my right and I saw what seemed to be a Hitchcock armchair.

"You all seem to be busy so I will go my own way."

"To the athenaeum?" This was the middle man and he spoke in a suffocating manner that gave his voice a ponderous quality, as if he dutifully weighed and apportioned each painful word. "We understand you have been frequenting the place. I am speaking of the library, in case you did not understand."

"I am not stupid," I snapped. "But I am confused by your interest."

He spread his chubby hands and looked to his left and to his right. The man on the right, hunched, lanky and gloomy looking, said, "We are always interested. That is our function."

"Our prime function." The man on the left, who had the posture and size of a scholarly imp, emphasized his point by raising and then flicking his index fingers in the direction of the chair.

I did not fully trust them, skulking around in a gloomy room. "I prefer to stand here by the door if you don't mind."

"I insist," he said with a petulant frown.

"And I decline."

They looked at each other for a while before the head in the middle asked me in his rustling wheeze, "Shall we begin, then?"

"You can do whatever you want. It's your room." Even as I said the words, I knew that my curiosity would prevent me from leaving. "However, if you insist, I can delay for a short while."

"Excellent. That's an excellent first step. We prefer to do things the simple way. It's less messy." I walked over to the chair if only to confirm which of the three was speaking. The chair's sloping seat was glass-smooth and I crossed my legs and grasped the armrest to avoid sliding. From this angle, I noticed that the person in the middle was fleshier than his companions and in the gloom, this made him seem more important. His features were flatter and when he popped something into his mouth and swallowed, he resembled a picture of a basking amphibian I had seen somewhere or other. The other two swallowed with him, their jaws seeming to hinge and unhinge in unison. The fat one opened his mouth and tucked his head this way and that. It was a remarkable display and I wondered if he was trying to unsettle me. "There's nothing to be nervous about," he said. "You are one of our…how shall we put it…one of our special guests. Some have been lost, unfortunately, but we are happy you are still here. You have tested us more than anyone in recent memory, but that is…"

He turned to the lanky man who said, "Outweighed by your ability to continually fascinate us."

"Why should I be nervous of three old heads?" In the small room, my question seemed too provocative, so I added, "But I am pleased by the status you have accorded me."

The man in the middle looked to both sides and said, "Good, good. Let us begin once more. We understand you have been frequenting the library. Researching books on memory loss. Is that correct?"

"Is that so?" I certainly was not going to reveal my activities to these three.

"Let us refresh your memory, then." He leaned to his left and the man there passed him a book. "Here is one of your favourites. It deals with the loss of episodic memories." He flipped through the pages and read. "Here is a subset on what you must have surely memorized. Autobiographical memory discrepancies." He flipped again and I wondered how he was able to read in this dark room. "And another on procedural memory."

"It sounds very interesting."

"Interesting, you say. But it's not part of our –" The middle man placed his hand abruptly before the imp, cutting him off.

"Of our what?" I asked.

They glanced at each other before the man in the middle said,

"Let's not concern ourselves with that. Do you know why you are here?"

I hesitated before I answered. And, during my moment of silence, I thought that if I had known more of you and your motive in consigning me to this place my answer would have been more straightforward. You will understand that I felt I had no choice but to tell them, "I cannot say."

He reached for the book and held it before him like a fat praying mantis examining its prey. "Would we be wrong in asserting that it is from these books you got the idea your auto-biographical memory has been damaged? But not your procedural memory. Very convenient, would you not agree? You can remember everything once it's not connected to you?"

"Why would that be convenient to me? Or to anyone for that matter?"

The impish man leaned forward and I saw that his chin was so pointed it looked like an inverted triangle. "Because it's a perfect escape hatch."

The man in the middle said, "At first, we were not convinced, but your research in the library, your solitary walks, your –"

"Am I under surveillance?"

The gloomy man fluttered his fingers as if he were a sleepy magician. "We try to keep on top of things."

"That is an admirable attitude, but I cannot see how it involves me."

I was trying to keep my cool but the imp slammed his tiny hands on the table. "Inspector Instant or the Legendary Legerdemain or whatever comic book name you have given to yourself this month, we are not here to play games." But his puckish appearance and his diminutiveness made it seem as if he was doing exactly that. I may have smiled a little.

The middle man placed a hand on the imp's shoulder and

patted him gently as a father would a child. "Do you still hold on to your claim that you recall events only from the previous three months?" He seemed to be asking his friend the question, his tone curious yet chiding.

"I never claimed any such thing. And I never called myself any of those names, either. I believe you have confused me with someone else." Even as I said the words I knew how ridiculous it must have sounded to these three who were somehow apprised of my amnesia.

"Ah yes," the middle man said. "According to our calculations, your new cycle" – he made an air quote as he said "cycle" and I felt that to a child he would appear the perfect monster – "your new cycle began a little over a week ago." The gloomy man whispered in his ear. I heard the word *cake* and I felt this was the centre man's name. Cake added, "My apologies. My apologies. Nine days." He emitted a sigh and his partners did the same. I felt I was in a pantomime. I would have left at that point, but I wanted to hear them out. In an odd way, it was interesting. It became even more so when he continued, "If we are made singular by our memories then you can be a new person four times in a single year, just like that. Anyone you want. No guilt, no regret, no apologies, no lessons learned. Just a new man. A new model, maybe. Very convenient. It's perfect. Perfect. Is there anything you want to say?" When I did not reply, he added, "We are waiting."

He was right, you know. I have no idea of family, parents, ancestry, culture, traditions. No memory of pain or pleasure, of guilt or satisfaction, of failures or accomplishments. No idea of what I am and who I should be. A man with no identity and no purpose. In limbo, as I mentioned to you. "I am flattered by your interest in me, but I am not certain I deserve it," I told them eventually.

"You are an intelligent man, so you must understand our skepticism. Perhaps you want our sympathy."

I realized then they were baiting me. They seemed to have some understanding of my condition although the period it encompassed was too expansive. I decided to wait them out in the hope that some familiar gesture might spark a smidgen of familiarity.

"Let's see if we can shake your memory," continued Cake. "This Compound is not my home and I will stand apart. They have constructed a world –"

"They have constructed a world," the imp broke in, "That exists only in my mind..."

And now the person to the right. "My watchfulness will keep me inviolate. My invisibility will preserve my sanity. I will not be a tapeworm in a petri dish, my head incessantly lopped off. I am and will always remain...and so on and so forth."

I was shocked. Had they read my letters before I regained consciousness? As you well know, this was the opening to one of the letters I had found in my jacket. I believe the letter was addressed to you and I was once more reminded of your complicity in my imprisonment. They may have noted my reaction because Cake, managing to sound bored and admonishing at the same time, said, "You should not be so alarmed. We are merely pointing out that you have never exhibited the symptoms that should be associated with your circumstance. There is an element of calculation in your determination, is there not? I am, I shall, I will, I must and so forth."

The man on the right almost breathed out the words through his nostrils, "It is remarkable. Remarkable and worrying."

Cake withdrew a watch from his jacket and placed it on the table. The imp leaned closer to look at the time or the model or just to seem important. "Let's go through the routine once more. We are obligated to do so even though we know the outcome. What is your name?"

I didn't like his lecturing tone. I remembered one of the trio remarking I could choose to be a new man and so I told him, a bit spitefully, "Remora the Remorseless." I have no idea where that name sprung from.

"Do you have any relatives, Mr. Remora?"

"It's possible."

"Wife or children?"

"They are not here with me."

"Do you know the year we are in?"

"One year is just like the other so it does not matter."

He sighed and continued, "Can you describe your place of birth?"

"I am sure it has changed by now."

There was a brief pause before he continued, "What of your childhood? Did you spend your time in one of the sanctuary towns? Or were you one of the lucky ones who escaped to a bamboo hut or a stone cottage? There are still these heritage sites, you know. An igloo, perhaps?" The imp giggled at the word *igloo* but these were questions I had asked myself and for which I had no answers. I still held the hope that some slight clue from that period might spring other answers.

"During a previous encounter, you described a ring of mountains and an overpass. You claimed the mountain was crumbling and the people on the overpass were jumping or falling down the side. Can you add to this?"

When I said nothing, another one continued, "There is an explosion, and light that is solid crimson and aquamarine, falls in globules that attach to the ground and make everything slippery. There are hedges and fields of intersecting burrows and communities of inquisitive animals staring upward at creatures that resemble them. But these creatures are flying and exploding."

I heard the rustle of pages before another interrogator spoke, "The sky is ablaze with dripping clouds that incinerate everything beneath, the fields and meadows and the furry animals. And from within the blaze there comes the chug-chug of a train. Miles and miles of carriages that are empty but for the group of soldiers in one carriage and the assassins in the other. Or they may be connected chariots rather than carriages. Each assassin looks exactly like the other."

"But maybe the other carriages are not empty. Perhaps there is a group of madmen trying to escape. Maybe they are running away from their diagnoses. Do you know the train's destination? Is it perhaps going in a loop?"

The gloomy man leaned over, holding some sheets in his hands, which were very long. Cake stretched his head up like a tortoise as I stood to take the sheets. They were filled with familiar drawings and even with those that were new, that I had not seen in my room, I saw a similar style. "Tell us about these sketches," Cake said. "How did you arrive at these scenes?"

Here, I must pause in my account to tell you this: People with unreliable memories are more hamstrung than those with useless limbs or impaired senses. Those disadvantaged folks can at least see, or know, what they are missing, but for men and women like me – if others exist – it's like being forever poised on the rim of a void. We are forever teetering and we retrieve and grieve in granules. We cannot make connections because the synapses spark and sputter and die. This may sound dramatic to you but it's a helplessness worse than any other kind because you can see neither the beginning nor the end. Tracks pulled away the minute you have crossed them. You have no idea if you are travelling forward or constantly looping back.

In case I have not made this clear, the simple truth is that I have no verifiable recollection of my previous residence. I sometimes dream of frigid volcanoes with caves leading to luminous larval creatures that I also see later mewling and wreathed in silk in a market square or bazaar or circus where men and lithe women are hoisting tramcar wheels above their heads and whizzing through the stalls and alighting nimbly on flagpoles and leaping off and vanishing before they hit the ground. There is blood on the ground or something red in starburst splotches. Someone is always crying in melodious bursts like a medley of plucked bows. And always, there is a child, hovering just within the range of my vision. Sometimes I recall these scenes as if I am hurtling through the air and watching a flurry of misaligned boxes whizzing by in the opposite direction. At other times, I see blue-skinned beings floating above two battalions that seem poised to attack each other. The beings are shedding tears that seem to transform into leaves as they touch the ground.

I was so taken up with my own thoughts that I barely heard Cake prodding me about the source of my inspiration or the gloomy man saying in his gloomy voice, "We are interested in what's going on inside here." He tapped his head. "Is it madness or something more?"

"I don't know if I can help you –"

"Do you know that tapeworms can retain their memories even if their heads are lopped off?" The imp made a cutting gesture and Cake patted him, a bit more roughly this time.

"Ignore my little friend for the moment. Tell us something about yourself." His tone was almost conversational. "Why, for instance, are we gathered for this meeting? What's your function here in this Compound?"

As you may well imagine, this is the thought with which I awaken and the last thing lodged in my mind before the dreams begin their drumming. It started, as I mentioned, that morning when I awoke in my room with welts on my legs and a light-headedness that caused me to stumble to the ground as I tried to walk to the minuscule kitchen and, once I got there, realized that I had no idea who had outfitted my cupboard, stocked my closet with clothes that fitted me somehow, left a note on the escritoire. *You are in possession of your notebooks and letters and the drawing implements. You need nothing further.* I then discovered the letters in my jacket. The letters, twenty-one in all, filled some of the gaps but added to my confusion. Half a dozen were addressed to you and they appeared formal and lecturing, but a few hidden in the inner lining of my coat and addressed to myself possessed one common thread: they were filled with warnings of *an imposter who takes on a different guise whenever it is necessary* and who would *pretend to be all things to all people.* I will assume that we both know the identity of the imposter. I cannot tell you how often and long I stared at the illustrations on the walls and tried to understand their connections with the dreams or visions or wedges of memories.

I heard Cake saying, "We are waiting."

I decided to give a neutral response. I told him, "I am here now."

"That is beyond doubt, but it is not what we asked."

"I do not believe I wandered here by mistake."

"Sarcasm aside, we will have to agree. But it does not answer our question." I told him the truth: that I did not know. They conferred for a while before Cake continued, "And how would you rate your progress?"

"I keep to myself if that is what you are asking."

"Would you like to describe your interactions with the others?"

"Which others? I just stated that I keep to myself."

"What about outsiders? Former patients. Escapees."

"Patients and escapees? What is this place?"

He ignored my questions and repeated his own. "Were there any contacts?"

"With whom? The escaped patients? Why would I want to contact them?"

"Perhaps it is because you consider yourself an outsider," the gloomy one said. "A man unable to walk on firm ground and for-ever looking for signs that he belongs."

"I am just as real as you are."

"That was not the question, but we are glad you brought it up," Cake said. "One of the books in the athenaeum contained an intriguing account of a man who believed he had set the stage for a perfect crime by creating an exact replica of himself to take the fall. He foisted all his qualities onto this double but as usually happens in these cases, he soon began to wonder who the real man was. Himself or his double. We are aware you have borrowed this book. Several times, in fact. Do you know the writer?"

For a minute, I felt he had been referring to you. Then I realized this was another trap. I had not borrowed the book in question. Why then did he pose the question? They seemed to be awaiting my response so I said, "Perhaps we all fantasize about discovering someone who reflects all our attributes. A twin or an exact off-spring. It grants us a kind of modest immortality. What do *you* think?"

"What we think is not an issue. Do you still insist that your memory losses are presaged by cephalalgia, vertigo and tinnitus?"

I said nothing. Following another conference, the imp asked, "Do you feel guilt for any of your actions?"

"I believe it's impossible to attach emotion to events you cannot remember."

Cake laughed suddenly, and in the enclosed room it sounded like the hollow clatter of coins. For once, his companions did not imitate him. In fact, they appeared confused. "You have answers for everything. But they are not really answers. Riddles stuffed into riddles. It's like a game to you, is it not?" He still appeared amused. "If our circumstances were different and the universe was an oppo-site place and I were forty years younger and not in charge of rediscovering what we have lost I might even enjoy our little conversation. It would be one for the books. Yes, one for the books."

I was a little confused by his change in demeanour. I told him, "I am not the only one speaking in riddles here. I have told you all that I remember. If anyone is withholding information, it's you all. Perhaps I can answer more truthfully if you speak more plainly."

"Our function is not to provide information." This was the gloomy man. "That would be counterproductive."

"We assess and adjudge and verify. You may consider us remote interlocutors," Cake said. "But let's proceed." He seemed to be thinking of what to say. "You claim to not recall anything beyond three months. I am using the period to which you have referred during our previous sessions. Do you have any sense of your life before this breach? For all you know you may have committed a terrible act before you were hustled to this place. You may have suffocated your wife and young daughter. Wiped out the witnesses. Revealed state secrets. Led an insurrection. Instigated a genocide. Carried a lethal strain of an incurable disease. The sole survivor of a cataclysm. Concocted the perfect crime. Placed innocent lives at risk. A rapist and pillager. Take your pick?"

After a while, I told them, "Everything is possible but if that were true you would not be so comfortable with me in this isolated room."

"We are not as defenceless as we appear."

"Nor am I."

I said this as an act of bluster but it got their attention. There was a little conference before Cake said in an almost conversational manner, "I suppose you are right. You must be resourceful to function in this place with just a three-block unit of memory to play with."

"I manage."

"That is admirable." I hoped he would elaborate but they grew quiet. The room now seemed brighter than when I first entered and I saw Cake licking his fingers. I waited for him to withdraw a sheet from the folder but he continued licking.

The man on the right swivelled his chair so that he now faced me and I saw that he had a rather large forehead. He looked like someone on the verge of making an unfunny joke. He began speaking. "The mind, in isolation, is a funny creature. It is eternally leaping, snarling, stretching and crouching. Sometimes it rolls over and pretends it is dead. For what purpose, we may ask?"

I considered his question. "It's interesting that you have equipped the mind with a form and shape." It really was, you know. I added, "Maybe it just wants to survive."

I thought the trio would be satisfied with my response but Cake's frown spread on either side until all three were all gazing at me in exasperation. Because of their advanced years, this expression made them appear grumpily senile. I may have grinned. "You may find this amusing," Cake began, "but we do not. We do not." His companions nodded in agreement. "Imagine, if you will, a holding tank filled with the softest, most amiable creatures extant. Or a rustic pond, for that matter. Now consider what will happen if an alien species, some troublesome nettle-like creature, finds its way there."

"A tapeworm," the gloomy man said, prompting a smile from the imp.

I ignored both. "These pleasant pond dwellers will lose their torpor and find a way to survive. They will adapt. Are we now concerned with aquatic life?"

For the first time the gloomy man smiled. "Perhaps they will all get along? The benefit of one becomes the benefit of all."

I didn't know what he was getting at. "Maybe," I said.

"What you are saying is that sterility, though good in the short-term, closes the door to progress and adaptation. Very interesting. Yes, very interesting."

"If you say so," I said.

"Yes, yes, very interesting," Cake continued. "So we need the tingle of madness. Yes, yes."

I couldn't understand why he was so excited. The gloomy man said, "The dreams that inflame us."

I waited for him to complete his sentence, but it was Cake who spoke. "Tell us of your dreams. Use as many adjectives as you choose. Colour them whichever way you like."

The imp produced a notebook and a pen. "Begin."

I knew they were trying to trap me. "My dreams are no different from yours."

"Oh, we doubt that," the gloomy man said. They did their conferencing once more. And as they did so, they recited a litany of questions, not giving me an opportunity to answer any. Would you leave the Compound if the opportunity presented itself? Do you maintain a journal? Do you relate everything to an accomplice? Or to acolytes? Is there a routine that you follow? Are your dreams only of the previous three months? Are you afraid of pools of water? Do you only believe the last person with whom you speak? Is it easier to remember to forget or to forget to remember? What happens when an agitated mind merges with another that is stable? Can some approximation of immortality be achieved by preserving our consciousness in an external source? Do you blame anyone for your situation? Do you blame us? Where would you go if you were allowed to leave the Compound? What would happen if everyone stopped dreaming?

I suspected they were trying to get through a list of prepared questions with the hope that I would choose one. Then I felt they were trying to rattle me. I said nothing. Not even when they said, in tandem, that they were aware of the various stages – the word they used was *incarnations* – I pretended to go through and that they had learned to prepare themselves for any contingencies.

"It may interest you to know that the worse type of criminal is not the man who gloats in his darkened room but the man who is blind to his felonious acts. Why, you ask? Because he feels no remorse and will repeat his actions over and over and over. There are men like that, you know. Men, who in pursuit of a presumed obligation, have sent hundreds to their death." I did not like the gloomy man's magisterial, lecturing tone and would have departed then but I wanted to understand their interest in me and determine the nature of our prior familiarity. "They were only performing their duty, you may counter, or maybe there were special circumstances, but do you truly believe either should guarantee absolution?"

"You seem to be having an argument with yourself," I told him. "Again, I will say that if you speak more plainly I might be in a better position to tell you what I believe or disbelieve."

"Well, let me be as plain as possible. Are there others here you may have tried to influence? To get them back on board? This is very important. Very important."

"I manage by myself. I already mentioned that a dozen times. And I have no intention of forming friendships in this place."

"Because you are superior?"

"Because I value my privacy."

"What privacy? Have you not maintained that you have lost and continue to lose all your memories? So tell me this: how can one value something that does not exist?"

"I will find out who I was. I will someday."

I had spoken defiantly but this drew a smile from Cake. "Is that really your intention? Or are you are groping toward another reinvention that will be amenable to you and your pursuits? Perhaps this is the real reason for your claims to a recurring selective amnesia."

He turned to the gloomy man, who nodded so shakily I was reminded of a puppet. "When you first arrived here we considered another possibility, but you soon put an end to that."

I am sure they knew I would ask about this other possibility and when I did, they engaged in a little huddle before the gloomy man continued, "During moments of extreme and prolonged distress we can conjure counterfeit memories into which we insert familiar faces. We reward these old friends with new roles."

"You had us for a while," the imp said with a malicious smirk. "Today I bake, tomorrow a new man make."

I saw Cake fluttering his fat fingers as if he were shaking off some viscous liquid. "We are led to understand that the most primal fear is of darkness and of the night. What if the night washes away our memories and we awake as someone else? Or in an alternate universe? What if our souls are stolen?"

"Djinns and zombies and spectres and jumbies and gnomes and –" Cake put a hand on the imp's shoulder to stop his flow.

I said nothing. I was aware they were all looking carefully at me. Perhaps they expected an outburst or another question. I knew they were trying to confuse me even further or perhaps lead me away from the truth. Eventually I told them, "You seem to know far more of me than I do of myself."

"Your statement is correct. Consider us your custodians."

"I do not need a custodian so it seems we are wasting each other's time here. Let's get to the point. What is it you really want from me? A man with an abbreviated memory."

"I am glad you brought that up. Let's say there's a man who claims to regularly lose his memory. Would you say that this man's condition is the result of sabotage or his own fickleness?" The way the words fell from Cake's tongue made me think he had rehearsed this particular question and everything previous was leading to it.

"I can't say. But I am willing to hear your conclusion."

The imp seemed so agitated I felt he would crawl onto the table. Again, Cake put his hand on the other man's shoulder. "What we want from you is very straightforward. Simple answers to simple questions." Once more he raised his head like a tortoise and I felt his question would be both silly and unanswerable. He did not disappoint. "What is the nature of the actual man? How can a man define himself when there are so many influences? If you create a false timeline are you then free to minimize actrocities and maximize small victories?" When I did not answer, he added, "You must understand we are here to help. But we cannot do that if you continue this pretence. Would it suit you if we chose some middle ground and work our way from there? We will even offer you the opportunity to choose this point. A month? A year? Three years?"

For the first time, he seemed a bit sincere. I knew it was another trap, yet I thought carefully of my response. Eventually I told them, "If I tell you that I do not know who I am it will mean nothing so I will say instead that I do not know who I was. And because that is the beginning of everything I cannot answer any other questions you may have." I was taken aback by my earnestness and wished I had said nothing. They engaged in a long conference and as they leaned closer, their skulls touching, I knew that if I sketched this scene later I would draw a three-headed man. Perhaps I would give the head in the middle – clearly the most important – pendulous drooping lips and tiny pointed teeth. I heard the scratch of pen on paper.

The gloomy man brought out a Gladstone bag – funny I would recall a brand – which he placed before him. "We have some material here," he said as he fiddled with the bag's contents. Eventually he retrieved a coil spring notebook and a clutch of pencils. He seemed to be inspecting everything and when he was satisfied he turned to Cake, who nodded, and he replaced the pen and notebook. "We would like you to have this."

I would have refused but the imp climbed on the table, gathered the bag and hopped toward me. I was startled into acquiescence and when the imp returned to the table I recovered to say, "What am I supposed to do with this?"

"Expose yourself." The imp clapped and received stern glances from both men.

"We would like you to record your dreams."

"In any shape and form."

"Light the fire."

I felt all at once that this entire encounter had the tenor of a dream. This uncertainty brought a brief surge of dizziness and I tried to steady myself. But during that brief moment I saw flashes of an old man disappearing whenever death came calling and another man caught in some kind of sandstorm and a blind woman pursued by a wolf and a ragged group on a train running toward some catastrophe. But each of these memories were separated by a second of blinding whiteness, like the blank pages between chapters.

What would they do with these images even if I managed to transcribe them on paper? They were gazing intently at me and appeared to have shifted their chairs so they now appeared closer. I suddenly thought of something: Was I part of some experiment? The men before me were trying to convince me I was not crazy while suggesting that I was not completely sane. They seemed to be leading me down different roads with the hope I would choose one and momentarily I felt they knew less of me than they claimed. I was convinced of this manipulation when Cake said suddenly, "We have decided to grant you your wish."

"Return my memory?"

"The most unreliable thing in our possession is our memory. And yet we invest so much trust in it." Cake smiled and the tip of his tongue slipped out. "But to answer your question, we cannot return what has not been lost. What we can do is to allow you to clear away the debris. Reidentification, if you wish." He turned his face to the gloomy one and said, "Our monkish friend has lately taken up with mutual causality. He is growing pious, I am afraid."

"*Paticca-samuppada.* We live, we die and we live again." The imp tittered at this but the gloomy one put his palms together and recited with almost strained seriousness, "A loop represents the most absolute design in nature. A spider's web, the veins on a leaf, the spirals on an insect's wing, the brain –"

"And so on and so forth," Cake interrupted. "You are free to go. Free to go."

The imp leaped to the table once more, stretched to grasp a string and the room went black. I stumbled out and five minutes later in my room I would have doubted this entire crazy encounter but for the Gladstone bag at the foot of my bed.

3. BALZAC THE BRUTE

I noticed the darkening sky when I was returning to my room and hurried along. I was certain I hadn't spent more than an hour with the trio, and I tried to push aside the notion that neither the passage of time nor the weather seemed to obey rules in this place. The night either took its time or went in a flash and the clouds always appeared like set pieces. I realized this was more likely due to my faulty memory rather than the paranoid idea that everything in the Compound was controlled remotely. Paranoia. The men seemed to imply that it was I who had been brushed by its claws while ignoring their own heightened suspiciousness of my activities and my retentiveness. I wish they had been clearer about whatever they wished of me. Still, I should have been more tactful with them; perhaps they would have explained the circumstances that led me to this place.

The section of the Compound that houses my room looks like shipping containers stacked alongside each other. The walls seem to be fabricated from a variety of materials: brick, metal, wood, concrete and what looks like hardened cardboard. Likely they had been built at different periods, but the general impression is either of deliberate neglect and decay or a place – much like the sabotaged library books – reconstructed in a wilfully discordant manner. I have no idea why I am placed away from the idlers I see roaming around, but for this I am thankful. There is a general statement: It is only in solitude that a man truly understands what he wants of himself. Perhaps you mentioned this to me at some point or maybe it was an aspect of my personality prior to my arrival. I cannot say.

I shut the door to my room and from habit I focus on the illustrations on the wall. After twenty minutes or so I close my eyes and wait for the rattle of approaching memories. Typically, they are just brief flashes, but perhaps the whiff of my recent encounter has stimulated some dying part of my mind and instead of the familiar and numbing ringing that always comes from somewhere behind my left ear, I hear an irregular whirring that reminds me of a flagpole beating against the wind.

I see a train station. Apart from a group of diminutive elderly men and women drained of colour, the place is abandoned. The group is gazing at the static clock and their arms are interlocked. The station is cold and smells of damp iron. Through the open window I can see puffs of smoke above a sheen of pink ice. The litter, embedded bottles and steel pinions give the ground a remotely apocalyptic look, as if the cold had swept over the city all at once. There is a row of concrete houses and inside, women with their babies frozen to their breasts. Perhaps there is a curfew in this section of the city. The greyish-black buildings are arranged in a sort of amphitheatre and the small wooded area before a jagged wall must have served as a courtyard. It would have been carefully maintained at one time, before the bush overtook the hedges and covered the benches. I see all of this through the station's window and when I walk outside, I am met by the mouldy odour of damp rot and neglect. A man is sleeping or frozen in a mess of oily cardboard squares. There is no one else. The memory shifts.

Someone is on a bus or a carriage with me. I cannot see the face of the other passenger, but I am afraid of him and I am fearful that our destinations match. And, in fact, he gets off with me to a derelict terminal at the edge of a town. Beyond the town there are fields of lustrous hay, golden red, that seem slightly suspended and when I walk to the terminal, I notice a child outside, watching through the bus's window. As the bus passes slowly, I can see that the child, with a wooden bow-shaped toy at her side, is drawing squiggles in the air. I cannot see her face clearly through the dusty window, but she seems to be looking fearfully in the direction of my fellow passenger who I now see has followed me to the terminal. Beside him is a grotesque black beast, its neck the size of its torso. The group at the terminal freezes when they notice the man. This vision seems to hold some connection with the dream from which I awoke nine days earlier, but there are these additional details.

I am about to open my eyes when another scene arrives, hurtling like jerky images from an unattended projector. I am struck again by my precise recall of something as arbitrary as a projector. It's almost as if every trace of autobiographical information has been selectively excised or muddled, leaving everything else intact. In any event, this slice of memory seems older; my recollection more flexible. A solemn couple is on their way to some function. The veiled woman is clutching a photograph of a child and she seems not to notice the little boy trailing them. She is focused on the man, slightly ahead and walking quickly. They are all dressed in dark funereal clothes and the boy hangs back as if he wants to be somewhere else. Or perhaps he was not invited. Now, the woman looks back, not at the pair but at the sky. She raises both hands. The photograph is torn away first, then, as she is spun around, her clothes. Soon they are all caught in a great turbulence, a cyclonic disturbance of swirling boars and bulls and giant fishes with deformed eyes and teardrop-shaped leaves.

This scene is so terrifying that I get up immediately to search the clutch of illustrations but there is no equivalent representation. Two hours later, still searching through the sketches, I am struck by a sudden thought: does madness appear quietly like a gentle pat on the shoulder or does it arrive full-throttle, all rage and muddy laughter? It's an important consideration and I wonder if this has been your aim from the beginning; a payback for some silly slight that you have never forgotten. So will it then help if I tell you that I am sorry, contrite, deeply apologetic, ashamed, disgraced and everything else you want me to be? I would tell you all of this directly if you were to suddenly appear before me, but you have hidden yourself well. I have this sense of you only as a presence; a spirit with a jangling bag of old frowns and grievances, a ghost running away from its pale shadow. You made certain I would never recognize you if you decided to show up either in memory or in person. Reading your letters was like shuffling cards in a game whose rules I did not understand. Sometimes I felt you were warning me to never trust you and at other times, you seemed to be saying the mistrust should be directed at myself. I realize that my limited memories may complicate ordinarily trivial descriptions, but I still wonder at your habit of writing in riddles. What are you really afraid of?

But there are more pressing concerns. If my memory of a terminal is real shouldn't I try to locate it? Walk backwards until I arrive at some familiar point? But what if I had done this before? The three heads claimed I was in some kind of three-month loop as far as my memory was concerned. My presence in the Compound would indicate I had failed to get to this point of familiarity.

An hour later, I fall back on my bed and stare at the walls. I think of cellblock inmates gazing at their enclosures and I recall, too, the heads describing the fear of the night and by extension the dulling of memories and consciousness as springing from some primal instinct. I don't want to be cornered by this sort of hysteria so I try to approach the drawings – which, together with the letters are all I have – differently; not searching for familiarity but attempting to guess at the mood that propelled their creation. I scan each, trying to determine if the instigating emotion was sadness or impatience or devotion. They all seem to be of different styles. The deviations are subtle – deeper brush strokes in some and minuscule shifts in the choices of colour – but as I look closer, I see in those placed lower on the walls the background details, the faces and the landscape are so blurred they appear to be echoes.

I get up and withdraw the other sketches from the basket and in these, too, there are fluctuations, from the broad leisurely strokes on some to the intricate and reflective pencil work on others. What if I am not really the artist, but have instead been thrown into the room of a lunatic? The three heads had suggested I was, apart from an artist, a madman and an imposter. I recall my first stable memory of the Compound and the listless people milling about as if in a slaughterhouse and my fear that the place was some kind of infirmary. This is a horrible possibility. I circle my room, trying to calm myself. Eventually I open the Gladstone bag, withdraw a sheet and try to sketch the three heads. The sketch looks like a child's cartoon so I erase it and try again but the result is no different. Maybe it is my frustration, but as I scratch and erase and scratch again, I am forced to consider the possibility the three heads may have been right: I am no different from all the listless and morose people scrounging around the place. Yet, what was their purpose in asking me to sketch my dreams? Was it a part of some remediation or was it something more sinister?

An hour or so later I gave up my attempt at sketching and decided to preserve the drawing, childish though it was. There was no space on the wall. I tried to shift the cast-iron safe closer to the door. The safe was too solid to budge and my efforts loosened a painting above, that of the woman and her child. The painting fell behind the safe and I attempted to squeeze my hand in the narrow space to retrieve it. I took the boomerang object from the basket and probed behind the safe. When I pulled out the painting, I saw that I had also brought out a chunk of some material that seemed to be a type of hardened cork with a polystyrene interior like vulcanized rubber. At first, I assumed I had broken off a bit of the boomerang but that was made of fossilized bamboo.

I had never seen anything like it. I wished there was someone to whom I could turn, but a man with no verifiable memories cannot easily trust anyone. Certainly not the three heads or the idlers scrounging around. I followed my usual pattern whenever I came across something unfamiliar and headed for the library. I placed the material into my pocket because I knew that even though it was still darkish outside, there would be idlers, always curious, hanging around. On my way through the corridor that led to the canteen, I diverted to a side path to avoid the row of cellblocks where I had encountered the three heads. There were a few men sleeping on the benches and a woman walking in even circles, but thankfully she was too preoccupied with her measurements to pay me any attention, so I arrived at the library unprovoked. Just before I opened the door, I heard the muffled flap of an overcoat but saw no one.

Once there, I set the material on a table and went in search of a relevant book. This took a while because the covers, as I mentioned, were misleading and when I returned I saw a man sitting at the table. He was staring at the piece of cork or whatever it was and because of his bulky physique and fixed expression, I was immediately cautious. Then I noticed his childlike manner as he reached out for the cork, holding it this way and that. "This is a very interesting thing you have here," he said in a surprisingly squeaky voice. "Now that you have my attention how do you suggest we proceed?" He smiled and the muscles on his jaw, tightening, popped up his ears a bit.

"What are you doing here so late in the night?" I reached for the material but he closed his fingers around it. "I didn't expect to find anyone here."

"The answer to that should be obvious. I was anticipating your arrival, although I must add that I am flabbergasted by this piece of implement you have here. Is it bait for a mousetrap? Well, I am not biting." He tittered and covered his mouth in an almost feminine gesture.

"Have we met before? Why were you waiting for me?"

"You, my friend, have committed a heinous crime. Most people have done something they are ashamed of. Even I have walked on the dark side. I am not talking about my colour. So don't go there."

"What are you talking about, exactly?"

He answered quickly as if he had anticipated my question. "Every three months we meet at this very spot with some new puzzle for me. Do you know that in the dreams of brutes there are things always floating around looking for attachments? Feathers for birds. Gillyflowers for plants. Children for parents. Souls for the purified." He plonked his hands on the table and I noticed the scars on his knuckles. "And speaking of the soul, what happens to it when all the minds are joined? How can one thing exist when it becomes another?"

"I don't know who you have mistaken me for but –"

"Nobody is interested anymore." There was a pinch of menace in his dim-witted smile. He seemed like a man who would commit a reckless act and laugh at, for instance, the spurt of blood or the severed finger. "I, on the other hand, am different. This mysterious substance here, for instance." He repeated the sentence with an even stronger lisp. "I am interested in the composition of things people carelessly leave around. What can it be? Did you get it from the flood? Could it be from outside?"

But for his childlike squeak, I would have assumed he was

mocking me, so I told him, "I have no idea. That's why I brought it here. I found it in my room. Besides, I don't know what flood you are talking about."

He thumped it on the table, leaning in, his face close to the object. Suddenly he bared his teeth and bit into it. He glanced up, the material caught between his teeth and elongating his smile. He spat it out and said, "Now that we have re-established our connection it will be ruinous if there is discord on a simple matter. Agreed?" I noticed his muscular shoulders and arms and nodded. "Okay, then. Let's proceed. Ask me my name. C'mon, don't keep me waiting."

"What is your name?"

"What would you think of a man who asks the same question a hundred times yet expects a different answer each instance? But I will bite. My name is Balzac. Now ask me why I am called Balzac the Brute?"

"Okay. Why are you called Balzac the Brute?"

"My first instinct is to tell you that it's none of your business and pound you for your impertinence, but we are sitting on opposite ends of the same table, so I will oblige. The simple answer is that I was a brute. I made that up myself, but it was you who put it in my head. Balzac the Brute."

"Could you explain how that happened?"

He replaced the object on the table and took a deep breath. His chest swelled impressively. "It is not my intention to delve into the past, or the future for that matter, but I will oblige. As you well know, the team you created was the most powerful in the universe, but they were all, in my respectable opinion, demented. All except the Brute. He was brutish when the situation demanded and erudite when he was not provoked. I respectfully submit that he was a man like myself."

"Can you tell me more about this team?"

"As an erudite man, I will treat your inquisitiveness as a sign of enthusiasm and say that we have undergone our training and have been waiting for eons for the magic word. In the meantime, one has absconded, another has turned invisible, a third rendered helpless and the others have been waiting in the shadows for your return. The longer we wait, the closer the brute gets. I can feel it rippling beneath my skin this very instant." He was still smiling but the words came out as a threat. "Do you know that at one time men would take one look at people like me and whisper the word to their daughter or wife? It was common. Even if they knew nothing about me. Brr-hoot."

"Why would they do that?"

"You are kidding me, right? It's there in all the history books. I read tons and tons of books when I was trying to keep the beast at bay. Let me tell you something. In the beginning of everything, they were unreadable and I wondered what kind of fool would expose all his dark days to perfect strangers. To wit, I will illustrate with an example. A man who created a group of brave heroes to fight all the old gods, a noble mission if I could say so, to pummel these tight-lipped, fossilized miscreants to dust…this man, instead, decides to send his creations to do his own dirty deeds." Looking at Balzac I felt that people who smiled while talking of violence were unpredictable and dangerous. "But I persevered. Then one night I decided to read the books as a brute would and I realized that the writer, a gangrenous miscreant himself, if you will permit me, had written his books especially for me. We were having a little rap session, just the two of us. Same with the next book. And the next and the next. After a while, I realized that all the books were created by the same person and that made the conversations easier to follow. I gobbled up the library in no time. No time! Where did you find the time to write all these books?" He got up and walked to the nearest shelf. *"Bullets and Bloodstains. Soliloquy with a Silent Strangler."*

"*Stranger.*" I corrected him. "And it's a library. The books are not mine. Besides, I am an artist, not a writer."

"I will have to be disputatious," he said. "One man hides inside another man and pretends neither is either."

Maybe it was his exaggerated lisp, but I felt like saying it's the sort of statement made by children. Instead I said, "I have no idea what you mean. Perhaps you can help me?"

"Now that is the kind of request that gets me thinking. Is it innocent or a double-edged sword?"

"It's a simple question."

"The only question before both of us here seated at opposite ends of the table is why you wrote these books and then disguised them by switching the covers. Why you have been disguising your own covers. I must conclude that you have been leaving clues that only you can understand. A puzzle with the pieces strewn about. A brute notices these things, you know." He seemed about to smile but changed his mind and the resultant look was one that made me think somehow of a llama. "If I was still a brute, I would have gone on a rampage and dismantled the entire collection, but in my erudite state, I am more perplexed by your trickery. What would you say if I told you I could read this book in one sitting? The entire thing." He grinned like a child.

"I would say it's very impressive. Most people wouldn't be able to manage it."

"Remember, I am not most people. I am a brute." He smiled in a shy manner and continued, "I was joking. Would a brute be able to remember the following? 'Hear ye, oh faithful. Awaken me not from my slumber, for though the heavens explode when I dream of the wind, when my sleep ends so do the worlds.' What do you think of that? Dreaming when we are awake and not the other way around. In the nights, I mean."

"It's very striking."

"Striking." He laughed heartily. "Only old fogeys with chauffeurs use that word. Or boxers. I don't know why you would bring it up. You are a strange man, if I am permitted to make this observation. I never noticed this before. I am flabbergasted, to put it mildly."

I did not want to aggravate him, so I said, "*Striking* is a word just like any other."

"There you go again! Words are power, my friend. Your book here, for instance. Written thirty years ago and yet I will spend thirty hours of my life with it. Do you think people will remember me in thirty years? Never going to happen. I don't know why people utter these fallacious things. It drives me crazy." He twisted his wrists and watched the ripple of muscles on his forearm. "The only thing keeping me from splitting them open is my vocabulary. I ask myself, 'Would a man with a lexicon of over two hundred thousand words act so precipitously? Would Balzac act in this manner?'"

"Did I also cause you to be named Balzac?"

"What are you talking about?" He was still riled. "That was way back. When I was born, my father took one look at me in the crib and said, 'Ballsack.' Then he disappeared. Completely. Well, not completely, as every couple of years there were sightings at the station. Always went looking but he forever managed to escape. I would have chomped his nose off. My mother used to say that he had a kind of sixth sense that allowed him to slip away in the nick of time. She herself was a whore with a knack for humour. Why you ask? She conjured and perjured all the way to this place where she signed off on me. And that is the true and abridged story of Balzac the Brute. But you already know all of this."

"Is it possible that you have mistaken me for –"

"Before, I used to get mad at everything. Now these same things just want to make me laugh. Why, for instance, would the old whore conspire to deposit me in this place? Why would I remember her with a different face and voice each night? Maybe it's funny." He giggled loudly as if to prove his point. "Here's another rip-roaring question: Why would a man with a noble mission change his directives every three months? Lead us to the ring and throw in the towel before the first bell. Three years ago, I would have already punched you senseless. I was an out-of-control maniac. A raging beast like a hyena or something. My jaw was capable of more bite pressure than any known human. My greatest joy was tearing into bone and gristle."

I tried to understand his rambling. "I take it you are happy with who you are?"

"I am stable. That in itself is a major accomplishment. I have banished the brute. Do you know how I have accomplished this astounding feat? I think of the child I once was and all the miserable little children swarming around with no hope in their eyes. I am afraid of them, but they keep me sane. Go ahead. Pick up your book and record it. It may come in useful when the lights stop flashing and you are wondering who and what you are." He seemed to be waiting for a reaction, but I was trying to understand his flow. "I don't care what you think of me, 'cause one man's opinion is as good as another. I could walk out from here in a straight line until I arrive in the closest suffocating camp and by the time I take the first bite, the attendant, who resembles a rundown mole cricket if you ask me, will have seen straight inside me. This poor brute has been granted a stay of execution to participate in a groundbreaking experiment, he would think."

Once again, I decided to say nothing. He too seemed a bit confused by his last statement, but eventually he said, "Free will. Remember the story you wrote? With this very world sitting next to others and the big man, the Timekeeper, the beardman, the dozing bugaboo, getting so old and absent-minded, he forgot which ones needed winding? There was a child in the story, too. A girl hopping from world to world. Poor thing couldn't understand why the beardman stopped listening to her prayers. Do you do that sometimes?"

"Pray?"

"Why would you do such a thing? Why should the beardman rouse himself only for you? I am talking about setting things in motion."

"We all do that sometimes, I guess."

"I was afraid you would say that. I really was. I think it's fundamentally wrong to think you are God, coiling up innocent people to suit your own ends. What if they decompress years after you coolly walk away? What then?"

"That's not what I said."

"Relax. I am not going to chew your ears off. Who would hear your screams? Not a soul. Not even the Managers. It seems as if you are inviting some dislocation."

"There is a Manager?"

"Don't play games with me, my friend. For all I know, you might be in cahoots. Managers and Timekeeper. A neat little group winding us up and setting us like simple playthings on the train hurtling to nowhere." He considered me for a while and added, "If it's true that God set his clock then it's also true that he set forth his Timekeepers. His interlocutors." He looked at me sullenly before he returned his gaze to the object on the table. "Have you ever noticed you can change the shape of an object by adjusting one small detail? This object here, for instance, is shaped like a bird. Now it's a snake. You can trick an erudite man with fanciness but never a brute. An erudite man will try to see every fallacious thing with his soft-focus eyes, but a brute can get to the jugular in no time. He cannot be distracted with loops and spirals spun by a fakir because to him they are just patterns. Nothing more, nothing less." He thumped the table and I jumped back. "People are putting things in my head. It's not right." He raised his shoulders and twisted his neck this way and that. He seemed to be trying to recall something and the expression on his face was suddenly painful. "I spent the first half of my life looking for my father. Sad to say he escaped. Now ask me how I spent the second half."

"How?" I asked cautiously.

"Even though your question is impudent I will oblige. I shifted my search to my creator."

"How did that go?"

"All these questions. It would be remiss of me if I did not point out that each time a man gives away a secret he hollows out a part of his soul." He reached down to retrieve the object and when he straightened, he said, with what appeared to be genuine sadness, "I know this is your profession but I don't know how you could live with it. Hollowing out people one scoop at a time until they become spare ghosts. You and your three friends."

"You give me too much credit."

"Credit for time served. I cannot tell you how often I heard that when I was strapped. It gets my blood boiling just to think of it and I get a hankering for gristle." He got up abruptly and walked over to the nearby shelf. He plucked out a book and sent it spinning against the wall. "Lies and porky-pies," he said, lisping heavily. He did the same with half a dozen books before he finally calmed down. "There is too much violence in this world. Can I tell you what the biggest vice in the world is? I will tell you if you promise not to interrupt. Do I have your word?"

"Yes. Go on."

"I am glad we settled that. If you will permit me, there is too much mendacity in the world today. This is why I keep to myself. In a rathole, if you want to know. My fortress of solitude. Apart from the remaining team members, I avoid everyone like a concussion.

Everyone packed in here and screaming of blue lights." He grinned amiably and walked over to the table. "The brute is gone for good. Inside I am as soft as baby blubber. I am smiling here but deep inside I am like the saddest person you can imagine. Now I am going to open up my soul to you and tell you something special. It is not rage that drives a brute but sadness. Yes, you heard correctly. Sadness at the circumstances that brought two living beings into this situation. Brute and prey. What do you think of that? No matter the outcome, they will be joined till death. This world is filled with sadness and there is nothing we can do to change that because the clock has already been set. I figured out that on my own." He twisted his neck and I flinched at the loud crick. "When the clock is already set the only thing left is patience. The Manager cannot comprehend this elementary truth so I am always one step ahead. One step ahead of the Timekeeper and Fakir and –"

I decided finally to put a stop to his maundering. I told him that I knew nothing of his Manager and really, I did not care. Perhaps this Manager, if he existed, was an expression of the beast threatening his composure; perhaps he was some security official with whom he had some dealing. Regardless, the Manager was a spectre not dissimilar to the father he had never seen. The members of his imaginary team most likely served some similar function. While explaining my assessment, I watched him cautiously; watched the way his fixed imbecilic smile conveyed so many contradictory emotions. It was like peering into a dark mangled kaleidoscope; and when something new stiffened his smile for just a second it was too late.

It happened so quickly, the shuffling of anxiety for rage and hurt; and in the moment before I passed out, the stark distress on his face.

When I came to, he was gone. It seemed that he had made an attempt to repair his damage as my chair had been pushed back to allow me to lean forward on the table and a bloodied handkerchief was next to my face. When I stood up, I felt a lancing pain in my jaw. I was certain he had broken it and I looked around to see if he was still about. He was gone and so was the piece of cork I had brought with me. I walked out of the library, shading my face with my hand. Everyone seemed to be staring at me. Alone in my room, I bandaged my jaw with an old sock and when it slipped, I lay on my bed and tried to block the pain by slowing my breath. But there was a more pressing discomfort. I was certain that Balzac's last words to me were, "Forgive me, Father."

4 THE WET NURSE

I spent the following three days mostly locked in my room, nursing my broken jaw and watching fearfully through the window. Early in the mornings, I sneaked into the canteen and hurriedly brought my food to my room. There was no doubt Balzac had mistaken me for a writer with whom he had some previous issue. Maybe this writer had pointed out his brutishness and for that reason, father and writer were joined in his mind. Now, you may understand why I suspected your hand in his mistake. First of all, he had demonstrated a faulty memory of my appearance. And secondly, I am an illustrator, not a writer. Even at this very moment, recording this is torturous. Quite frequently, I struggle with my expressions and wonder if there is, perhaps, an idiom from some other language that might work better. (I imagine you chuckling at the thought of someone who remembers nothing of his life yet is able to simultaneously write and possibly translate – albeit in a stilted language. Over the past days, I have wondered whether this, too, is part of your game: watching me struggle in an unfamiliar milieu; annotating all my missteps.)

Once again, I am confused by the trouble you must have gone through to carefully set up this parallel universe populated with people pretending some familiarity. But your motives aside, my encounter with Balzac introduced more immediate concerns. He had mentioned a Manager with whom he felt I might be aligned, yet I had no knowledge of his own accomplices who could very well be roaming around the Compound. My room, as you already know, is equipped with a wooden door and iron bars on the single window, neither of which would deter a steadfast interloper. Certainly not Balzac with his bulging, almost cartoonish muscles. Picturing him in this manner reminded me of someone or something and I went to the sketches in the onion-skin envelope. There, I found an illustration so exaggerated it could have been drawn by a child. The upper body was too huge; the lower ridiculously tiny. The man's forehead was big and his neck thicker than his waist. The books in the background looked like bricks and the walls seemed to be collapsing on each other. I took out a pencil and tried to improve the sketch, idly at first, by shadowing the background and pencilling in the details of the foreground. When I was finished, I saw that I had modified the drawing to create an accurate representation of Balzac standing by the table. But I had gone further. Between the two aisles I had pencilled zigzagging patterns.

I put the sketch on the table, poured out some porridge into a bowl and crumbled bits of bread into the mixture. When I was finished with my meal and was dusting away the crumbs, a swift glance at the sketch seemed to transform the zigzagging patterns into a cartoonist's depiction of atmospheric electricity. Where I had seen this occurrence, I had no idea, but when I held up the drawing I got the crazy idea I had been trying to represent a swift, blurry motion. Perhaps some part of my brain was working covertly to tell me something. This might be utter nonsense but the more I stared at the wavy lines, the more certain I grew that just before I passed out, I had spotted some vaporous movement behind a shelf. I had assumed that Balzac tried to repair his damage by setting me upright on the chair, but was it possible that someone else had picked me off the floor? Apart from Balzac, the only other person I had ever seen in the library was the naked man on the stool, but I was certain that he would not move so quickly.

The next morning, I tried to convince myself that Balzac's business with me was done; that he had returned to wherever he had sprung; that the bamboo boomerang I carried would fend him off, yet I was extremely fearful as I made my way to the library. Twice I turned back. On the third attempt, I steeled myself by thinking that I should know if in this forsaken place I had a friend. Someone who might be able to fill in all the gaps in my recent past. Tell me how long I had been here and perhaps the manner in which I had spent my days. (On a related note, I realize that harnessing a traumatic incident to an account that lacks any personal details will perhaps feel incomplete. But you understand my situation.) When I arrived at the library, I stood by the door and called out with the hope of drawing out the person. And Balzac, too, if he were still around. I heard my voice echoing – the furthest iterations like tin drums – and I was reminded of how huge the building was. Eventually I walked inside with the boomerang in my jacket.

She was sitting in one of the two reading rooms adjacent to the stockroom with her back to the window, wearing a white sundress that gave the illusion of light passing right through her. I didn't show myself but she glanced up as if she was aware of my presence. I remained behind the shelf when she got up, walked over to a cart, plucked out its single book and held it to her face as if it would soon disintegrate. There was something graceful and tragic about her gestures and as I stared at her, I felt that it was not the book – a ragged-ear elephant with a broken tusk on its cover – that was in danger of dissolving. I wished I had bought my drawing pad. When

I stepped out from behind the shelf, I saw a slight tremor ruffling her body and I decided to sit some distance away. I must have spent an hour or so there and even though she would have been aware of my gaze, not once did she look at me. But I kept a discreet observation. There was a kind of limpidity to all her gestures and the manner in which she wrung her hands and slumped into her chair gave an impression of bonelessness and subtly shifting flesh. I thought of a gossamer fish hiding beneath a coral reef's limestone. I noticed, too, that she seemed to fade away whenever she leaned back out of the light. I wanted to say something to her but felt she would jump like a startled cricket if I got too close.

I tried to think of some way I could begin a conversation and I wished I had some memory of how I may have handled this sort of thing. Eventually I got up and walked over. "Hello," I told her. "I have never seen you in the library before. Are you new to the Compound?" When she did not reply, I added, "I don't mean to be rude but I am curious. I might also be grateful. I was involved in a little incident the other day."

She seemed quite dismayed, although I could not say if this was due to my presence or to the memory of Balzac's barbarity. I was dismayed myself when she got up with the book and replaced it on the shelf. And she did this with all the misaligned books and those on the floor, gathering, replacing and adjusting. Some she held against her chest as if they were special or had provoked some special memory. She seemed to fade with each step away from the window and then she disappeared entirely. I stood up and walked through the entire gloomy building; through the main room littered with boxes and torn-off covers, through the other reading room with its overturned tables and chairs, to the stockroom where I had climbed onto a stool to gaze at the town. But she was gone.

The next day I brought one of the blank sheets from the Gladstone bag, hoping that I could get a more thorough idea of her from my sketch. Once more she was seated by the window, but she had hauled a desk before her and she was wearing some sort of mask or blinders. I dragged a chair to the opposite end of the room and if she heard, she gave no indication. Perhaps she was asleep; and that was how I drew her: with her arms limp on the desk and the light filtering through her body. When I was finished, I got up, still undecided as to whether I should make another attempt to begin a conversation. Eventually I walked over. "Are you okay?" I asked.

There was no reaction and I felt stupid standing there. I decided to leave her alone.

"Someone is always rearranging the books. Every three months I have to start over."

"Do you work here?" I asked her. "I thought the place was abandoned." I noticed a book, *The Worm Runners Digest*, before her and I wondered how she was able to perform her tasks with blinders. "I can help, if you like."

"It's hopeless. No one cares anymore."

I reached for the book and the jacket slipped off and I saw another title on the front cover. *Adjacentland.* The book was a mess of torn pages. "I am afraid this cannot be repaired."

"Nothing can be repaired. I was bruised so many times." Her voice suited her appearance. It was thin and reedy and seemed perforated with dark gasps like someone breathing inside a winding tunnel.

"I am sorry. Did someone harass you?"

"Yes. They never allowed me to finish my job."

"Was it someone from the Compound? Is that why you are hiding here?"

She offered a soft sigh. I thought of a baby wren being strangled. "I don't know if it's safe anymore." She took off her mask and got up. Her eyes were milky and blank like a blind animal's. "I need to gather my thoughts. I must go now. I have to find someone."

After she had hurried out of the library, I returned to my drawing pad and when I drew a series of fractal shapes tightening around her, I grew worried for her safety. I looked at the drawing and here at least I felt that my artistic flaws did not diminish the work. She seemed without bones and her limbs were positioned at impossible angles. The next day she was not in the library and I hung around for a while before I walked to the canteen to load up my stocks for the week. On a whim, I circled back to the library. She was at her usual spot, one arm raised at the side of her face in a protective gesture. When I walked over, she glanced up in alarm and then quickly looked down. "I am waiting."

She said this as if she was unsure, so I asked, "Are you waiting for someone? Is it the person you wanted to find the other day?"

"I am alone now." There was a nervous ripple in her voice.

"Well, I won't bother you. I just wanted to ask about the people who were bothering you."

"I am alone now," she repeated. "All alone. There are no children anymore." She glanced around with her milky eyes. "No, that's not correct. There's one. A girl."

"Is that who you were looking for?"

"Yes, that's right. But she, too, has disappeared. Did you see her? I used to be her mother. I am sure of it. Am I your mother, too?"

"I am a bit too old," I said surprised. "And no, I have not seen the girl or any other children. I don't think there are children here." She was crumbling her coat's cuffs as if she was impatient for me to leave. "There is something I would like to know. Was it you who helped me the other day in the library?"

"You had passed out."

"Yes. From an attack."

"You were sitting alone. You must have fainted and hit your face on the ground. Your left ear was bleeding."

"I was attacked. Did you not see a brute around?"

"You were alone." She seemed to be pleading. "All alone. I didn't see any cannibals."

"Did you say cannibals? He may have left, then. In any event, I would like to thank you for helping me."

"I used to be a wet nurse. I tried to help as best as I could." She said this in such a dispirited manner that I felt she had been cut adrift from her family at an early age and that she had never filled this void with stable friendships.

"Do you work in the Compound, then? In a dispensary?"

"I tried to help everyone in need. It was difficult. I couldn't manage. So many died."

"The mothers or the children?" The question upset her even more, so I said, "I am sure you tried your best."

"I couldn't keep up." She shook her head and I imagined some terrible tragedy in her life. "I couldn't keep up. They took away the ones I wanted to keep. They kept them sleeping forever. These poor children who had stopped dreaming. Why couldn't they understand that?" Her voice seemed to hold a trace of accusation when she added, "Why are you here?"

"The Compound? I am not sure. I was left here by someone, but I cannot remember if I had been tricked or drugged. The person may have been a friend, so perhaps I trusted him too much."

"What is trust?"

"It's when you place your faith in someone."

"Faith?"

"It's something you expect but cannot see. I suppose you can sense it." Before she could ask, I said, "Sense is like faith in a way, but the outlines are clearer. Are you testing me?"

"Maybe. Yes. Yes, I am. I don't like when people put things in my head. I don't even know what is real anymore."

I wanted to say, "Welcome to the club," but she seemed too distressed. So I told her, "I come here to find out about things I have forgotten. Would you like me to leave?" She said nothing and I asked her, "Do you have any friends here?"

"No one cares. There are no babies anymore. They have all been taken away. Haven't you noticed?" She got up so suddenly I felt I had offended her in some way. And when I returned the following day, I decided I would not add to her distress by attempting a conversation. I fetched a casebook on infectious diseases from the shelf and sat at the corner of the main room. Fifteen minutes or so later she came out with a clutch of books that she replaced one by one on the shelf. Then she gathered a couple from the floor as gingerly as if she were gathering shrapnel. She moved with such tremulous forlornness I felt that when she disappeared behind some shelf she would be gone forever. I said nothing to her during this entire process and when she did not return from one of her trips, I got out my drawing pad. About forty minutes later, I looked at my sketch. It was of a woman kneeling, her face tilted slightly upward, her lips parted, her hair divided so the nape of her neck was visible. Her posture suggested a woman fulfilling some obligation from deeply honed reflexes. In the drawing, she seemed a frail automaton devoid of joy or passion.

"Is it real?"

I did not detect her approach and I could not determine if it was a question or statement as the three words seemed to have been wrung from layers of uncertainty. "I thought you had left." She was still staring at my sketch so I told her, a bit disingenuously, "I don't know who it is exactly. It might be anyone."

"Some...soma...somebody. Is it real?" she asked once more.

"I can't say. I sketch things to see connections I may have missed. I try to trick my mind."

She peered closer and I saw a scatter of moles on the back of her frail neck. From the angle, they looked like tiny holes that went right through her body. "Must I be like this? What has happened to me?" She covered her lips with her fingers and rushed away. I considered following her, but I had no idea what I would say. Nevertheless, I went to the canteen hoping I might spot her there. I saw a stocky woman with a metal name tag reading, "Barbita," quarrelling with a group I had seen marching in the early mornings. I felt that if I were drawing a portrait of that group I would include outlandish costumes and capes and fancy headgears. The stocky woman would get a fishtail protruding from her mouth. She must have noticed my smile because she came over and told me angrily, "You think you are special, but no one here is better than anyone. Chew on that."

I left hurriedly.

The following day the delicate woman was at her usual spot in the library but now she was smiling. This was encouraging and I walked over. "I saw you at the canteen yesterday," she told me when I came up. "You were drawing something."

"I didn't see you."

"But I was there."

"Oh, I don't doubt it." Nevertheless, I wondered how I had missed her and I had this sudden image of her sitting alone in the gloom, this sheer woman who refracted light.

She said nothing for a while and I returned to the book before me. "I have twilight vision. Would you like to know what I see here, all around us?"

An hour later, alone in the library, I tried to recall some of the woman's descriptions; and as I did so, I began to sketch amphibious creatures emerging from a swirling lagoon with multicoloured, fernlike plants and dust clouds embossed with unstable variegated colours. I had never done an illustration like this before and I wondered if this type of instability might be similar to a scene of all my memories tumbling out, unstoppable and overwhelming and pushing me further into darkness. You may laugh but that was how I felt. I walked to my room contemplating this and when I got there, I added to my drawing an almost imperceptible outline of the woman. I was curious about her real environment and I imagined the walls painted in a faint carmine colour and the curtains, a shade darker, blocking most of the external light. There would be abstract paintings on her wall and ghostly silver ornaments on the shelves and on the table. I felt she was careful to return everything to their precise positions when she was dusting or cleaning. Before I fell asleep, I imagined her kneeling before her bed with her ankles pressed tightly together. There were two pillows on her bed and sighs that looked like confetti were cascading around her.

And this was the image in my mind when I walked to the library the next day. I decided I would ask her if she lived in the Compound or in one of the houses in the town that lay beyond the massive wall. Maybe I would bring up the subject by stating that I had recently discovered a layer of some corklike insulation on my walls. When I got to the reading room, I saw that she was once more wearing her blinders and I made a fair bit of noise as I dragged across my chair to sit opposite her. There was a fixed smile on her face and because her eyes were hidden, I could not determine if her expression was blissful or maniacal. Perhaps she was meditating, I thought.

"I can see you there. You are wondering about the mask. It sharpens my senses."

"A recalibration. Like pirates wearing eye patches above deck to improve their vision in the darkened lower decks."

"Yes. That's it exactly. How did you know of this?"

"I have no idea," I told her truthfully. "Maybe it's something I read in a book and forgot about."

"How can you forget something like that?"

I made a sudden decision. I told her, "My memory does not

travel very far. I don't know how far exactly, but its span exceeds eighteen days. Maybe it stops completely at three months or reforms into something else. I really do not know."

"It's the same with me. Then everything that has been erased returns. Sharp and cutting with pools of blood and dried-up little babies, and aunts with spiteful eyes, and missing fathers."

Her response, morbid as it was, encouraged me to say, "Sometimes I worry that every new bit of information that I glean squeezes away an equivalent amount of memory. It's as if I am being calibrated and rationed."

"So, are you afraid of learning anything new?"

I thought for a while before I told her, "I am more interested in remembering forgotten details. I don't know if that counts. But I am never sure. To be truthful, there is little that I can be certain of."

"Was there an accident?"

"If there was I have no memory of it. I would like to find out, though."

She still had her fixed, slightly maniacal smile when she asked, "Do you recall anything at all?"

I felt it was safe to tell her what I had withheld from the three heads. "I believe there was a woman and a child. One was dead and the other was searching...I don't know which..."

"Did you kill your family?"

"No! No, I would never do something like that. I am not capable. Besides, I am sure I would have some memory of their deaths and the funerals. It would be impossible to forget something like that. Maybe I was absent, away at work, in another city." She pressed her hands against her face and her skin seemed to ripple like an alert animal. She appeared suddenly frightened so I told her of the drawings on my wall and the painting of a woman and her daughter with the inscription: *The child is the heart of reason.* I mentioned my decision to record each new day with the statement: *Today is a new day and yesterday is the same day.* "I have been trying to understand the significance of the drawings. I didn't put them there, but they are all familiar. Maybe there are recurring patterns. Perhaps they are a sort of diary, a journal written by a –"

"A lunatic?"

I was disappointed. "No. Someone recovering from a coma. Or perhaps a man who had awakened drunk in an unfamiliar place. Someone in limbo."

"Limbo." She seemed to be considering the word. "Do you think someone is also looking for you? If she has not died like everyone else. Do you have a mother? A daughter? A wet nurse?" She asked this with genuine sadness and before I could answer she added, "You mentioned a child. We must find her."

"It's just someone from the painting in my room."

"Can I see them?" I felt a flush of anxiety about taking the woman to my room, yet I was disappointed when she added, "I shouldn't. It's not right. Will you describe them for me?" I described those of the dead city and the train station and the little girl with two bodies in the background. I included the more recent sketch of the trio and she grew suddenly frightened.

"We must find her," she said.

"The child? It's just a painting –"

"We must warn her. We must warn her of what is happening."

Her words left me frozen. I had heard this admonition before. Here I must interrupt this conversation to address you directly. I cannot say if the statement had been issued from me to you or the other way around, but I know it had been attached to desperation and panic. When I recovered, I asked her, "What should we warn her of?"

"They are going to take her away because she is different. She can see things…colours and shapes and ghosts. Monsters hiding beneath bridges and candy houses and flying horses. Yes. And a woman in the water. She has a snake's body and can fly through the air over a man with chains on his feet. Poor child. We must warn her. Is her foot fixed?"

I was a bit disappointed. I told her, "I only know this child from the painting."

"Then I must do it myself. Will you help me?" Before I could defer she began to explain what we were going to do. I was intrigued; and for the next hour, I guided her around the library. She described the targets her fingers touched and asked me to assess her galvanic responses from her pulse rate. The next day we did the same. She told me that her compassion was nourished by creating direct connections with objects and our exercise was to prevent further erasure; and when we returned to her chair, her fingers softened on my wrist and I realized she had fallen asleep. Her lips parted and I heard a string of snores followed by a gentle gasp, all of which sounded like little secrets to herself so I waited for a while before I left. The next day, she recounted a dream in which children were descending from scorched wombs.

I began to look forward to meeting her and I imagined us outside the library, perhaps even outside the Compound where I pictured bushy hedges overlooking cobblestone pavements and grassy trails. Eventually, we would wander to a terminal or station and return, both of us separately, to wherever we had come. But she grew quiet when I mentioned this and I felt that she was afraid she would disappear in the sunlight.

Then one day, a little over a week after our first encounter, I saw her with huge sunglasses instead of her mask. Uncharacteristically, she had on a feathery wool sweater and a weathered grey toque. She seemed upset and I noticed how birdlike and capricious her gestures were. I asked if everything was okay. "I am ready," she told me, adjusting her sunglasses and holding out her other hand.

She was extremely nervous and I was afraid she would faint.

Outside, I steered her away from the loitering groups and the main buildings – the canteen enclosure, the block of rooms, the chapel, to what seemed, from a distance, a knoll but which I saw was an overgrown cemetery.

"Where are we now?" she asked. When I mentioned the old cemetery, she added, "Can you look among the tombstones and tell me what you see?"

"Numbers but no names. Maybe those crumbled away."

"So there are no children?"

"I cannot tell from the numbers."

"Numbers," she repeated slowly, tugging me away from the place. Her steps were as unsteady as when she wore her mask and I was certain that her eyes were closed behind her sunglasses. I also wondered whether her admission of twilight vision was not a cover-up for some kind of blindness. As a means of encouraging her, I said that when we immerse ourselves in nature we soon realize that not everything we see is idyllic. I pointed to blight on a tree, to a tuft of dried grass, to a clearly injured gull hopping around, and as I described each, I explained that when we observe these apparent imperfections we understand that we are part of a broader canvas. Sadness usually comes from the notion that we have been singled out for persecution. Careful observation disproves this, I said. I told her she was not alone. When she asked how I could know all of this with my faulty mind, I tried to explain that it was mostly my autobiographical memory that had been erased. Perhaps I was boasting but my observation unbolted more questions about my long-forgotten occupation. Also, how did I know of these empathetic connections?

"You can recall every scene until you step into it?" She thought for a while and added, "But how can you truly know anything unless you step into the picture? And what if it changes when you leave?"

"I can remember dry facts like faces and events and places, but

I can never arrange these into any meaningful pattern." I told her that the fragments of memories I recalled were like dreams that were vivid upon first recall but which quickly receded because – like the events of the dream – they could never be rearranged to represent a real experience. "It's the same, I think, but I am not certain of anything. Not even of my dreams."

"You can still dream?"

I nodded. She was the first person to whom I had tried to explain my condition and I was a bit excited because listening to myself seemed to better clarify my situation. "I try to stitch together scenes until they make some sense," I told her. "But even then, I cannot say for sure if they really happened or if I have compromised particular occurrences." She said nothing for a while and I wished I could go on. Perhaps she did not believe me or, more likely, felt I was like all the other loiterers roaming the Compound. "I want to know more of my prior lives," I told her. "I know the beginning was far from this place."

"How do you know it was far off?"

In one of my letters, there was this description: *Everything is frozen but for the flakes falling outside my window. They fall in dancing patterns and when I close my eyes, I can hear their music: tinny and plaintive and ethereal. I wish there were faces imprinted on each flake so that I could collect them all and form a pastiche of my memories.* I told her, "My romantic and childlike view of snow tells me that I am from a place where there is never ice on the ground."

"Describe what you mean by romantic."

"It's a way of thinking. Of using the imagination to –"

"Imagination?" She stopped suddenly.

"The dreams dancing in our minds. I don't know how else to describe it. Maybe it's like looking at that hawk up in the sky and trying to imitate its vision."

"Is the bird trying to imitate ours?"

It was such a childish question, but I glanced up and noticed the circular pattern of the hawk over us. "I think it's simply curious."

She said nothing for a while and I felt she was recollecting her own life. As we walked away from the cemetery, up the hill, her steps, surprisingly, became surer and when we got to the top, I stopped. She took off her sunglasses and her milky eyes swept the scene beneath us. For close to half an hour she said nothing, then she began to describe what she saw, felt and heard. A drizzle resembled a cavalcade of bees. The light units on the abandoned railway track beneath seemed like a pack of wolves. A shifting cloud formation looked like spreading cancerous cells. Marigolds appeared to be pods for the souls of aborted babies. She grew excited and the world she witnessed was both grotesque and wondrous. There were curlicues and whorls of colours and a slow liquefaction of rocks and cobblestones. And babies everywhere. It seemed as if she was peering into a dimension that gathered new contours as it violently reformed itself. She had asked about the imagination but her outpouring suggested no deficit in this respect. Maybe she had been waiting for a moment like this, I flattered myself. "Leave me here," she in a surprisingly resolute tone.

"Are you certain? I have nothing to do otherwise."

She stepped away and because we were so close to the edge, I grasped her hand. "Please." Reluctantly I released my grip and when I walked away, I felt I would never see her again. But she was there the following morning, waiting for me in the library with her sunglasses and her wool sweater. What followed was the same as the previous morning – inquiries about the numbers on the tombstones – and when she asked me to leave her, I said we had already seen everything this angle had to offer and that together we should explore the town outside. I mentioned the first time I peered from the library's stockroom. I described the play of light from the misaligned lampposts on the sloping roofs, but she pulled her shoulders up and seemed to close herself against what I was saying. I left her hunched up and when I glanced back, I saw a woman who seemed to be gazing at a coming storm.

The next morning when we left the library, we were shadowed by three men who soon gathered their own followers. I steered her to the main gate but she pulled away. Her hand was trembling. She asked me if I had ever been outside and I described my shifting memory of what I assumed was the town outside. The roofs could be perpendicular, the fretwork beneath the gables might be intricate with intersecting ringlets, the upper walls may very well have been streaked with a pale-blue luminous coat, there could be bales of lustrous hay on the porches and the entire scene could be distorted by funnels of bright red dust. The colour was never the same, I explained.

I expected disbelief but she seemed enthralled, nodding her head and when the group of men who had been following us came up to listen to my description, she said, "I don't want to be here." Yet she resisted as I directed her to the gate, the soles of her feet fairly scraping the ground. I pushed open the huge gate and stepped onto a plank bridge that led to a narrow path bordered with ugly croupe-shaped flowers. Beyond the flowers was an asphalt lot. From a distance, the town appeared to be a mélange of grocer's shops with blocky lower floors all fixed by narrower upper levels with deep rectangular windows. This was quite different from the drawings on my wall and the tremble of her fingers added to my own nervousness as I reflected on how often I had imagined this view.

Now it was she who was urging me on and as we walked on, she asked me to describe what I was seeing and I told her that we were now at a promenade with three concrete statues of men partially crouched, their hands in some sort of defensive gesture. One of the figures had toppled and it seemed to be digging into the pale grass. I explained that the street signs were all streaked with blue and, as in the Compound, the missing letters made them impossible to read. I added that the place seemed completely abandoned. "The colours are odd," I told her. "They seem unstable. Maybe it's because we have been cooped up in the Compound." I did not mention the brightness added a good twenty years to her face or that she seemed to grow older with each step we took away from the Compound.

"The other day you said you had come from far away." I nodded and she continued, "Was it from Adjacentland?"

"The place from the book? I wish I knew," I told her. "For all I know it may not even be a real place."

"They brought babies from there and put them into schools and squeezed away their dreams. Poor children. I don't know where they have all gone." As we continued walking, she said, "Tell me about the light." When I did not answer quickly enough she asked me in her slight voice, "Is it green and violet and smashing into each other and forming new colours? Is there a woman in a silk gown detonating some device? She is on the ground and her face is missing. Someone is turning her over with a laced-up boot and her lips are somewhere on the pavement. There are dead babies everywhere."

"Are you recalling something that happened to you?"

"I don't know. Maybe it hasn't happened as yet. Is it real if it has not occurred? Why should one be real and not the other?"

"Because we remember the things that have passed by. We can only speculate on what is yet to come."

"You said you couldn't remember. Are you not real?" She posed the question as a child. I would have smiled but I felt her fingers tightening around my wrist. "What is that sound?"

"Perhaps it's the wind." I looked up. The clouds were stationary but a hawk was flying overhead. Then I heard a faint buzz.

"There is someone here. Can you not see him?"

I glanced around. "The place is completely deserted."

"Are you certain?"

"I believe so."

"Then you should leave me here."

"I can remain for a while."

"This is where we always separate. I must go now."

"*We* always separate? Did you say we?"

"I must find the child and warn her. Thank you for helping me. I must go now. Can I get a hug?" When she embraced me, I tried to feel some substance beneath her clothes, but she felt as slender and lifeless as a mannequin. "What is that you are hiding in your jacket? It hurts." I withdrew the bamboo boomerang and showed it to her. "Is it a bird?" she asked.

I had not noticed that one end was frayed like a plumage. "It's a boomerang."

She passed her fingers along the ribs. "Does it always return as a different creature? Or fly in circles and never return?"

"I never threw it at anything."

"Then you should not." With each pronouncement, she took a step away from me, and as she had done in the library, she seemed to disappear with each step. I called after her and I heard my voice echoing through the empty streets and then a soft tumble of sounds: from one of the upper windows I heard what sounded like a rattling clockwork jingle followed by a child's laughter and finally a series of flat thuds like bodies falling into each other.

A wave of sadness fell over me and I could not say whether it was connected to some long-lost memory – a child's dangerous toy, a mother absconding – or whether it was the notion that I would never see the wet nurse again. I peered over the bushy hedges, all the while shouting to attract her attention in case she was hidden in one of the houses. The temperature outside the Compound was a good five degrees or so colder and I regretted not wearing a thicker coat. There was a strong breeze, too, which kicked up several spirals of dust that smelled of spilled diesel or perhaps machine oil. I put my hands against my nose and continued my search. Yet I arrived once more at the plank bridge even though I assumed I had been running in a straight line. Just before I stepped on the bridge, I had a sense of someone behind me and when I turned, I saw a lanky figure in an overcoat that was blowing upward in the wind. Then the figure was gone.

I knew it was not the woman, but I recalled that she had mentioned seeing someone in the town. As I ran, the shadow seemed to be moving with me, keeping its distance until I arrived at a street where the buildings, taller and narrower, were so close to the road that tenants on opposite sides could easily carry on a quiet conversation. I glanced up and felt a sudden crush of claustrophobia, as the buildings appeared to be slowly sliding toward each other. Again, I saw the bird and I felt like throwing the boomerang at it. Instead, I stopped, took a deep breath and slowed my pace. I wished I knew the woman's name and I felt silly to stop every five minutes or so to shout at buildings that seemed completely abandoned. I suppose I was so taken up with my observation of this area I had no idea I had once more arrived at the promenade. I stood there to rest and to puzzle over why, in spite of my trajectory, I was right where I had started.

When I returned to the Compound's gate, the group of men who had been following us cleared a path. One of them, a chubby man with a hanging lower lip, said, "You are in big trouble."

"Did you see a woman returning through the gate?" I asked him.

Someone from the crowd shouted, "What woman? Can I have her?"

"She went out with me."

"Maybe you killed her," the fat man said.

"Can I have her?"

"You must be reported to the Gatekeepers. They are not here today. You are lucky. But only today. Lucky only once."

This was the first I could recall ever addressing one of the loitering groups and I tried to control my annoyance. "Look, I don't have time for this. There was also a figure by the asphalt lot. Did you see anyone?"

The man who had shouted, stepped forward. Everything about him was grimy but for his hair, neatly oiled and brushed. "Do you know how long I have been here? Make a guess."

"I am more concerned with the person outside. There was a woman and I am afraid he may have –"

"May have what?" the fat man asked. His companions came up closer, surrounding me. "Did you do it again?"

"Do what?"

"The same thing."

"Would you mind describing what that same thing was?"

"Why describe it if it's the same? The description would be the same, too."

"The same thing is the same when it is not different."

"Everything that is the same is different when it's not the same."

So this is what conversations in this place are like, I thought as I stepped away. "Don't bother," I told them. "It was most likely my imagination."

They all applauded and grouped into a huddle. Then the fat one said, "How can you tell what occurred after did not happen before?"

And a man with a smug and almost cherubic look on his small face added, "So it is written and so it is said." When I walked away, he shouted, "The childkiller has been cancelled. End of text."

"Erased."

"Everything will be erased."

"You, too."

When I hurried away I had a sense of someone from the group following me so I circled around the block of containers in which my room was located and walked through the canteen to the other side of the Compound where there was an abandoned sporting field with rusted javelins and iron balls strewn about. I didn't want anyone from this place to know the location of my room but when I was returning to the container-like cells I stumbled on a figure turning a corner at the same time. He was a severely whiskered man with a face too round for his slim body and he seemed extremely startled at our minor collision. "Were you following me?" I asked.

He tried to look aggrieved but was undone by uselessly pushing his hands into his waistcoat's pockets and adopting a stiff, almost official posture. His hat, I saw, had a hole in the centre of the brim. "Give me five good reasons why I would do something as stupid as that."

"Because I saw you with the group of men a while ago and now here you are."

"Go on. Let me hear four more. And please hurry as I am busy." He glanced at one wrist then the other, even though neither had a timepiece.

"Never mind. Please step out of the way."

"I was here first," he said, but as I sidestepped he did the same, first to the right then to the left.

"What are you doing?" I asked him.

"I am following your lead." I made a move as if I was heading to the left but swiftly shifted to the right. "Not fair," I heard him saying. "Next time I will be more prepared."

As I hurried to my room I glanced back but I did not see him. For the remainder of the day and half the night I worked on my drawing of a woman striding away from an explosion. Early in the morning, I erased the woman's face, lightened her outline, rolled up the sheet and took it with me to the library. She was not there, but on the desk she had always chosen was her mask. I pushed it into one of the drawers with the frail hope she would return. But I already knew she was gone; and when I left in the late evening, I tried to lessen my disappointment by convincing myself that she had arrived at the stage where she was confident enough to step out into the world. And I had helped her. Before I arrived at my room I decided that I would seek her out in the place I had thrust her; the town and beyond it, the terminal and the world it led to. I thought of how she had been acclimatizing herself, during our recent trips, for a journey to find this child who may or may not be dead. I reflected too on her questions about the imagination.

5 THE SOLICITOR

Distressingly, I have a few times encountered the man who blocked my path the day the woman disappeared. He calls himself the Solicitor and he has taken to lugging around a battered satchel, which, he insists, is stuffed with his briefs. During our last encounter, I was eyeing the group at the gate when he snucked up behind me and said, "I can represent you." I was startled and I turned to see him with his briefcase and smile, both battered and useless. "Both of you. Two for the price of one." I glanced around but there was no one else.

"I have committed no crime so I don't need any representation."

"Really?" He looked up at the sky and uttered a dramatic chuckle. "That is not for you to decide." There was a full growth of hair sprouting from his nostrils and an equivalent growth on his negligible chin. Because his big nose elevated the centre of his face he appeared much closer than he really was. Instinctively, I stepped away.

"Look, I am very –"

"Hear me out. I have the perfect defence." He tapped his brief-case. "Madness. I can prove that neither of you were in full control of your senses. Diminished responsibility. It's perfect."

"I am not interested. And you should stop talking in plurals."

"You were commanded by the almighty. There were voices in your heads. You saw snakes everywhere. You were innocent proxies." I hurried away and heard him shouting, "You were sods and idiots. Sleepwalking. Demons in your dreams. Call me. I have represented half the people in this place."

I don't doubt it, I thought bitterly as I entered my room and locked the door.

That was seven days earlier and I have avoided him since. It's now twenty-one days since the woman disappeared. And I have been stuck in my room for most of the time because of the so-called Solicitor and the groups of idlers I see, from a distance, at the gate. They, too, seemed to have taken a disturbing interest in me. So, helplessly cooped up, I have been trying to understand the events of the month and a half since I awoke in this place. Each morning I sneak to the canteen to collect my rations for the day. Usually the place is empty but this morning I saw an old woman sitting by herself and staring with the fixed gaze of the blind at the area before her. She appeared to be in her late seventies and although she had misaligned the buttons on her coat and her scarf lay too loose on her chest, she had taken her time with her hair. She seemed to be expecting someone and I waited a while expecting a caregiver or matron would arrive to take her away. Half an hour later, I walked across to her table and without any hesita-tion, she told me, "It's time to go but there is no one to fetch me."

I asked her, "Have you been waiting for a long time? Someone should come along shortly."

"It's time to go. And there's no one to take me." Her voice was angry and she began to shout after me, "Take me! Take me away!

I cannot go by myself." She began to pull at her hair and when I stepped back, she grew calm once more, her features frigid yet remote.

I left without collecting anything to eat and on my way out, I saw four or five old men with the same blank expression. Once more, I wondered what I was doing in a place where everyone but me seemed crazy and whether their behaviour would appear normal to someone with a functioning memory.

It's surprising that an old woman, a disturbed stranger, should affect me, but the face of the old woman remained with me. I tried to regain my focus by looking at the illustrations on the wall, at the scene from my jalousie, the pattern on the iron safe. I tried to determine if, in some way, her obliviousness to her situation mirrored my own condition. There was something else: I was seized with the idea that the focus of old people narrowed so minutely that everything but the pain, the growing feebleness, the grasping for scattered memories, was deflected. You may say this was an overreaction – likely incited by my uncertain age and memory – but I couldn't help wondering whether this fixed regard of more able-bodied people involved a recollection of better days and an annoyance at how swiftly they had passed, or whether the blind gaze was just that, blankness and nothing more.

Over the following hours, I tried to consider a mind even worse than mine, where connections were constantly eluded, where thoughts died the second they were born. Many of the people in the Compound looked passive and solemn as if they had been tranquilized and I wondered if I, too, had experienced some type of deceptive calm the moment my memory had collapsed. I got out a sheet of paper from the Gladstone bag and reproduced the scene from the canteen and when I was finished I noted how very similar, in my drawing, the gazes of the old people were to those of apes; I saw the same mix of muddled curiosity and helplessness.

Perhaps I was just a few steps away from this unavoidable and irreparable debasement. Perhaps I was already there. Two centuries ago, I would have been lucky to reach fifty and I knew that the degradation had already begun in ways I had missed or more likely forgotten: this numbing grind of life. Not for the first time, I wished I knew how old I was.

I have this memory of explorations of solitude; of pastoral tracts extolling long replenishing strolls and closely guarded seclusion and fastening the mind on fixed objects to achieve some sort of peace. I cannot say how I may have reacted when I first read these descriptions but now I am sure that when there is no other choice, this hallucinatory calm is just a prelude to a complete relinquishment of the spirit. I know this sounds awkward and overly dramatic and I would not expect you or anyone not similarly afflicted to understand. Time and again, my mind returns to the old woman sitting alone and confused and I feel that there should be a better way for a life to close. Surely, she must have relatives, grandchildren whose births she may have witnessed and whom she must have seen running around the place.

You may laugh at my sudden decision to get out of this place that was prompted not by my encounter with the creepy trio or the intrusive Solicitor or the loiterers but by an old and harmless woman. In order to accomplish this, I had to more fully understand the Compound.

That very night I began with the area with which I was most familiar. I studied all the illustrations on the wall, staring at them for hours, from different angles, walking from wall to wall, closing my eyes and rearranging the images. I am not sure if, to the normal, inspiration or solutions arrive in an instant from an equilibrizing of linked memories, accepted facts and common knowledge, but in my case the moment of understanding was slow and uncertain. So slow, in fact, that it took a while to notice the connections between the slight man seated before a desk, walking alone in a cloud-filled valley, relaxing with his eyes closed and the dungeons with spike traps and lopsided streetlamps illuminating capsized lorries frozen in steely blue ice. On another wall, there were men and women alighting nimbly on flagpoles and leaping off and vanishing before they hit the ground and above them, blue-skinned beings shedding tears that seemed to transform into leaves as they touched the ground. I studied them all, panel by panel, not as individual drawings but as an unfolding narrative, each image connected to the next. As I did so, I literally grew dizzy with excitement and I had to sit awhile just to go over what I had learned. There was a writer. He had composed a tale of strangely powered individuals. The batch of drawings with these men and women – almost an entire wall – that had so confused me was an illustrated representation of this story.

But three hours later, I was on my bed, my head bent, my mind frozen. I had been misled by my breakthrough because the succeeding panels reverted to the writer, lightly pencilled and in the background yet unmistakably present and surrounded by his creations. I saw him conversing with the blue-skinned beings, leaping with the airborne men and women, cavorting with amphibious creatures. But stranger still, I observed that each succeeding drawing brought the writer more into the foreground while portraying his companions as increasingly bent and helpless so that in the end they were nothing more than twisted brutes. Why was this so? What was I supposed to take from this? Were they clues left for me to decipher? Additionally, there were several drawings that seemed completely out of place: an elephant with a thick pencil instead of a tusk, a couple standing forlornly before a tombstone, a group of men gazing at a mess of diagrams on a blackboard, an old house that seemed to be sinking in the ground, sketches of bags and grips and arcane medical equipment. And the child with her mother. For two days and nights, I walked from one end of my room to the next. But there were no answers and I felt that my partial insight had only served to introduce questions beyond any understanding. This was far more frustrating than my previous ignorance. What was the writer doing in the middle of his story? Had I misinterpreted everything so far? Other questions arose and I thought bitterly that trying to recover lost memories was like searching for flecks of gold in a fast-flowing, muddy stream.

Another week has passed and I have shifted my examination from my room to what I know about the Compound. This is what I have come up with:

1. The Compound is possibly a kind of infirmary but if so, I cannot see any type of security. The huge gates are unlocked and unguarded and I am confused why no one, especially the group of idlers who hang around that area, has attempted to leave.
2. This may be because the Compound is situated in a deserted town – as determined from my brief foray outside – and it's likely the security is stationed at the outer perimeters of the town.
3. There are three old men who either are administrators of some kind or have taken up this designation capriciously. Their base of operation might be in the town but more likely it's further afield.
4. There might be even more dangerous men roaming about. One I met in the library pretends to be a shy hoodlum. There are others who seem to be gazing at me from a distance although this may just be my imagination. You understand why I am pushed to this sort of paranoia. The people with whom I come into contact, like the Solicitor, claim to all know me in some form or fashion. I cannot determine if they are working in tandem or if this preferred familiarity is a symptom of whatever ails everyone I have met so far. If it's the former, I cannot ascribe any motive other than their wish to unsettle me. The most memorable person who issued this claim has disappeared.

5. I have lost the ability to draw. This is the most distressing blow so far. (If I still possessed this ability there would have been little need to narrate this account to you.) Mercifully, none of my motor functions seems impaired.

6. My memory does not go back far enough to determine whether the Compound is a kind of temporary holding cell or a lab of some kind or an asylum. But the place is huge and I have avoided any extensive explorations because of the clusters of idlers I see everywhere. This will have to change, as I cannot keep stumbling against the same wall.

From the above you will understand that my exploration was a difficult undertaking as, even in the nights, there were always people loitering around, some of whom misunderstood my interest in the place and decided to walk in lockstep with me.

One evening the Solicitor sneaked up on me. "Are you planning to escape? If that is the case it is my duty to forewarn you that it will be seen as an admission of guilt. The offer still stands. Two for the price of one. It's the best I can do."

I focused on his first question. "Why would I want to escape? And where would I go?"

He patted his briefcase and I noticed he was wearing two left shoes. "I have all the information here." He unzipped his briefcase and pretended to read from a page he half-pulled out. "To the scene of the crime. It's where all guilty people go. Shall we all meet there?"

"The only place I am going to is my room," I said as I walked away.

"Have you seen my hat?" I heard him shouting.

After that encounter, I avoided the common paths and instead trudged between the trees and cisterns and abandoned wooden buildings. I soon discovered the Compound was even bigger than I had imagined. I had walked with the wet nurse to the cemetery overlooking an abandoned railway station, but there were gravel tracks on either side of the graveyard that led to long sheds. It seemed a miniature functioning town with its own pond, animal farm, fields and mills all powered by chugging machines in a huge boiler room. I chose the early mornings and the late nights and one night when I was climbing up a rugged hill, I heard a voice saying, "We are most inventive when we are forced to account for our actions."

The voice was not the Solicitor's and it had come from one of the slopes that led to a shallow ravine. I thought it was one of the other loiterers, which was strange, as everyone seemed to stick to the main areas. Someone was climbing ahead of me. He had a cane and when he noticed me, he pointed with it to the sky and said, "Look how fiery the clouds appear. The dry branches are scrambling the light. It's as if someone flung a colony of ants against the sky. The diffusion makes everything seem alight. Can you see it?" I tried to match his view but could only see a gnarled tree clinging to the other side of the slope. "There are little ravines running through the clenched roots," he continued. "Do you think there are animals living there? We should investigate." But he stood there pointing with his cane.

"It might be dangerous," I told him.

"If you can spot the possibility of danger then you should also notice its counterpart," he told me. "Astonishment."

"What are you doing here?" I asked.

He ignored me, jabbed his cane into the ground and took a couple steps up to a ridge in the hill. "This is a place of abandonment," he said, gazing around. "No, of extinction. People come here to fade away."

I managed to get closer and asked him, "What are you doing here so late in the night?"

"It's the only thing left for me."

"I do not understand."

He plunged his cane into a crack and levered himself up. "Let me assure you of an indisputable fact," he said, breathing heavily. "When a man arrives at my stage, when there is little to look forward to, then this man begins to repopulate his world. He remembers old buildings and terminals and benches. But they are all empty, you see. And this old man, or woman, for that matter, tries to put people into the places. Familiar faces, accustomed gestures. He does this slowly and with utmost care."

"And when he is finished?" I asked him.

"When he is finished? Then he must begin once more."

He could have been referring to my memory cycles and I told him, "There seems little point in this. Why do the same thing over and over?"

"Isn't that what we all do? Ah, look at the view from up here."

We were now beneath the highest ledge, but it was so narrow there was room for only one person. "Do you mind if I remain here?" I asked as he pulled himself up with a surprising agility.

"You can if you prefer, but you will miss everything."

It was a relief to speak to someone who seemed relatively lucid. I told him, "Perhaps you can describe it for me."

"It won't be the same. I might include details that are important to me but meaningless to you."

"I am just three yards or so beneath you."

"I see sheds built at odd angles and cows grazing on the sides of trees. A man is unfolding an umbrella and when he is done, a woman appears at his side. They have left now but there is a child running about looking for them. Do you think it's a game?"

"All I can see are the trees and long rows of some type of spiky plant."

"We are looking at different things. You are searching for the beginning and I for the end." He was so close to the edge I felt I should caution him, but he said, "Ah, there he is. A child and he seems not to notice the adult's departure because he has found his own playthings. New friends. He is playing with them and now his mother returns alone. No, it's not his mother. A woman, a nurse or nanny of some kind. His new friends are dancing around her, but she cannot see them."

"How do you know that?"

He ignored me and said, "She seems confused because the boy is imitating his friends, in the manner of children. It looks a little cruel as if he is mocking her. Poor boy."

"Should your sympathy not be directed at the nurse?"

He sounded a bit irritated as he said, "You don't know anything. The boy has been left alone by his parents once again. What else do you expect him to do? His friends are interesting, though. One can turn invisible, another seems to be very strong and the other can fly. What do you think would happen if I flew off this ledge?"

"You would be smashed on the rocks beneath."

"You disappoint me terribly. You see only disaster and tragedy. What if I suddenly discover I can fly and swoop and soar?" Actually, it was he who was the disappointment. I did not want to tempt him by prolonging this subject. He grasped the protruding root of a dead tree – a palm of some kind – and hoisted himself onto a gravelly protrusion just above the ledge. He glanced down at me struggling to keep up with him and said, "The boy tugs away the nurse's umbrella and makes a running jump as if it can propel him upward. He has stumbled and he glances back to talk to his friends before he tries once more. The nurse seems to be pleading but his friends are encouraging him. He is running faster and farther and he opens the umbrella but beyond my field of vision. Where has he gone?"

"To find his parents?"

"Yes, yes. But why would he look for a father who abandoned him for his new wife? I think the boy wants to disappear and become someone else. Not his little stepsister, for sure, because she is part of the scheme, too. Clutching all the affection. They would be better off without her."

He was now so close to the edge that I felt he would surely slip over. I was about to warn him when I saw that what I had mistaken for a cane was really an umbrella that he had unfurled. He was waving it around and pointing this way and that. "You should be careful," I told him. "It's windy up here."

"Then it's perfect. Perfect."

And standing there, pointing his umbrella at the area, pausing frequently to search for some sign of the boy, he told me the most amazing story. He professed to be a writer who had changed the industry because of his creation of psychoneurotic heroes. But the industry, levered on the muscular shoulders of unambiguous automatons, did not pay him much initial attention and they were caught by surprise when each issue drew long lines at the bookstores followed by fevered discussions of these frenetic heroes' battles with vaguely familiar government officials and wealthy industrialists. The nine members of this group always prevailed by accessing their nemeses' memories, learning of their strategies, and pre-empting their moves. This was not a seamless operation, however, as the empaths invariably tapped into repellent memories. Absent mothers, bullying fathers, conniving siblings, unresolved sexual issues. Frequently the team delivered their death blows while sobbing uncontrollably. The readers loved it because it mirrored their own lives.

Then the writer disappeared. There were several rumours. He had been shipped beyond the walls where he had died from either malaria or a bullet. He had been stricken with a debilitating disease. He had been taken out by an envious competitor. Or by the government, which had grown uneasy with his sweeping depiction of corruption. This last view got the most traction because his villains, motivated mostly by greed, intolerance and hypocrisy, could have been drawn from any government office. Soon he was forgotten; or more accurately, he was written into legend.

Having this conversation up in the mountain was the craziest thing yet in this crazy place. Yet he did not show any surprise at my presence and I could not push aside the suspicion he had been waiting for me. I asked him suddenly, "Do I know you?" When there was no reply I asked, "Was it you who left the note in my room? Who left me here?"

He paused to ask me, "Do you know that each object carries with it the imprint of all those with whom it has come into contact?"

"It's important that I know. I have recorded everything so far. As I will this encounter." My voice was loud and insistent.

"The world is filled with little connections. Spirals bearing the faint whiff of sulphur. I can assure you that the further we cast our gazes the more we see of ourselves."

"Was it you?" I screamed.

He leaned over and his umbrella caught a tiny whorl of breeze that spun him around. He laughed as if it was great fun and continued, "When I discovered that the stories did not spring from my own fertile imagination but were planted there, I knew it was time to stop. How could I continue? I was nothing more than a tool and a plant. My stories of empaths and superpowered beings and multiple dimensions and cosmic rays and underground labs were planted to desensitize my readers. To prepare them."

I was terribly disappointed. He was now talking in a manner that would impress Balzac and the rest of the Compound. I tried to calm him. "And you have written nothing since?"

"You don't believe me," he said, speaking softly now. "I can see that. But to answer your question, a writer develops a particular way of looking at the world and even when he stops writing, this particular orientation remains. He never loses this madness."

"Why would you categorize it as madness?"

"Oh, it's just my way of talking. Madness, in a perfectly ordered world, is simply a different vision. Wait, what am I saying? I believe the altitude has made me reckless because I am going to reveal a secret. As a young writer, I imagined that my inspiration had come from the most prosaic of things. My asthmatic childhood. Being bullied each day. A father who claimed that his epileptic fits were communions with an angel and a mother who was jealous because her own visions were only of the life she should have lived. A step-mother who disappeared each time I sought affection. A little sister I daily planned to murder. And when I wrote in a haze with no conscious will, I assumed that this was the method of all geniuses. A senior editor once told me that my stories had the potential to change the world. He could not have known how correct he was."

"Correct about what?"

He sighed and said, "Let me make more plain what you refuse to understand. What I had taken for normal inspiration was far more." He then revealed that his stories sprang from voices in his head. During the height of his fame, he had been thrilled by the fans' reception, but as their adoration and tributes grew, he began to feel there was something bigger at play. People began quoting lines of dialogue, dressing up in his heroes' costumes, writing to him about the changes in their lives. Once, a young girl accosted him outside his office and told him he was a prophet. This in itself was not unusual, as some of his fans had begun to worship him with reverent silence when he entered a public place or presented him with unanswerable questions as if he carried some great wisdom. He began paying more attention to the voices directing his stories. He recalled the precise moment when he realized he was a tool. It was late in the night and the voices were beating about in his head. He was working on an instalment in which his heroes were transported to a dimension that corresponded to an earthly paradise. But this was a paradise with layers of rules, each layer more intractable than the other. He remembered getting up from his desk, turning off the light and returning to bed. But the story followed him in his sleep. He awoke the following morning with a clear decision: he would no longer write this story. But each time he tried another story with other heroes it was chased off by this particular plot. There was only one course of action open to him: he had to stop writing entirely. But even that was not enough. He had to repair the damage he had done by warning his former colleagues.

Here I will admit that I had decided that this madman was not you. He was now perilously close to the end of the ledge as he continued his story.

"At first, they listened patiently," he told me. "Later, I noticed their embarrassment and shiftiness and I concluded that they too were infected. Soon, I was met by security guards or confronted with locked offices. When I realized my entreaties were useless, I contacted the radio stations and newspapers. Finally, I turned to government agencies. The result? My associates cut me off. I was flushed with antipsychotic drugs. It left me shaking with involuntary motion. I lost control of my tongue and lips. I felt like a character in one of my stories. Eventually I was shipped off to an asylum. And it was there that my lucidity returned. I started to see clearly what was happening. And I began to see the end."

"Are you referring to the Compound?"

And that was when his story got more astonishing. He told me that during his years in exile, when his fans were hoping for his return, he had created another gallery of heroes. Among those was a postman whose gift of invisibility had been scuppered by his concurrent blindness. A hemophiliac who invented a serum that gave him extraordinary strength. A sensitive and nervous woman who awoke one night with the ability to fly. I asked why he had never published comics with these heroes and he told me, "Don't you see? They were all compromised. The invisible man struck with blindness had become a traffic hazard. The hemophiliac superman constantly ruptured blood vessels while lifting his heavy objects. Did I mention that he also suffered from high blood pressure?" he asked. "Or that my beautiful nervous woman would no longer fly as she was often paralysed, in mid-flight, by vertigo?"

I told him, "They were flawed heroes, then. Much like your earlier ones."

"These were not flaws. They were fatal defects that effectively neutralized their powers."

"So they were forced to be ordinary men and women. Just like you and I. I think that's very interesting."

"Was it? My own views are different. In any event, they could not be published. They were dangerous nonsense."

He seemed a little annoyed, so I told him, "What I meant was that your heroes were faced with choices that many of us, in the real world, are subject to. Power, but at a cost. It's a long-familiar phenomenon."

"If you are trying to say that I had created conditions with which real people could identify then I will have to agree. Unfortunately, in a place like this the distinction between what's possible and what's not is not too clear. As you have learned by now it's quite easy to inhabit another person's memories."

"So you wrote the book or books here? In the Compound?"

"My years of exile, I try to think of it. My period of exile in a little sanctuary. A sort of writer's retreat. During my early years here, I had a fair bit of time to think about my life, about the industry I had abandoned and most of all about my period of success. I have tried to understand the precise point at which fulfillment and happiness intersect and why this joining can never be sustained."

I didn't know what to make of his story and I waited for him to elaborate. As a means of encouraging him I said, "I have figured out the illustrations on my wall. They are like panels in a comic but not everything adds up."

"Destroy it," he told me. "It's utter nonsense. Dangerous nonsense." He looked up at a bird circling overhead and for the first time he seemed a little frightened. "You need to stop bothering me," he shouted, either to the bird or to me.

"Careful," I warned because he seemed so agitated.

"The child has returned and the nurse tries to take her umbrella. He pokes her in the eye. Poor boy. He does not know what is in store for him. He will be locked inside his room, chained to his bed and prescribed the vilest concoctions. Poor, poor child. I must warn him. It must come to an end now."

I had now managed to get alongside him and when he opened his umbrella and jumped I instinctively clutched his coat. Our fall was slowed by his umbrella and I closed my eyes and waited for the crash and the pain. I felt the wind across my face and when I opened my eyes, I saw that we were floating above the Compound and then above the old town. The town was barricaded with a wall that led to a ravine and a short distance away some sort of cathedral. Then we were beyond the town and I saw a small bus terminal in a field that went on for miles and miles and which was dotted with derelict buildings with rubble strewn about. My eyes began to burn and I felt I would lose hold of the flying man's coat as we flew over a derelict mansion and across what appeared to be small volcanoes emitting some kind of sulphurous dust. In the far distance, I saw what looked like an abandoned train station.

Throughout this, the flying man was silent and I looked up to see if there was some mechanical attachment to his umbrella. I saw nothing, just a man with his arms raised. In my shock, I lost hold of his coat and I fell.

STAGE
TWO

6 THE WATCHER AT THE WINDOW

Three days have now passed since I awoke in the lower floor of a two-storey house and discovered your letter. You have not revealed yourself – as I hoped you would – but I am now convinced that I am not alone in the building. Each evening following my exploration of the immediate area, I see the curtain shifting but whenever I stand outside and gaze at the windows, the place is as still as it should be. On a side note, my scrutiny has thrown up other details. From a distance, the building had seemed a brick-and-mortar store, but up close it appeared fractional, as if it was an adjunct and some big part had been knocked down and the debris carted off. It reminded me in this respect of a chapter house. These precise observations have convinced me of my former profession, but everything else is a mystery. I might want to speculate that there is a punctuality to the act of shifting the curtain and it is possible this unknown person's outward gaze has nothing to do with me. Perhaps it's an old man grown habituated to gazing out whenever he took his nightly medication. Or maybe it's just a draft ruffling the fabric.

I have no idea how I found myself in this town, this street, this lower-floor residence that smells of something aged and viscous, like resin-soaked linen stored in canopic jars. This determination tells me that it is only my autobiographical memory that has been expunged. There are a few detailed geometric diagrams on a wall – of buildings and crosswalks and trails and landscaped terraces – that seem familiar but only in the sense that I may have seen similar diagrams at some time. On the opposing wall, there is a charcoal illustration of a slouching ape transitioning into an upright man and another of a man gazing at his older self in a mirror. The younger man is confused; his older self, his lower jaw thrust out with grim determination, seems to know what he wants.

Now to your letter. There was no date and it was addressed rather formally: *To Whom It May Concern.* Here's the gist in case you cannot recall.

It is my wish that this lodge will finally bring you the peace that you claim I have stolen.... It is my additional hope that you will begin to remember in an orderly fashion...risky, I know...I have learned to forgive a side of you but your other associates, I fear, are not so understanding.... I believe you will be safe here and more significantly so will everyone else...please record everything that occurs and any anomalies you may observe...omit no details.

And so on. Apart from the references in your letter to legacies and visions and more visions, it is littered with veiled warnings. I take these to indicate that you are afraid of me and I should feel the same way about you. I have to inform you, though, that your letter omitted the most significant detail: how did I find myself in this place and why can I not remember anything? The bleeding from my left ear has stopped but I still hear a ringing each night and an occasional bang as if something in my head is breaking loose. I am not being deliberately dramatic because I sense a shuddering memory skulking in the dark with each crescendo.

Some of these involve a temple or monastery and flattened wings falling in spirals on a surging dam. Following one of these cranial bangs I was jolted upright not so much from the imagined sound but because this memory was so distinct I could actually visualize it. A man is released from a mechanical chair into a room where he stares for hours at a sliver of light as thin and frail as a child's finger. As it is the only object he can see, he focuses on it the minute his eyes open. Hours pass, perhaps days and weeks, and the sliver of light moulds itself into a puddle from which tiny insects swarm before it briefly reshapes itself into a knife or a key. The trick repeats itself over and over, the light taking other forms but always it's a threat followed by a means of escape. Perhaps it's simply a nightmare; a man in my circumstance is permitted to have a few of these.

You have left a supply of tinned food in the cupboard that should last a month or two. For this, I am thankful. But that is the only bit of gratitude you will get from me.

Yesterday morning, as a way of pushing aside this worry about my curious circumstance, I decided to walk through this neighbourhood. I suppose I hoped I would come across someone who might march me backwards to the point of my injury, but the place is completely deserted. I returned in the afternoon and, not meeting anyone, I began to pay close attention to the buildings instead. As I strolled along, I felt that in another season, when the first showers rendered the light soft and diffuse and unreliable, it might be possible to glimpse the original rural tones of the town. I slowed to a stop several times and saw where wood had been replaced by stones and then brick, wooden windows with glass, and stone walls with hedges and wire fences. The renovations, over the generations, had been done piecemeal and frugally and it was possible to distinguish some of the features of the partially knocked down buildings – the eroded arches, buttresses and cantilevers. As

I walked on, I discovered the only objects that resisted the architectural extemporizing were the statues: they were simply neglected, folded away between shrubs or staring from their lime-green bases.

I was a bit surprised by these precise observations and they convinced me that in my former life I might have been a rustic poet or, more likely, an architect. This determination restored a bit of my confidence and I convinced myself that it might be a prelude to the restoration of my memories.

You dedicated half your letter to visions so I will now tell you that when I was returning to the building in which you had set me up, I believed I saw a face behind the shifting curtains in the upper window. It was a bit gloomy and I assumed it was a trick of light or something. Surely, I would have heard some sound to indicate a life above me. Nevertheless, I went to the upper room and knocked on the locked door. There was no answer and I walked down the stairs, believing it was merely my hope I was not alone in this abandoned place that had provoked my vision.

Three days have passed since I saw the ghostly face and my knocking on the door has yet to yield any result. Once, I tried to force open the sturdy door and stopped only when I considered that the presumed watcher from the window may have some good reason for not showing himself or herself. It's driving me crazy, as you may well imagine, and I have now moved to imagining this person from the style of the window: multi-paned and set off with a protruding arch at the top, and beneath, a narrow ledge, the correct size for a potted plant. The sturdy boxiness of the lower floor suggested the structure could have once housed a shop; a shop specializing in haberdashery with bolts of faded cream and yellow fabric stacked against a dusty wall. Perhaps the proprietor had been an oldish man with forearms made wiry from constant snipping. He may have had a gentle moustache that set off his sad eyes and he wore neat clothes because his customers were mostly middle-aged women. This man, with or without a felt hat, had moved upstairs after the failure of his business or from some tragic event and he now lived alone, surrounding himself with carefully arranged pictures on his mantelpiece. Here my imagination failed and the pictures remained blank: meaningless white pages contained within frames. This omission was distressing and it reduced all I had learned about the house and its occupant.

I focused on the lower floor where he would have once conducted his business. The life-size mirror standing at an angle reflected the dusty trinkets, pale silk flowers – perhaps oriental lilies – and the willowware set at an angle in a deeply stained cabinet. Each time I pass the mirror I glimpse myself and when I notice my skin, which possesses the pallor of the silk lilies, and my face, which seems more aware and confident than my present situation warrants, I am forced back to your letter. One night I had the suspicion that the man upstairs had a tiny peephole through which he was tracking all my movements. I pulled up a stool and examined the ceiling, inch by inch.

The following evening, on my return from exploring the town, I noticed the uppermost leaves of a raggedy mulberry bristling and walked over to see if a tiny animal was burrowing at its roots. I was about twenty yards from the house. The watcher at the window must also have noticed the trembling bush, and because of this shared observation of the burrowing animal, I felt that I could call out to him with a degree of familiarity. "Hello," I shouted. "I can tell you are watching me." When there was no response, I took a couple steps closer in case he was like many old people, partially deaf. It then struck me that he might be a man accustomed to privacy and might be annoyed at my attempts at familiarity so I stepped back and pretended I was investigating the mulberry.

Here is a confession. Sometimes I recall trivial events that have no apparent connection with me; and as I was poking about, I remembered someone, somewhere, claiming that old people buried their valuables in view of the front window. (Was it you who had mentioned this?) I wondered if there was some hidden treasure beneath the bush. Perhaps that was why he was keeping his watch. The moon was full or close to full and the leaves, swaying gently, resembled a scatter of coins. Because of this, I was uncertain if a piece of whitish paper had been dropped in the centre of the bush where I could not retrieve it. When I walked away, I considered also that the Watcher – which is how I began thinking of the person – might have feebly thrown some object at me.

The following night, another piece of paper fluttered down immediately after my arrival. I went at once and picked it up. There was a single figure: a date scratched over so many times the final year was indecipherable. I waved in the direction of the window and when there was no response, I felt a bit silly and walked a short distance to a building, which, covered in dried vines, resembled an overturned basket. I assumed the building was abandoned, as the vines seemed to have sewed shut the windows. But there was a cat, tawny-brown as the vines, curled up at the base of the front step. The cat must have sensed my gaze as it got up and stretched, scratching the stone with its impressive front claws. It did this for close to five minutes before it limped off into a tunnel of shrubs and withered twigs. I waited a short while for its return before I walked back to the chapter house.

I stood outside the window for an hour or so and just when I was about to leave, another sheet flew from the window. On this was another set of numbers, 6 x 9, the x suggesting dimensions of some kind. When I got to my room, I placed the pages side by side and tried to make sense of the messages.

During that week, at exactly 6:39 every day, a tiny crumpled sheet fell from the window. A couple times, I waved but there was never any response, as if, for the Watcher, the single word or number, and later, the short phrases – like *penalty catalogue* and *trust deed* and *power of attorney* – were enough. I was confused by his actions. Was he trapped in the house or had he been waiting for decades for someone to pay him some attention? I suspected they could be meaningless words comprehensible only to the aged person who had released them and that I should bother no more, but I could not get it out of my head there was some as yet not understood purpose. I even entertained the hope that I could discover something about myself, but what could a man living alone, at the end of his life, tell me about myself? However, in my situation everything has to be considered.

Every night I reviewed what had been written. I tried to understand at first if there was some stand-alone significance before I placed each addition alongside the others. Sometimes I rearranged the pages hoping to spot an anagram or acrostic or some riddle but I could find no associations.

Soon, as with any unsolvable puzzle, my interest dwindled and I simply collected the bits of paper and placed them in a heap. Each day I wandered farther afield. The town seemed without end but I soon discovered that the maze of cross streets had sent me in a series of loops. The streets are named, but in a confusing manner with letters of the alphabet randomly assigned before the word *Tree* so that there is an A Tree Street and a K Tree Street and so on. The town was either a neglected prison that had deliquesced into a backwater refuge – holding a pastoral charm perhaps to a normal man – or my lopped-off memory could not yet put all the pieces together. During my explorations I began to pay more attention to details, and also to place a leaf from the mulberry at each intersection to mark my track.

Earlier this evening I came across a concrete wall that seemed to rise higher with each step. There were old signs plastered every ten yards or so extolling the value of solitude and warning about prying eyes. Perhaps as a means of emphasizing these warnings, lower down, a narrow ditch ran parallel to the wall. I followed this ditch for close to two hours until I concluded that the town, as far as I could determine, was completely barricaded. The only interruption in the ditch-and-wall cordon was a dark, forested area where there were lianas wreathed around tall spindly trees that resembled bamboo. Beneath were ferns, nettles and spindly shrubs that looked like mossy crabs. The entire area appeared excavated from some tropical zone and plopped down at the town's end. While I was wondering if this anomalous patch was an abandoned herbarium that had spread over the years, I heard a frightful cry, a sort of full-throated ululating from within and I hurried away.

Thereafter, I avoided that area. However, I couldn't help but wonder what lay beyond the wall and each day I tried to approach it from a different direction. That was how I came across a huge gate formed in the shape of a fierce-looking albatross holding an hourglass between its claws. I was excited when I noticed two men stationed at the gate because it was my first direct glimpse of anyone else in this forsaken place. Both were clutching cigarettes that emphasized the arcs of their furious waving and when I placed my hand on the gate, the shorter, a runty man with prickly marsupial eyes told me, "I wouldn't advise it, buddy."

Before I could reply, his companion added in a mocking voice, "Entrance denied." He pumped his cigarette up and down as if he were stamping a form or something.

"What are you guarding?" I asked the pair. "What is inside the wall?"

"Question denied." The taller one plopped the cigarette between his lips and withdrew a soiled and folded page from his overalls. He made a great show of flapping it open. His companion did the same and they both glanced at each other expectantly. The shorter one backpedalled with a little flourish. "Might we interest you in an elegy? It's a distillation of our observations over the years. Each year we add a line."

"I have nothing else to do," I told him with the hope that he would answer my questions when he was done.

He brought his page close to his eyes and read, "The first man was a superman."

His friend continued, "The second man was a thief."

"The third man had a battle plan."

"And still they came to grief."

They both did a ridiculous shimmying routine but stopped when they noticed my attempts at remaining serious. The taller one said, "This is most disgraceful. You people will never appreciate refinement. It's useless. I don't know why I even try with you people." He tugged his friend's ear and dragged him closer to whisper something.

"What do you mean by 'you people'? There's no one here but us."

"You people!" The shorter one screamed. "One, two, three, four." He pointed to different parts of my body. "And they all came to grief."

The taller one released his friend's ear. "You think you can fool us with your new clothes and voice and face, but we can see through everything."

His friend drew circles around his eyes and squinted as if he were peering into a telescope. "We are the Gatekeepers. Everything must be recorded." He took out a crumpled notebook from his pocket. "We have been duly designated and empowered."

"All must be recorded."

"Did a woman go through these gates?" I asked suddenly.

"A woman?"

The tall man placed his hand over the other's mouth and bent to whisper into his ear, looking at me all the while. When he was finished, he opened his notebook and told me, "Describe this woman. Spare no detail."

"Was she lactating?"

"Was she bleeding?"

His lanky friend looked at him harshly, but I had no idea of this woman's identity, if she existed at all, or from where the question had sprung. "I can't remember. I guess I forgot."

"You forgot what a woman is?"

They did their conferencing once more and then stood side by side, their arms hanging stiffly. The taller man coughed into his cupped palm. "A woman is…"

He stepped back and his friend continued, "A woman is a…" He too seemed stuck and his friend dragged him back and took his place.

"A woman is another thing." He said this with a tremulous flourish as if he were caressing a cactus. His friend applauded. "Now who or what is this woman?"

"Don't bother. What are you guarding inside those gates?"

He withdrew a box from his fob and held it against his ear. "It's silly to pretend that you do not know the rules. I have been stationed here for three years. Or six or nine." He seemed to be speaking to his box. "Oh, I see. You are better than everyone, you say. Do you know how often I have heard that line?" He glanced at his friend as he continued. "And do you know what I always say in reply? I say that you did not create me, so I am my own man. I can choose whoever I want to be."

His friend, with his hands on his waist and little chest puffed out, the stance suggesting some sort of military posture, glared at me. "We are exempt."

"Exempt from what?"

"From interference." The taller man returned the box into his fob and snapped the elastic lining loudly. "Conversation terminated."

"We have orders to shoot on sight."

"You better believe it!"

As they were prattling I caught a swift glimpse of a brutish-looking creature beyond the gate and I asked the pair, "Is there someone at the back? A hulking man?"

"Hulking?" The taller man rolled up his sleeves and flexed his hand. The shorter man tiptoed to touch his flabby biceps admiringly. I left them shimmying around one another. On my way back, I was curious as to what the two jokers had been guarding. The walls seemed to enclose a compound of some kind, but it was odd that such a place would be set on the outskirts of an abandoned town. When I was approaching the chapter house, I noticed the usual movement at the curtains. This was curious because my watch showed the time to be 7:06. I walked to the spot where the sheet had landed and another fluttered down. And another. Soon there was a cascade of pages. A couple fell just beneath his window and a few floated over the mulberry to embrace the lamppost. It took me about fifteen minutes before I collected all that I could and when I was finished, I looked up and saw that the curtain was now drawn once more.

The pages I had collected previously were of numbers and cryptic phrases, but the new set seemed different. There were illustrated depictions of tacks of lamplight, wheels and cages, clocks with missing hands, dollhouses, lanterns, brass knuckles and mallets, and items of clothing possibly from a different time. On some of the sketches, there was a figure hunched inside a rectangular box balanced on cogs. Late in the night I awoke and got out of my bed. I went to the table and looked at the pages I had spread there a few hours earlier. I stepped back and saw, unmistakably, a man perched atop some sort of wheel. Beneath the man were empty cages and he was focused on these rather than on the pile of items stacked inside a huge box made of ice or glass.

Here I will confess an idle thought: It is likely that for those with a normally functioning mind, insights arrive after long reflection and consideration, but for me, with less time and fewer resources from which to draw, they are sudden and often startling. (Should it be the other way around?) And, looking at the illustrations, I knew immediately it was a ledger of sorts. I took the illustration to the table and shone the light and I saw clearly an accounting of a life by a man who needed to be certain he existed. He needed this certainty because it was time to leave. (But why had he placed all his possessions in one cluttered area? And were the empty cages representative of the giant gaps in his memory or did they point to his unaccomplished goals?) I could not sleep after this and I paced around my room until the first splinters of light edged through my window. I couldn't understand why he was throwing everything away and what exactly he wanted me to do with the litter. I noticed a lizard gazing at me from an indentation on the ceiling. It was making an odd clicking sound as if trying to communicate. "Just two of us here," I mumbled. "Maybe your companion is hidden."

This was really an act of frustration – talking to this reptile – but it brought the sudden feeling that I had been sharing the house with none other than you, Mr. Letterwriter. It had to be! But why? Unless it was a complicated game whose rules I could not understand, it seemed unnecessarily cruel. I resolved to confront you. So, up the stairs I went, and I began to bang on the door. I decided to continue until you showed yourself. When my knuckles could no longer keep up with my banging, I turned the doorknob.

The man standing at the doorway, less than two feet from me, was exactly as I had pictured him except that he had a thick, grey beard and a full head of hair, also grey. He was of smallish to medium height and his eyes, made smaller by the saggy skin enveloping them, seemed both despairing and hopeful. I had thought to bring along your letter and I shoved this before him. "I would like to return your letter." He blinked slowly, his attention directed not to the letter but to the intruder standing outside his door. He seemed terribly out of sorts, like a patient with a terminal illness. I felt I had made a terrible mistake, yet I asked him, "Did you write this?" Now he gazed at the letter, at the same time feeling around in his tweed jacket for something. Maybe a monocle, but to be safe I stepped back a bit.

He, too, stepped back as if he was imitating my movement. But he left the door open and I followed him into the most choked room I had ever witnessed. (Not much to draw from with my limited memory, but nevertheless.) On every wall were shelves built at odd angles yet miraculously holding suitcases and briefcases. There were more bags and chests on the ground packed atop each other so they formed fences that seemed impossible to get through. The only items of furniture were a lopsided table and a purple sofa and these, too, were laden with old leather briefcases and portfolios. It seemed he had spent most of his life planning for a trip and I asked the only question that I could think of. "Are you leaving?" He seemed to be nodding, but when I saw his hands shaking, I felt it was the tremor of an old man. He pointed unsteadily to the suitcase nearest to him, a bulky black unit with the remnants of torn-off stickers. "Would you like me to help you move this?" I grasped the metal handle and heard the rattle of the objects within. "Where would you like it?" He walked slowly to the door. "Downstairs?" He did not reply and I took the suitcase through the door, waiting for further directions. But he waved twice and closed the door. I stood outside his door for close to five minutes, and when he did not return I called out a few times.

Eventually, I took the suitcase down the stairs and placed it in the hallway close to the door. I left it there when I departed the house but all the while I was wondering what he had packed inside. Weapons and body parts? Tokens and amulets? Tinctures and bandages? When I returned an hour later, I immediately went to the suitcase and pushed up the metal clasps. Inside, I saw a pair of trousers, an assortment of sewing needles stuck into a sponge, a piece of tailor's chalk and a couple bolts of black thread. I held up the trousers and noticed that they were marked just above the hem. Beneath the pants was some silky material folded neatly around what seemed to be a cloak's clasp. At the bottom were nine pieces of fabric on which were stitched insignias of some kind.

As you might well expect, I was a little disappointed. It now seemed likely the old man was a tailor and his suitcases were stuffed with fabric and half-finished clothes and sewing material. Perhaps his business had dried up when the town's inhabitants had moved away. I closed the suitcase and even though I knew that the world, in its present state – if I could judge from the town – might well be filled with tradespeople for whom there was no place, I felt sorry for this old man trapped in a house with suitcases that would never be moved until he was dead. "It's nothing," I told the lizard, which was still on the ceiling, clicking away. "People like him living alone must be dismayed by the idea of all their possessions being calmly audited and thrown away after they passed." I contemplated this state all night; the passing of a life with nothing to show for it but accumulated debris, insignificant and useless to anyone not familiar with the prior owner. Tokens and mementoes and other objects burnished over the years reduced to junk.

The following morning, when I walked up the stairs and knocked on his door, this thought was still with me. The door was unlocked and when I entered his room, I noticed that the curtain was drawn and he was nowhere in sight. I worried he had stumbled somewhere between his suitcases and had fatally hit his head. I had this image of a stiff body with a gaping wound covered in dried blood. Then I saw him on his sofa, his head thrown back. There was a greyish pallor on his face and the scatter of blue veins on his wrist seemed like the fingerpainting of a child. I walked over and asked if he was okay. He fumbled to raise the leg of his trouser and tapped his feet on the floor twice. I now saw that he had taken some time with his grooming. He wore matching socks and his shoes were shining. As I took in his jacket, adorned with cufflinks, a thought that could be considered unfair crossed my mind; I wondered why he had taken the time. An old man, his life almost over, with nothing to look forward to. Waiting for the end and a witness to see him through. Or perhaps he wanted more than a witness. It was a disarming thought but for a mere second the darkness shifted and something sprang to life.

I was young and the world was rushing by so swiftly I felt it would soon come to a grand and dashing end, like a merry-go-round or a cartwheel that had lost its mooring, spinning faster and faster. This is how the end would be, my younger self believed, not a steady and stumbling decline but a frenzied keeling before the final crash. This young man had no idea of life dwindling away, of decay and deliquesce, of bloated organs and strangled veins and a heart not willing to work as hard. I wished I could see him clearly and take in his features, this young man; I wished I could understand his optimistic belief that his life would end as swiftly as it began. It was the starkest and – in spite of its brevity – the most distinct recollection of myself I had so far dislodged. It seemed to have come from another place and it was the first recollection not associated with the disarming banging in my head.

My little reverie was interrupted by what sounded like an animal groan from the couch. I rushed down the stairs and straight out of the front door. Perhaps it was dread that instigated my panic but the farther away I walked, the sharper the fleeting sense of this young, indifferent man grew. How many years passed since I had been cloaked with that naïveté and how many more would have to pass before I transformed into the old man whose house I had fled? This old man, unburdening himself of all he had gathered over the years, waiting for the end. Travelling light, I thought.

But at the moment I was more interested in this unexpected retrieval; I wanted to sustain and prolong it. So I walked through the town, pretending I was seeing it for the first time, as a newly arrived resident would. And as a newly arrived resident, I tried to summon some bit of nostalgia, some remembrance, some regret about the place I had left behind. This *must* work, I thought as I stumbled through the uneven lanes and byways, the narrow pavements overtaken by hedges and shrubbery. But there was nothing more. And I was left with an aching envy of this young man who measured his life not in years but in velocities.

As I was returning to the house, I tried the same approach: to see it as a stranger would. This was not easy because from the moment my eyes opened in the lower floor of the chapter house, I had forced myself to look for familiarity. But gradually, I began to see it differently; I saw it as a building that had shaken off its mooring and was floating on a churning lake. Doubtless this was because of the blanket of mist that had pooled over the road and around the tree trunks. I imagined the old man looking out from his window and waving as from a departing vessel. Eventually I turned away and crossed a path to a bench partially hidden by a stooped and forlorn-looking willow. I dusted off the dried stems and the leaves that, at first glance, appeared to be nematode worms, and sat. The entire town seemed conjured from the mind – from the *minds*, I corrected myself – of a committee of deranged dreamers. I looked up to the sky, watching tiny, furry tufts of clouds appearing to reform around a larger mass that resembled a sinking vessel. I must have fallen asleep and, as I was rubbing my eyes, I noticed that the clouds had not shifted their positions for the duration of my nap: the furry bits were still detached from the larger mass. I must have dozed off for just a few seconds, I thought, even though it felt much longer.

A few minutes later, I walked up the front steps of the chapter house and opened the door. I saw my housemate standing at the top of the stairs. He was smiling but in the stunned manner of someone who had just suffered an injury and had not yet decided on a reaction to the pain. I looked at him carefully but I did not climb the stairs. The young man who had appeared so unexpectedly and briefly might have imagined that the deteriorating senses of the old, blinding them to their worn-down bodies, were blessings. The much older man standing at the base of the stairs saw something else: he knew there would be all these attempts at preservation, like embalming in stages. I felt ashamed to be thinking of this, just beneath this man with blue veins and skin so sallow and loose it seemed bloodless. I looked away and considered going into my room. But I knew he had been waiting for me. When I glanced up, I saw a slanted roguish smile now, as if he had read my mind. (But, more likely, a reflex from an earlier time.) He walked slowly to his room and I climbed the stairs. As before, he tottered between his suitcases, glancing this way and that until he tapped a grey bag. I felt we should talk and discuss his former profession, but he seemed impatient for me to depart.

I opened the bag in my room. I had been expecting more sewing supplies, but I saw bottles and brass cans, all wrapped in cotton. There were lotions and tinctures and balms, and in a small purse, a pair of pliers and a steel brush. The commingled odour of ammonia and sulphur reminded me, unexpectedly, of a hospital's waiting room and I paused for a while to agitate any memory of the duration and purpose of my visit to such a place. I returned to the bag several times in the night and by the next morning, I was impatient to get to the old man's room.

Yet once again, he was not interested in my questions. I delayed, told him that I had no use for whatever lay within the portmanteau he had tapped and that, furthermore, the lower floor was small and already cluttered, but he just stood silently with an impatient look. When I was leaving, he withdrew a pair of snuffers from his trousers and smiled his roguish smile.

"Do you want me to take this?" I asked. He continued smiling and there was something unnerving about his fixed expression. Perhaps all of us, normal and afflicted, old and young, associate this rigidity of emotion, the absence of gestures with death. I repeated my question just to dispel my uneasiness.

I left his room a few minutes later with the same unease and by the time I got to the bottom stair, I was determined to end my visits. But I turned up the next night. And the night after. Each night I observed his deterioration, the blue discolouration and puffiness on his body, the scratches on his wrists one night, the bruises on his cheek the next. But I continued going up the stairs; I suppose I wanted to see how it would end. (Maybe, as an infant learning of the ebb of life by observing the increasing immobility of favoured grandparents.)

In the meantime, I cleared out a fair bit of his room until the lower floor was stuffed with suitcases and bags. Some of the larger items – a globe with a tilting axis and with all the continents but Europe painted over, a reading lamp with an angel base, two old lanterns that seemed plucked from a lighthouse, a brass goddess with a crack around her neck, a pocket watch with the hands stuck at three, a medallion with a circle or a zero in the centre, a mandolin (it may have been an ukulele) with a crudely drawn figure of a dancing woman on its lower bout – I placed on my shelves; the rest, mostly primers on euthanasia and methods of illustrations – two completely opposing sets of manuals – I replaced within their containers. It occurred to me that while I was arranging his stuff he was perhaps doing the same; settling which item he should give me next. I told this to Little Clicker, the name I had given to my companion on the ceiling.

One night, I asked the creature, "What exactly is it that he wants me to do with all his junk? It seems as if he had been waiting for me to show up. No, that's almost as crazy as talking to a lizard. He has been living alone for so long he is just relieved that anyone would show up." A few minutes later, I decided to do what I should have done from the beginning: I returned with some of his smaller items. The door was open when I got there, and upon my entrance I was quite startled to see him standing rigidly before me. He seemed different somehow and instead of walking through his stuff, he stared silently while I replaced the items I had brought to their shelves. He did not seem unduly offended – or even appeared to notice – and when I was done, he pointed to a sturdy brown musical instrument case with brass clasps fashioned in the form of knuckles and bound with rope. I had resolved not to take anything from his place, but he walked to the grip with his slow steps and a lopsided smile and I decided that he would no longer have use for the organ or whatever lay within. Although it was smaller than the suitcases I had lugged from his room, it was surprisingly heavy. When I was leaving, he extended his hand and I noticed he was wearing a tan suit that seemed brand new and which fitted him perfectly. I made a joke and asked him if he was leaving for a trip, but he said nothing. I saw him staring with his lopsided smile at the knotted rope securing a grip.

An hour or so later, I placed the case on my bed and withdrew a packet of porridge from the cupboard. While I was heating the porridge, I wondered how the old man had managed in his frail state to cook and care for himself. I could not recall a stove in his room but with all his junk, I could easily have missed it. While the water was boiling, I closed my eyes and tried to imagine him in his younger days. I saw a man who looked dandyish and spritely. He seemed to be in transit and although he was alone, both his dress and his air of expectancy suggested he was on a rendezvous of some sort. I had no idea where this image sprang from and it may well have been a slice from my own past. (Or from yours, related to me.)

I regretted my weakness in taking his instrument case. I finished my porridge, returned to my room and, as I had done so many times, I reread your letter. Perhaps it was my mood but I felt we may have been friends once.

I put away your letter and walked up the stairs. The Watcher was sitting on a sofa. His skin was startlingly pale and he was gazing lifelessly at the floor. Next to him was a Gladstone bag. "I came to thank you for the tools but I can no longer take any of your stuff." He said nothing and I added, "Perhaps there is some other person who might find it useful. Is there anyone else?" I was surprised I had not thought of this before. He shook his head so ruefully it seemed more an admission of regret than an answer. "I am going to leave now." I turned to leave.

"Baa baa baa." I jumped because he had actually screamed and when I returned I saw he was crying. He was grinding his teeth as if he was trying to say something but he uttered the same distressing animal sound.

"Is there something…something you want to say?"

He rested his hand on the bag.

"I am sorry. There is no space downstairs. I thought at first that someone might have come for your stuff. Please understand."

"Baa baa baa." He now seemed quite frantic and he settled only when I grasped the bag's handle.

I left his room with a fair bit of trepidation, wondering about the bag's contents that had distressed him so much. I took it to my own room and immediately opened it. I was relieved to see a stack of record albums. There were singers and musicians, posing with their harps and guiros and ukuleles and accordions and other equipment I could not place. I decided to stack them on a shelf but when I was moving the pile, I once more noticed their lightness. I replaced the albums in the grip, withdrew the one on the top, *The Tawny Leopard*, a calypso collection by an old man with a slanted hat and I felt inside. At the centre of the phonograph record was an illustration of a little girl with her arms stretched over her head.

Many of the jackets were missing their records but they all held sketches, old, faded and creased. A few were discoloured at the edges, most likely because they had been removed from a frame or from a photograph album and half a dozen, all of the same girl with a square, dirty face and a scatter of curls, were unfocused as if drawn from a distance. There were other sketches on onion skin, of men flying over burning cities and prostrate women in some kind of cornfield and a man dragging a wolf and a creature with three human heads and a train hurtling down a mountainside and a deluge that had trapped an entire town. Although a different style had been deployed with each sketch, I could see from the firmness of the brushes and pencils, the broad strokes and the proliferation of dots and crackles, they had all been done by the same person. I wondered if the artist had been trying to experiment or to mask his style, but then I realized they been sketched over a protracted period as the girl had been portrayed at different ages. When I examined the drawings more closely, I saw that the crackles were really huddles of skinny children holding out bowls of some kind. Soma, the name at the bottom of each picture, I took to be an identification of the subject rather than the artist's signature. Beneath each illustration was this confusing statement: *Today is a new day but yesterday was the same day.* The last picture I replaced in its jacket was of a dashing young man in a military outfit. It seemed a self-portrait and I was confused by the familiarity of its subject. Eventually, I concluded this was so because the military man was a younger representation of the Watcher from the house. This picture contained another odd adage: *Nothing exists until we deliver our verdict.*

I replaced everything carefully, pressing down on the contents so that I could properly close the bag. In doing so the lining came undone and I saw another page, folded so many times it resembled a table's temporary wedge. When I unfolded it, I saw it was the upper half of a letter. Or it may have been the lower. It bore the same handwriting as that on the portrait and if anything, it was even more confusing. *I wish I could introduce you to your younger self so you could see what you alone possessed and what you wisely hid for most of your life. You tried to warn them but they would not listen. Too late, they understood your concern but expect no gratitude. Be careful. Do not ignore anything as the clues are always before us. Think of what might be rather than what has passed.* The last sentences were difficult to read, several words obscured by the creases. *They want from you what they have cast aside themselves.... They are dead souls walking.... I cannot say more.... In time you will understand the reason.... Ignore the words meant for others... They have constructed a world that exists only in your mind....*

I spent the night reading and rereading the letter. Was it addressed to the old man or had he himself hidden it in the bag? Did he even know of its existence? And the most pressing question: Was it meant for me? The writing matched the letter I had found earlier – did that contain the words I should ignore? – but I could not understand why it was hidden so carefully. As I am writing this I keep hoping you will walk through the door of my room and explain everything. But my only companion is Little Clicker who is at his usual spot on the ceiling, his head turning this way and that, following all my moves. Poor thing!

Early the next morning I walked out of the house. The air was morning-cool but it felt different and, as I walked on, I felt that warm ribbons of wind had stolen inside the breeze that came at first in hesitant spurts before levelling out. In my hand was the Gladstone bag. I believed I would understand its contents better in a different setting. What did the writer mean by instructing me to ignore the words meant for others? It all seemed so covert and unlikely. But really no less unlikely as awakening in this town with a lizard, a cat and a senile old man. And three idiots loitering at a gate.

Maybe they might help. With bag in hand, I walked past the forest where I had heard a horrible wailing and to the promenade that led to the albatross gate, but when the two jokers stood to attention as they noticed my approach, I turned around and retraced my steps. And I looked at the roofs, walls, porches and hedges and tried to pretend you had placed me into this quaint town of so many architectural styles because of my old profession; to spark a memory.

This has been very frustrating as you can well imagine. There is a smidgen of familiarity about everything, but these memories are shuttered and because they are linked to no other remembrances, they shatter as soon as they are born. I feel that alongside the promised revelations hinted by the letterwriter, there is another hand at play; one designed to keep me perpetually confused. I say this because the town, as I already mentioned, is designed in a series of loops, almost as if the intention is to perpetually keep its inhabitants here. Unfortunately, there are just two of us and one seems to be on his way out. (Not out of the town, but I guess you understand my meaning.) I am writing this seated on a bench between two cypresses. They look like old aunts and I cannot explain why I remember something so arbitrary. I can see a cathedral's spires in the distance. The cathedral seems to be built into the wall that stretches for miles. Less than half an hour earlier, I had discovered that its front doors were secured with three huge deadbolts. And so here I sit, bag next to me. Just before me, in a sage mulberry bush, I see a hat stuck on a branch. I want to retrieve it for the old man since he is the only other person in the town but it's too high. Besides, I am a bit tired. This has been my longest journey in the town so far. I must do this more often. Maybe I will discover a way out of the town.

On my way to the chapter house I decided to confront the old man and ask about the contents of the bag and if he knew of the enigmatic letter. As I approached the house, I saw a woman sitting on the front step and stroking a bobtail cat on her lap. Before I could issue a greeting, she told me, "I never believed the stories about murderers returning but here you are."

To be honest, that killed all my excitement about seeing another person.

7 THE SHERIFF

From a distance, she had appeared much younger but up close, I saw that she was in her mid or late forties and that she was gazing at the bag in my hand. "I didn't expect to see anyone here," I told her.

"Yes, I can see that. I must have taken you by surprise."

"You showed up from nowhere. I just returned from one of my treks to see if there was anyone else so it's strange seeing you here." I didn't mention that her vague familiarity, from a distance, had stoked my hope that, somehow, she was here because of me.

"A trek?" Her lips turned up in a smile and her eyelids crinkled down at the same time. The expression added a few years to her age and also granted her more assurance, as if she was a woman of great experience. "You make it sound so adventurous. It's just a forgotten place. Which is not surprising, with all these billboards complaining that Big Mouths Tell Big Lies, and Don't Whisper Too Loudly, and Beware of Fake News." She spoke with her fingers against her lips, regarding me carefully and I wondered how I had missed her during my explorations. "Who would want to be placed here? Well, Old Boy, apparently. And you."

I decided to not tell her of my faulty memory. "It's quiet."

She laughed, something rustling and hoarse, and I saw how easily she had changed again, now to a world-weary, rugged woman. "If you believe that then you are missing everything."

"What do you mean by 'placed here'?"

"Well, did you come here all by yourself? Traipsing along in a merry caravan?"

"I believe I may have had some injury and was left here by a… a friend, to recuperate."

"And where is this loyal friend now?"

I had gone over that from the day I found myself in the chapter house. Perhaps an accident or some emergency had delayed you from showing up or maybe this period of isolation was a part of my therapy. Yet, I suspected that neither of these was true. One night – it may have been my third – I had awakened from a nightmare of being forced to drink massive decanters of liquid before a blue light that was so bright I could feel it searing my face. "I manage by myself," I told her.

"That's not what I asked." She seemed to be waiting for a response, but I said nothing. "By the way, my name is Soma." She opened her legs a bit and allowed the cat to snuggle against her belly and I saw why I had, from a distance, mistaken her for a younger woman. She was lithe and athletic in her hiking boots, khaki skirt and her vest, the hood thrown back and partially exposing a sinuous tattoo running down her neck. Her casual disinterest seemed, up close, quite deliberate. "Are you finished gazing?"

I surprised myself by saying, "I was trying to guess your age." The cat rubbed against her belly and I saw its fur matched her own colour.

"You have been alone much too long." She said it as a joke, but her face was hard and remote. "What have you been doing all this time?"

"I don't know how long I have been here. I have lost track of time."

She glanced skeptically at me. "I always feel people are hiding something when they say things like that. 'Lost track of time.' As if they have secrets hidden away in all its folds and creases."

When your memory is as short as mine, everything is a secret. I almost mentioned this but instead I told her, "I have been trying to find other people in this town. But there's just me and the man upstairs."

"The man upstairs is supposed to be eternal, taking all his different forms...in different eons...but our man has misbehaved..." She leaned back, regarding me. I couldn't understand if she was joking but she seemed so seasoned and watchful, I felt this situation was not entirely new to her. "He's still on the couch. Slumped forward like a heathen praying."

"The old man from upstairs?"

She stroked the cat's neck but looked up at the sky. "There's just two of us in this place." She pointed to herself and to me and leaned back. "The corpse is upstairs."

"He's dead? He seemed very ill but I didn't expect him to die so suddenly." Not knowing what else to say, I told her, "I am sorry."

"What's there to be sorry about? He was here and now he's not. Happens all the time."

"How *did* it happen?"

"How should I know? I just got here. Why don't you tell me?"

I decided to return some of her suspiciousness. "That's quite a coincidence. Your presence at this time."

"As is yours. Sauntering by with your bag. What do you have in it?"

"Nothing of interest."

"Why don't you open it, then? Let's examine the contents."

"There are some personal items."

"Maybe you have vials of poison. Or a strangle-cord."

"Or maybe my toothbrush and slippers."

"Were you thinking of leaving, then? Did your job and moving on?" She was looking at the bag rather than at me. Released, the cat sprung away. She glanced swiftly at the animal and added, "Or maybe you are a mortician with your implements packed away in your mortician bag. You look like one, too. So tight with frowns and disapproval."

"Well, it was nice meeting you. I'm sure you need some time alone." I tried to steer some sympathy into my voice. To be honest, she was a real disappointment after all my searches in the town for another person.

As I was climbing the two front steps, she told me, "Hold on. How did you know him?" She lit a long cigarette and watched me through the smoke.

"He lived upstairs. It took a while before I discovered his presence. I have no idea how he cooked or took care of himself."

She reached into her blouse and brought up a beaded necklace. She fingered the beads in a studiously idle manner before she tried to get it around her neck. From my position, I spotted a scatter of moles on her shoulders. "Was he lonely? What did he do all day?"

"I don't know. He was in his room all the time. Surrounded by all his mementoes. Grips and bags and suitcases. He never said anything to me. Maybe all old people are like that...counting their words carefully, I mean."

"What did the grips and bags contain?"

"They are all in my room." Even before I finished the sentence I knew she had already been through those; her focus remained on the bag in my hand.

Suddenly she relaxed and asked, "Are you like that, too? Counting your words?" I had no clear idea of my age, but she seemed to be slotting me into a category older than I had imagined.

"I count the *days*. Looking for familiar things. When I first saw you from a distance it seemed as if I had seen you before."

My statement must have surprised her because she fumbled with her necklace and when the clasp disengaged, she sat with her chin cupped, staring morosely at the beads rolling down the steps. She glanced up with a hint of accusation in her eyes, as if I were responsible for her mishap. Eventually I stooped and collected a couple of what looked like dried berries. "Jumbie seeds," she mumbled to herself. "Protects me from the spirits." When I dropped the dried seeds into her open palm, she said in the same quiet manner, "Will make something new from it. That's how life is, you know. We are always recasting the remaining bits so that we can forever remain the same little girl in the same yellow rocking chair. Straightening out the bent edges and repainting the furniture. Rearranging the beads. The games are the same, as we grow older. Only the skin changes."

I didn't understand what she was talking about. It seemed as if she was putting up an insincere defence against my remark about her familiarity. She seemed to be waiting for some response so I asked her, "How did you know the old man?"

"I can't recall saying that I did."

I persisted. "Was he your father? Or an uncle? Some relative?"

"He may have been one or the other at different times."

With her evasiveness, I was beginning to disbelieve her more with each passing moment. "I am not sure I understand. When did you last see him?"

"A few minutes ago. He's still on the couch. I came out here for a smoke and this cat just came up to me and claimed me as if it knew me all its life." She snapped her fingers a couple times and the animal returned with a tiny mouse in its mouth. "Oh, Tonkie," she said. "There's no need. I understand." The cat deposited the mouse by her feet and she flicked the rodent over with her finger and in an abruptly playful voice said, "See what you have done, you crazy cat? Did you consider that the taste will remain in your mouth for months? Who will cuddle you then?"

"Are you not disgusted by the mouse?" The cat had chewed off a leg and an ear.

"Why should I be disgusted? Tonkie didn't know what he was doing. He knows it's what cats are supposed to do." She held up its tail and flicked it expertly into the mulberry. The cat ran after it and she got up and dusted her thighs. "Would you care to accompany me?"

"Perhaps you need some time alone with your father or your uncle or whoever –"

"I can see you do not believe me and I must tell you that I can match and raise your skepticism. So we are equals." I was about to say we were not, when she added, "Let me tell you a story. Once upon a time, there were two men living alone in a town. Half died and the other half pretended ignorance. Soon a sheriff came upon the scene. What do you think she would deduce?"

"Are you the sheriff?"

"Are you the other half?" She dipped into her shirt, feeling and fondling. Eventually she brought out an old star-shaped medallion caught on a necklace. She seemed to be awaiting an answer, but I walked away. I had had enough of her. Maybe she really needed time alone; perhaps all mourners were infected with suspiciousness. At the lamppost I decided to walk to the gate where I had seen the two jokers and behind them, a beastly looking man skulking around. On my way there I saw someone trying to dislodge, with a pole, the hat I had earlier spotted on the shrubbery. As I got closer I saw it was a man with an impressive nose that made his tiny, close-set eyes and his nip of a chin almost irrelevant. For days, I had not seen anyone else in the town and now, within a few hours, I had come across two. "Hello," I said.

Immediately he said, "My hat just flew off and I can't get to it. Can you help me?"

"It's been there for a few days at least," I told him as I took the stick he was flicking at the branch.

"That's not possible," he said, drawing close and looking me up and down. "Can you climb? My feet are not equipped for agility." He glanced down and I noticed one of his feet was turned to the side.

"What are you doing here?" I asked. "Did you just arrive?" I wondered if he had come with the woman.

"I heard there was going to be a death. I am the Mortician. Do you want a death certificate? An obituary?" He picked up a battered briefcase and pretended to be fiddling within. "A floral arrangement? I can get you an impeccable wreath."

"I am still alive so why would I –"

"Yes, you seem alive. I will grant you that. Can I then interest you in my embalming expertise? I can recreate the man you were thirty years ago. I can also make you look thirty years older if you so choose. Anything you can…can imagine." He hesitated and added, "I have the gift."

"I am not interested, but there is someone who might be. A woman who just arrived in the town was asking about a mortician."

"A woman? Then I must be off." He snapped shut his briefcase and limped away as fast as his deformed foot would allow.

"You are going in the wrong direction," I told him. "What about your hat?"

"Keep it!" he shouted.

I decided to return to the house to inform the woman I had seen a mortician. When I entered the room, I saw her sitting next to the old man. I almost apologized for intruding into what appeared a quiet little domestic scene. "Is anything different?" she asked. "Is this how you last saw him?"

I recalled him uttering his strangled animal sound and wondered if I had mistaken suffocation for anger. "He was still breathing."

In a matter-of-fact voice she said, "That's because it's difficult to kill someone who has been forever staring at death. You never know whether they are gone or not."

"Perhaps you finished him off," I told her stiffly.

"Perhaps. A perfect pair now." She leaned across the body and patted the couch. "Would you like to sit?" She noted my discomfort and added, "When last have you been with a woman?" She wiped the corner of her mouth with the back of her palm, her eyes twinkled, and I wondered at this shift in her mood. "I can tell everything about a man from the way he responds to that single question. Does it surprise you?" She smiled a little and turned to the corpse. "Or perhaps you are nervous about the body. It's just an empty vessel now, you know. Look at this." She shook the body and it fell directly onto her. I quickly walked over, straightened the old man and pulled him to the end of the couch, away from her. When I was finished, I saw not gratitude but suspicion on her face as I stepped back by the doorway.

"You shouldn't play with the dead like that," I told her.

"Unless you plan to reanimate the body it's just a piece of junk now. Is that your intention?" She must have noticed the confusion or shock on my face because she began to laugh in quick exhalations, the nasal sound seeming judgmental and harsh rather than jovial. "What do you think we should do with the body? We could leave him in one of the empty houses. Or bury him in the back garden."

"We?"

"Well, we could always leave him here. Preserve him with some embalming fluid and grant you a perfect companion. Like a sturdy piece of furniture. Decorative and useless. The things you could talk about!" I almost told her about the mortician, but my trust was fading with each minute. "Or we can always return him to the Compound."

"The place with the albatross wings?"

"You should stop pretending, you know. It gets predictable after a while."

"I am glad you mentioned predictability because I have been wondering how you knew the old man was dead?"

"He's been dead a long time. In a manner of speaking we all are when the spark is gone. He was waiting."

"For what?"

"For you, for me, for us both...who knows?" She leaned across and pulled the dead man's lips into a smile. "I wish he were this pliant when he was alive. Someone told me that whenever we identify too closely with a dead body we trap some of its loosened memories. But we never know because we assume its empathy or something. What do you think?"

"I am not an expert on memories," I told her. Far from it, I almost added.

"I have met people like that. Once, an impossibly savage man told me that he knew when he was about to forget something significant because he could actually feel the cauterization. He didn't actually use that word because he had been reduced to a simpleton when I met him. But he described the smell of something burning, the heat in his head, the dullness of his eyes, the coldness in his heart. Soon after, a woman mentioned that the gaps in her memories were filled with elegant deformities. She claimed that what she lost had been compensated with twilight vision. Crazy, you say?" I was about to agree when she added, "The savage had killed his father and the woman her child. Everyone I meet seems to be a criminal or an accessory." She turned to the corpse. "What crime do you think Old Boy here committed?"

"I thought you knew him."

"Not as well as you. I didn't share his house. And he didn't give me the gifts he threw your way." She glanced at the Gladstone bag I had placed at the doorway.

"If you are so interested in the bag you can always get a warrant. If you are really a sheriff."

I said that with the hope it would compel her into an admission but she told me, "I don't need a warrant. It's already mine." She spoke grimly as if there was no doubt in her mind. Then suddenly her expression softened and she said, "I feel as if I have been circling this town for years. Can I tell you something? Would you believe me if I say that sometimes, if you are a wanderer, during your wanderings you unexpectedly come face to face with a house that you know will see you through to the end? You can see yourself coughing out your last miserable drop of life there."

She looked toward the body, ruffling her hair away from her face and her profile, her thin lips and high cheekbones, reminded me of someone I may have known. For a second, I had this image of her watching from a canoe and behind her, a panorama of clouds that seemed attached to the boulders beneath. Someone was seated beside her, a child, and she seemed to know that before they touched land, one would be dead. "Where have you been during your travels?" I asked her.

"Why would that interest you?"

"When you are stuck in one place for a long time everything looks the same."

She took her own time before she told me, "Everything looks the same from the outside, too. After a while, the borders get blurry and everywhere looks alike." She seemed to be addressing the old man. "Travellers are less interested in adventure than in finding something familiar in an unexpected spot. We move further and further just to belong and to know there are these connections everywhere and we have not been abandoned. It's funny in a way. Travelling further and further just to get home." She looked away from the body. "Were there any conversations or anything?"

I did not want to tell her about the cryptic messages he floated down. "We did not get far. His death came in the way."

"'His death came in the way.' What an odd thing to say." She repeated the phrase once more and looked at me with a bit more interest. "Do you know what I felt when I saw him here? I believed he was napping and when he awoke, the world would shift in some crazy way. Some little adjustment that was too easy to miss. I imagined him being obsessed with this and spending hours staring out of the window, noticing the smallest thing. Like the drizzle of tiny insects against the window and the last tremor of wind in the few seconds between evening and night." She sighed as if she were releasing some great pressure and I noticed her blouse tightening.

I couldn't tell if this new pose was genuine or not, but I felt a flicker of sympathy for her. Even though I had already decided she was no sheriff, I couldn't yet determine her association with the old man. I suspected she too was trying to gauge my own connection. I told her that whenever I saw him he was always immaculately dressed. As if he were stepping out or expecting a visitor. When I was finished, she said, "It's exactly how I imagined it would be. Standing before two windows with reflecting panes. One showing the road travelled and the other the journey still to come. If you sit down with pen and paper, you could look forward just as easily as you look back. Figure out how it will come to a close, too. Maybe he was doing that. What do you think?"

"I can't answer that. You know far more of him than I do."

"That's not true." Unexpectedly she began to cry, the sound, stifled by her palm, fluting, intimate and almost melodious. For a second I felt I should grant her some privacy, but when she looked at me and I saw her eyes, inflamed with sadness, I walked across and sat next to her. She slid closer, dusted my collar and leaned in. Here I must make a confession: because of my memory situation, I cannot say with any assurance if all men of a certain age find women who are secretive and who flirt with lies alluring because of the sense that something deep inside is broken and can be fixed. But at that instant, looking at this woman, a decade, perhaps two, younger than me, I felt unexpectedly drawn toward her; drawn toward her difficulty in presenting herself; drawn by her breath on my neck and her fingers on my chest. I have gone over what happened next and I am not yet certain who took advantage of whom. When she shifted her position to straddle me, I assumed she was simply manoeuvring to adjust the body at the end of the couch. I could have pushed her off or remained neutral; instead, I placed my hands lightly on her neck. I felt overpowered by her energy and her ferocity, her pupils rolled back so that from my position her eyes appeared to be milky and wistful and maniacal. Up to that point I was transfixed rather than overpowered, but when she wrapped her fingers around my throat I began to struggle, almost passively at first by trying to free myself, but as I began to suffocate, I pushed upward and just before I blacked out, I slapped her with as much force as I could muster. She screamed and everything went black.

When I came to, she was on the couch, a knee to her chest as she adjusted her clothing, clipping the buttons in such a remote manner we could have been strangers who, sitting opposite one another, had just finished our meals, straightening our clothes and dusting off the crumbs. "What just happened?" she asked me in a gentle voice.

But I was having none of that. I sprung up and when my pants fell over my knees I stumbled between her legs. "What happened? You tried to kill me."

"I can't remember...I don't think it was me...I wish I could sleep now." She slid down to rest her head on the couch. "I can't remember what just happened, but I remember everything else." She patted the seat and asked sleepily, "Would you like to hear what came unstuck?"

"I prefer to stand here if you don't mind."

And in this tranquil state, her eyes still half-closed, as if she was nodding off, she began with a land where she claimed people lived and died in a blink.

8 THE WORLD OUTSIDE

Standing a safe distance away, alert to any sudden moves, I listened as she proceeded to tell me the most unbelievable story. She had grown up in a shack between two scrapyards in a faraway land where she claimed, "Man-sized rodents walked out from the deserts on two legs." When she was thirteen and rummaging through the scrapyard for metal, her mother revealed that her biological father was not the grizzled man who was shovelling some distance away, but someone who had disappeared years ago. Her mother brought out a photograph and she felt that the sun sluicing through the latticed fretwork of an abandoned building made it appear as if the photo's subject was peering through the bars of a cell. "Where is he now?" she had asked.

Her mother addressed the question half a year later in an eating house. "He's gone," the older woman had said. "He was supposed to take us, but he disappeared in the night." She remembered the eating house in every detail – the flies on the ruffled tablecloth, the lachrymose couple seated across, the pear-shaped mole on the waitress's nose, an animated argument between two drunks outside the glass wall – but nothing of her mother's expression.

Following that conversation, her mother began to disappear in small instalments. In the beginning, "her gloves and long boots seemed emptied." One evening in the kitchen, while her mother was knitting, the older woman's hands disappeared completely. "I was astonished to see a piece of thread commanded like a puppeteer's string." Shortly, her mother's quiet smile, her wide-eyed stare and her eyebrows, one higher and more severely arched than the other, were wiped out. Gone, too, was her sweetish odour of milk and sweat, replaced by the odour of steeped arsenic. The opposite took place with her adoptive father. She now noticed that the features on both sides of his big imposing nose matched entirely. Sometimes she looked at his nose as a kind of spirit level reflecting the perfect symmetry of his features. "I felt he was mocking me with his beard and hair. I felt he was saying, 'Look at you. Just like your mother. No wonder. Look at her!' I tried but she was mostly gone by then. Not much to see."

She had paused in her story to lean forward, her chin on her knee. I was still affected by our very brief moment of intimate violence, but I suspected the mother's "disappearance" was due to the daughter's shame and her desire to tune out the older woman. She told me that one day her mother disappeared completely. And once again, she recalled only the surroundings, the noisy back door creaking shut, the steam rising from a saucepan on the stove, the eyes of the man whom she had assumed to be her father watching out from the door jamb. This final disappearance was unfortunate because her mother had been describing the person from the photograph. "Then poof, she, too, disappeared with her story inside her. Erased. First her insides hollowed and then the rest of her."

She paused for a while and I wondered if the man her mother had been describing was now lying next to us, dead and cold.

"Do you think it's possible to suffocate from too many strangulated stories?" She glanced at the body and continued. She was seventeen at the time and fled her mother's house early the next morning. "When I looked back it seemed as if the sun had fallen on the house. I didn't care." She moved to a small town. Every single person was crazy and starving and dancing. She followed a troupe to another town. Everyone was moving at the time and she did the same, although she had no idea of her destination. Soon she fell in with another group, another town. And another. "The caravan grew larger with each stop. And more frenzied. But I couldn't stop." Over the next year, she repeated these moves, journeying farther from her mother's place. She mentioned places: bright streets, dirty basements and motel rooms, arguments and knives. She described all of this but little of the people she met. I felt that she may have been a prostitute and that she had blocked off her clients as she had done her mother, but then she said, "Everyone was running away. Those who had forgotten got new reasons from those they met on the way. Until every single person had the same story. Those that survived, anyway."

"What was this story?" I interrupted.

"Dead parents. No water. Empty syringes. Diseases not yet named. Deserted bazaars and blood everywhere. The world was ruled by bullies who were as funny and depraved as a bad stepfather. All rules and obligations and penances." She glanced at the body before she continued. Sometimes she came across battles where weapons were constructed from the most intimate items. "I remember green and violet clouds smashing into each other and once a woman in a silk gown detonating some device. There were dead babies everywhere. You didn't know who to trust. One day your friends became enemies and the next day they could be either. All around there were towns not fit for ghosts. Yet that was all that was left. Ghosts." Then the scenery in her story changed. Suddenly there was water, "The waves crashing down and picking themselves up and crashing down again in the same way and with the same shape." The caravan had thinned considerably by then; some had given up and returned, and others fell at the sides of the road, gazing at the sun. The sea voyage was even more perilous. Boats were flung in the air, spilling out their passengers like insects before the vessels fell to earth, crashing against the rocks. There were scuffles that led to outright mutinies, and these captainless boats drifted away from the convoy and disappeared. "Then we saw the outline of this place we were all moving toward. It seemed covered with pale dust and trees that had not spreading boughs, but formed perfect triangles. As we got closer, we could hear a mechanical clanking in the distance. I am sure everyone must have been wondering if it was all worth it. Five percent of us had made it to that point and while we were lined up on the beach the dead bodies of our former shipmates floated around us. It was horrible. How did I forget something like this? Or the containment camps we were pushed into while we waited?" Her voice was softer and I couldn't tell if she was addressing the old man. I was still not sure I believed anything she had said.

Still, I asked her, "Waited for what?"

"There were men in iron costumes asking us questions. Showing us pictures…crazy pictures of puppets with women's clothing. Mallets and lanterns and brass knuckles, too. A few were drawings of wheels and cages."

I was astonished; she was describing the illustrations the old man had flung from his window. Yet, I also suspected she had been through my things. I asked her, "It seems odd that after that dangerous trip, you all would be presented with pictures –"

"Yes, it was. What's even odder is that I was the only one let through. The rest were packed into boats and…and sent back. Or sent somewhere."

"Why did they let you alone through?"

"I can tell from your voice that you don't believe me, but it doesn't matter. In any event, I was just thankful. All I know was that I was too exhausted to answer their questions about the images. I told them they were meaningless."

She seemed flustered with my questions, so I told her, "Sounds like a perilous journey. You are lucky that you made it through." She glanced again at the old man and I felt she was really telling this story to him; emphasizing how much she had suffered. "Sorry. Please go on." This – real or not – was my first picture of the world outside and it was both horrendous and fascinating.

"Finally, I was let through the gate. There were lights everywhere, an unstable bluish light and I wondered why there were so few people and why there was so much silence. I was taken to a building and made to sit in an enclosed room. This bluish light was more than a light. It curled around me and I felt it entering my mouth and nose. I lost consciousness. When I came to the only thing I was wearing was this necklace." She fingered her sheriff's badge and I realized she had possibly found it when she had been searching for metal with her mother. "I was moved from place to place. This procedure was repeated at each station. I can't recall much of that period. Maybe it was the blue light." She began to rock back and forth and instinctively I stepped back. "Soma. That was the name they called me. There were others who had been let through at an earlier time. We were all given the same name."

"What did it mean?"

"Who knows? Something? Someone? Some? I wish I could remember my real name." Then she stopped her rocking and said in a slightly excited voice, "There was a mountain."

In spite of my skepticism I was enthralled by her description of the place. The narrow roads were bordered by steep ledges overlooking dungeon-like canyons and foaming water that, from a distance, appeared to be boiling. The mountain, metallic blue in spots, seemed carved from a luminous material she had never seen before, but, as she got closer to the top, the colours were loosened and everything took its hue from the clouds that were so low they obscured the finger-tipped birds that flew out abruptly from hundreds of crevices. The winding road fell suddenly at times and, because the entire area was misty, the experience was like dropping from the sky. In fact, she felt as if the mountain were attached to the clouds. The sky seemed so vaporous that after a few days she could not gauge how far away it was.

Her account, although familiar, had the distance of something not experienced but heard. Perhaps I had read this somewhere. I closed my eyes and imagined I was before a canvas looking out at the scene and I saw instead a hunched man sitting before a desk, spitting and cursing and writing in a journal. "Are my accounts so tedious?" she asked me lightly.

"I am trying to see what you are describing. To see it as a memory fragment. I do that sometimes."

"Well, the next fragment won't be pretty. When I reached the summit, I realized that everyone there was disfigured in some way. I felt at first that they too had come from outside, but these were children too young to have made the journey." She described a series of interconnected camps that seemed more like orphanages. Children struck with diseases and horrible nightmares were dragged along at regular intervals. "At first, I turned away and swore at the children who came close. 'Get the fuck away,' I told them. 'Go find your mother or something. Where's you father? Did you kill him, too?'" But they were everywhere. "I am not your caretaker," she said to a girl with one eye, even though she had already begun to suspect the opposite. Eventually she relented. "The first child I treated had shoots growing out from her feet. It was so sad. I felt this was the worst thing that could happen to a little girl. Then I realized that the shoots were also growing inwards. She was in so much pain." She seemed to be waiting for me to say something and when I did not, she continued, "I told the child that she was becoming a beautiful plant. That God had chosen her as his special shrub." This seemed like a horrible thing to say to a suffering child, but I kept quiet. "And it worked. She died smiling. I told her she would bear the most adorable flowers." She pressed her palms against her cheeks and offered her own elegiac smile. "I told her that when the flowers floated in the sky she would be able to fly with them."

Then there was the description of another young girl – the camp seemed to be stacked with young, diseased girls – who was stricken with an abdominal parasite. "Such a pretty child. And so strong." She explained how she evacuated the worm by perforating the abdomen through the navel and encouraging the extruding worm to curl around a twig. "Each morning as I gently twirled the twig, I felt the worm resisting my pressure and retreating farther into the child's abdomen. On the third day, the twig snapped and the worm retreated."

"Did the child survive?" I had no idea why I asked the question because I could not believe her account of this orphanage place to which she had been sent or assigned.

"She died. And in that moment, so did I. I fled. I ran and ran and ran. Sometimes I heard the voices of my pursuers and their machines and I felt I should just stop, and at other times I stared over a gorge and closed my eyes and wished I could take that final step. But I had sacrificed too much to get in. So I continued, hiding in the shadows, stealing scraps during the nights…"

As she trailed off I said, "Surely someone might have helped if you asked."

"Someone? There were no someones. One night while I was skulking outside a café I watched this family smiling at each other and nodding…and the group at the table opposite doing the same.

I had seen the men in uniform acting in that manner but felt then they were just following protocol. They all seemed connected, as if they each knew what the other was thinking."

As fascinating as her story was, it made no sense. Was she a sheriff or a woman on the run? What was her relationship with the old man? And how did she find her way here? She seemed to have guessed my thoughts because she got up and watched through the window. I asked her, "How did you find this place?"

"It's no use. You wouldn't believe me. I can see you doubt all that I have revealed so far. I would doubt it, too."

Maybe it was her last statement, but I wanted to believe that she, too, was struggling with her memories. Yet hers – if true – were different from mine, which were disconnected and useless. "I don't know if I believe you, but I would like to hear it to the end."

Now she turned toward me. "You asked if anyone helped. There was a child." She said this abruptly as if she had made a sudden decision. "A child. It was a child that led me here. At first, I felt she was one of the orphans I had treated and I called out to her, but she kept disappearing at will as if it were a game to her. Sometimes I would see her in the distance and when I got there she would be farther ahead. I couldn't understand how she managed to move so quickly."

"Did you think it was the girl with the shoots growing out of her feet?"

"Yes. That's who I thought it may have been. I remember her name now. Dawn. No, it was Dyenne." She put her hands to her cheeks, covering her mouth as if she were horrified. "That's all I remember," she said softly through her fingers.

"Do you know why she led you here?"

"Maybe we were headed to the same place. I could have told her of my destination at the orphanage…if she was there among the children. Or maybe she read my thoughts like all those people

I saw who knew what the others were thinking. Did I tell you how we met? My first sight of her was awakening and seeing this ragged little face above me. I had been interfered with –"

"In what way?"

"Someone had dragged me to the other side of the road." She turned once more to the window and I felt she was either hiding something or trying to come up with a more convincing story. "It was not the girl," she said eventually in a flat voice. "It was not her. She couldn't have done it."

When she turned away from the window I was surprised at the look of satisfaction on her face, in spite of all she had just said, the muted smugness of someone granted restitution. I asked her as soon as the thought came into my head, "What did you expect to find here? Did you return here to make sure the old man was gone?"

I could see her thinking. Eventually she told me, "Who knows what goes on in the minds of those whose memories are fading? Perhaps he was spooling his life backwards and expecting everyone he knew to reappear at their appointed spots." She paused, as if waiting for me to add something. "It's something I heard my mother say before she finally vanished. About life spooling backwards. Poor woman." There were several questions on my mind, but I noticed her clasping and unclasping her fingers and I realized she was considering some confession. When she spoke, though, her voice was steadfast. "The minute my mother revealed her story, throughout all my journeys the one constant question has been whether personal responsibility can be washed away if the memories of these infractions are gone. Can guilt be weighed on the same scale as recollection? How can one survive without the other?" She looked away from me and now focused on the body. "Should someone be accountable for something they cannot recall? But what if the loss is not complete and they are presented with recurring slices of their crimes? Can guilt then be measured in percentages?" Now she fixed her gaze on me. "What if they are pretending? What about the consequences?" She had spoken in a rehearsed manner, with a slight lilt as if she was imitating both words and tone, as if all she had just revealed was pointless. She kept her gaze on me and I realized she had been working her way to this question and it was not idle reflectiveness. She wanted an answer.

I, too, wanted an answer. But to an entirely different question. "The world you have described seems divided into two sections. What happened?"

She shook her head. "How should I know? It was always this way. The only thing I know for certain is that those of us on the outside were feared and scorned. But we also possessed something of value. I puzzled over that during the time in the orphanage."

"Value as caretakers and servants?"

She took her time in answering, pausing, as if she was still working her way to an understanding. "In the place I left, we believed that imagination was not a pliant, fanciful thing that could be coloured by our mood, but was...was the store of memories passed down from generation to generation. No dreams, no fancies, no visions, no pretences. Just memories...and if the memories were wiped out...the imagination followed."

This determination was so staggering I could not believe it had come from this elusive person whose story had so many gaps. While I was considering what she had just said, my mind ran to you and I wondered if she was part of your game, this woman who had appeared from nowhere, claiming to be a sheriff, refusing to acknowledge her relationship with the old man, claiming, too, that our little moment together had somehow loosened these astonishing memories. Yet I wanted to believe her; I wanted to believe that if I had shared her harrowing experiences I would have been just as elusive, just as distrustful. I told her quickly before I could change my mind, "I have no memories."

"You cannot remember anything?" She seemed disappointed.

"I remember the functions of things. I know how to light a stove, for instance, but I have no memory of myself ever doing that."

"That's it?"

"There are other memories, tiny, slippery fragments that are so random and impersonal they may mean nothing. Nothing to me, I mean."

Once more she leaned her head against the backrest. "I have this sense that I spotted you in one of the ships. Holding on to the rigging like a wet rat."

She said it with her eyes closed, half-smiling, and I adopted the same detached, amused tone when I said, "I hope I would remember something as stark as that. In any event, you are lucky you made it through."

"I am not sure I did..." Her voice trailed off.

"You seem tired," I told her. "I am going to look for someone. He says he is a mortician."

"Here? In this town?" She seemed alert now.

I noticed the lizard on the ceiling and pointed to it. "I will be back. There's Little Clicker to keep you company."

Before I could move she rushed out of the room and I could hear her hurried footsteps on the stairs. I didn't like the idea of sticking around the body alone, so a few minutes later I decided to follow her. The cat was sniffing about in the mulberry but it darted away and scuttled up the lamppost. When I got there, I could not see it, so I glanced around to see where it may have jumped and called its name a couple times before I gave up and walked in the direction of the Compound. The farther I moved from the chapter house, the more my skepticism returned. I had the vague feeling that the woman had killed her parents and absconded, but I could not recall the exact utterance that had fired my suspicion. Perhaps it was her shifting personalities and her evasiveness. I still could not understand her purpose in the town and could not believe she had been led here by a child who somehow read her mind. I could not believe that her memories were unexpectedly loosened by our little bout of intimacy.

When I drew close to the albatross gate I decided to ask the two clowns who sprang to attention when they noticed my approach.

"Halt!" the shorter man said. "Step no farther."

"I am looking for a woman."

"A woman?"

Too late I recalled my last conversation. "Did anyone pass through these gates?"

The taller man said, "You are not authorized to ask that question. Now stand down."

"There was a woman at my place –"

"There once was a woman at my place," the short man interrupted, his index finger springing up.

"Who set out looking for grace," his friend continued.

"Instead she uncovered."

"An expired old buzzard."

"The man she swore she would erase."

They conferenced for a moment and said together, "And secrets stuffed in a case." Both applauded and linked arms, dancing and goose-stepping.

It was useless talking to the pair so I decided to return to the house. On my way, a silly thought popped into my head: I hoped the woman would stay for a while. We would plant a backyard garden and every evening we would stroll through the town and I would point out all the quaint designs and she would tell me more of her travels and of the world outside. And maybe one day, we would both leave.

This little fantasy did not last long, though. When I got to the room, both the woman and the body were gone. I recalled the clowns' limerick and rushed downstairs to where I had hidden the Gladstone bag. When I opened the bag, I saw that everything I had packed inside was gone. The linings were torn away as if she had been looking for something specific. The only item left was a drawing I had not seen before. That of a little girl with her hands against her back. She was gazing straight ahead rather than at the two bodies on the floor. The artist had drawn just the feet but I could tell the bodies were of a man and a woman. Between both bodies was an object that resembled a boomerang.

9 THE DISAPPEARING BODIES

Following my encounter with the woman, I felt more trapped than usual. I assumed what I was feeling was similar to a normal person's reaction at being left behind and I could not put out of my mind all the fantasies I had briefly entertained of our life together. Forget what I said about being trapped. I was haunted; and I wished I understood what might lay inside the mind of those with stable memories. Would I soon forget her, too, as I had forgotten everything of my prior life?

All the old questions rose in my mind, joined now by new misgivings. Was there something tying me to this dead town? Could it be possible that I had actually spent my entire life in this place? Was the sense of some distant familiarity, recently sparked by the woman's extravagant descriptions, just a way of looking at things through her eyes? Was she joking when she said she had spotted me on a ship looking like a wet rat?

Each evening, I walked through the town, memorizing all the little details of our encounter and what she had told me of the world outside. A place of mountains and deserts and man-sized rodents and trains and waves crashing against a boat. As horrible as her journeys were, I wanted to experience this sense of moving, of going somewhere, anywhere. I wanted to be in all these places. It was now twenty-one days following her disappearance and this evening while I was wandering around the town, a crazy idea hit me. What if she was laid up in one of the deserted houses? She had even mentioned that one of the town's abandoned houses would be a good resting place for the old man's body. It made sense because the town seemed completely enclosed, interrupted only by the albatross-shaped gate that housed some kind of compound, and on its opposite end, a cathedral built into the wall and a dense and possibly dangerous forest.

The next day, I made my way to the gate. Once more, I met the two jokers intent on play-acting their responses to my questions, but I could not summon the patience for their silliness. I resolved to check the town's houses one by one. I began early the following morning and was astonished at how unfamiliar the place appeared. I felt as if I was seeing it for the first time and I worried about whether my mind was in the early stages of shutting down once more. But as I walked on I realized it was a trick of the early morning light that had hollowed out the shadows cast by the eaves and gables and had interfered with the town's rustic charm. Now the jumbled styles seemed indulgent, and although I knew the renovations had been done over the years, I had this sense of frenetic improvisations by homeowners who, mired in poverty for a long while, had suddenly come into money. The money, I felt, went into the houses; grand projects and impractical restorations. Then, just as sudden as it had come, the money was gone. Glass louvres stood next to old wooden shutters with rotting sills, paint had been splashed to settle fraying mortar, pipes and wires snaked in and out of the gables. On some of the creaky porches with mismatched newel posts, I imagined men so frail-looking they would soon wither and blow away in the sunlight. I thought then of an epidemic that had passed through so swiftly that when the symptoms appeared no one could attribute a single causal agent. As I walked through the town, I reasoned that many of the buildings were workshops that had been converted into living quarters.

Looking at the buildings in this manner made me unexpectedly distressed by the notion of precious time slipping away. I got the sense that, even though our eyes point out shapes and structures, it is our mood that shades and adds depth. When I approached the chapter house, I tried to push aside the hope – as I had since she had disappeared – that I would once more see the woman sitting on the front step. I wondered how she had vanished with the body so swiftly and whether she was now holed up or trapped in the Compound. Yet she didn't strike me as someone who could be easily imprisoned. Maybe she had found her mortician and they had swiftly taken the body to a funeral parlour that I had somehow missed. I decided to divert to the spot where I had seen him reaching for his hat. When I got there both the hat and the shrub on which it had been stuck were gone. I walked closer and noticed a huge hole where the mulberry once grew. The inner diameter of the hole was serrated with sharp ridges and it appeared that the person wielding the shovel had done his or her work carefully so that the plant had been withdrawn in a single clump. Who would remove an entire tree and for what purpose?

A few minutes later I entered the house and from habit, I stood at the doorway where I had last seen the woman. She had not touched all the grips and suitcases in my room and I assumed she too had been confused by the odd assortment of manuals detailing what looked like surgeries of the brain and other tracts on community housing. Such a strange combination! As I had done each night since her departure, I opened the suitcases and walked around each, occasionally reaching for a particular tract, flipping through the pages, smelling the jackets, passing my fingers along the spine, gazing at the illustrations, holding the book at different angles, hoping somehow to spark an errant shard of memory. I have to tell you that as I was doing so, I also considered that you had deliberately left the books there for me. (Though why you should leave anything for which I was so unprepared was beyond my understanding.)

The only book I could follow was titled *Common Spaces*. It described in a complaining tone the tendency to arrange towns around the idea of private space; where fences and hedges demarcate property boundaries and where small public areas are set aside for commingling. I state the relative simplicity of this book not as an excuse for my intended intrusion – how harsh the word sounds! – but rather to say that most of the town's houses, constructed at a much earlier time with their shared hedges and overlapping eaves, would have been designed for common entry; built for people who knew and trusted each other. I imagined that the occupants, before they were struck down or moved away, must have regularly visited, checking up on each other's health, bringing over some freshly baked pie, helping to adjust a piece of furniture, or just following some ritual from their younger days. During my earlier explorations, I had never actually ventured inside but had looked through the front windows and observed that most of the living rooms were organized for entertaining, with couches set together and bordered by coffee tables.

What harm would there be if I carried my explorations inside the houses?

It was three days before I actually ventured inside a building. And another three before I felt comfortable doing so. Once I was inside, I made a fair bit of noise, slamming the door and banging the furniture to awaken anyone who may have been sleeping upstairs. Only when I was sure the house was empty did I examine all the downstairs rooms, the kitchens and annexes and toilets and closets and storerooms. And during this process, I always thought of the men and women who may have once wandered about the halls and occupied the couches overlooking the lower windows. Some were easy: the cluttered living rooms of the smaller dwellings suggested a single person, a widow or widower gone to ruin, while others pointed to some sort of social life with regular visitors. There were a few, however, that withheld their secrets; in these, I lingered until I arrived at some understanding. In one of these houses the dining room was painted in white but there were quilted red borders around all the wall ornaments and the old pictures of trains and steamboats. The carpet was thick and dusty and gold rugs hung on the stairwell. It seemed the house of a happy family until I noticed the knives hidden in the steamboats and the neat cuts on the rugs. Another house was filled with steel exercise equipment and benches with cables and pulleys. It resembled a torture chamber and I was confused by its familiarity until I judged it might have once served an alleviator. Yet in this house, too, I saw signs of sabotage, with the pulleys loosened and the cables discreetly cut. A block away, I discovered a room that was bare but for a triangular cabinet with a circular revolving base. The cabinet was set at the dead centre of the room and it was congested with a gramophone, two radios, a guitar, a trumpet and a quartet of miniature drums. Beneath the drums were a couple of notebooks with limp damask bookmarks but when I flipped through to the marked pages, they were all empty. There were also no photographs to clarify the image I formed of this musician whose social life must have dried up as he or she got older. Two houses down, the entire space was filled with plastic plants, all decorated with hanging ornaments that resembled bereft little eggs. It seemed to be the former residence of a spinster and at the base of a plant, I saw a photograph of a woman with a long face further hardened by prominent cheekbones. I rummaged around for pictures of children but found only ornate sketches of deformed animals – elephants with missing tusks and toothless jaguars. In a street hidden by an overgrown weeping willow I saw a single house that was completely bare of furniture. The only sign of previous habitation was a doll on the step and a telescope on a window ledge. For some reason, it seemed the saddest place in the town.

I tried to memorize every single scene that caught my attention; every house or lane or piece of shrubbery that presented itself. I knew this was a way of preserving a part of my memory, but I also held the faint hope that all these images, viewed together, might trigger some type of understanding as had the pages the Watcher had thrown from his window.

Each night following my exploration, I tried to imagine a conversation with the occupants of the homes I had visited. Sometimes I fell asleep with these thoughts spinning in my head and when I awoke, with Little Clicker gazing at me, it took a while before I readjusted to the reality that the conversations were not real. I was disappointed because, for those brief moments, I felt I was not alone.

I must mention here that all my explorations were confined to the lower floors but one night while I was flipping through *Common Spaces* I noticed a line I could recall previously reading. "For those of advanced years for whom a stairway can be problematic, and indeed fatal, it is advisable to entertain guests on the upper floors." It was on the last page, a curious placement, and the paper was not as yellow as the rest of the book. The next morning, I entered one of the houses on P Tree Street. It was the musician's and I had brought along the calypso record by The Tawny Leopard as a gift. I called a few times and when there was no answer I placed the record on the gramophone. Perhaps the musician was bedridden.

The calypso began with a scratchy brass prelude. Then there was the singer accompanied by a guitar. His voice was steely yet humorous.

> *Late last night while I was walking down the street.*
> *You wouldn't believe who I happen to meet.*
> *Was a fella with a face just like mine*
> *And rightaway this fella start to opine.*
> *Nothing is old and nothing is new*
> *Even me standing in front of you.*
> *We meet one time and we go meet again*
> *Everything we do is already ordain.*
> *As he continue his nonsense I say mister stop*
> *You talking in parable like old Aesop.*
> *He start looking around anxiously*
> *As if he trail by twenty jumbie.*
> *He say the only thing he could confide*
> *Is that they looking for something they cast aside.*
> *I ask him what this thing could be*
> *And he say Tawny is your melody.*

I couldn't determine the chorus because the needle was jumping over the grooves. Maybe the musician upstairs knew the words. I called once more before I walked up the stairs. I anticipated coming across an ailing musician or items of a personal nature, perhaps clothes or diaries. The last thing I expected was a dead body, appearing so natural and peaceful on the bed I thought at first the man, his grey hair and beard neatly groomed, his hat on his chest, had been sleeping.

I left in a hurry, running along the street and bolting the door to my room. All night I thought of my discovery. How long had this body been there? Was there a mourner hidden in another upstairs room? Was the old man really dead? I had not looked closely and perhaps he was in need of some assistance? I could have waited till the morning to verify this and as I was walking out of the chapter house into the dark street, I tried to convince myself I had been unnecessarily frightened simply because I had been so shocked. Twenty minutes later, I was able to confirm that he was indeed dead, although it appeared his body had been shifted so that his hands were now crossed over his chest rather than at his sides. I could not remember, either, a mandolin at his side. His face seemed familiar and I realized I had seen it on the cover of the calypso album.

I called a few times before I walked down the stairs. On my way to the chapter house I heard a shuffling alongside me, behind a hedge. I shouted and when there was no answer I decided it was the cat snuffing around. As I passed the house where I had seen photographs of trains and steamboats I noticed the front door was slightly ajar. I walked up to close it and decided to check the upstairs rooms. Again, there was a corpse, this one outfitted with a mariner's cap and some sort of blue uniform. A whistle hung over his chest.

That night I entered every house I had previously explored and in each I discovered a dead body. And in each upstairs room the body matched the paraphernalia I had discovered on the lower floor. A man wearing a one-shoulder wrestler's costume. An old woman plastered with kohl and lipstick. Another woman wearing a necklace of birds' eggs. A body encased in a pink dress, its face hidden by a black veil, two dolls beneath its masculine arms. It was early morning when I returned to my room. None of the bodies showed any signs of decomposition and I could not understand how they could all have died at the same time. Since they were the only occupants in the houses, who could have groomed and arranged them? The only people I had seen were the woman and the idlers at the gate and none gave the impression they would engage in such an onerous task or that they had the skill to preserve the bodies. But there was someone else. The mortician! It had to be.

I had decided to avoid the men at the gate, but my unease at being the only living occupant in a town of old preserved men and women overrode the irritation they aroused. When I got to the enclosure the gate was locked. I called a few times and when there was no response I considered climbing over. The gate was more than twelve feet high and I placed my feet on one of the lower bars and tried to hoist myself to the upper crossbar. I was halfway there when I heard a distant growl and noticed a horrible black beast running so quickly toward me I felt it would crash against the gate. I jumped down in a hurry, tumbling on my back. The beast was too big to get through the bars, but I immediately got up and moved away some distance. From its massive head and muscular shoulders and haunches I felt it was a boxer. It was interesting that inside my faulty memory still resided some knowledge of canine breeds. Surprisingly, the animal was wagging its stumpy tail and its low growls now seemed playful. I took a few tentative steps forward and the dog pushed its snout up as if to greet me. Some of its teeth were missing and I felt it was in some distress. "Here, boy," I said, clicking my fingers. "What happened to your mouth?" I was now a few steps away from the animal, holding my hand out as if I had some treat. Suddenly, the dog reared up, its bark no longer playful. Foam was dripping from its mouth.

As I hurried away I considered my luck in not making it to the other side. I wondered what it was guarding. Perhaps the place was an abandoned prison. The rows of cellblocks and some sort of turret at the far end certainly suggested something of this nature. I decided I would restrict my explorations to the town. Over the following days, I made my way to side streets leading to little cul-de-sacs and crescents where the plants were stragglier and the flowers curled like mauve snails on the paths, and in each of the houses I found a dead body on the upper floors. Once more I thought of an epidemic that had raged through the town, even though I knew this couldn't be the case as the bodies on the beds were all dressed and decorated. Could they have been strangled by a homicidal maniac or by a vengeful group of thugs? Again, this seemed unlikely.

One night while I was on my bed, watching through the window, I saw the hedge separating the two houses on the opposite side of the street rustling. My lights were off and I was watching though the curtain. It occurred to me that I might be under some kind of observation and I remained there for close to an hour, hoping the person would reveal himself or herself. I went to bed with the distressing thought that the observer was waiting for me to die so I could be dressed and perfumed and placed in the upstairs room. "Do you think someone is spying on me?" I asked Little Clicker.

The following morning, I walked to the hedge and even though I had managed to convince myself it had been a scurrying animal I decided to explore the outer reaches of the town. As in the residences closer to the chapter house, I also found bodies in those areas, but they were not as carefully coiffured, the arms stiff over faded clothes and the bedsheets rumpled. It seemed as if the mortician, or whoever, had been in a hurry. I still expected to find him and I had the feeling he was always one step ahead of me. I tried to walk gently as if I might catch someone powdering a corpse. One mid-morning, unexpectedly, I came across a house with a small group. They were not at all startled by my presence in the hallway and they soon resumed their quiet conversation while they brought miniature porcelain cups to their lips. They held this pose in their oversized overcoats, not drinking or moving, as if they were waiting for a photographer's flash. There was something familiar about the group and I stood by the window trying to determine why this was so. "I am sorry to interrupt," I told them in the gentlest voice I could summon. "Were you all moving from house to house fixing all the dead men and women?" They seemed so startled by the question I almost regretted asking, but I pressed on. "I can't understand how there could be so many dead bodies in a place and all so carefully preserved."

"Are you here for the show?" This was a small man whose wrinkled chin seemed to be folded over his cardigan.

"What show?" The man who had spoken looked toward a woman and she too looked to her left. The entire group performed this pantomime before they looked toward me. "Have I seen you all before? I cannot remember where exactly…" They relayed their glances once more as if each was expecting the other to reply but no one spoke. "Do you live around here?" I asked.

"Oh no, no, no. We are here for your show."

"My show? I don't understand."

They leaned closer to each other and a tiny man with freckles on his bald head said, "We have to leave now." They all put down their cups, but so gently I could hear no clinks. I noticed they all had pale circles on their wrists as if a watch or bracelet had been recently removed. A tiny woman with a silver brooch on her coat got up, smiled sweetly at me and went into a room I assumed was the kitchen. She was followed by a man who could have been her brother. He offered a little bow and departed. One by one, they left and when they did not return, I went through the door and saw that it led to a backyard with an open gate.

I was surprised, given their years, at how fast they sped along the road. At an intersection shadowed by a billboard with a silver eagle that resembled the gate I had seen at the end of the town, the painting badly frayed so that one wing seemed torn off, they diverged into different streets.

As I tried to keep up with the group, I heard a faint scurrying sound like tiny lead boots on a tin crossway. I followed this sound, weaving in and out of alleyways for about twenty minutes and at a downslope, I was extremely startled by a prolonged gasp as if a reservoir had suddenly emptied of its last ounce of water. I froze and looked to the manholes but could see no gushing water. It was then that I noticed a flickering light on the horizon, blue and red spiralling waves that intersected into lambent crosses.

I walked in the direction of the light until I came to an old railway platform. But the light was farther away and as I continued to what seemed like the end of the town, I wondered how the group of old men and women were able to manage this distance, particularly the steep hill before me. I had explored most of the town but had never come across an abandoned railway or a hill. When I climbed the hill, I was rewarded with the sight of a vast basin partially covered with a huge billowing canopy. On one slope, a bus was overturned and on the others, there were small craters that seemed to be caused by projectiles. The light I had witnessed earlier was coming from under the canopy and when I walked down, I saw an amphitheatre beneath the tent and the group I had seen in the house sitting next to skinny, robotic-looking objects. At that moment, the sky lit up and a booming voice said, "Prepare to be amazed. Witness the spectacle of a man driven to multiple worlds of darkness and despair. Not one world, not two, not even three…wait for it." The last words were drowned by a crescendo of cymbals. I chose an empty seat at the back.

The film began with a room enveloped in blackness, gradually lit to reveal an emaciated and bald man sitting in a cubicle surrounded by objects that all seemed to be oval. The camera focused on the objects one by one and the man, though perfectly still, eyeballed the camera's focus. Then the camera pulled back and revealed that the room was bubble-shaped. And from this freeze-frame shot, a voice began to talk about machines. For the first few minutes, it seemed very technical and I wondered what the families in the theatre were making of this, then the narrator – or perhaps the person in the middle of the room – began to talk about how our trust in machines would lead to our extinction. He seemed to be struggling in his seat – as if he was strapped down – while he explained that machines granted too much power would draw resources for their own efficiencies rather than for what would always elude them: the coming climactic changes and to the diseases already on their way. "We have surrendered before the battle has begun. I have been punished for speaking the truth. They have stolen everything from me." He got extremely agitated as he said this, looking this way and that. Eventually three men walked ponderously into the camera's focus. The man in the middle was short and wide and he moved slowly, his pace matched by his companion on the right, a lanky man. The figure on the left was hopping about as if agitated. One of the trio stepped forward and sprayed something into the man's ear, the second into his eyes and the third into his nose and mouth.

This was a horrible image and I couldn't understand the chuckles I heard around me in the darkness as the man bemoaned his loss of freedom. The chuckles grew into joyous laughter as, looking directly into the camera, the trapped man began to scream that all the material collected about him would ensure more would be known about his life long after he was dead than was identified at the present. "But what would they know? Will it be real? Will it be me or something else? What happens to the soul when minds are tied together?" He was quite riled up, although clearly weakening from whatever he was forced to ingest. The audience was enjoying it, even though the laughter had a canned quality. Before the subject began to convulse, he managed to sputter something about insanity being the only antidote. "Let them decode that," he said before he grew still. For a while, there was only the crackling sound of a projector, then the canting head of a goateed man appeared. It was a close-range shot and he appeared to be the cinematographer examining the lenses. I was certain of this when his eye occupied the entire screen. "I touched them and they felt pain. But they grew used to the pain and turned it against me." There was a sharp sound and the eye snapped shut. I heard an unspooling whir and I thought the film had ended, but the three men now reappeared in another scene sitting by a table. One of them, the centre man, looking directly into the camera, said in a low and regretful voice, "In times past, people like you were seen as special. Extraordinary. You saw spirits and gods and you spoke with angels. Your delusions made you remarkable, your craziness coloured the heavens, your paranoia gave you special insights. And so on and so forth." He seemed to be speaking to the audience.

The man to his right added gloomily, "You banned and banished and blackballed."

I assumed they were talking about the man who had been strapped in his chair and I felt that this bit had been spliced into the original movie, as the lighting was different. The centre man issued a prolonged sigh that seemed to expand his body like a toad's and said, "You are a psychopath. Nothing more, nothing less." The three men began to laugh as if a joke had been made. "Here is the result of some of your inspirations." Once again, there was a whir, followed by two minutes of grainy footage that depicted a woman removing the limbs of a child and trying to graft them onto an eviscerated adult. She went about her task in a grandmotherly way while she fitted the bones. The scene faded slowly with the congested voice of the centre man saying, "It's time to send you back...back...back." The voice echoed until the screen went black.

I heard someone before me saying, "That mamma is a miscreant. Even I do not have the lexicon to express my shock at this brutish act."

Another voice said, "Behold the return of –"

"Should we hide?"

"Shh," another voice said, and I saw two floodlights criss-crossing the area above the screen. A ladder descended into the lit area and a man with a cape climbed down with some difficulty until he was able to stand on the top of the screen. He slowly loosened his hold on the ladder and placed his hands on his waist in a heroic pose. Then he set his feet farther apart and raised his hands over his head. Some sort of metallic wings flapped open but they may not have been properly attached because he began to teeter and when he realized he might fall, he tried to grab the ladder. There was a sickening crash and the lights went black. From the speakers came the voice of a man saying, "That's the story of a man named When."

And another, "Whose closing act was to suspend."

"His failure to hitch."

"And stitch and bewitch."

"Has brought us now to the end."

I recognized the voices and felt I had wandered into a show meant for the inhabitants of the Compound. Yet I could see no one as I walked to the front. "Hello. Is anyone there?" I heard a stifled grunt and as I wanted to be certain the mishap was not a part of the show, I added, "Was this an accident?"

"An accident, my friend, is simply an unexplored possibility." I asked if he needed any help and he told me, "I am okay. I have broken a few bones and my wings are crushed but they should be mended by the morning. I fell on a blind woman. Now, I must be on my way. My herald is waiting." There was an abrupt whoosh as he rose before me. One hand was clutching the rope and the other waved as he rocketed into the night. He plummeted briefly to ask if I had spotted a little girl running around the place before he ascended once more. When I recovered, I searched behind the huge screen but all I saw was some sort of pulley machinery. I looked around for the woman who had broken his fall, but she must have been carried away.

I would have returned to the chapter house then because it was almost 10:30 p.m., but I saw a figure running up the side of the basin. I decided to follow it and half an hour later, I came upon what appeared, in the gloom, to be old carriages and discarded wagons and engines. At the far end of the junkyard was a huge billboard with a white, washed-out illustration of an orange-tinted man who seemed to be tap dancing with his cane. I was trying to distinguish the words on the billboard when I saw some movement to my left, a figure jumping out from a carriage. The person was followed or chased by a huge black beast. "Wait!" I shouted.

He was wearing a cap and a long overcoat but I knew immediately that he was the performer with the defective wings. I shouted after him, "Wait! Where are you going? There was a group of old –" I stumbled on some kind of pinion wheel and when I got up, the man was gone.

I walked back tiredly in the direction from which I had come. Half an hour later, I felt I should have brought along my mulberry markers because I was lost. I knew I would be going in an endless loop until the light of morning. At each street, I shouted even though I knew no one would respond. Then I saw the cathedral's spire in the moonlight.

"If you keep this up the roused spirits will be upon us."

I jumped. It was the performer. "I am sorry. I think I am lost."

"So it shall be in the beginning and so at the end. The situation that presages our existence and the last one that slips away with us."

"I meant literally. I am lost. I can't find my house."

"First you have to find yourself." His voice was low and melodramatic like an actor's. His statement even sounded like a line from a movie. "Let's look at it this way, brethren. You are no less than the man you imagine yourself to be."

"Are you practising for your next show?"

"We are forever practising, but to what avail? Will we be ready when we are called upon to account? But to get back to your question. You are no less than the man you imagine yourself to be and no more than the man you would like to be. You are who you are at this moment. Nothing more, nothing less. A man standing on a three-foot piece of earth. Is he changing while everything around him remains constant or is it the other way around?"

"Again, I have no idea what you are talking about."

"There are no easy answers, my friend. If there were, bodies would be piled up in never-ending heaps. We need this itch is what I am saying. Decrees and destiny. It's a harlequin spin, I tell you. A prescribed solution would stop you dead in your tracks. And that is where you would remain." He grinned and his eyes seemed more sunken. "There are no coincidences and no luck and no randomness. What there is, if you will allow me, is wilful blindness at all the connections floating before us. And the consequences. There, I have said my piece and I feel no better for it. My work here is finished and I must move on. We will meet again, though I must say that the time and place is not completely within my purview."

While he was scratching his dog's neck, I asked him, "Did we ever meet before? Your voice sounds familiar."

To his dog, he said, "Did you hear that, buddy?" He loosened his hold on the collar but continued talking to his dog. "When you have travelled around for as long and as far as we have, you develop a feel for things, don't you? Let's say you are sitting at the back of the bus, minding your own business and thinking dog thoughts, and lo and behold, who should enter but the very man you are looking for. The question arises as to what measures you must take, wouldn't you say? Should you seize his soul or should you carry him to his abode? And since you are a dog, are you willing to spark the blood of someone you are authorized to protect? These are important questions when you are fighting for the very people who misunderstand your mission." He walked a few steps then turned to me. "I am going to break all the rules here and tell you that nothing is complicated if we adjust the angle. What you are looking for is closer than you imagine. It always is." He walked toward the cathedral and I was about to tell him that the door was securely locked when he added, "But you are going in the wrong direction." He fished out a huge bunch of keys and opened each of the locks. I followed him inside. "Spring cleaning, brethren. The seasons are upon us." He kept up his jabber as he walked through the building, which was much bigger than the front had suggested. He went into a little room and emerged wearing a frock. "Have you ever studied a man without faith, brethren? His face is slack and purposeless. If you look long enough you will notice the eyes swollen with greed and the lips trembling in anticipation of some perversity. If you look even longer, you will see that every square inch of this man is marked by envy and dissatisfaction. Listen to how such a man talks," he said, moving about with a rapid stride, adjusting lectionary, cruet, paten, ciborium and other objects. "You can actually hear the schemes swishing around. For such a man has a heavy tongue. Now tell me this – are you a man of faith?"

This was an interesting question to which I had never previously given much thought. Eventually I told him, "I cannot be certain."

"Then you are lost."

"I cannot dispute that. What are you doing?" I asked him as he tried to adjust the lectern.

"Replacing everything to their correct positions. We need these markers is what I am saying. We cannot shift things to suit our present circumstance and I will tell you why. Are you ready? It is because forgetting comes naturally to us. There, I have said it."

Eventually he came to a vestry and opened its back door. Red light, splotched and speckled, flooded the place. I backed away, reeling from the burning odour of sulphur and coughing into my hands. I was about to sit to settle myself when I heard another cough from one of the pews and turned to see three figures sitting close to each other. "Hello," I called out. "I didn't notice you all there." My eyes were still burning and I could not distinguish their faces.

The middle man said, "We notice what is convenient at the moment." His voice was so stifled and ponderous I asked if they were monks. The man on the left, shorter than the others, seemed riled up with my question. The middle one patted him lightly and continued, "We are here to gauge your progress."

The only thing I could say was, "Really?"

"Yes, really," the man on the right said gloomily.

"And would you mind revealing your prognosis?" I assumed they would offer some theological nonsense, but one by one, in tandem, they began to explain that although my memories were not repeated in three-month cycles as I claimed, they were in fact disjointed and the connections random and arbitrary. They seemed to be suggesting that this was not uncommon with extreme paranoiacs. One of them said, "A bit here and a bit there with no true understanding of precipitating events or consequences," while another added, "There was no sequencing or pattern and so no objective reasoning and analysis." Finally, I heard, "Your memories were never lost after a specified period. Rather you lost the ability to make connections between everything that you recalled. The only connecting thread was your willingness at encouraging others to participate in your paranoia."

"And who might these others be? I must be very persuasive." I wondered how they knew of my memory loss.

The little man tittered and said, "Ordinary people coloured by your own obsessions."

He glanced up at the middle man, who added, "An extreme form of prejudice, you might say." He uttered an unnecessary sigh and added, "You, sir, have succeeded in fusing your life's work with your actual life. Now would you be kind enough to tell us your name? Is it still Remora?"

"I believe you may have confused me with someone else." A name came to mind, Cake the frog. Instead I uttered the name of the dead calypsonian. "The Tawny Leopard. But I am more interested in the tall man who walked through the vestry's door. I followed him here." The impish man stood on the bench and both his companions pulled him down. "He was here just a minute ago." I wished I could see their faces more clearly. "I believe he is a performer or something." The man in the middle folded his arms against his massive chest and his companions did likewise. I waited a minute or so for some clarification and when they said nothing, I told them, "I am going after him. I believe he may have found a way out of the town." I was surprised by my declaration, although I suppose it had been my intention all along. So I left the three men in the pew and walked toward the vestry.

LO THE HARLEQUIN SPIN

On the vestry's wall was an engraving of a half-dozen fused figures, their eyes cast upward. I went inside and noticed a swaying rope attached to a bell on the rafter. I half expected to see the performer dangling there but it was more likely he had gone through the thick wooden door at the back. I headed in that direction, opened the door and was buffeted by a powerful breeze blowing up spirals of what smelled like carmine particulate. It was peculiar that I would know this, I thought, as I shaded my eyes with my palm and saw miles and miles of field that bore the same reddish hue as the dust.

The edge of the town! Inside one of the town's houses, I had seen a snow globe of a man chain-strapped to a rock. When I shook the globe, he seemed caught in some atmospheric agitation, and, looking at the world outside, I saw a similar kind of turbulence. I took a deep breath and stepped outside. The air reeked of sulphur or iron pyrites that had been pulverized and the mere thought of inhaling this poisonous dust made me nauseous, but I pressed on. I must have walked for about twenty minutes before I came to a bus terminal with sketches of birds on every inch of the glass. I stumbled to the enclosure and saw the man just beyond the terminal. He was holding his animal loosely and seemed unconcerned I may have been following him. Perhaps he felt secure in the presence of his pet, and for this reason, too, I kept my distance. While I considered my next move, I realized that what I had mistaken for birds were really the hats worn by bushy-bearded men whose faces were arrayed in a circle. In the centre was a naked woman, the men looking away from her. My error was due to red blots on the glass, but also to the odd style of the drawing: thick brush strokes and intersecting dots that brought to mind the electrical crackle that might precede an explosion.

I heard a distant whine, like an underground turbine, and I noticed the man watching the road. When the bus appeared on the horizon, it seemed quite tiny; and focusing on the vehicle, I saw how much the surrounding fallow resembled bloated pillows as if air had been pumped from underground in precise instalments. The man whispered something to his dog and stepped into the middle of the road. For a moment, I feared that the driver would knock him down, but the bus stopped at the last minute. The dog bounded in, pulling his owner to the last seat. When I followed, I saw that the driver was the man who claimed he was a mortician. But now he was wearing an eye patch and he pretended not to recognize me. He seemed a bit annoyed and I wondered if it was because this abandoned town lay on his route. I asked where he was headed but he ordered me to my seat with a wave of his hand. I looked around for a coin receptacle and finding none, took a seat in the middle. The bus pulled off with a lurch that flung me forward. I remained in that position, leaning on the backrest before me just so I could surreptitiously keep an eye on the dog, and when I heard a low grumbling, I glanced back and saw man and pet conversing. The bus bounced along at a steady speed and in my forward position, I soon dozed off.

I awoke from a dream of monstrous animals with metallic claws and a sequence of explosions and limbs scattering in elegant patterns. Walking within this carnage was a frail woman with a mask and some distance behind, a little girl. All the scenes were contained within frames, like a cartoonist's sketch pad. It took a while before I adjusted to the fact that I was actually on my way out of the town. How often I had dreamed of this! Just to be sure, I looked back and saw the man waving to someone outside even though there was not a single person in sight. He got up in a rush and began pounding the window, and the driver, clearly annoyed, brought the vehicle to a stop. The man ran out of the bus, leaving his dog behind. I looked out hoping it was the woman, Soma. The driver slid down on his seat, opened an aluminium Thermos and withdrew a revolver that he smelled before replacing it. As he was doing so, the passenger returned, his cap and coat covered in white dust. The bus pulled away and I heard my co-rider slapping his coat and talking about "a mighty combustion" and "a vanished dryad" to his pet. He quieted down when we came to another stretch of derelict farmland but resumed his conversation as we approached a town that was as grey as the previous settlement had been white. The entrance to the town was through an archway on which someone had written *Major Manor*.

The name seemed familiar, but I could not recall the broken-down grey buildings with steel pipes protruding from jagged concrete. Most of the buildings were – or had been – high-rises and although there was no one on the roads, the lanes and byways must have been congested with people at some point. We entered a thoroughfare with a series of open manholes.

"There's no doubting it." I looked back and saw that the man with the dog had moved two seats ahead. A couple minutes later, I heard some shuffling and turned to see him closer to me. His jacket was torn off at the shoulders and the decals and stickers on the pockets and collar reminded me of a dream, or vision, of over-turned and burning vehicles similarly decorated. I could not see his dog and I hoped it was securely tied. I noticed the driver glancing in the rear-view mirror and I feared he would stop his vehicle and order both of his passengers out. I felt I should establish some connection with him so I mentioned the emptiness of the bus. He glanced back, but too quickly for me to gauge his expression. It was the man with the dog who answered. "If you pay attention, brethren, you will see faces everywhere." In the confined bus, his voice sounded low and hollow – like spare iron poles beating against each other – but this made his statement seem even more ridiculous. When I glanced around instinctively, he added, "Not like that. You can't see anyone like that. Let's take it to the field outside." He must have leaned forward and I felt his breath on my shoulder. This intimacy was disquieting and I shifted in my seat and looked out the window. "What do you see?" What I saw was a mountain ridge with light-coloured seams that were too regular to be natural. Perhaps they were roads and the cottony balls were pack animals. "Would you like to know what I see?" He didn't wait for an answer. "I see a procession of people. What's the word? A *kerry-van*. A kerry-van moving slowly along. Maybe they stopped right there." He knocked on the glass and I made out a ripple in the land, two parallel valleys that crested into a maze of inter-locking trees. It was some distance away and I was about to answer when the bus pulled up and the driver got up and stared sullenly at us. He seemed set to say something but instead he adjusted his cap's peak and limped outside. "If the driver knew there were a hundred faces following him, do you think he would still take a leak here and deface this sacred ground? Why is it sacred, you ask? The answer is that every burial ground is sacred. It does not matter whether death comes blindingly from above or creeps invisibly like a wildcat, thinning out the infants and the old. It's all the same. But everything carries a consequence." The word *consequence* rolled off his tongue lightly and I felt that this was an important word to him; one he had nestled in his mind for a while, pulling it out every now and again.

The driver returned, pushed in his gear and the bus rolled off. "What about you? Do you live around here?" I asked the man.

"That's a good question and I have only one answer for it. My answer is that I am just tripping like a nomad. Or a paladin to be more precise. I move from world to world, restoring the unbalanced to their rightful positions."

I tried once more. "Do you belong to this area?"

"*Belong*. Now that is the sort of word that is not in my dictionary. Can I tell you why? It's a word with boundaries. Do you see what I am getting at, brethren? No? Well, let me explain. It's a trap word." I noted the rhythm in his voice and I realized that what I had first mistaken for richness was really the rustic quality of a man who talked to himself a lot. "It's like this. If I ask you where you belong, you have two choices. You can answer quickly or you can speak the truth. My quick answer is that I belong everywhere because that is the life I know. The other answer is that I belong nowhere. I own nothing and no one has a claim on me. I am, if you will allow me, sacrosanct. Do you follow? On another note, did you see that stump there?" He tapped the glass. "Well, I have to inform you that it is not a stump but a totem. I don't expect you to notice this in the night so don't take it as a criticism. As a matter of fact, I am still waiting for you to answer my question."

"Would you mind repeating it?"

"If it will make you any happier I can strive to do exactly that."

"Go on."

"Now that sounds more like a demand than a request. The question is what if you see connections that don't yet exist? Are you a madman or a visionary? But there is a bigger question looming." He pulled the dog's ear and whispered into it. "Should you bite your tongue or howl to the heavens with the full knowledge you are heading toward a crucifixion? There are always consequences."

He began to murmur to his dog and I looked out the window and tried to establish some familiarity, but the rolling fields offered no information. "Where is the bus going?" I asked him.

"We are going exactly where you expect. Not a fathom more, not a fathom less."

I tried again. "Where does the route lead?"

"A route is a sticky business, brethren. It can lead to the future if you are willing to risk the mountains and to the present if you keep on a straight line. Don't ask about the salt pans and craters unless you are interested in the commencement." His attention was caught by a Ferris wheel and he added, "There was a truck stop there. Grew into an amusement park because the truckers often rode with their families. Was like a little piece of magic if I am allowed to exaggerate. But magic only works when you can't see what's coming next. Same with miracles, I have to add."

"What happened to the park?"

"Trucks stopped coming is what happened. People expect families to always appear the same as if they are trapped in photographs stuck over a fireplace." There was a new note of anger in his voice. "Nobody asks the most important question of all. The question is what happened? What happened to all the people who lived here at one time? What rules were there in the nights? What did they speak about when they awoke in the mornings? What was the breakfast arrangement like? What were they thinking during that early morning dip in the river? What did they see in the water? Trouble arising from upstream? No one asks the important questions. Not-a-body! But there are consequences. Do you know what keeps me going? The rule breakers, that's what I am talking about.

They must be rubbed out. The spirits pelted away so the hosts can get a second chance. And when the spirits return, I will be awaiting. There, I have said it all." He patted his dog and whispered in its ear.

With my limited memory, I could not be certain if the passenger was deranged, edified or comical. I felt it was the first and I tried to shift the conversation. "What happened to all the farms?"

"Stolen by the man who promised redemption with every utterance. A silver-tongued charlatan who bought everything before he burst into orange flames. But I am relieved that you put that into words because it shows you have a soul. So, I am going to be frank with you. How do you save the living? Allow me to answer your question. You do it by making choices. I can already hear you asking if that is the only option and I must answer that regrettably, it is. Cubes and die. It's a harlequin spin. One day I am going to put that into song because I hear it singing in my head." I heard him humming to his dog before he said, "Your questions tell me that you looking for someone."

"Would you pipe down there?" The driver's voice held the disinterested – bored, even – tone of a man accustomed to delivering this particular request.

Surprisingly, the man got quiet and in a low voice, he told me, "His name is Fuckjowl and he transports the inhumans. We are natural enemies even though we are, at this moment, engaged in an identical undertaking. I could force the life out of his body with a single clap, but everyone has a function. Here's a question for you to consider. How would you deal with a man who levelled a village not because he enjoyed the sight of squirming children but because he believed it was his duty? Do you believe in consequences, brethren?"

In the same whispery tone, I told him, "I don't know what you are talking about, but was it you who did an act with wings of some sort? In the town we left?"

"You have hit on one of the most unassailable laws of the universe. We are forever performing and forever judged by our last performance. I am truly amazed at your insight."

"That's not what I said."

"You, my friend, are too modest. I, on the other hand, shout from the treetops." He had spoken loudly and I noticed the driver eyeing his Thermos. A few minutes later, my nose began to tickle from the smell of sulphur. "This is the quietest place in the world and for this and no other reason I travel this route. Still as a statue with living eyes and a lost soul." He got up and told me, "Please keep an eye on my herald."

I was about to protest when he walked to the front, scrambled the driver and flung him out of the moving bus. For a second or so the act seemed funny. Then the man got behind the steering wheel and, in his remarkable voice, said, "I return things to their rightful positions. You can say that I shorten the pilgrimages by cutting out all the deviations." He watched through the window. "There's a humming in the air tonight. Do you feel it, brethren? Do you understand that because of this we are all joined like birds weathering a storm? When we glance at the face of a stranger it's only because we are standing too close."

Panic began to set in. "Why did you do that?"

"When all is said and done, I am nothing but a performer. Did you by chance see a little sprite about?"

I got up. "You might have killed the driver. Why did you do that?"

"I have returned him to his natural environment."

"There is nothing outside. Just red dust."

"There is a house somewhere about."

"Where? I can see nothing."

He began to talk to himself. "A travesty is what I would call her. A sprite who talks with the birds but soon she will lose this gift when I catch up with her. A matchstick placed at the wrong angle can bring down the entire universe. A mutational meltdown. No one can outrun their consequences is what I am saying. There is too much fluttering in the world. Stability is what we need." I heard his dog growling and I realized I had no choice. I got up, pushed open the back door and jumped out.

STAGE THREE

11 THE GIRL BEHIND THE DOOR

I vaguely remember a bus and a burning field dotted with underground vents that threw up some kind of vitriol that clung to my throat and eyes. I remember walking within this conflagration and falling to the ground and pulling myself up only to fall again. I have no idea how long I kept this up before I arrived at this house. I have this image of a child helping me along, but I realize this is impossible because no one could have survived the crash in this desolate, volcanic place. I am using the word *crash* because I assume it is this event that had left me stumbling on the road, my memory wiped away. Three times over the last few days, I have attempted to retrace my steps to determine if there were any survivors or even luggage and equipment left behind – if in fact the vehicle is still there. And each time I was forced back by the wind, which whips up red spirals of dust so thick and foul they feel like burning mantids crashing to Earth. But my brief moments outside afforded me a sense of the house in which I have found refuge.

When I piece together the hurried glimpses from outside, I come up with a three-storey wooden house with a large attic that seemed to be collapsing on itself, giving the structure a strange inward curvature. My first view had seemed to show irradiating scales painted or carved on the walls, but my subsequent observations revealed the pattern had been caused by leaves from a huge sycamore tree blown against the house and stuck to the resinous wood. The house seems to have been built a century earlier and it shows in every square inch: in the lopsided windows, the rotting walls, the dented roof and attic. The sort of exterior that suggests a caved ceiling and piles of rubble, but its interior is remarkably well preserved. At first I felt that the last occupant had tidied up for a sale and I wondered who would ever choose to live in this area. I considered it might have been an archeologist of some kind. But that was before I discovered your letter and the notebook in which you instructed me to record my observations.

Because I cannot recall anything before the accident or crash or whatever had sponged away my memory, I have tried to determine our connection and, more precisely, the nature of our collaboration. Why were you expecting me? Were we working on some scientific project; perhaps a measurement of the wind or an examination of the red dust it throws up or an investigation of the vents or geysers? I have tried to push aside the solid fear that we may have been travelling together and you had perished in the accident. I hope that you will soon turn up and explain everything.

In the meantime, I will follow your instructions in the hope that I may discover why we were heading to this place. My investigation of the house so far has revealed that it is stocked with food for a month or two. I have also ascertained that it been previously occupied by a scholarly person as there were two sturdy desks set on opposite ends of the room, both bookended by wooden filing cabinets. On the desk on which I found your letter and notebook, I saw an old Russian-made camera and a pair of heavy binoculars, and in one of the drawers, I discovered three dozen rolls of film scattered among a compass, a measuring tape and a spirit level. The other drawers were either locked or shut tight from the warped wood. Beneath the desk, there is a Gladstone bag with what appears to be antique medical equipment – rusted forceps and terrifying amputation saws and trephines and an assortment of syringes. The bag had some red stains in the inner lining and I pushed it with my feet closer to the wall.

A thick cream curtain hangs behind one of the cabinets and when I first moved it aside, I saw a bookcase that had been built into the recessed wall. The books bore fascinating titles and they all seemed concerned with demonic possessions, lobotomy, bloodletting and etherization. There were also slim periodicals with obscure articles on trepanation and childbirth and others with diagrams of electric chairs and pulleys. The books were strange, to say the least, yet they all seemed familiar.

This morning, while I was waiting for you – or some rescue party – to show up, I plucked out two books from the middle shelf, *A Sentimental Journey Into the Mind of a Cannibal* by Mausi Rampart (translated by the Reverend Thomas Loft), and *The Miserly Mind* by Anonymous. I placed these aside with the intention of reading them later and walked around the huge room, observing the interplay of gloom with the light reflecting from the slanted wall mirror next to a fireplace with surprisingly fresh logs. There was a sturdy couch close to the fireplace and when I sat, I saw my reflection in the mirror, that of a smallish man in his mid or late forties with a puce colouration, as if my skin had collected all the dust blowing outside. I also saw what I had previously missed: the reflection of half a dozen clay figurines arranged on a window ledge just above a beige couch. The figures seemed to be of a man, each more disfigured than the previous. The last was so deformed it seemed to be of a centaur-like creature with extra limbs.

These figures, as well as the books and the Gladstone bag, seem out of place in the house of a geologist and I can only infer they have been left there by a previous owner. I have not yet explored the entirety of the building so I cannot say if there are more surprises. I have been to the basement, though, and I can tell you that it is huge and one end seems to lead through a short tunnel to a garage or a stockroom. The other end holds a small darkroom. There are trays and canisters of some colloidal substance and five packs of linen printing paper. While I was looking at the equipment, I realized that my familiarity with the procedure for reproducing the photographs and my ignorance of the tools in the drawers upstairs suggested I may have been your photographer – while you roved around collecting samples of rocks or calcified lava.

There is also an upper floor that I have been unable to explore even though there are two sets of stairs – leading to the same area! However, both are so rotted they are impossible to climb.

Last night I pulled out a slim tract from the recessed bookcase. *Organ Stop* by RH Bromedge, and when I opened it, I saw detailed illustrations of medical experiments and surgical procedures. The writing, in a cursive script, was too tiny and extravagant to decipher and the illustrations were not to scale as there were huge heads, small bodies and engorged organs next to withered bones. Sometimes this was reversed. Some of the medical implements reminded me of those in the Gladstone bag I found beneath the desk. In one of the illustrations, a man with flowing hair was in a transparent water tank that resembled a huge aquarium, his organs floating in the liquid and connected to his body by what seemed to be an electrical current. Three men were seated before a desk, observing the man.

There are also slim manuals on madness. The books seem to be collaborative efforts as there are three names on the jacket of each. One of the books, *The Worm Runners Digest*, described in a breezy manner a procedure for memory reassignment in planarian worms and astoundingly hinted at a process for storing memories outside the body. Because of its style I could not tell if it was fiction or not. Same with one of the manuals that reported an experiment where a crazy woman was forced to regress through hypnosis to the most traumatic events in her life. The woman, not given a name, was described as if she were an ape or some laboratory animal. It was only at the end that I read she had been found guilty, some time earlier, of infanticide. A companion book with the same faded green cover with intersecting lines detailed a similar procedure conducted on a woman who had murdered a man after he had abruptly presented her with the news he was her father.

Because of the missing and rearranged chapters, the books are difficult to follow and I cannot determine if the criminals who underwent these unusual rehabilitative procedures were plucked from a brutal place called Adjacentland or if they were eventually sent there. I have to wonder at the choice of reading material in this library. Take this pamphlet, for instance, with its long and meandering essay that seemed to posit the existence of points when the past and the future merged. At these intersections, the writer claimed, it was possible to modify the future.

Another article, torn off from a book and rolled between blank paper in an almost secretive manner, described something called a pivot point, that, as far as I can tell from the few pages, is the point at which creative geniuses snap, their brilliance replaced by psychoses. These psychoses are manifested through hallucinations that carry the whiff of their previous work. The stricken do not, according to this view, gradually descend into darkness but stumble swiftly into paranoia. The final paragraph speculated that there may be some tripwire in the brain that is activated when the inflow of information is too great for the neurons to handle.

Most of the manuals are similar in the sense that they all begin in a reasonable manner before they divert into hypotheses that are completely hare-brained. For instance, in *The Miserly Mind* there is a section that promises to discuss the process that madness, used interchangeably with the imagination, can hold the cure for a world gone sterile. It's perhaps the most intriguing of all the books. Unfortunately, apart from the preface, the rest of the pages have been torn out.

The books have clearly been interfered with; it's as if someone, clearly deranged and offended by the focus on the many forms of insanity, has pulled out entire chapters and switched random pages and covers. The more appalling alternative is that they have been placed here to deliberately confuse me.

It has now been six days since I have been holed up in the place and this morning after I finished a periodical on schizophrenia and demonic possessions, I noticed there was a lull in the wind with the red particles blowing weakly on the road. I decided I would try to retrace my steps until I arrived at the accident site. I took the binoculars and hurried out.

On the road, I heard what seemed to be the cries of an oboe, scratchy and interrupted as if it was played on a springy wound-up gramophone, but I soon realized the sounds were from the gusts of steam shooting up from the geysers. (Which really appeared to be small mud volcanoes.) All around were red lichen and battalions of tiny shrubs of the same colour. I must have walked for a mile or so before I felt a ruffle of wind and suspected that the lull was over. I scanned the outlying area with the binoculars and seeing nothing but serrated ground, turned back.

I was coughing badly from the particles blowing around by the time I spotted the mansion. From a distance, it resembled the sort of building that would startle children who instinctively grasp for lines and order and connections. (From where did I deduce this?) I could not recall locking the gate and while I was fiddling with the chain, I entertained the brief hope that you had somehow found your way here. The chain was rusty and I had to stoop to free the bolt. This task took close to ten minutes and when I glanced up, I saw a wicket door on the other side of the gate blocking my entrance. This was strange, as I should have noticed the door when I departed the building. I stepped back to get a better view and saw that it stood apart, not connected to the gate or to any discernible base. It was quite solid, too, with bevelled seams and a thick knocker on the side facing me. I felt it would topple over if I pushed so I decided to squeeze to the side, as I did not want to damage anything on the property. But as I moved sideways, the door shifted with me. I was quite startled as I was sure that someone was blocking my entrance. "Hello," I called out. "Is it you? The geologist? We were on the bus together. It may have been some other vehicle. Please step aside." When there was no response, I grasped the knocker, tapped it a couple times and called out once more. Eventually I placed a leg against the base and pushed hard with both hands.

"Please don't do that." I jumped back. The voice was airy, curious and female. Childish almost. "Why are you trying to get in? Are you looking for someone?"

"I've been here for the last week or so. Were you travelling with us? Were there other survivors?" When she did not reply, I asked her, "Are you alone? Where are your parents?"

"How should I know? I was flying at the time. They dropped like stones into the sea. You saw them pushed off."

I noticed her fingers tapping the sides of the door as if she was waiting for me to challenge her story. "Were you injured in the accident? We should go inside. Maybe there is some medication that –"

"I knew it! That is how you got everyone else."

"I didn't get anyone, child. Now you should really step aside."

"There was a big party before we left and everyone was dancing and drinking pink wine from blue glasses. The glasses were huge." She began to hum a low mournful tune and I felt sorry for this girl who had been traumatized by the accident and had been wandering around for close to a week. Perhaps she had survived by eating whatever she had gathered from the bus. "The mangle men came and they took everyone away and I hid and saw the worms they made disappear into everyone's ears when they pushed them into the flying cars. Did I leave anything out? Oh, I tried to follow the cars but I couldn't fly as high."

"Do you know where these mangle men took everyone?"

"How many times must I tell you? To the other place. To the adj…the adg…"

"Adjust? Adjective?"

"No. They don't like the last one you mentioned. To the adjay…"

"Adjacent?"

"Yes, that's it. To the Adjacentland."

"Do you know why the ambulance…sorry, the mangle men, took them to this place?"

"They were looking for…no… I am not going to say anything more."

"Are there any other survivors? Did you find yourself here all alone?"

"And I am not going to say a single word, either, about all the monsters you dreamed up."

I decided to humour her in the hope she would step aside. "So there are monsters about?"

"Don't pretend. The are from your dreams. All of them. The brute and a man without a tongue and a lady who can see ghosts and a thief. The Citizen Brigade caught them and took them away. All but one. The major monster. I think he is too strong for them. Haven't you seen him? Or maybe heard him as he is always clanking and grinding like this." She uttered a low sound as if she was clearing her throat. "I think he is building a nasty bomb."

"Then we should go inside the house quickly in case he makes his way here."

"Too late! He is already here. They were trying to vaccinate him with the worm when he got away. Did I pronounce the word correctly?"

The question was asked in such an infantile manner that I felt a renewed concern for the girl. I asked her, "When last have you eaten or had a shower, child?"

"Not going to answer any rude questions. Not even going to hear them. Right now I am pretending to stuff my fingers in my ears." After a while, she said, "I can fly. I already told you this."

"Yes, you did. You also mentioned the Citizen Brigade." I felt she was referring to the ambulance's attendants and I told her, "Maybe we should go inside and wait for them. There's no need to be afraid of me."

I noticed the fingers of one hand moving up and down as if I had reminded her of the door's weight. "Have you ever killed anyone?"

"What sort of question is that?" I asked.

"It's a very simple question. Now answer."

"No!"

"Maybe you forgot. Have you ever tried to kill someone?"

"Listen, child. I think you knocked your head in the accident. You shouldn't be out all by yourself."

"I am not by myself. I am looking for my pet cat. It helps me get around. It tells me who to avoid."

It occurred to me that she was afraid of me, a stranger. "Am I so scary looking?" I asked her and when she did not reply, I added, "Why would I do something so horrible like killing someone?"

"Because of the other voices telling you what to do."

"What other voices, child?"

"Stop calling me a child. The voices from the other people you have joined up with."

"I haven't joined with anyone. If you move away from behind the door you will see I am alone."

"Stop pretending. You know you can't see the others. They are behind your forehead."

"I see. Did I put them there?"

"They are always there." She paused and I felt she was peeping at me through a chink in the door. "Or maybe you did. You look old and wrinkly."

"Thank you. That makes me happy."

I heard a low giggle before she said, "When everyone got joined together the voices started."

"So everyone hears the voices?"

I saw a finger drumming against the door's side. "Some were fixed and those who couldn't be fixed were packed into Adjacent-land. All the monsters." Just then, there was a rumble of thunder and she whispered something about her monster.

"It's only thunder," I told her.

"It's when the monster comes along."

"There is no –"

I jumped back when the door fell forward and a ragged little thing stepped forward. She was wearing a hood that covered her face and a frayed serape studded with wilted flowers was wrapped around her shoulders. I guess I was too surprised to stop her when she turned the door over and jumped aboard. There were roller bearings on each end of the door and she kicked with one foot like a toboggan rider and sped down the road singing, "Round and round the mulberry bush." When I collected myself, I shouted for her to stop but she continued kicking until the door gathered speed on the downward slope. She was wearing boots that were ridiculously big and there was a clutch of what looked like marigolds poking out from the top of each. A bird-engraved boomerang hung on a necklace almost to her waist. She shouted something about the monster. Then she was gone.

I stood there for a while, awaiting her return up the hill before I hurried in the direction she had disappeared. I saw a series of vents and tunnels and must have called out for close to an hour, stooping to peer inside the vents. I wondered if she had taken her rations to one of the tunnels and I recalled the passageway I had discovered in the basement. I hoped that she had somehow managed to locate another entrance to the house.

Eventually I had to give up. The sky was grey with dark pouches hanging beneath the clouds. The sacs resembled wreaths of buoyant jellyfish. All at once, the pouches seemed to explode and icy rain fell with such velocity I felt I was being pelted with leaking needles. I covered my head with my hands and called out once more to the child before I was forced into the old house.

1.2 Kothar the Magnetician

The ice pellets were stinging my back when I ran onto the porch. I could hear the pellets crashing against the glass windows behind me like canister shots. Nevertheless, I stood there for a while, thinking of the little girl caught in the storm. I hoped she had found some safe spot to ride it out. Thrice I sprinted to the front gate hoping that she might be standing outside but rushed back to the house when a flurry of wind sent the leaves and twigs catapulting through the air. The wind also drove away the clouds and soon the storm let up a bit. I continued my watch from the porch before I opened the door. I couldn't understand the nature of the storm and especially the ice pellets in such an unbearably hot place.

"You are becoming careless." An imposingly tall man was standing before the fireplace waving two brushes in both hands like a conductor. His pupils were opaque through his dusty metal-framed goggles and I could not determine the exact area of his gaze.

My first thought was you had showed up, so I said, "I am sorry I left the door open. I was trying to get to the accident site. There was a child on the road. How long have you been here?"

"Just as long as you have."

"Is there anyone else? Where have you been all this time?"

"Waiting. For you."

"Are the tools yours?" I motioned to the assortment of geological equipment on the desk.

He issued an abrupt whinnying laugh and goose-stepped his way to the desk. The drawers would not open and he grew agitated and pulled so violently I expected the cabinet to come crashing down on him. Eventually, he managed to free the lower drawer and from inside it, unhinged the upper. "A heretic's fork," he whispered. "Whips and restraints. Corkscrews and collars. A dame's bridle. Dippel's oil." When he turned to face me, his neck seemed elongated by his plaid tie's severe loop. "What do you have in store for me?" His overgrown Vandyke and his peaked homburg accentuated both his height and his face's angularity. For a second, I imagined him silhouetted against a red sky, a battered flamethrower in his hands.

My hope it was you swiftly faded. But I had to be sure. I told him, "I am sorry. Have we met?"

"You do know that men like me are designed for dungeons. If we are lucky, we secure the employment of carnivals and circuses. Can you guess who told me that?"

I tried to steady my voice as I asked him, "I really cannot say. How did you manage to find yourself here?"

"I am here. You are here. Let's begin."

"Begin what?"

"Begin to repair your damage and return my life." He stabbed a finger behind one of his goggles' lenses and plucked out something. "Begin by weighing the efficacies of garrotting as opposed to poisoning. I am a master of both trades. I also dabble in basketry, cobbling, pottery, metalwork and magnets." He whirled suddenly and I jumped back. I tried to determine if he was joking but his face was practically hidden by the goggles. "Let's proceed, then." He pointed to the couch near the fireplace.

"You must forgive me, but I don't have the faintest idea who you are. Are you the owner of the house?" When he did not answer, I tried again, "Are you the caretaker or the gardener?"

"I purée mealworms and berries for nourishment but if you want me to be the gardener today, I can. Your move." He gazed at me above an open drawer.

I tried to explain. "I was in a bus that crashed on its way here. I assumed I was the only survivor, but there may be others."

"Where are the others?"

"This is what I have been trying to explain. I have been trapped in the house because of the wind and the sulphur or whatever it is that blows around. I believe I may have suffered an injury during the accident, as I cannot remember anything prior. You may have been travelling with us, but if that was the case, I have no memory of it."

He laughed deep and long as if there were a rusty spiral lodged in his long neck. "Once more, my name is Kothar and I am a magnetician. My aborted experiments are, as you well know, associated with electromagnetic pulses. You will get nothing more from me."

"Tell me, Kothar –"

He clasped his hands over his chest and adopted a look of solemn pride. "I prefer, as always, to be referred to as Kothar the Magnetician."

"I am afraid I have no knowledge of your field. Were you part of the team?"

"You know very well that I was."

It occurred to me that he may also have been affected by the accident although his memory was better than mine. "What happened to the others? Did they survive?"

He pushed up his goggles, took out a snuff box from his coat and poured its contents over his eyes. "Helps with my blindness." He continued rubbing the snuff over his face, then sprang up with a hearty bellow and glanced at me with bloodshot eyes before he eased back into the couch and replaced his goggles. I asked my question once more and he said, "They are around. Waiting for your call."

"My call? Was I the leader of the team?"

"Are we going to go over that again?"

"I cannot recall anything, as I mentioned. Was that the cause of the accident? An argument?"

He stretched out on the couch and began to wave his hands above him. "You were assembling a squad of differently abled people. And I was a virtual lightning rod, magnetizing all the irrational voices troubling your team to create a perfect power source. Don't you recall what you said to us over and over? That madness is the only pure state. That we were all gifted and you would make us famous? That there were those who wanted to drain and bottle our exuberance because they had lost every drop of it?" He seemed to be talking to himself and I was relieved that he had cooled down a bit. "Here is what you do not know. You did not give me my powers. Like every important discovery, mine was accidental. The discovery of reverse levitation by Baroness Simula Phykou. The kaleidoscopic uniscope by Professor Norman Ballard. The self-playing violin by ErPhu. The oscillating speculum by Monsieur Amygdala Carafe. The exploding spirit stove by Sir Rodney Hogarth." He twirled his whiskers so that both ends were stiff on his cheeks.

I felt I had underestimated the extent of his trauma. "I am talking of the team from the bus. Geologists or volcanologists. I may have been the photographer?"

He dragged his goggles over his forehead and turned to stare at me with bloodshot eyes. "Can I tell you something? I am beginning to understand you better." He grinned. "Much better. Would you like to know how?"

"Please do. I am just as confused as you are."

"Kothar confused? Well, let me tell you that I learned things in the wilderness you have not dreamed of. Have you ever audited a spider's web? I thought not. You believe you are smart, but I know how to deal with you now." He tugged off his boot and removed some sort of metallic encasement from his toes. Next, he brought out a miniature cast-iron box from his pocket. There was a key at one side and when he twisted it, I heard a little tinkle. He held the box before his goggles, fiddled with the key and produced a strange little gadget. "Do you know what it is?"

I didn't want to get too close to him, but I was able to see that within its recessed top were three cogs surrounding an unsteady hand. "It seems like a mariner's compass. Perhaps a gyrocompass, judging from the wheels." With my fractured memory, I was surprised I could recall such a precise object.

He grinned. "It's my usher and soulmate."

"So you were the team's surveyor?"

He got up and told me, "You cannot break me because I am stronger now. My mind is a free-ranging fowl." He seemed to be awaiting some comment but I allowed him to continue. "I know all your tricks. I learned things while I was waiting for you. I learned that, at a given moment, five people standing in a circle are always thinking the same things. I learned that soon we will dream in maps and decimal points. I learned that colours are not to be believed and that birds and locusts are news carriers. I have it all stored up here for the coming battles. Let them try to drain it! Let them try!"

I tried to steady my voice. I told him, "Mr. Kothar, I think you have been wandering around too long. You need to simmer down."

"Simmer down?" My suggestion seemed to rile him up. "You think you are clever, but you no longer control us. Hiding in your house and trying to joystick the world. Making us do things. Unmentionable things. I am going to be more thorough this time." He rose from the couch and came at me with stiff outstretched arms. I tried to step back but his hands were too long. He held on to my ears, growling as he did so.

"Stop that!" I kicked his knee, but there was some metallic plate so I banged against his chest, which seemed encircled beneath his coat with some type of chain. All the while, he was laughing. In desperation, I reached into his coat, hoping there was a weapon within but only came up with a brass swivel locket.

He stepped back immediately. "Give me that. You have no right."

I glanced at the locket. It was quite old and engraved with what appeared to be a kneeling ape. When I sprung the clasp, I saw that there was nothing inside, but Kothar put on a magnificent act: he backed away, shielding his eyes with his wrist. Then he fell on his knees. And it was in that pose that he reversed through the front door. I stood for a while, contemplating my near escape and rubbing my ears. When I looked outside, he was gone.

I stood at the window, gazing at the spirals of dust, trying to see where Kothar had disappeared. I remained there until night when it was impossible to see a few feet beyond the porch, all the while going over my encounter with him and with the child I had seen at the gate, trying to make sense of everything. We had all been affected but in different ways. It was unlikely that the crash could have altered all of our minds so there had to be another causal agent. The likeliest cause, I felt, was the red sulphurous dust that sprung from the vents and was blown about by the strong winds.

This determination brought me no joy because I had to consider the possibility that Kothar, in his maddened state, could easily have wiped out everyone else. In which case, neither you nor anyone else will read these entries I am making in your notebook. But at this time, I am more concerned about the little girl. She had mentioned a monster stomping around and I am convinced she was referring to Kothar. Poor child. That was why she had been hiding all the while. I decided that I would search for her in the morning.

I locked the windows but did not feel safe enough to sleep so I got some of the books I had placed aside earlier and went to the couch on which Kothar had stretched his long body. I began with one titled *The Monster in a Circle*, but when I opened it, I discovered it was a children's book with squat illustrations of ogres peeping behind hedges at goats and turkeys and children at play. Nevertheless, I found its childish sincerity quite funny and I caught myself smiling at the ogre's earnest speculations about the taste of everything arrayed on the other side of the hedge. I finished it in an hour or so, placed it aside and reached for another, *The Exuberant Life*.

It was thicker than the others and the illustrations, in fountain pen, were more detailed with lush, swerving strokes delineating the contours of every object. It began just as the others with fairies and monsters and ogres gambolling around but around the middle of the book, the young narrator began to doubt his own sanity when he realized that no one shared his visions or believed his accounts. Though the events described were fantastical, the descriptions – charged with anguish – had the feel of a memoir. Eventually, he grew to believe he was trapped in a topsy-turvy world where he was the only one outfitted with some kind of self-consciousness. He was hauled by his – in his account – unsympathetic parents from one expert to the other and they each prescribed the same remedies. Séances, special roots, peculiar baths, bloodletting, cauterization; one quack after the other. He began to suspect that his parents were not interested in a cure but was hopeful that he would be institutionalized so they could wash their hands of him and turn their attention to his little sister. His anguish at this parental betrayal turned to outright hatred when he realized that the experts, so attentive to his accounts, were part of the plot. He ran away, was caught and locked in his room. He ran away again, getting farther this time, but once again he was apprehended. Now he was chained to his bed. Then, one day he escaped and managed to outrun his pursuers. He continued running, hiding in the bushes, slogging through ravines and hills, catching small animals and eating fruits that sometimes left him sick. He was so emaciated that by the time he arrived at a massive wall he was able to slip through a narrow tunnel at its base. Still, it took him close to an hour to get to the other side and when he emerged he gazed at the wild and wondrous land before him and thought: Is this the place everyone tried to scare me with?

Apart from five mostly undecipherable drawings that seemed to depict an enclosure of some sort, a topsy-turvy little town with a confusion of architectural styles, a castle that resembled this house, a derelict train station and a scene with fishes leaping over a stream and fruit-filled trees – most likely, a representation of this new land – the book ended there. I examined the spine to see if a part had been torn off, but it was so old and crumbling, this was difficult to determine. I was puzzling over the book when Kothar walked in. I sprung up immediately, wondering how he had entered so surreptitiously. I felt through my pockets hastily for the locket I assumed he had returned for and I was close to panic when I discovered it was not there. But Kothar pretended he did not see me as he walked to the centre of the room, folded his hands above his head and began what seemed like a lethargic dance. He seemed to be singing, too, and when I listened more closely, I heard him babbling about a boy who was dragged from hive to hive by his beekeeper mother. This went on for several minutes before he tried to do something dainty with his long legs, almost toppled over, and continued his song in a slightly crouched posture.

He remained in that posture for a while. I asked if the song was about himself and he looked up forlornly. And here I completely astonished myself. (This disbelief lingers even now, as I am recording the event.) I walked to the doorway just in case and, keeping a close eye on him, explained that he had, most likely, at that young age formulated performances to reduce his sense of abandonment. Perhaps he had systematically neutralized feelings of attachment, of remorse and empathy. I suggested that while his mother was occupied and he was gazing at the hives, he fantasized about other lives and positions. I asked him if he was familiar with disintegrative shaming and I submitted that his belief in an epidemic of madness was a means of exteriorizing his own malfunction. It was a cry for help from an intelligent man.

With his hands on his head, he gazed at me with astonishment, but I must admit that I was far more shocked than he was. From where did this fluent knowledge come; from where did the phrases spring? The books I had scanned had helped, certainly, but my smooth assessment was confounding. I pressed on, the urgency in my voice due to my excitement at this flow of information and my fear that it would fade away if I hesitated. I explained the concept of operant conditioning and said that his pretence at being part of some scientific experiment was really a search for symmetry. I ended by telling him, "The most integral law in the universe is that of cause and effect. It is what keeps everything in balance. The universe is constantly rebalancing itself and sometimes we are caught in its oscillations. All we have to do is anticipate the ripples and ride out the waves." Again, I must stress my astonishment; it seemed for a moment as if Kothar was absent and I was addressing myself. The voice seemed to come from elsewhere and I had a sudden flash of three old men of different shapes lecturing in a room of unstable dimensions.

In any event, Kothar was not impressed. "I gave you a fair

chance," he said in a regretful voice. "You think I am mad. Unbalanced. A freak pretending to be a man. You are speaking in the same old language. Trying the same old tricks. Hoisting me up and pulling me down. Banning me from the group. Discarding me like a monster."

I was disappointed by his reaction. "Listen to me," I told him. "I am trying to help. I really am."

"Kothar knows who he is." His shoulders slumped. He seemed to be waiting for me to say something. When I did not, he said, "The buried should not be remembered. Ghosts should not walk upright. I have spent the last six years trying to figure it out. Now I know. You taught us to remember and then to forget. You and the managers."

"The mangers? Are you talking about the scientists who sent us out to –"

"You and them both were pretending to help us while all the time sabotaging our progress. We were your golems, given enough life to carry out your biddings. You wanted to see how far we would go. But it did not work. Death came in the way."

His last statement seemed familiar somehow. I told him, "I am sorry you have experienced this, Kothar. The person you have mistaken me for seems horrible. What happened to him?"

"Can I have my locket, please?" When I pointed to the desk, he got up and walked across. "You have managed to escape but be forewarned. The others will come for you." He took the locket and pushed it in his jacket. "You cannot bring someone to life and cast them aside when their tasks are completed. You cannot spark a fire and simply walk away. Be forewarned. When next we meet, a life will be snuffed out. The ripple you started will never end. Guess where I got that from?" He walked toward me without answering his question. I stepped aside quickly but he opened the door and walked out as if I were not there.

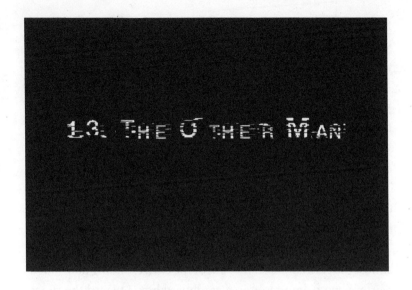

13: THE OTHER MAN

After Kothar's departure, I decided it was no longer safe to sleep on the couch in the lower floor. Kothar had sneaked in too easily and he could well do so once more while I was asleep. I decided I would try to climb one of the rotted stairways to the second floor. The one on the left creaked and shook with each step and halfway up a section of the riser caved away. I held on to the bannister and made my way down. I was extremely careful with the other stairway, testing each board and holding on to the bannister tightly. Eventually I managed to make my way to the top. I walked up and down a few times to know the safe spots.

There were three doors on the floor and I guessed the door in the middle, which was the biggest, led to the main room. I tested the door on the left and when it opened, I saw a little cot in the centre, and next to it, a tiny table with a water jug. The room was bare and I assumed that articles of small furniture might have been removed. The room on the right was furnished in the same manner but there were shackles hanging from the cot and just before the window was a wheelchair bolted to the floor. The cot was over six feet long and here, too, was the odour of scorched paper. This odour was absent in the main room and when I opened the door, the first thing I noticed was the paraphernalia of photographic equipment – camel-hair brushes, rolls of film, drying clips and a Zenit camera – at the base of an empty cage that hung about four feet from the floor. Behind the cage on the wall was a flashy photograph of a tree with spectacular scarlet flowers each enclosing an assortment of clocks. Turret clocks, pendulum clocks, water clocks and sundials. There were charcoal squiggles at the base of the tree and as I entered the room, I saw that someone had sketched in the outlines of miniature horned men with severed limbs.

On the other side of the photograph was a closet that occupied almost the entire wall. At the foot of the closet's sliding door was a pair of fawn balmorals atop a cardboard box. I placed the shoes aside and opened the box. I was surprised to see several novelty items, bagged and itemized. X-ray spectacles, a ventriloquist's whistle, a bag of desiccated sea horses and a bill for the purchase of a miniature submarine. The previous owner either had a playful side or he had been collecting the items for some purpose. I was certain of this when I noticed a notebook filled with insignias and single capital letters, each enclosed within a different shape. They seemed vaguely familiar and I guessed this was because the insignias seemed based on a lunar calendar. I replaced everything but took the shoes to the bed. The right shoe was stuffed with some paper that I placed in my pocket before testing the pair. They fitted me perfectly and I got up and walked around the room, listening to the light echoes of my footsteps. I noticed that the bedsheet was rumpled and I pulled at the ends and tucked these beneath the mattress. I walked around the room, wearing the previous occupant's shoes, gazed at his mirror and noted the reflection of his cage and his photograph. I went to the adjoining room with the shoes and watched, through the window, the view outside, the gate and the track that led to it. In the moonlight, the red dust appeared luminous and I wondered how he had managed to live in this forlorn place.

I guessed from the shoes that he was my size and – judging from his books downstairs – was concerned with the instability of the mind. Certainly, he shared my interest in photography. I returned to the middle room, slipped off his shoes and reclined on his bed. Now that I had some idea of the owner's possessions, I felt like an intruder in the house of this man who had chosen this desolate spot to carry on his studies. I closed my eyes and I tried to imagine him. In my half-drowsy state, I pictured him to be slim and slightly built. He carried with him a wince that he tried to disguise with a beard, but which was there for all to see in his smallish eyes. Most likely he had developed the habit of making his eyes even smaller, looking away when confronted by others and this aversion, though it had made him seem evasive, even shifty, had granted him the ability to quietly observe peripheral details; details he later patched together to see the real person rather than the figure that had stood before him. Perhaps this, rather than the books he had struggled with over the years, was his true gift. This gift grew over the years and gradually he turned his gaze outward, away from the person once energetic but now presented daily with less of everything.

I opened my eyes and gazed drowsily at the walls. The house must have been purchased for a nominal fee and the original owner may have assumed that only a fool would want to move to this condemned town; and he would have been surprised to be met by a man who spoke in careful and considered sentences. The original owner must have left quickly in case the purchaser changed his mind. But the new owner, who had travelled for miles and miles, had found exactly the place he was looking for and he soon set about removing the old furniture and bringing in or building new pieces. This would have taken a month or two and soon he had exactly the house that he needed. He would have walked through the house noting everything in his precise manner; looking not at the age of the fixtures but at their angles and the intersection of their shadows and the way the smell of mahogany was displaced by that of moist oak. He would have passed his fingers over the oak in the manner of a blind man testing for declinations and angles. I wondered if he ever had any visitors, perhaps a colleague who shared his interest. When I reclined on the bed I heard the rustling of the paper I had found in the shoe and placed in my pocket. There were five words that seemed to be hurriedly scrawled on the crumbled paper. *Look between the frames.* Just before I fell asleep, I thought of the cage and the shackles in the adjoining rooms and I remembered Kothar mistaking me for someone he believed was responsible for his state.

What I am about to describe has the texture of a dream, but I am not altogether convinced. (Even though it is logical to assume that my reflections of the previous owner of the house had brought it along. In any event, you can judge for yourself.) It began with the shoes still on my feet when I fell asleep. I have the sense of getting up very early in the morning and climbing down the stairs. On the lower floor, I walked from one end of the building to the other trying to see – and feel – it as it had been by the man whose shoes fitted me so perfectly. I checked the doors and windows and when I was sure they were locked, I turned to the recessed bookcase and tried to understand the owner's interests more precisely. I had left the camera on the desk and I took it with me to the darkroom, sprung the latch and withdrew the film. The counter had indicated that nine shots had been taken. An image began to take shape on the linen paper floating on the tray.

The appearance of details in a developing negative has an almost ghostlike quality as faces and bodies and background details coalesce and register from the liquid haze; and this is how I felt while I bent over the tray, watching the appearance of a man sitting on a gnarly stool and looking through the back window. There was a book on the table behind him and a half-empty glass. It was a perfectly composed scene and I wondered who had shot the photograph. I fished out the linen paper and I saw that he was staring at his feet and the photograph had been taken in one of the rooms upstairs. I flapped the print a few times and walked up the stairs to the room with the bolted wheelchair. I held the photograph before me while I walked around trying to determine the exact spot the photographer must have stood. I pretended I had a camera in my hand instead of the print.

This is where it got confusing. With the picture of him in my hand and his shoes on my feet, standing in the same spot as his photographer, we began a "conversation." First, he introduced himself. He knew too little of his father who disappeared for long periods and too much of his mother, a hypochondriac whom he soon realized had been taking medication prescribed for her absent husband. So, at an early age, he had to take care of his mother and at this early age, too, he developed a narrow hatred for both parents, and sometimes they blurred into a single person. It was easier for him to concentrate his hatred toward an overexacting guest. But he had put all of that aside to work on an important project.

What project, I asked?

The solution to the most intractable problem can be found by asking the simplest question possible, he told me. How do you get enemies to agree? How to come to a common understanding in a world torn apart by antagonistic views? How to bring about peace? How to stall the quality we are all born with?

I told him I did not understand and waited for an explanation. After a few minutes, I opened my eyes and glanced around. While I waited for his reappearance, I studied the photograph from every possible angle but there was nothing new. Then I thought of something. I rushed down the stairs so quickly I stumbled on the last step and fell to the floor. But I picked myself up and hustled to the basement darkroom.

In this newly developed photograph, he was seated at the kitchen table. There were two books and a bottle on the table. I searched for the books and placed them in the exact spot as in the photograph. I rummaged about in the cupboard until I located an empty bottle of wine and I put it alongside one of his figurines, that of a three-headed baby.

I closed my eyes and heard him clearing his throat with a sound that felt like hollow air pockets. I felt that what he was about to say was important, but the minute I opened my eyes he disappeared. I apologized and shut my eyes. He thanked me and then began to talk. He explained that the anxiety he had never been able to displace mirrored that of every other afflicted person in one profound way: the inability to answer some central question. The question would vary, he was telling me, but the outcome was always the same in that it pollinated other doubts. The first question, could be: Did my mother hate me? This would lead to the second question: Was it something that I did? Inevitably, he would then wonder whether he could have averted this maternal displeasure by modifying his behaviour, or if this flaw had affected others with whom he came into contact. I heard him leaving but this time I knew what had to be done.

Five minutes later, I walked to his bookcase, positioning myself from the photograph in my hand. He glanced at me with some irritation as if I had kept him waiting, before he continued. He told me that the bitterness about his being singled out for persecution had voided all his assurances and allegiances. I heard him saying: One central question with no easy answers. Just one. And the misery begins. He lowered his head. But you know all of this already. I am saying nothing new.

I told him I was happy he had decided to reveal himself. He took his time to reply. He said when a person lives alone for too long, he ceases to exist. He must have seen my skepticism because he immediately added that it is only our interaction with others that gives us a being. This seemed quite silly, this view that we are shaped wholly by the judgments of other people as if we are nothing but hollow men and women waiting for life and I wondered if he had stated this simply to examine my reaction. I was certain of this when he gave me the example of someone living in complete isolation, such as man marooned on a deserted island, slowly losing whatever personality he possessed. Vanishing in instalments, he said with a muted sadness. This sounded familiar, but I said nothing. For a while, he, too, was silent and I felt that he had regretted his talkativeness for he was undoubtedly a man accustomed to quietness. I decided to give him some time alone so I went into the kitchen and made myself a cup of tea.

I returned with my cinnamon tea and settled onto his couch with one of his books. I saw him, hands folded against his back, staring at the book from the photograph, *The Handbook of Alienism*. I apologized for rummaging through his bookcase and assured him I would soon replace the books I had taken out to their proper positions. I asked if the book he was reading was any good. After a brief pause, he told me that although it had been written three and a half centuries earlier, its contents bore the same relevance as it did then. I assumed that he was complimenting the author, but he said that years from now people would look back on this period as a continuation of the Dark Ages. All we have accomplished is to modify the nature of the restriction by substituting physical restraints with pharmaceutical immobilization. Treating a patient is now like putting him in a car without brakes. Should he stop by crashing against the tree, the ditch, the hydrant, the group of children or should he continue speeding down the road in the hope that some more amenable barrier presents itself? We are the modern diviners, the soothsayers, apothecaries, thaumaturgists. Some might call us charlatans, too, and they would be half right because we are always operating in the dark. His voice was controlled by a new eloquence and I felt that he had waited a long time to utter these words. Our profession, he added, can never be clearly defined because we constantly nibble at the edges of other disciplines. I saw frown lines on his forehead and a cynical twist to his lips. He waited until I was finished to tell me that he drew his diagnoses from a meticulous observation of human nature rather than from some moth-eaten prescription. I asked him why he had chosen to live alone in this house in an otherworldly setting.

I reminded him that he had mentioned questions but had provided no answers. I said that I felt I knew him but there was a barrier preventing a fuller understanding.

There had been a misfortune. He said the word gently as if it was something soft and unformed.

What type of misfortune? I asked.

The usual kind. The kind that time always brings about.

I noted the minute wince to his lips; the hint of regret and pain. He turned a page in the book and told me that following a period of complete numbness he began to live each day in expectation of the following. He could not wait for the day to be squeezed out to make way for the next. So I was always waiting, he told me. Waiting for what surely must be better, improved days. Sometimes, I skipped over a day or two or a month, or years, even, and then I saw myself as an old man waiting for death. To see myself like this, like the people who lay on my couch was unbearable because I knew the outcome. I had seen it a hundred times. He was glancing at me in a sideways manner as if he was trying to come up with an answer to the questions on my mind: What was the cause of the misfortune and how had he been affected?

I watched the veins in his hands seeming to shift position. He uttered a phrase: *The passing of smaller things.* He then spoke of his inability to trace fragrances to their sources. No longer feeling the tingle from running his fingers along the grain of an oak table. Looking at a photograph and not being able to separate appreciation from acceptance. Smaller things, he repeated. But they began to add up. I know you want something impressive here. Like a suicide. A striking devastation. But you will be disappointed. I am my own man.

We all are, I told him, just so he would continue.

I am the same person no matter where you choose to place me. A train station, a grotesque mansion, a town of ghosts, a compound. I will always be the same.

Me? Why would I place you anywhere?

He seemed quite annoyed and I felt he wanted to be alone. I went to the window and gazed at the drizzle, so wasted and crimson it seemed like a kind of vapour: the shell of some object that had long dissipated and which put in mind the swift second before an explosion. I walked up the stairs and left him to his book.

When I awoke in the early morning, I recalled every detail of the dream, which was unusual. It took a while before I concluded that I had unconsciously been setting pieces together to come up with a picture of the owner of the house and that my dream was really a tendering of all this understanding. Perhaps, too, I had been influenced by the words written on the paper about looking between the frames. I felt I had spent too much time cooped up in the house and I decided I would clear my head by stepping outside, as it seemed relatively calm through the window. I put on the shoes I had found in the closet and walked out of the house. When I crossed the gate, I looked around for the tunnels I assumed the little girl was using to shelter but they had all been covered over with the red dust. I walked on, testing the ground with my shoes. After a while, I began to cough and I returned to the house.

My eyes were burning and I washed my face in the kitchen sink and went to the bookcase. I got out a book that at first seemed to be describing this area, but as I read, I discovered it was about a compound of some kind. The place described was part of a town, the existence of which was hidden from cartographers and regulators and tax collectors. The compound was set in a town of interlocking streets and rows of identical houses and had once been the old administrative centre of the town. In this compound were scientists, writers, painters, teachers and musicians. I was thinking that it was some kind of retirement place; a retreat for burnt-out men and women, but the book seemed to suggest that they were surreptitiously monitored and were not free to leave if they chose. As I continued reading, I realized that the compound was not a retreat but a sort of holding house for men and women overwhelmed with madness and, moreover, they had been carefully chosen. But why? The book seemed to suggest that men and women with a particular sensibility, those who endlessly tried to find answers to abstract questions had been gathered there and carefully monitored. I tried to follow if this was so because their obsessions had transformed them into zealots, but the book's tone shifted and it now appeared that these men and women were constantly forced into bouts of regression to the precise period when their inspiration scattered into lunacy. It was a rambling and evasive account and the last chapter gave a hint at the reason for this fogginess. The writer admitted to using a *nom de plume* because he had once been a psychiatrist at the place and following his decision to abandon the institution, he had been hounded with the rumours that he was delusional, had suffered a breakdown, had identified too closely with his patients at the place, a background check had revealed he was a criminal and so on. One of the more cutting accusations was that he was categorizing extreme irrationality not as an abnormality but as a vital spark only because he had himself been infected. The rumours spread among his associates were not the end of it and here the author hinted there may have been attempts on his life. He had been forced to hole up in decrepit little towns, constantly on the move.

Now you might also be wondering if the haunted psychiatrist had finally found refuge in this forbidding area. The texts certainly suggested this and those that described barbaric medical practices may have been smuggled out of the compound as evidence. Perhaps Kothar had followed him here or had been brought along. But all of this was just speculation. I went to the bookcase and tried to see if there was some journal hidden away between the books. When I found nothing, I took my search to the rooms upstairs. I was about to give up when I thought of the undeveloped negatives in the darkroom.

There were six and I placed two into the developing tray. As the photographs took shape, I saw a man with a crook in his thin lips that suggested the permanent imprint of some horrendous vision. The man's mouth was partially open and I could see neither teeth nor tongue. I waited for the film to fully develop, for the features to fully emerge, but the man's features remained the same. I fished it out of the tray and held it up against the lamp.

You are looking at it the wrong way, came the voice from the end of the room. I was startled and I called out Kothar's name, but the voice was not as abrasive and rusty. In fact, it was remarkably similar to that of the dream man. I heard the voice again saying, when you measure everything in time, you see nothing else. You see only the hours and days and years falling like blank slates on a concrete floor. You can see the cascading slates but never hear the sound of them shattering on the floor. Death is the end of time. It's as simple as that. And what happens before is of little consequence.

I cannot understand why this is so hard to grasp.

Once more, I called out but there was no answer. I felt I saw someone standing at the end of the darkroom. The figure seemed to have absorbed some of the gloominess and appeared a light shade of blue, like a plant from a sea cave. But when I walked to the area, I saw it was a canister perched on a stool. I returned to the developing prints and once more, I heard the voice but from another side of the room. When a child is born, it looks around the room to determine its contours and how far away the walls are and the depth of the floor. Everything else is irrelevant to its tiny eyes. And years later, we endlessly repeat this act when we already know the answer. This is how we live our lives. Marking and measuring. Setting boundaries. Circling the wagons. It's how we measure our lives. Beginning, middle and end. Death is the end of time. Everything else is an accessory, a fable, a conversation with ourselves that possesses no real meaning. Why won't you understand?

I felt stupid saying, "Is that what I am doing now? Having a conversation with myself?"

In the second print shimmering in the liquid, I noticed the downward turn of his lips and I tried to determine if, in his smile, there was despair or contempt or skepticism. I hung the print on the drying hook.

The sequence is wrong. You have arranged the prints in the wrong order. You need to reverse them all.

I wondered if I had inhaled some of the red dust on my brief trip outside. I put the last print into the tray and I saw the outline of a slim man taking shape, the shoulders slightly hunched, the thinning hair swept back. I held the print against the lamp – before it could completely dry – and I saw the same figure. I carried it upstairs and held it against the window, hoping that in the natural light I would see it correctly. It had developed further to show a crook in the man's thin lips that suggested the permanent imprint of some horrendous vision. The subject's mouth was partially open and I could see neither teeth nor tongue. But it was unmistakably a photograph of myself.

I was confused and, I will admit it, frightened, as I returned to the basement to develop the remaining film. Half an hour later, I saw they were all blank; the glossy paper overlaid with red ripples that resembled an ocean rising against itself. I tried to convince myself that, in my haste, I had probably mixed the developing liquids in the wrong proportion and so the photographs had been undeveloped. Likewise, the one I took upstairs had been overdeveloped.

I rummaged around the shelves to see if there were batches of fresh print paper and as I did so, I heard a sound from one of the tunnels. I called out a couple times and when there was no answer, I assumed it was the fierce wind blowing through the vents. That night, though, I was sure I heard voices downstairs, but twice I checked and saw no one. The third time, I saw a man looking through the window. He had a hat that seemed too big and when he turned I noticed his striking nose. "What are you doing here?" I asked just to be sure this was not another vision.

"I am fixing everything," he said. "The titles must be arranged alphabetically."

"Where did you come from?" I asked him. "Were you part of the team?"

"I am the Librarian," he said in a fussy manner. "The books must be arranged properly. They are all out of place."

Given the situation, it seemed silly to apologize for anything, so I told him, "I didn't expect to see anyone here." He continued replacing the books. I thought of something. "Was it you who was hiding in the shadows and –"

"I am the Librarian," he replied with some irritation. "Did you read everything in their proper order?"

"What order are you talking about?"

Instead of answering, he hurried down the steps to the basement. I noticed he had a funny limp. After a while I decided to follow him. "Hello," I shouted. I heard my voice echoing in the tunnels and the patter of footsteps. I followed the sound, calling out every minute or so. The tunnel was damp and the odour of sulphur increased with each step. I was about to turn back when I came to an opening. Three men were seated close to each other on what looked like a bench cut from the wall. I was both startled and relieved. "Are you part of the rescue team?" I asked immediately.

The man in the middle laughed in a funny way, like the forced unscrewing of a rusty nut. "Yes, you may consider us in this manner."

I walked closer so I could get a better view in the gloom. "What are you doing here? I was looking for someone who called himself the Librarian. It's lucky I followed him. Are there others?"

The little gnomish man on the left tapped the side of his head and said, "Inside here." He began to titter.

"I meant other survivors." I wondered if they had been affected by the sulphurous dust and needed some time to recover. "I believe there may have been someone else here. Not the Librarian."

They leaned closer so I could not catch their whisperings. Eventually the middle man cleared his throat and said, "Yes, we are familiar with your friend." As he said *friend*, the little man made two air quotes and he looked like a child climbing a wall. "Believe it or not but most of the inmates have their own special companions. Your own, we have to admit, is more unique." There was another huddle before he continued. "We believe your previous profession allowed you to add layers that gave him more..."

He seemed to be searching for a word. His own companion on the right said, in a sombre voice, "Heft. Height, weight, expressions, personality, background details and –"

"And so on and so forth. We know what you are thinking. Why would I do this?" He managed to sound both bored and melancholy.

Now the impish one took over. He related a story about a writer who, years after he had committed the perfect crime, created a fictional double to whom he could relate the details of this crime. "Pan has goat ears," he finished with a giggle.

His companions did not share his amusement. "What we are getting at," the middle man said, "is that for men with your condition, the creation of a friend, a protagonist, an acolyte – call it what you will – is not unusual. What is unusual is the attempt to augment the phantasms of others. When you use your imagination to fill in the –"

"I believe you all should rest for a while," I told them with utmost sincerity. "The air outside might be poisonous."

"Let us continue, please. When you use your resourcefulness to convince others of their own imaginary friends. When you shade and shadow them. We believe this is a way of controlling those less resourceful than you."

"Again, I must suggest you all rest for a while."

The middle man acted as if he had not heard my request. He said, "Our theory is that whenever you find something that is propelling you toward the truth, you sabotage it. You burn, disfigure and rearrange." He tapped his head and added, "Your friends inside there don't want to be spurned."

As they did one of their huddles, I asked them, "How did you all get here?" I was now certain that they had been affected by the dust, but their presence indicated a rescue vehicle not far off. When they did not answer, I walked to the door and added, "Please wait here."

"We have all the time in the world. All the time. Before you leave, can you tell us your name?"

I had no intention of alerting them of my memory loss. I recalled the authors of all the books in the recessed library and gave them a composite name. "Don Velesco Alejo Tomas Pascual Garibay."

"This is more inventive than usual," one of the trio said in a gloomy voice.

I took a deep breath, pulled my jacket up and pressed the collar against my face, and walked out of the house. Ten minutes later, I realized I had made a mistake in leaving, as I could see nothing but swirling dust. When my face began to sting, I pulled my jacket farther up to cover my eyes. I felt this was what trying to breathe in quicksand must feel like. It felt as if I were walking on quicksand, too, as the ground felt soft and unstable. Soon, I could see just a few feet ahead of me and it was becoming almost impossible to breathe. Twice I stumbled and each time I recovered, I saw a tiny figure standing some distance ahead. The second time, I tried to call out, but my mouth immediately filled with dust. It was too late to turn back so I pressed on and when I saw what appeared in the distance to be a man with a wolf, I felt it was my mind playing tricks. This is what death looks like, I thought.

STAGE FOUR

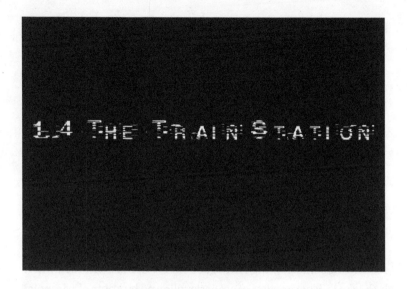

1.4 THE TRAIN STATION

I have to conclude that I am a director. Not of a company or a business of some kind, but a movie director. Your instructions were very vague and I hoped that I would get a clearer understanding once my drug-induced haze had passed and I could better grasp what I was doing in this old train terminal and why I could recall nothing of the film and, more alarmingly, nothing of how I found myself here. But as the morning progressed, I realized my amnesia had either been instigated by some potent cocktail of drugs or something more serious. What that may be, I have no idea.

I have tried to spark my memory from your instructions scattered across the storyboard. *The actors are not professionals. They need firm instructions. Be firm but patient. Learn from them.* It would have been helpful if you had included an actual summary of the plot because I have decoded three or perhaps four separate narratives from the storyboard. The first, of a madman endowed with a vast array of powers he was reluctant to use because each heroic act transported him to some earlier trauma, I discarded altogether. The second was the story of a group of ragtag second-grade superheroes who grew increasingly frustrated because they were summoned for mundane tasks like locating lost buttons in retirement homes and reading to old ladies and repairing obsolete appliances. They hungered for some truly heroic mission and increasingly they grew disconsolate and depressed. This narrative was told from the perspective of a psychiatrist into whose office they filed and whom they assumed was the leader of their team. The underwhelming name they had given him was Adequateman. (Likely because he possessed no powers.) The third and most intriguing involved a comic book writer who grew increasingly convinced that all his creations sprang from an external source, which had been using him to desensitize and perhaps prepare his readers for some coming Armageddon. His spiral continued when he began to have pockets of amnesia followed by bouts of paranoia, which he attributed as attempts by the entities – in the storyboard, they appeared as blue divine beings – to pre-empt any broadcast of his unexpected insight.

Some of the images in the storyboard make no sense. There are flexible machines and troops of flying monkeys and a blue man on a chariot that appears to barely skim the ground, and above him a figure that seems to be dancing in the air, unconcerned about the havoc beneath. But the next page depicts the dancing figure shedding tears that transform into leaves. On the succeeding pages, I see men dressed in robes straining with huge bows and these same men witnessing the immolation of horses.

The sketches are mostly hurried with explosions represented as starburst splotches, although there are a few that are remarkably detailed. One of these depicted a scene in which a man is strapped in some kind of machine in a bubble-shaped room while three scientists watch through a glass door as the images – drawings and photographs – flash before the trapped man. Another shows a child on a mountain throwing a boomerang while water spouts from fissures into the valley.

This old abandoned train station with its desultory and dystopian appearance, its crumbling pillars and tunnels, and the stream-leaking manholes and the surrounding amphitheatre which must have been some sort of waiting gallery, seem most suited to the third storyline. If there is some way the three storylines come together, I have missed it altogether. Perhaps this is a prequel of some sort. So far, I have not noted the presence of either the actors or anyone from the film crew. There is an old bus in the parking lot, but the trains must have been out of service for decades.

I hope the rest of the crew arrives soon because I have almost used up the stock of stale chocolates and candies in the vending machines. Additionally, I have no desire to continue sleeping on any of the concrete benches in the terminal. It's now late at night, although I cannot tell the exact time from the clock just above the ticket counter. It's stuck at nine-thirty and the hour hand beats like the claw of a dead bird against whatever malformation is blocking the cogs within.

I had hoped that sleep would return my memories but this morning I am no closer to recalling anything prior to the moment I awoke on the bench facing a useless clock. I went outside to see if there was any sign of the crew and, seeing no one, I decided to explore the passageways. Most led to platforms where I saw dead trains sitting on the rails. There were three tracks and the trains were parked parallel to each other. As I explored, I discovered the doors were locked and when I peered through the lower windows, I noticed the long seats at the end of each carriage. They would be infinitely more comfortable than the bench in the station so I moved from carriage to carriage, testing all the doors and windows. This took several hours and I was about to give up when I skipped across the track and tried the doors of the carriages on the middle rail. At the end of the lot, almost half a mile from the platform, I came across an unlocked door. I climbed on and peeped through the little porthole at the adjoining carriage. I saw that it was a canteen with half a dozen tables scattered around. Most of the tables were occupied. Everyone glanced up when I walked in and, because they seemed either impatient or annoyed, I explained that I had been in the station and I had no idea it was the meeting area. I did not mention anything about my amnesia because I still hoped it would wear off. They all had a ghastly pallor as if the makeup had been overapplied. I wondered if this was residue from a previous film where they had all been cadavers.

For a couple minutes, no one said anything, then from one of the tables a youngish man with a drooping nose and soft-looking ears that made him appear like a drowsy marsupial came up and told me in a rather dramatic voice, "My name is Knife. I am an amputee and I stabbed my father with my phantom hand. Thank you for asking." He left a drawing of a floating limbless being.

When Knife returned to his table, a harassed-looking middle-aged man said, with a trace of irritation, as if he was in a hurry and I was delaying him, "I am Shad." I nodded and he said quickly, "Shad the Man. I am still trying to discover my power. It has something to do with shadows but I am not sure." He was followed by a delicately built doe-eyed man who blew into his palms and whispered to his fingers, "I am a trappist." They both left their own sketches, the first of a man strapped to pieces of junk and the second of a dog lying on its back.

I realized these were your actors and I wished they would elaborate beyond their roles, but I recalled your note explaining they were not professionals. I saw a woman walking up to me. "I am the Countess Conferrer," she told me. "People used to stop me on the streets all the time and ask me to do the countess accent from *The Ritzy Waltz*. I was Clara Carrington in the series."

"Your gift. Tell him," someone shouted.

"Would you like to hear? I have nothing better to do, anyway."

I felt I should return some of her haughtiness so I told her, "You may as well. I have nothing else to do, either."

"You are an odious old cotter. But I will grant you your request. Can you see my aureoles?" She fingered a necklace of teeth-shaped beads. I glanced away. "No? Well, they are usually blue but with bands of yellow when there is an illness or grey when there is confusion. But I don't blame you for your blindness. No one but me is cursed with this gift." She then proceeded to describe her gift. During her first year on some kind of "oculus" show, strangers came up to her on the streets to tell her how she had changed their lives. At first, she had taken this to be normal fan adulation, but one night a middle-aged woman swore she had recently abandoned her abusive husband because of the show. "You are like a shaft of light," the woman had told Clara, or whatever her real name was. When the woman departed, Clara came to the conclusion that she had been speaking literally and on the set, she began to visualize a beam of light flowing out of her body. The beam felt limber and hot, like liquid ore poured through a translucent cylinder. "During the three years and three months the show was on, I healed thousands. But who's counting?" Nevertheless, she confessed that she used to rigorously scan the newspapers for miraculous lyses and she had established connections between particular episodes from her show and these recoveries. Soon, she convinced herself that her aura was not only beneficial to the sick and wounded, but had also provoked acts of altruism from formerly bored celebrities. "Favoured people unflinchingly putting their lives in danger for potty-faced orphans. Building wells and hugging ugly little lepers. Can you believe it?" She examined her long nails. "I shouldn't take all the credit, though. All I offered was redemption." She formed a triangle with her fingers and peered within.

I looked behind her. A little line had formed. A stocky man wearing a hard hat told me, "The name I go by is the Dismantler. I break apart everything that is incomplete. That is all I am prepared to state."

He was followed by a man with protruding teeth and tiny narrow-set eyes. "I am the Toeman. I am a proponent of the Theory of Everything. TOE."

I decided to ask him about his preparation for his part and he sat immediately as if he had been expecting my question. A watery ripple of worry creased his forehead. "I have spent most of my adult life trying to locate its Cartesian coordinates."

"Of your role?"

"The man before you is a fake." He unbuttoned his coat and revealed his sunken chest and his pot-belly. "What you see here is but a shadow."

He seemed a little worked up, so I told him, "I understand the process of preparing for a role and transforming yourself into a new man."

"Right now as we speak, in a parallel universe our doubles are carrying on this exact conversation. My mission, you see, is to locate the real Toeman."

I wondered if he was talking of a stunt double and I asked, "Can you describe your part?"

"I am developing a hole-o-meter. With luck, my travel through that warm and pleasurable tunnel is imminent. Thank you for asking." He closed his eyes and began to breathe quite heavily. When his eyes opened, he began to bawl, "I am coming. Don't hold me back."

I told him, "There will be enough time for that later on. It's better if we get to know each other first."

A well-built middle-aged woman got up from her table, grabbed Toeman by the scruff of his neck and dragged him to his seat. He was still shouting, "Goodbye, my friends. I have discovered the coordinates of the tunnel's palpitating entrance and I shall soon hurl myself within. Wish me luck."

When the woman returned, she gazed at me accusingly before she said, "You shouldn't be encouraging him to misbehave."

"I didn't encourage him to anything. In fact, I was trying to determine the precise role to which he had been assigned."

"Exactly. He keeps shifting from one to the other. This happens to all of us, but his case is extreme."

"Don't you all know who you are supposed to be?"

"Yes, we do. But the other memories keep stirring in our minds. Even after we have been scrubbed."

"I understand. You carry the flavour of your past performances. So sometimes it's difficult to pull away completely from the old roles and slip into the new ones."

She sat. "Yes, that's it. I never thought of it in this way, but you are right. How do you know all of this?"

"Well, I am the director. At least I believe I am."

A tiny tendril of fear flicked across her face. "What's our new mission? Toeman mentioned we might be taken to the other side. But he is crazy. That will never happen."

"What other side? Another studio? A new location?"

"What do you have in your bag? Maybe everything is there." She got up suddenly and walked away.

She was right, though. I decided to consult the storyboards before any further introductions so I got out the ledger in which they were contained and walked to the last table, which was occupied by a hulking man, his face flat on the surface. I glanced through the illustrations. The man said, "You are a man of many surprises, my friend. I would not have guessed." The squeaky voice seemed familiar but all I could see from his sleeping position was his impossibly big ears twitching like a dog's.

"I was trying to determine the personas of everyone here. Who is the heavy, the ingénue, the villain, the hero, the –"

"A man's field of vision is determined one hundred percent by his interests." He raised his head and I saw his wide forehead and simple smile. "There are others who will be interested in renewing your acquaintance. Ask me who these others are?" When I did as he requested, he got serious and said, "It's funny that you should say the very thing that is beating around my head. You, my friend, are amazing. The Amazing Acolytes."

"What?"

"Your team. The Amazing Acolytes. Your creation, if I may venture. It would take a callous man to stand aside and not exhibit any concern about his wild and wondrous universe. One of them, anyway. Correct me if I am wrong, but I do not believe you are a man of such callosity." I was about to explain I was the director rather than the writer when I noticed him clenching and unclenching his fingers. His knuckles were scarred in neat patterns. "It may surprise you to know that I comprehend your indisposition one hundred percent. People look at me and see a sloppy brute lumbering around, but they miss something important. Can you tell what it is? C'mon, make a guess."

"I have no idea."

He leaned back and folded his arms. I now noticed he had a rugged knapsack on his lap. "A creator with no ideas. That's a new one, my friend. It's crazier than a god who cannot see the future. Or a Timekeeper who cannot tell the time. If you will permit me, I must chuckle a bit." His chuckle did not seem forced in any way and I felt that he was very convincing in his portrayal of a dim-witted and unpredictable brute. He gestured to the tables. "Look at them. They have been waiting eons." I could not understand his exaggerated way of speaking and I felt that his proper speech had been arrived at after much practice and coaching.

They all looked ragged and disconsolate. The man opposite reclined his head on the table and I opened my ledger once more, trying to fit everyone into the story. When the groups saw me consulting the book, those at the far table got up and formed another line. One by one, they walked to my table. Some just shambled before me and said nothing while others spoke in rapid and incomprehensible spurts. A pudgy woman whose dark velvety skin made it impossible to guess her age sat with a prolonged sigh and placed a bulky sequinned fish purse on the table. She fiddled with the handle before she opened the purse and withdrew a piece of paper rolled up and secured with a rubber band. She blew into the cylinder formed by the paper as if she was determining what to do. "I not always so forward but I know you will understand." She rolled off the band with a snap and passed the page to me. "I could bother you to read this, please?"

"It looks like the inside cover of a comic book."

"Read it, please."

"The next issue will feature the long-awaited debut of the Spiritmaster."

"You understand now? All the time, I waiting and waiting." She got up tiredly. "But nobody calling. Why nobody calling?"

She was followed by a little man who offered his own sheet of paper. I now noticed all of them were holding pages, some of which were folded neatly and others crumpled into balls. He was followed by a man with long dirty fingers. "I am the Bookbinder," he told me. "I can make a new story with any old book." He began to shuffle the sheets in his hand. "Voila! New story." Next, a man who introduced himself as Boing bounded up and claimed to be continuously trailed by tapirs and sloths. "But nothing can harm me," he said, handing me his own sheet, which contained a cartoon cat perched on a parapet surrounded by a pack of hounds. "Not even a steamroller."

When everyone had returned to their seats, the man opposite asked, "Did you pick anyone?"

"I didn't know that was my function. Were these extras?"

He raised his head and stared sullenly at me. "It takes a man of extreme callosity to wind up innocent victims and walk away unperturbed. A Timekeeper without a conscience. I thought I had seen everything."

"Am I missing something?"

I hoped he would shed some light on the nature of the film, but he told me, "You miss all the pain knotting up and embroiling into a giant fungus that forgot it should stop growing. Now, the question you want to ask is whether this pain is friend or foe. The simple answer is that it is both. Before I realized this, I was a raging lunatic. Or should I say before we realized this." He smiled and his ears popped up.

I saw him glancing around and I asked, "Are we waiting on someone?"

He said nothing for a while but just sat looking over my shoulder with a sad smile plastered over his broad face. "We have all been waiting. Patience is not the aphrodisiac some would attest it is. It gets in the way sometimes and then you forget what you are waiting on and remain frozen in a wide-legged stance that leaves you open to any kidney punch coming your way. Easy pickings for every manager in sight. Now ask what we have been waiting for."

I asked his question.

"It's funny you should ask that, and my answer would be for the right moment. Waiting for that perfect second when you see everything coming toward you in a slow-motion dream. Perfect pitch and rhythm and the air slows for just that moment as if it is holding off for you. In that instant, you become faster than any living thing in sight. It would be remiss of me if I did not point out that it was you who drummed that into our heads. Remember your favourite admonition? Every man has a mission, but to understand his mission he has first of all to understand what he has hidden away and forgotten." His voice had changed a bit; had become more solemn. This made him sound more deranged.

I thought of something and asked, "Are you a grappler?"

"I am what you want me to be. A brute. Balzac the Brute."

"And are you all in character? How long have you been practising?"

"That's a good one." He said it as a joke but did not laugh. "You are smarter than that, as you full well know, so I will oblige you by concluding that there must be a reason for this pose. If I may be bold enough to say, a man does not signal his uppercut by crouching low. That would telegraph his intention and his antagonist will load up with a roundhouse right and pummel him straight to the ground. That is the way the world operates."

"Should I take that as a yes?"

He reached into the knapsack hanging on his leg. The tiny round object wrapped in foil paper he brought out looked like a bird with a broken wing. "It took a while before I figured it out. A piece of some substance that is both porous and solid. Light and dense. Weapon and armour. Something and nothing." He was slowly unwrapping the object as he spoke and when he was finished, I saw it was just a piece of cork. "It was a paradox until I realized that it represented everything. A paradox no more," he said, lisping severely. "How can something be a paradox if it includes everything? How can a man run away from what has not yet occurred? How can a boy be an orphan if his father is still alive? There's another. How can a madman see the world in more shapes and colours than a man with a thousand books before him? Is that why we have been probed by every means possible?"

I assumed these were declarative statements but Balzac seemed to be waiting for an answer. "I would like to help you but

I am afraid that all I have is the storyboard in my ledger. To be honest, I had been hoping you all would help." I tapped the ledger and added, "It makes no sense. There are too many storylines."

After a while, he said, "It makes perfect sense. Ask me why."

"Why?"

"Your question reeks of impudence but I will pretend I did not notice." He turned to his knapsack, unhitching it and plopping it on the table between us. "An erudite man always tries to find the correct answers to his puzzles because he knows that the minute the answers stop, the Brute will return. Sometimes I feel it bubbling beneath my skin." He reached into his knapsack and brought out a mask. "It allowed a woman who was incomplete to balance out the world. With the mask on, she was able to neutralize everything. The oppressive world she imagined, the people she believed meant her harm and finally, her own frailty. She became sightless and so she could choose whatever vision she wanted to dance in her mind." He sounded unexpectedly lucid. "Your own words, if I am allowed to quote." I guessed he was quoting from the script. "Strangely, she was the only one who could tell what was real and what was not. A sightless siren unswayed by visual prejudices," he said, lisping heavily. Next, he withdrew a piece of crumbled paper. "Placed strategically in the centre of a silver plant. Symbols and allegories and…" He was trying to pronounce *hieroglyphics* and growing more frustrated with each attempt. Eventually he gave up and closed his eyes. "A man taking account of his life."

He brought up other pieces of junk. When he said he also had a Gladstone bag in his carriage, I felt I had to stop him. I opened the storyboard ledger and tried to locate the connection between the sketches and his junk. While I was doing so, I asked him, "Are these artifacts part of the plot? I cannot see any references here."

He glanced at my notebook and said immediately, "To be quite honest, I would have once found that question to be rude and callous. I would have gone berserk, as brutes are wont to do. I would have bitten off your ears and chomped on their soft tissue. Did I ever mention that its consistency is similar to gizzard?" He laughed, three unfocused chuckles. "That's a joke, my friend. I would have done far worse. But I have changed. I am no longer roused by your pretence about these artifacts, as you put it. The brute inside wants to tear you apart for leaving these mementoes behind. Like in the story you told of the girl who kept reappearing to remind us of our humanity. Or maybe to keep us in check. I can't remember everything when there are all these voices whistling in my head." He placed both palms on his chin and twisted his neck. "But a man with a lexicon of two hundred thousand words is patient. It's an obligation. Now I must repeat my request."

"What is it exactly?"

"Here we go again. Let me point out that a brute never asks for directions because it's there etched in his thick skull every minute of the day. He knows what he wants and he moves toward it. There is no shame or guilt or remorse. See, want and take. That was my credo. During those dark days, I would not think that a simple request might deflect the carnage."

I noticed him straining to look at the ledger and I told him, "Just some sketches."

"Can I?"

He accepted the book, gentle and expectant and timorous, as if it were a newborn. He took a while, studying it, holding the book at different angles, before he opened it and turned the page. But soon his excitement took over and I could see him flipping the pages quickly, returning to a previous page, murmuring to himself, nodding and casting glances at me. Then he was finished. "The source of everything. Divine wisdom." His squeaky voice sounded almost reverent. "Creation and destruction in the same act.

Dancing gods lying low and peeping with their hidden eyes. Then jab after jab after jab. Bam! Kidney punch followed by a thumping clout. I don't know what to say," he said, his squeak so hushed it seemed as if he were whispering through a closed door. "Just when I felt you were incapable of doing so, you have delivered a knockout punch. Floored me plain and simple. It will take some time to completely digest all of this."

He closed the ledger, placed it on the table with exaggerated reverence and reached for his knapsack. I told him quickly, "I need that ledger."

"I must admit that I am completely befuddled. Did you not set forth all these parables for us to decipher?" He looked genuinely confused. "If I am free to opine, I will have to say that I find this most unusual. Most discourteous. What would the others think?"

"What others? The producer? The cinematographer? The –"

"C'mon, don't be doing me that." His voice held a slight lilt and I wondered if he was imitating some other actor. "We have gone through this, let me see, a hundred times." He stared at my outstretched hand. "I must admit that you are a slippery pugilist. Bobbing and weaving and playing possum on the ropes. The only thing that prevents me from plugging you is the worthy thought that a being of your calibre must have a righteous reason for these gambits."

He returned to the ledger and began murmuring something about acolytes. I could not recall a religious angle in the storyboard and I asked him, "Are there acolytes in the team?"

"Amazing. That word adds everything. Amazing Acolytes. Without this pejorative, we would be like everyone else. Maudlin and jabbering, as you yourself said." He tapped his head. "I mostly remember the things I am supposed to forget. Do you know why? Because I operate on instinct. I have a sixth sense about most things. People look at me and see a rank savage, but little do they know that inside the mind of this savage, there is always a sweet melody. It's what preserves me. And preserves them, too, I must add." He motioned to the others, who were looking at me intently. "Do you know how long we have been waiting? Thought at times they were delaying tactics or, worse, setting things in motion like a callous Timekeeper and coolly walking away from the decompression. But the brute within knew you were hitching and coupling everything. Waiting for the pitch perfect moment to reawaken your team."

I told him quickly before he verged into another ridiculous tangent, "I, too, have been waiting. Now I need the ledger."

I assumed he would put up some resistance, but he gingerly pushed the book across the table with his fat thumb. "It would be derelict of me if I did not point out that an idle army can become very fidgety. What is the point of allowing your Golem to sleep till the end of time? Or your brute, for that matter."

I shoved the ledger into my coat pocket. "Very well. When is the scheduled date for the first shoot?"

"The first shoot. I like that." He offered his broad grin. "No one's going anywhere. We will all be here waiting."

"Where do you all rest?"

"Each man chooses his own bed?"

"A different carriage?"

"Each man chooses his own bed. Free will, if I may opine."

I decided to find a suitable carriage, possibly not too close to the others. I recalled your note stating that the actors had been practising forever and I felt they were too close to their roles. Dangerously wound up from waiting. (For your appearance, perhaps?) I got up. But before I left, I asked Balzac, "Do you have any idea of the script? There is little continuity and to be frank, a fair bit makes no sense. There seems to be too many stories here. Too many voices."

His grin widened even further, threatening his ears. "I can oblige you by attempting an honest answer, but I will most likely be far off the mark. My perusal of your notebook was too swift for even an erudite man to assess, much less a brute. That was a joke, in case you didn't notice. Here's another joke. If you put a gun against my head, I may tell you that we were reassembling for the most dangerous mission of all. The Origins issue. That split second between creation and destruction when everything is in perfect harmony and when gods are formed. One second off and we will be somewhere else. Someone else, I must also add. Do you remember what you told us? That parables are God's puzzles. His little gifts to us. Like scattering matchsticks before an ape." He smiled almost sweetly.

I tried to force a requisite smile as I got up. I spoke loudly, addressing the entire group. "It was nice meeting everyone. I have to consult the storyboard to see how it all fits together. Oh, and the sketches you left with me. Shall we meet here tomorrow, then? The same time."

"What time?" the woman who referred to herself as the Countess Conferrer asked. They all glanced at their bare wrists.

I remembered the stuck clock in the terminal and I told them, "I will be here in the morning."

Toeman said, "Each universe has its own time. We have to be careful because one can scuttle the other. Who knows what will happen when parallel dimensions collide?" He seemed to be reflecting on this crazy possibility. "Face to face with your doppel-gänger and wondering who is real. Sometimes I feel I have stumbled across that barrier, you know. Did I tell you that my double is a man of incredible strength, honesty and beauty?"

"You all have had enough practice for the time being," I told them in a joking fashion. No one seemed amused.

I pushed open the door at the rear and as I walked from car-riage to carriage, I wondered if among the group were stuntmen and boom operators and costume designers and sound technicians and prop makers and so on. To be honest, they all appeared to be extras with leading-men delusions. As I walked on, I thought of other tasks and I realized that my memory of functions and facts had been untouched. It was only my autobiographical memory that had been short-circuited. I wondered if this deficit pointed to some more serious problem and moreover if I had been similarly affected previously. I wished I were closer to some medical institution rather than in an abandoned terminal.

I decided I would finally get a good night's rest and think of these issues in the morning. Nine carriages down I took off my jacket, hung it on the back of a seat and prepared to rest. But when I lay down, I heard a voice from the seat at the back. "Lolo need a cuddle." I got up in a hurry and saw a little man stretched out, his feet curled up like a baby's.

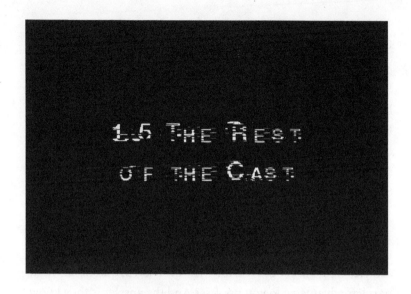

1.5 THE REST OF THE CAST

Before I could apologize for my mistake in assuming the carriage was empty, Balzac walked in and hugged the man, at the same time lifting him off the seat and depositing him onto a narrow table. He seemed to coo as the brute was transporting him although it may have been a suffocating sound. "At this moment in time, I present the Stenographer," Balzac said, rather formally.

The man began some sort of finger-dance but I soon saw that he was pretending to transcribe something onto an invisible tablet with an invisible pen. "I didn't see you earlier," I told him. "Are you part of the team?" He pointed up and the brute gazed in that direction. Both men seemed to be studying the patterns on the carriage's roof. After about two minutes or so, I asked them, "Could you explain what we are doing?"

Balzac looked down and said, "Lolo is the Stenographer. The only man to write an entire epistle on the surface of a lake. Water is his canvas."

"Are you quoting someone? It sounds very poetic in an old-fashioned –"

"There you go again, my friend. Words are power and the Stenographer can write five hundred a minute. His epistles are complete before the dissolving begins." I noticed the so-called Stenographer trying to demonstrate this ability by swishing his hands through the air like a martial artist. When he toppled over, Balzac scooped him up, replaced him on the table and peered between the man's spread hands. "Amazing," Balzac said. "How can anyone provide an answer to a question not fully framed, Mr. Stenographer? It is most befuddling."

"What is the question?" I asked. "And the answer?"

"I find your own question most impetuous. It's the sort of question only a gangrenous miscreant who tried to hide from his acolytes would ask. But I will bite. The question in question is what peculiar advantage do you possess? And the answer is they know what they are searching for but cannot recognize it."

Balzac seemed clearly annoyed, but when his friend began to chuckle with deep-throated trills, he pitched in with his own ringing giggles. At this point, I was forced to consider a possibility that had been nibbling away at the corners of my mind. The crew seemed to be seriously unhinged and I wondered, briefly, if the mass hysteria, or whatever it was could be, connected with my own amnesia. So when he told me that it was time to meet the rest of the team, I felt it would be best if I knew, one way or the other, exactly what I was dealing with. On the bright side, I might also get an idea of the nature of the proposed film. I wanted to make clear that I was not too keen on wasting time with men and women who appeared more confused than I was, so I told him, "After you. I can spend a few minutes."

Immediately, the pair stopped laughing. Balzac said, "Impatience, my friend, is no lesser vice than pride because they both spring from beings who believe they breathe a purer air." His friend began to swish and Balzac offered his translation. "Better to have a brute as your companion than a man who tries to jump ahead before the path is properly cleared." He was talking his usual nonsense but when the Stenographer struck him lightly with his rod, he calmed down and added, "I, too, once operated at this altitude so there is nothing to be ashamed of. Did I mention that I was once a raging brute who could chomp through wire like if it was raw chicken?" He scooped up the little man from the table and walked through the carriages until he came to one that was locked. "Mister Kurt, number one and top of all. Step forward."

The door opened and I saw a man standing by the window. His slouch was so severe I assumed that it was to offset his striking height but then I noticed his twitchy fingers, his manner of looking at the ground and, even through his bulky overcoat, the slump of his shoulders. He looked like leading-man material and I felt that he was best suited to play someone who had lately endured some traumatic event that had shot through his confidence. When we approached, I noticed that he towered over Balzac. "I am not sure anyone can help me, but I am willing to help everyone."

"You, my friend, are too modest," Balzac told him. His friend began to swish and Balzac, watching him closely, added, "When we are in the centre of the storm we assume there is no way out of the turbulence because we begin to think like a mindless brute rather than noticing the calmness just behind. So we plough forward."

"Not if it's a solar storm." I was surprised by the man's scratchy voice and his choice of disturbance. "Each day I feel my energy sapping away." He pushed up his horn-rimmed glasses, brushed an errant curl from his forehead and shot a swift glance at me. "In the mornings, I awaken alone and in the nights, I fall asleep by myself. People like me are no longer needed. We are meticulous, plodding and old-fashioned. We operate under strict codes of justice so we are constantly pushed aside to make way for more popular saviours."

I could not decide if he was describing his role or the details of his life as he spoke with an unusual gravity about the region in which he had spent his boyhood, once idyllic but now littered with abandoned farms and derelict manufacturing plants. "I come from a burnt-out world." He gazed around and I could see his eyes narrowing. "I was born in a place that no longer exists and sent here as a child. My foster parents are long dead and I am alone in this place. Useless and idle. Without purpose. How can a man with no purpose maintain his virtue? How can virtue be salvaged when its distinctness is constantly changing? How can I be a saviour when I do not know who I am?"

He was talking utter nonsense, even for a B film, but Balzac said in a respectful voice, "I do not blame you, my friend. We all have these brute thoughts because we have been waiting for eons for the button to be reset. But your destiny is about to change." The Stenographer did an elaborate swishing act and Balzac added, "There are multiverses awaiting us just behind the door." I assumed Balzac had mistranslated but his friend smiled and nodded.

"When you encircle your mind with the completion of small acts, you can accomplish nothing more." Kurt smiled nervously and added, "I need one final mission to rediscover my purpose." He said this in an apologetic manner but the words seemed quite dramatic, possibly because he had straightened during his little monologue but as he turned to leave, I noticed his slouch had returned, his stature diminished once more.

While we were walking to another carriage, Balzac said with some admiration, "When that being rediscovers his purpose no one in the universe will be safe. I hope you know what you are doing by reactivating the team, my friend."

I was about to remind him that it was he who had suggested this when the Stenographer bawled out, "Fingers!"

The carriage before us seemed empty, then I saw a boot and a man literally jumped through the back door as if he was caught in the momentum of a sprint. He stopped just before he crashed through the opposite wall and levered his head through the small window. "Quite a view here," he said in an almost disinterested manner. "It must be gentling to stand here at the end of a hard day. Particularly during nights as stormy as this. The view is quite spectral. Like peering into another world. I'm sure there are bats roosting in all the abandoned tunnels. Now, why have you summoned me?"

"The team is being reactivated," Balzac told him.

He turned quickly, his coat whirling around his legs. "I operate alone and I need no one." His stance suggested a midway pause in some untangling flourish and I felt that in his pose, there were both recklessness and evasion. "My job here is done."

I thought of something. I had assumed that Balzac was the film's villain but it was most likely this Fingers character. And Kurt was undoubtedly the hero. "What is your expertise?" I asked Fingers.

"The black arts," he replied sternly. "I can locate the connections between everything. I am an untangler unparalleled. A cosmic detective. A rippler, a rappler, a ruckus-maker. I can disappear at will." He ran through the door. A few seconds later, his head pushed through the doorway and he added, "And reappear, too. I can also decode echoes."

After he had left, I asked, "So this is the team? What about the technical people?"

"That's a very pertinent question you have asked. It shows you have been keeping your ear to the ground so I will reward your inquisitiveness by stating that we have half a dozen applicants waiting in the sidelines. Some you have met and others have held back because of their shyness. They are all worthwhile if this is what you are thinking." He scooped up the little man. "Follow me, please." I followed the pair three carriages down. Balzac said, "I present to you, Mr. Christof Crimpola. Please rise."

"There is no need for this formality," I said.

But the man was already up, one eye blinking uncontrollably, the other as stark and unmoving as a monk's. He set his stable eye on me and said, in a jarring monotone, "Nothing is hidden from an arithmetician. Do you know why? It's because we can calculate the distance between reality and trickery. Danger! Danger! It does not compute." He folded his arms before him and added, "I am a human cryptographer, constantly decoding the intervals between infinity and erasure." Balzac, who seemed to be enjoying himself, applauded once more and Crimpola continued, "I am the disentangler of perplexities. The issue is the path I should take. Should I assemble the future through algorithmic computations and Kalman derivatives or should I tack all the carefully sloughed bits of the past on a display panel. In the end, it's all the same. When we awaken, nothing will have changed. We will be just as before."

"I take it you are the accountant?"

"I am an arithmetician," the man said firmly, his eye blinking furiously. "There are worlds beyond worlds and only I can know of those we have left and those we are hurtling toward."

Balzac told the man, "I must apologize for our friend's bold statement." To me, he said, "The accountant is one carriage down. Or maybe he's an auditor."

Once more, I followed the pair. When we entered, a little man got up with a slouch so severe I assumed he had been partially paralyzed by spondylitis. He stared at the floor as if hypnotized by the steel studs. This gave him the air of an elderly man deep in concentration; and when he did speak, his voice had the gravelly, rustic quality of an asthmatic poet. "When one lays out a clutch of bills and receipts on a table, one encounters a life exhibited. Most people would see arbitrary purchases on the crumbled paper but when I look carefully, a sweet-sweet tapestry begins to emerge." He spread his gnarled fingers like an absent-minded conjurer and I noticed that his heavily veined hand was a pale ghostly blue. "One will never find more soulful music than the rustle of paper unfolding. I am the Auditor and I can see sweet-sweet connections."

The man resumed his examination of the bills. I asked Balzac, "Is there anyone else? A cook or a chef or caterer? What do we do about meals?"

"The canteen is stocked with tins of sardines and beans and we hunt rabbits in the tunnels. But I assume you are referring to Tiffin."

I followed the pair. "Tiffin!" I jumped as the Stenographer had shouted right into my ear. At the far end of the carriage, a man got up and a woman with him. He was walking rather quickly as if he was trying to evade the woman who, as they drew closer, I saw was quite elderly. The woman had an apelike look of bewildered despair and the man was very skinny, his clothes hanging around his body loosely. "State your role," the Stenographer barked, startling the woman.

"I am a breatharian," Tiffin said seriously. "I get my energy from inhaling nutritional microbes and from the morning sun. Food is an inconvenience I avoid at all cost." As he continued, it seemed that not only did he engage in extremely prolonged bouts of absolute fasting but also that each period brought about some pre-determined result. It was not easy to follow his story because he spoke in a nasal manner with an indeterminate accent, but I gathered that he was matching the dates of his fasts with the outset of droughts and famines and pandemics and other calamities, each occurring in some faraway place he called Adjacentland.

"That is an amazing gift you possess, my friend," Balzac said, but looking at me rather than at Tiffin.

"I thought you were the chef," I told him.

"We are mortal enemies."

"So you have an active role in the undertaking?"

"We are all active, my friend," Balzac said. The Stenographer began to swish and Balzac translated, "Once, we were asleep and dreaming of missions past and present but now that we are awakened, we shall plunge headlong into those multiple timelines and do battle with the old creaking gods."

At this point, I felt I had to reveal my memory issues. Everyone was talking about a film in which I was either the director or the scriptwriter. Moreover, they seemed wound up from waiting and rehearsing. Perhaps they were sleep-deprived and delusional. During my brief conversation with the woman wearing a medallion necklace I had spoken about actors sometimes falling so deeply into their roles, they carried the traits of their characters into their everyday lives, but this situation seemed an extreme form of mimicry. I was about to reveal my memory situation when the Stenographer began to swish. Before Balzac could offer a "translation," I asked the pair, "Is there anyone here who might have some idea of how we are going to proceed with the shoot?"

Both fell silent and gazed at me as if I had committed some transgression. Then Balzac said, "It would be remiss of me if I do not point out that you have everything set out in the tome that you refuse to share with anyone else. I should also hasten to add that parables become stale and mouldy when they are not passed on." The Stenographer did some swishing and Balzac nodded. "My esteemed colleague has advised that parables are the forte of a man who you have not yet met." The Stenographer swished once more and Balzac added, "He goes by many names. Inquisitor. Fakir. Paladin."

I had no idea what he was talking about but I decided to follow the pair in the hope I would eventually meet someone with a better grasp of the plot. So once more, I followed them. We came to a carriage with the curtains drawn so it took a while before I noticed a figure hunched in the corner. He seemed quite lanky and he was wearing some sort of priest's frock, which was odd, as on his head was a cap turned to the side. He seemed a bit familiar, although I could not determine if this was because of his features or his garments. Before Balzac had the chance to offer an introduction, the man said, "Have you ever studied a man without faith, brethren?"

I told the man, "My friends here believe you may have some idea as to how we can proceed with our undertaking."

He reached into his frock and brought up a torn-off page. He held it up before him and asked, "Tell me what you see?" There was a drawing of some type of vessel but the lines were blistered with dots and crackles.

I took the page. "It looks like a ship."

Balzac gasped as the man said to me, "It's an ark powered by faith and navigated by devotion."

I recalled my early suspicion that the storyboard pointed to some cataclysmic event and I reached into my jacket for the ledger. I flipped through the pages, searching for an equivalent illustration. The man got up and I saw that his head almost touched the top of the carriage. In the gloom, his eyes appeared sunken and I saw there were decals stuck on his cap. He stretched his hand, but I remembered Balzac's odd possessiveness about the ledger and I told him, "I will keep this for the time being, if you don't mind." I felt Balzac's breath on my shoulder and quickly pocketed the ledger. Once more, I looked at the man's torn-off page. "Is this how it's going to end?"

"It will end as it began," he said, and I noticed his voice had an almost musical timbre. "Lo, though the heavens open up and the sky bleeds, the sanctified shall yet find refuge. They shall be shepherded into the waiting zones with the glorious promise their lives will be returned. They shall be born and born anew. The others can expect nothing for they are nothing." I assumed this was a line from the film and I hoped it was you, not I, who had written this stilted dialogue. "I walk the land when there is trouble afoot. I right the wrongs." Just then, there was a low growl from the back of the carriage and the Stenographer tightened his hold on Balzac. "Dog dreams," the Inquisitor said. "They are more pernicious than anything you can imagine."

"I think we should leave now," I said. "I should find a suitable carriage in which to rest." I walked away before Balzac could offer any suggestions. As I walked on, I turned to see Balzac and his little companion watching from the tracks so I skipped across to the third line of carriages. Nine carriages down, I located an unlocked door.

16 THE MAN IN THE CARRIAGE

I locked the door, took off my jacket, hung it on the adjoining seat and stretched out with the ledger in my hands. I hoped that a good night's rest finally might cajole my memory. It was too dark to properly see the storyboard, but I was familiar with the illustrations, anyway. I flipped through the pages and tried to establish some connection between the drawings and my conversations earlier in the day.

I hoped to recall something of my prior association with this dystopian fantasy because – even with my faulty memory – I felt no connection with this type of story. Nevertheless, I attempted to come up with some semblance of a plot. I recalled Balzac's chatter about a team of super beings or acolytes or some nonsense and I felt that Kurt, the hero who had lately languished, had been summoned with the others for a mission that would imbue them once more with a sense of purpose. But what was this mission and what were the obstacles in the way? Based on my interaction with the men and women in the carriage it possibly involved an ark and a cataclysmic flood and alternate universes and battle between gods.

Was there anything else? Maybe a story concerning a brute with pretensions of acuity. It seemed there were several broad plot outlines and I was supposed to either fill in the inciting events and the resolutions or, more onerously, tie everything together. You will forgive me for believing that you wisely absconded after saddling me with this half-baked script that possesses neither instigatory event, motivation, nor resolution. It was late in the night when I closed the ledger and placed it beneath the seat's cushion.

I fell asleep almost immediately but my dreams were not of parallel universes and superpowered teams, but of a wide-open field. The ground was sandy and littered with bleached, pliant bones. When I looked down, I saw water swirling around my ankles and the bones took life and swam away. In the distance, I could hear a rising drumbeat as if opposing armies were assembling in formation. When I stopped to listen, the drums seemed closer and the beats were coming from all directions. I panicked and tried to escape but the water had risen and the waves were now around my chest. I saw the bones were converging around me and through the swirling water, in the distance, I saw hundreds of soldiers from opposing armies advancing toward each other. Their modes of transport were antiquated chariots and horses and elephants, and as they got closer, they also appeared to soar upward. Maces and spears and arrows cleaved the air, some dropping just beyond me.

I tried to swim away but the current carried me closer to the battle. I was on my back, floating on the red water. The battle was now in the air and the opposing armies were arranged in constantly shifting formations that resembled eagles, turtles and wheels. From beneath, it was a wonderful spectacle, almost a dance, and I soon forgot about the blazing arrows dropping all around my body. Then the bodies began to fall from the sky, flaming downward. One by one, they fell and those that seemed to see what was happening, tried to gain altitude by flying upward but they, too, crashed down. Soon the sky was empty and I felt the hands of the fallen fighters holding on to my limbs, dragging me down.

I awoke in a panic. I had no doubt that my nightmare had been elicited by my perusal of the storyboard. I was sweating in the enclosed carriage and I got up and opened the door. The night air was cool and refreshing and at this late hour, I knew there would be little possibility of meeting anyone, so I stepped between the tracks. In the moonlight, the abandoned carriages looked like hulking metallic monsters. I smiled at the thought; this refreshing night stroll was a good respite after my conversations with a film crew who had waited too long and practised too much. I recalled your instructions that they needed firm directions and I felt unexpectedly sorry for them. They really appeared to be awaiting some guidance as to how to proceed. Yet they appeared unpredictable and altogether dangerous. My limited memory is a big handicap, as you might well imagine, but I have decided, from my interactions with the actors, that men and women with a faulty or incomplete vision of their roles and propelled only by a vague sense of some remote mission, could either relapse into worthlessness or become ticking bombs. While I was preoccupied with this thought, I saw a figure running some distance before me. Too big to be an animal and too small to be an adult. But what would a child be doing all alone in the night? Could he or she be lost and looking for someone, as I myself had done the first week in this terminal? I followed the figure until it slipped into a carriage.

When I went into the carriage, I saw it was a smoker and empty but for a couple dozen books scattered around an iron safe with a knuckle-shaped handle. I looked through the windows for the child and I was about to step outside when my eye caught the safe's unusual handle, a closed fist. I kneeled before it, turned and pulled open the heavy door. Inside, I saw an assortment of 8 mm film reels and a projector. You will understand that I was extremely excited with this discovery and as I hauled out the projector and attached one of the reels, I began to suspect that this old terminal likely functioned as some sort of studio. Why hadn't I thought of this earlier? It made sense, with the storyboard left in my care and a bunch of disoriented actors wandering around and no one else in sight. I held the hope that the stock of old films might give me some idea of the kind of movies made in the studio and I was a bit disappointed when the projector failed to turn on, either from a wasted battery or because it needed cleaning. I poked around the pile of old books to see if there was a spare battery pack or perhaps a missing part of the projector.

I was soon diverted by the books themselves, which all bore interesting titles, but when I turned the pages, I found that torn-off chapters had been placed haphazardly into most of the books. They were all similarly sabotaged and I wondered who would have done this. Books detailing medical experiments shifted into fairy tales and romance novels into religious tracts. One of the books, slimmer than the others, bore the interesting title *The Miserly Mind*. The early section was missing and the first page I read described a boy whose sister had died when she was nine years old. In short order, his father disappeared and his mother committed suicide. The boy was adopted by a man who was not named but signalled by a hyphen. This - was an astronomer of some kind and he seemed quite cruel as he explained to the boy that the deaths of both his sister and mother had been caused by "snuffles," a form of madness. He himself, it emerged, was not entirely sane and as his cruelty increased, the boy decided to run away. A section was missing here but it seemed that the boy may have been searching for his father during this period. Close to the end, the boy – now a man – found his father in some kind of home. The old man was demented at that point and for two pages, he ranted

at his son (whom he did not recognize) until an unsympathetic –
and possibly conniving – nurse came and took him away.

Again, there were missing pages, but it seemed that the narrator
was finally brought along to his adopted father's view and was convinced the world was filled with madness. Surprisingly, he did not
apply this diagnosis to himself, especially as he began to fuse the
older man's research with his own musings as possible solutions
to this epidemic of craziness. There were cryptic references to Cold
Spots and Dark Flow and consciousness drugs that might allow
glimpses of parallel universes and alternate realities.

I got the impression the narrator was searching, literally, for a
world not tarnished by guilt and regret and I wished I knew how
the story ended. There were clues that neither his mother nor his
sister had really died and as it was not an autobiography, I wondered why the writer did not deal with this more directly rather
than leaving clues in the later sections. However, I had scanned it
hurriedly and with the missing section, it was likely there were
connections and little clues I had missed.

I put down the book and when I poked around some more I
saw a leather bag with a battery pack. I fitted it to the projector,
turned on the unit and I heard the sound of the reel turning. The
film was animated and within a few minutes, I discovered it was a
representation of the book I had recently been reading. And like
the book, it was incomplete. In fact, both ended at the same point.
The only difference was a partial depiction of the sister in the background of some of the scenes, animated as a blur of cotton or some
soft cloth surrounded by leaves and flowers. The next film was
grainy and orange-tinted. It showed experiments of some kind
being performed on men strapped to chairs or bolted with helmets
onto cots. The camera was static and the frame rate was about four-
teen per second so it had the feeling of both a documentary and
an old-fashioned comedy. I couldn't decide until a voiceover began

to talk about biomechanically weighing, isolating and expunging guilt and regret and other disorders I couldn't follow.

The granularity in the third film was so bad it was almost impossible to follow. It began with a ragged old man wandering in some desert. Every now and again, he would stop either to shake his fists at the sky or to turn and gesture as if he was trailed by followers. This went on for about fifteen minutes until he came to the edge of a cliff. He tore off his rags, spread his arms as if he intended to fly and jumped. Once more, he turned as if he was beckoning some unseen person. The film ended there. I withdrew the reel and placed it on the floor with the others. The three incomplete films each bore some resemblance with the books and I rummaged through the pile to locate the equivalent texts. I put aside *A Sentimental Journey Into the Mind of a Cannibal* by Mausi Rampart (translated by the Reverend Thomas Loft), *The Miserly Mind* by Anonymous and *Organ Stop* by RH Bromedge, with the intention of carrying these to my room.

"You should not be so surprised. Like most psychopaths, they are quite clever. They manage to convince others that they alone hold the key."

I got up in a hurry. "Hello? Is someone here?" The sombre yet mellow voice was familiar. I walked through the carriage in the hope of locating the speaker. I glanced around and saw a figure hunched on a seat blocked off from the moonlight. He was looking out the window. "Hello," I repeated. "I did not notice you before. Did you just get in?" When there was no reply, I added, "I did not expect to find anyone here at this late hour. Were you with the group I met earlier? I was just looking at the films but they are just as confusing as the books. Someone took the time –" I stopped when it occurred that he may have despoiled the books. "I have put aside a few to read later on. I apologize if they belong to you. I assumed the carriage was empty."

"You are wasting your time with those books," the person said. "They will tell you nothing. Better to listen to a story crafted by a nine-year-old."

"You might be right. The films I managed to see are no less confusing. Were you here all the while?"

"I am always here."

"I didn't see you. Is this where you sleep? If that's the case, I am sorry for intruding. I was walking by and I noticed the smoker was unlocked. There is a group of actors here, too. We are supposed to be making a movie, but I honestly have no idea because the storyboard is so fractured." You may say this was an unnecessary rush of information, but for the briefest of moments I felt I had encountered no less a person than yourself. But, as you will see, the conversation soon proved otherwise.

"Fractured. Yes. I can see it."

"The film?"

"It constantly spools backwards. Over and over."

"What's the point, though?"

"The process will continue until they find what they are looking for."

"The actors? Like some kind of rehearsal?"

"They are searching for the end by returning to the beginning."

"Really? I do not understand that process."

"They hope to find the spark before it splintered."

"What spark? Inspiration?"

"Interesting. I didn't expect you to understand. The spark of inspiration before it splintered into madness. They would like to bottle that moment. Study and replicate it. Determine why it sputtered. Why it always does. There is the theory that the world operates with myriad checks and balances to ensure that nothing happens before its ordained time. So, there are accidents and premature deaths and madness. The first two are intractable but the last can be interfered with. Adjusted to speed things up." He chuckled lightly.

I had assumed he was talking of the actors but he sounded just as disoriented as the others I had met. Besides, I had never heard of this strange theory. I tried to steer the conversation back to him. "How long have you been waiting here?"

"Just as long as you."

I was about to tell him that I had been here less than three weeks when I was struck by a rather horrible idea. I had assumed that my memory loss coincided with my arrival at the terminal, but what if I had been wandering around, just as confused, prior to my coming here? For months, maybe, or years. I still had no idea how I had ended up in this bleak place. No idea if I had a family or friends somewhere or an office to which I would trudge every day. No idea if I was a man with a soiled past or someone who had been lauded with accolades. Maybe I was just an unremarkable person whose days followed each other in the same pattern. A failed writer or frustrated director whose projects had long dried up.

Balzac and the others acted as if they knew me and I took it for granted this was because they had mistaken me for the screenwriter or the director. Eventually, I asked the man in the carriage, "Did you write the script?"

He turned as if the question interested him. The meagre light hollowed his eyes and his mouth. "It's not finished. It never is no matter how many times we travel back. They are wasting their time. They believe memory can be stitched and joined." When he walked away, I saw that he was my size but I still had not fully glimpsed his face.

I left a few minutes later. There was a reddish tinge to the sky and I realized that it would soon be morning. The sprigs of red tumbleweed blowing across the tracks looked as if they had bled from the sky. I had spent half the night in the carriage. I hurried along so I would not meet anyone on the way. I had mentioned to the crew that I would meet them all in the morning, but I needed an hour or two of sleep. Perhaps I would meet the man who had been silently viewing the movie with me and he would explain his odd utterances and hopefully connect it with the film we were supposed to make.

When I entered the carriage, I saw the cushions on the floor. Someone had been rummaging around. And the ledger was gone.

17 THE CONDUCTOR

I could not sleep after the discovery of the intrusion. I locked the windows and the door and double-checked everything, but I still felt insecure. What if I had been sleeping in the carriage during the intrusion? I remained inside reflecting as to how I should approach this situation. At first, I resolved to confront the group and reveal that someone had broken into my carriage and stolen the ledger. I would then explain that the confusing movie they were all ranting about could not proceed without the storyboard. I quickly changed my mind about this approach not because the ledger had been useless so far but because I had no idea how Balzac and Fingers and the others would react in their demented state.

When I went to the canteen, it was empty. I had with me the three books from the previous night because I feared they would be stolen from my carriage. Half an hour later, Balzac walked in. He was followed by the group I had met earlier. No one said anything, but I was aware that everyone was looking at me, and from the corner of my eyes I noticed some of the group moving to tables closer to mine. Balzac and the Stenographer were now at an adjoining table and the little man was holding on to Balzac's arm like an infant.

I got out *Organ Stop* and began reading. The man who had been introduced as Tiffin came across and asked, "Where did you get those books?"

I glanced up and noticed his bony face, the doe eyes, the high nose and thin lips. Unexpectedly, I felt angry with the group. "That is none of your concern," I told him.

I heard Balzac saying, "It takes a callous man to be so cagey about his actions." To Tiffin he said, "Tell him why you are so upset."

Immediately Tiffin said, "I lost control during my fasts. There were innocent victims." He proceeded to describe a child who had died following one of his fasts and a young woman who had jumped from her balcony following another. "I have an obligation as you well know."

"Tell him how you discovered your power." Balzac tried to prompt him out of his sulkiness.

"I found your book in an old phone booth. There were drawings. I could not understand the messages at first, but after reading the book, I felt stronger and faster. I knew it had been left there for me."

"Tell him about the book," Balzac said.

"Yes, it was about a man who got his strength from a phone booth. He always came out stronger and faster. But one day he discovered that all the booths had been destroyed overnight. He built a new booth and another, but it was useless. You know how it ends."

"He moved to another town?"

"That is unnecessary, my friend," Balzac intervened. "You know full well that the man could not recover from this backhander. You know full well that he lost his appetite and ended up like a lion caught in one of those drought places. Mangy and demented and famished beyond belief."

Balzac seemed to be waiting for me to say something. When I

remained silent, he transferred his gaze to the Stenographer. "I myself could never possess such power because I am an eater. The tear of gristle and the crunch of tender bones is what gets my engine going." The Stenographer swished a bit and when Balzac patted his shoulder, he began to purr, at the same time pointing to a nearby table.

Maybe it was Balzac's threat or the Stenographer's purring or my dismay about my memory, but I felt my anger growing. I took a deep breath and said in a voice loud enough for the entire group to hear, "There are a few things we need to address here. Clear up some misconceptions. I should have done this earlier and I blame myself for not doing so. When I met you all earlier, I got the impression that you had been awaiting my arrival. I mistakenly assumed everything would become clearer, but so far I am no closer to determining the cause of your error. Secondly, I have not written any book or script. Not the one to which you, Tiffin, mentioned, nor these before me." I tapped the books on the table. "And before you begin to jump to your usual conclusions I will tell you that I discovered these in an abandoned carriage. They were there with a dozen old films, some of which I managed to view." I heard a gasp from the group and I continued, "And finally, last night someone broke into my carriage and stole the ledger that contained the storyboards. I am less concerned about the loss of the ledger than with the realization that there is someone within this group who believes it's okay to intrude into another person's space. A thief."

No one said anything. I got up and walked away but my annoyance remained. I passed the smoker carriage and when I glanced back, I got the distinct feeling that three men in white flowing coats were following me, so I walked down a platform into a narrow hallway and slipped into a tunnel that led to sturdy concrete stairs. Across the road, I saw a building with crumbling pillars. I walked across quickly and hurried down a long stairway that led to an underground pathway. I picked up my pace until I was running and twenty minutes later, I came to what looked like a whistle stop. There was a small waiting area and when I entered, I saw a row of old men and women sitting quietly on a long bench. They seemed not to notice me and I guessed they were waiting for the station clerk to return to the empty booth. They all glanced at me and I observed how tiny they were, almost shrunken in their overcoats. "What are you all doing here?" I asked. "Isn't this place abandoned?" They were all smiling in a tranquilized manner. The man on the edge said, "We are waiting for the train. The others have left. Every day the train takes a dozen." He glanced at his companions and they nodded. "But thank you for asking. Thank you. No one cares anymore. Soon we will be forgotten." They resumed gazing at the window.

"Where are you going?" I asked them. "This place looks abandoned." I glanced at the clock stuck on nine.

"We are close to the end so it does not matter." He closed his eyes and I saw that they all had tiny strips of bandages on their arms. The group looked exhausted and when I left them, I wondered how long they had been waiting.

"Where are you going?" I asked once more.

"We were the last ones," the man said. "We tried to warn them, but no one would listen."

"Warn about what?"

He looked so distressed I regretted asking the question. But he said, "Children who could no longer dream were no longer children. We warned them, but they would not listen. Men who followed a single directive were no longer men. We warned them, and they laughed at us. Women who forgot they were girls were no longer women. We warned them, and we were punished for it."

"I don't understand. Who punished you?"

"In the beginning they were harmless. They were our caregivers and chauffeurs. They made life easier."

"I don't understand who you are talking about," I told the group. They looked too old and frail, but I asked, "Are you here for the film, too? Would you like to join the other actors in the carriages?"

"Each time you ask us we tell you the same thing. We are tired. Tired..."

I decided to leave them there, as I wanted to explore the area to see if there was a waiting vehicle. My mind was still on the group when I came to a sort of junkyard littered with engines and over-turned hulls. In the distance, I saw what appeared to be a forest, but after half an hour or so, my feet began to hurt from my stiff balmorals, so I decided to return to rest awhile with the group of old men and women. Maybe they would explain if a bus or some other type of transportation came weekly to this dead place. They were not there, which was odd because I had not heard the sound of a vehicle. I looked around for a while before I made my way back. I got lost a few times but eventually I saw the line of carriages.

There was no one around and I headed for the smoker carriage where I had spent the previous night. I looked around for the man who had been sitting silently viewing the films with me before I attached a reel onto the projector. The first was some sort of dance routine featuring two men. It began with the shorter man shim-mying around the taller, who was chewing a cigarette. Then the taller man sprang into action, contorting and spinning so that his companion had to duck. The dance was a compendium of styles with stamping and pirouetting and curious eye movements and finger-twirling. My exasperation from earlier faded as I watched the odd pair's antics. Half an hour later, I attached another reel. Here, a very tall man was placing metallic plates across his chest and fitting some sort of goggles over his eyes. He looked perfectly mad as he glanced every now and again at the camera. Suddenly he rushed forward and the camera must have fallen, for the man now appeared in a vertical position. He stepped back, raised his leg and the film went black. The abruptness of his action was exceedingly funny.

I expected the third film to be just as funny. A man was walking around an abandoned town, the camera following him from a distance, as he talked about religion. "Those afflicted with religious delusions are the most difficult to treat as their fantasies frequently spring from some biologic blemish. Undifferentiated schizophrenia, bipolar disorder or epilepsy that renders them impervious to counselling."

He paused before a hedge before he continued. "In every other profession, these men would be condemned and punished, but in the cathedrals, their sobs amplified into soaring arias, they are embraced with great fondness." I tried to understand what he was saying. Following my encounter with the rest of the crew, his utterances were no less startling and in an odd way – perhaps because of my limited memory – they seemed reasonable. "Most delusions can be whittled down by explaining to the patient that there's no context in reality to sustain their fantasies. This is not possible with those suffering from religious delusions because these patients immediately adopt an adversarial tone during a deconstruction of their apparitions. The one trying to help becomes an agent of the devil, testing their faith."

At a mulberry bush, he paused to glance up at a chapter house's window. "Everything is predicated on the presence of trust. The impaired must have faith in the proposed remedies, and the alleviator must believe his words have magnetized pockets of rationality, however deeply recessed these may be. Do you understand why it is impossible to counsel an acolyte? Or, for that matter, someone who cannot accept his insanity?" He offered a prolonged sigh as he glanced around. "The so-called custodians fail to understand this simple truth."

I recalled Balzac talking about the Amazing Acolytes and felt it curious that the film had also referenced the word. "Even with my disdain of this medieval belief in possession and sorcery, I am still in awe of the sturdy discipline and forbearance of men whose lives are tied to their faith. And I am not ashamed to admit there have been rare moments in my own life when I lamented the absence of an omnipotent figure." Suddenly he began to run, weaving in and out of streets. "I am not going to do this again," he shouted. The camerawork was shaky here and it was only when he got to the edge of what appeared to be a basin and turned that his face was shown. "No one is perfect," he screamed. I replayed this bit several times to be certain it was the man who had been in the carriage the previous night.

I turned off the projector and got out a book titled *The Sacred Heresies*. I chose this book because I felt it would mirror the last film, but so many pages were missing it was impossible to arrive at a thread. I must have fallen asleep and when I glanced through the window, I saw it was already dark. On the way to my carriage, I jumped when I felt a hand on my shoulder. It was still dark and the hand felt rough and heavy. I spun around and the man released his hold. In the gloom, I was able to see his big ears and squat figure but nothing else. "You shouldn't be sneaking up on me at this ungodly hour, my friend. What if I had not properly recognized you and dismantled you limb by limb?"

I recognized the voice as Balzac's. "What are you doing here so late?"

"Although your question is most impudent, I will grant you the courtesy of a straightforward response. I am a nocturnal creature. In the nights, I allow the beast to roam free. It's the only way I can keep him under control."

I told him, "I wouldn't want to get in the way, so I should leave now."

"Far from me to disagree, but before you do, may I ask where you have been all day?"

I decided against mentioning the films. "Exploring the terminal. I met a group of old people there, but they have left. I should be on my way now."

"You, my friend, are amazing." I suspected that Balzac used this statement when he had nothing else to say. "You have seen something where there is nothing. It is a paradox worth examining."

"Well, you will have to do that by yourself because I have not eaten all day." I dreaded the thought of going to the canteen because the group would surely be there. When I entered, I saw Fingers, Kurt, Toeman, Tiffin, Boing and the countess woman sitting together. At another table was the group of men I had met in their carriages. And sitting alone was the Stenographer. I glanced at everyone quickly, not making eye contact before I gathered tins of meat and beans.

They all looked so expectant I felt a twinge of guilt when I left and I steadied myself by thinking that I needed some time alone to determine what I was doing in this place and my connection with the group who had been awaiting my arrival. They could not all have mistaken me for someone else, yet I had not the slightest sense of familiarity with any of them. That's not true, though. Every now and again, I got the sense that I had heard some of Balzac's nonsense and the man who called himself the Inquisitor had spoken in a rich voice that seemed familiar. The woman with the medallion had an odour that set my mind to an intimate act but surely neither of us would forget something like that.

I have not addressed you directly for some time, but I wished you had left something less meagre than the instructions for the film. Anything at all, even slender clues. That night I occupied myself by trying to make sense of the three books. It was close to midnight when I realized that even though they were of several genres, they all possessed common stylistic tics. Long sentences, semicolons, an abundance of adjectives, random paragraph shifts and so on. I cannot overstate my excitement as I tore off the pages from the three books and tried to create some sort of chronological sequence or at least a pattern. This jigsaw was not an easy task because I had before me a children's book, an archaic medical manual and a religious treatise. Yet slowly, a sort of similitude emerged. All three were involved in a search for perfection by walking backwards and attempting to exorcise points of trauma or doubts or dislocation. All three books mentioned a process called either *lethal sequencing, remote pivoting* or *resetting*. You will forgive me my exhilaration; in this crazy situation, this was the first riddle I had come close to understanding.

There was something else: one of the paragraphs in a science fiction story reminded me somehow of my conversation with the group of old men and women waiting for a train.

It began harmlessly. The machines helped us. The old, the lonely. The disabled. Then we gave them new tasks. We asked them to perform surgeries. Assuage our boredom. Make decisions. We asked them to show us the world as if we were lizards that had been living under a rock. We delighted in pretending to be children with adults who were forever obedient. We allowed the machines to think for us. Dream for us. We made them smarter. Then they made themselves smarter. And the dreams changed. Then they stopped. The machines began to edit us, removing cancerous cells, obesity genes, fallacies, illusions, visions, empathy. They anatomized our molecular information and determined what should be excised. We entrusted them with everything, with the certainty their values would mimic those of their creators. And they did.

My discovery of these books and the proper sequencing of the pages brought other problems. I had no idea who the writer was and why he or she had disguised the books' genres and had compounded this fragmentation by rearranging chapters and covers. I thought of the man in the smoker talking mysteriously about regressing to the precise point of madness to reset the switch that had precipitated the trauma. (I also briefly considered that you may have been the instigator of some convoluted prank before I decided that the other players were far too convincing to be part of such an elaborate ruse.) When I left my carriage, I took the books with me because there was no way to lock the door from outside. Halfway to the smoker, I saw sparks shooting upward. I broke into a run and even before I got to the fire, I knew it was the place to which I was headed. By the time I got there, the fire had burnt itself out and when I looked through the window, I noticed that even though the steel structure was impervious to the flames, the interior was completely destroyed. A bat was flying in a circular motion. I walked back quickly to my carriage and locked the door. I was certain that the fire was set deliberately and I also knew it was no coincidence that it had occurred so soon after my discovery of the books and films. Someone was trying to impede my progress, which was confusing because I had no idea what I was looking for. Like the previous night, I went through a list of likely suspects. It could be anyone.

I slept in snatches that night, awakened by the slightest noise. I decided I would find some other sleeping area farther away in the morning. It was still dark when I set out and when I stopped by the destroyed smoker and looked through the window, I had the horrible thought that the man who had been inside with me had been caught in the fire. I opened the door in a hurry and was relieved when I saw no signs of a burnt body. I was about to leave when I noticed the safe was locked. I could not recall if I had done this myself or if the man had locked it. I tried the handle and after a while, I managed to open it. Inside I saw some kind of bamboo boomerang.

I took the boomerang and set out for the area I had visited the previous day. Once again, I hurried along in case I was being followed. As I was passing the junkyard, I was startled when a figure rose up from a mess of cardboard on the sidewalk. He was not one of the crew and I had not seen him with the group the other day. In any case, he was so ragged I felt he had been hiding out in the junkyard for a while. "What are you doing here?" I asked him.

"Ah, brother," he began as if he had been waiting there forever for that question. "Ah, brother. The walk of life. It's a funny thing when you think of it. Everybody's walking away from each other. Hadda time" – he made snipping gestures at the buildings and I noticed that his eyes were bright and unsuited to his badly creased face – "hadda time when only music was streaming from the decks. First was real slow music. Frilly like a ruffled hem. I used to think of it as mountain music because of all the peaks and valleys. That lasted a long time but it got taken over by music of the plains, you know, 'cause everything was one tone. Lotta weeping about broken hearts. Then the crying stopped. And the hollering began. Popping out slow in the beginning from every pocket. Spreading everywhere. Savannah music it was. Then that, too, stopped. I was waiting, patiently, brother to hear some new sound but it seems there is a chink in the groove."

"What do you mean?"

"Clip, clip, pop." He lay down once more and drew a slim piece of cardboard over his head. "By the way, brother, Conductor is the name. Don't have a calling card as yet but working on it. Can I tell you something? Every single time you ask the same damn questions. What happened to the woman? Why is the place so quiet? Where are the others? Always on the run or looking for someone. The two don't add up. Dunno what you are expecting, brother. There is a way in the world that leads to nothing. This is the way it is and the way it will be. End of text."

He fell back on the pavement and pulled his cardboard blanket over his head. "Wait," I told him with some urgency. "You said I asked these questions previously. When did we meet? Did you ever answer?"

"There is a way in the world that leads to nothing. This is the way it is and the way it will go down. I try to stitch and join and hem but the patches are getting bigger. I have the answer, but no one asks the proper question."

"What is the question?"

"The question is why do they now search for the very ones they discarded?"

"And the answer?"

"Because we got something they want. Something they lost. We got the music, brother. We got the crazy dreams and the funny songs. We got the ups and downs and the topsy-turvies." He pulled at the end of his ragged coat and bit into a dangling thread. "I shouldn't be telling you any of this. There's a little bat roaming about. You better avoid her." I saw his hands on either side, grasping pieces of cardboard and fitting them over his body. I stood there awhile, hoping he would emerge from the junk. I called a few times and eventually I walked on to the waiting area where I had seen the group.

As I expected, the place was empty. I decided I would head for the forest I had seen the previous day. Perhaps there might be a little town there. I paced myself by resting at twenty-minute intervals and at the fifth stop, I saw someone standing on the brink of a hill. I was a bit disappointed that someone from the group had found this area. I hoped it was not Balzac but as I drew closer, I saw it was a slim man in a grey overcoat. He was leaning on a parasol and looking up. I hurried in his direction but just before I got there, he jumped.

18 THE GIRL WITH THE BOOMERANG

I scrambled down the hill as fast as I could, but there was no sign of anyone. I looked behind the rocks and boulders and peered inside the crevices and between the spiky shrubs. Could he have been caught on one of the ledges? I glanced up but saw no one clinging to the sides. Perhaps his parasol had enabled him to ride an air current and he had landed some distance away. Even though I knew this was highly unlikely, I hurried to a field with rows of spindly, bird-shaped plants. I called out and hearing no response, I ventured within. The protruding stalks were stiff and I had to constantly brush these away from my face but soon they grew softer and more oval and I realized I was in another type of field. Here, there were leaning palms with twisted fronds and hanging epiphytes bearing wispy blue flowers and, most strange of all, clumps of miniature bamboo. "Hello," I shouted once more.

"There's no need to shout. Everyone can hear you for miles and you have scared away all the parrots."

I saw a slight movement behind one of the clumps. "Hello," I shouted once more.

"How did you find this place? Did the Citizen Brigade send you?"

I saw a face peeping from behind a bamboo shoot. Although I could not properly make out the features I was sure it was not an adult. "What are you doing here by yourself, child?" The figure stepped out and I saw it was a girl of about eight or nine. Her hood was studded with blue flowers and I added, "Are you collecting flowers for a game? You know you shouldn't be here all alone."

"What are *you* doing here? It's not even a sector."

"I was looking for someone. I think he floated off on an umbrella."

"Floated off on an umbrella? I knew you had been done." She seemed a bit demented and I asked where her parents were. When she did not reply, just regarded me skeptically, I inquired if there was a town close by. A little grin fitted itself on her face and she said, "You shouldn't pretend, you know. Or maybe you have been done just like all the others."

"Done? Which others? The film crew?"

"You think they are all actors? Really?"

"What else would they be? I have the script. Do you know what the word means?"

"I am not stupid. Where is it?" She took a step toward me.

"Someone stole it."

"Hah! I knew it." She stepped a bit closer. "I see you have brought my boomerang. Can I have it?"

"Wait a minute. Did I see you the other day? Running among the coaches?"

"No one will ever catch me here. I know all the trails and burrows that no one else can see."

"I have no intention of catching you. I already mentioned I was looking for someone."

"Or maybe it's just a trick." She looked at me with suspicion.

I decided to be firm with her. "This is not a game, child. Someone –"

"Floated away on an umbrella. Now can you throw me my boomerang? And don't try to trick me because I can talk with parrots and armadillos. Can you do that?"

"No, I cannot. And I am not trying to trick you. I am simply concerned that a child such as yourself is wandering about all alone."

"A child such as yourself? Who speaks this way?" She tittered and covered her mouth with her dirty hands. "Does everyone who has been done talk like the stiff people from old mothy books?"

"Why don't you tell me?" I asked her. "You seem to know everything. Hiding about and talking to your animals."

"I knew you were mean. I knew it would be a matter of time before your meanness showed through."

She took a backward step and I told her, "I am sorry. I shouldn't have said that. It's just that I am looking for someone who disappeared –"

"Yes, yes. I know. The man from the Compound and the old house and the haunted place with the monster and the train."

"Was he the same person from the smoker carriage? I didn't know that. He might be hurt. Did you see him?"

She shook her head and some of the blue flowers fell to her feet. She gazed at the flowers and told me, "I never saw his face. He died hundreds and thousands of years ago. I think during the war when there were yellow and red clouds on all the streets and machines were pretending to be men and the animals that could not have babies died out. They told me that with their own beaks. Do you know what else? It was the man from the house and the train who invented the do machines. Serves him right if he's hurt."

"What did he invent?"

"The machines that joined with people and made them act

strange. I think the machines did not work all that well because it made monsters, too. I read that in the books with pictures. Are you one?"

"You tell me. Do I look like a monster?" I asked, smiling.

"Maybe. A little. But I never saw one up close. I run away whenever I hear them coming."

"Really?" I decided to humour her. "So it's a little game? Like hide-and-seek, maybe."

"It's not a game, you silly old man. The Citizen Brigade checks to see if there are any new monsters and then sends them to live with other monsters. I know all the secrets because they can never catch me. Do you know why?"

"I am in the dark."

"That's a funny thing to say. They can never catch me because I can talk to birds and cats and lizards. I think I am…"

"You are what?" I asked.

"Alone. They can't feel what I am thinking, but I can see everything."

"Can you tell me how you manage to do that?"

She took a tentative step forward. "If you throw me my boomerang, I will tell you. Wait. Kick it to me or it will just fly back to you." I tossed the boomerang lightly to her and she grabbed it and pushed it somewhere in her clothes. "Bye, sucker." She ran off. I had to smile at her childish scheminess. I decided to return to the terminal when I heard, "They put other people's stories in your head."

"Really? Why would they do this?" I asked.

"Because they don't have any of their own, silly. They want to see what will happen when all these stories join into a big great story."

"So they can tell it to each other in the nights?"

"I already told you it's because they don't have any of their own."

"And why is that so?"

"Because they lost them, silly. So now they are looking for them."

"I see. And where do they get these stories to put into peoples' heads if they have lost –"

"From the books that they stopped everyone from reading because they said it made everyone mad. I think it's wrong to steal other peoples' stories and have them stuffed inside your head."

"And why is that so?"

"Because you believe they belong to you, silly."

"I see. And who puts these stories in? A monster?"

"No, silly old man. The three horrible men. One looks like a nasty toad and another looks like an imp and the last one like a sor…sorcerer. They will never catch me."

"Because they are from the books?" I asked her. "A fairy-tale book with a frog, an imp and a sorcerer?"

"No, you crazy old man. Because I can talk with parrots and armadillos. And I have a pet cat that's wild. Did I mention those?"

I decided to be firm with her. "Why are they trying to catch you? Do you think that maybe they would like you to rejoin your parents?"

"That's what they want me to believe. But I have no parents. I saw when they were done. And their brains taken out and stuffed into new parents."

"Are we still playing here? If so, that's a horrible joke to make."

"It's no joke. I was hiding at the time and when I ran away, they tried to follow me. They have been trying ever since."

"Hmm. Where do you live, child? I can take you there."

"Are you deaf? I have no home. Do you know how long I have been hiding?"

She stepped out and I saw her transferring the boomerang from one hand to the other. I wondered if the girl had strayed into the smoker and had viewed some of the films. It was likely because she had left her boomerang there. "And how does it all end?" I asked.

"It never ends because the toad and his two friends send back everyone, over and over, to do the same thing until they get the secret. And I know what it is, too." She looked smug with herself as if she anticipated my next question. When I asked her, she said, "They make these people pretend they are someone else. I think they want them to finish something that they started, but they never finished. I know what you are going to ask and I already told you that they want to see how the stories end. It's there in the books in the carriage."

"Is that where you read of the war? And the people whose stories were stolen and the strange machines?"

"I know what you are getting at, but I can tell the difference between a true story and a made-up one. That's why I am hiding here. All my stories are my own and no one will take them away. I know the name of the machine that made everything think the same. Would you like to hear it?" When I nodded, she said, "Birdie." As she spoke, I wished I recalled more of my own childhood. Perhaps at one time, I was like this child. I have to say it was interesting listening to her fantasies even though I felt guilty at delaying her return to her home. Then she said, "That is why only I can remember in a straight line. They can't steal my remembering." I tried to ignore her boast but I immediately thought of my own memory loss. I recalled my strange dreams of dungeons and lopsided streetlamps and blue-skinned beings shedding tears that seemed to transform into leaves as they touched the ground. I thought of my nightmare where I was floating on a sea or lake and watching armies fighting and falling around me. In some of my dreams, those that lasted a minute or so, there was a compound filled with lunatics and a man who looked like a zombie in an old house and a completely insane man in another. They were as disconnected as the proposed film scripts in the stolen ledger and I surprised myself by wondering if the insertion of foreign memories could have caused this fragmentation. But this was just a silly child's story. "Did you swallow your tongue?" the girl asked. She stooped to retrieve a flower that she replaced on her ragged lapel. "Why are you looking at me like that?"

"I don't know," I said, confused. "Maybe all little girls look alike. I believe you reminded me of someone...but I don't know who exactly."

"This is strange. People who have been done never remember anything. I should warn you that I like puzzles. I spend all nights solving them. I call them fuzzles."

"Then we are alike."

"What did you say? It's poor manners to talk to yourself. Even I know this."

"I said that I, too, spend all nights working on my puzzles."

"And?"

It may seem strange that I should reveal to a ragged child that I had found myself in a derelict studio with a group of actors who had memorized their roles for so long they had begun to believe they were these characters. I told her that I could not explain my presence in this sprawling studio set in an abandoned terminal, but I guessed I might have been one of the writers because I had been left with the storyboard. I told her of my dreams.

I saw her looking at me and stroking her boomerang and I felt she did not believe a word of what I had said, but she asked me, "I never talked to one of you. I thought you would forget everything. Do you think all these dreams are clues?"

I smiled. "I wished they were, but they are just bad dreams. Maybe people with bad memories try to fill in the gaps with –"

"Or maybe they try to not get mad. Like the people you are hiding from." I tried to recall if I had mentioned this fact. "The people from all these places, now in the train, are dangerous because all the voices are shaking in their heads and telling them different things."

"That's interesting. Did you read about that in one of the books?"

"I follow them around and see what they are doing and listen to everything." I saw her drawing circles in the air. "The toad and his two friends always send everyone back to the beginning."

"Of what?"

"Don't you listen? Of when the craziness started. They want to see if you will do the same crazy things."

I was about to tell her that trailing strangers was a dangerous game, especially with men like Balzac about, when I noticed a brief flicker of sadness on her face. I asked her, "Are you looking for someone? A friend?"

I thought she would run away and she made a few tentative steps before she returned, her shoulders slumping. "Not a friend. How did you know?"

"With most games, children are searching for something or someone."

"It's not a game." And here she told me an astonishing story. The men and women who had been stolen and their memories replaced had all been working on something important before they were forced to give up. I asked why they had stopped their projects and she thought for a while before she said it was because they wanted to come off the Birdie machine that joined everyone's thoughts. Her own mother, she said, had been studying plants and flowers. In her story, there were priests and scientists and writers and artists and musicians and athletes. All were sent to institutions. "That is how the toad and his two friends got them. I know something else. Only three months. That is how long they forget before everything has to start over."

I knew she was likely drawing her story from a film she had

seen in the smoker carriage and that it had probably been coloured by her own imagination, but I could not put aside my calculation that three weeks had passed since I awoke in the terminal, my memories washed. "What do you think will happen if one of these men escapes before three months?"

"It's impossible. The toad and his friends get them. They have a paladin man with a wolf. He calls himself other names, too. But I know how to get away from him. He is always talking to lizards and birds and cats." She tittered as if she remembered something funny and then I saw a strange almost adult expression cross her face. "How long since you woke up?"

"Did I mention that? In any event, it's less than a month."

"Hmm. I have a crazy idea. You should try to get away. It will be the first time ever and you can go to the other side and you can tell everyone about the toad man and his friends and they will break all the walls and set everyone free. I will help you."

I thought of the burnt smoker carriage and the stolen ledger and all the crazy men and women trapped in some movie role. I didn't believe a word the girl said, but she had come from some nearby town and obviously knew her way around. I told her, "Okay."

"Okay? I didn't expect you to agree."

"Well, I did. You lead the way and I will follow."

"Are you crazy? We can't walk. They will catch us when we get too tired."

"So how do you propose we escape?"

"The train."

I was swiftly reminded I was talking to a child. I told her, "The trains are all rusty and seized. They have been abandoned for a long while."

"The bus, then. The one the paladin man travels in. We can sneak on when he is walking about with his wolf."

"I haven't seen any working buses around. Besides, who would drive?"

"You! Don't tell me that an old man like you never learned to drive. Did they steal away that, too?"

"I don't know the route, so –"

"Are you making excuses to remain here with everyone else so you can get more crazy every day until you forget every single thing?"

"No, I wouldn't want that to happen, but I am not sure your plan is practical. What if you forget the route?" I saw the frustration on her face so I hesitated in adding other obstacles.

"Suit yourself. I will walk. All by myself. I don't need anyone."

"You are quite a smug little girl," I told her.

I immediately regretted saying this but before I could apologize she said, "'You are quite a smug little girl.' And why not? I am the only one who has managed to escape." She laughed loudly and cupped a palm against her ear. "The parrots are laughing, too. *Smug.* I must teach them that word. It sounds like a baby wren wrapped in a warm blanket. Smug." She turned and walked away.

"Wait," I shouted after a while and when I caught up with her, I added, "Maybe…"

"Maybe what?"

"How far away is the bus?"

"On the hill past all the old junk. We will have to leave when it's raining because that is when the crazy paladin takes his wolf to walk about." She skipped away. "In the early morning is when he goes."

19 THE TOAD, THE IMP AND THE SORCERER

When I got to my carriage, I was a bit disappointed that I had actually considered the girl's plan to leave the station. I was glad I had met her, though, because it meant there was a little village or town nearby. Perhaps I would explore the area and meet her parents or guardian. Or maybe she was an orphan and she had made up her wild story about the three men who had sent her to an institution or to her guardians or adopted parents. I wondered if her belief in the stealing of brains and stories was because she combined elements of her biological parents with that of her adopted parents. Poor child. She seemed tough, though, and resilient.

That night I heard the steady patter of rain against the carriage's window and I pictured her watching out from her bedroom, terrified of her paladin bogeyman. She was filled with stories, this child. I remembered her claim that the man who had leapt off the cliff had invented these horrible machines centuries earlier; machines used by the three men to steal stories.

I fell asleep, a bit amused at the girl's fantasies, but her description of the toadlike man and his companions instigated a nightmare that I will describe as best as I can.

It began with a bluish light from the corner of my carriage and in my dream, I asked, "Who is there?" There was no answer and I called out again. "How did you get into my room? I have a weapon."

"Please remain on your bed. There's no need to be unduly disturbed," a voice said.

I suppose I am more forthright in my sleep than awake because I demanded of the three silhouettes: "You waltz into my room while I am asleep and expect me to be fine with that. How long have you been here? How did you get in? I am not going to stand for –" I tried to get up to forcefully remove them but discovered that my feet were immobilized. I struggled to prise myself to a sitting position. My hands were tingling and there was a buzzing insect noise close to my ears.

"Please calm yourself," one of them said. "We are not here to harm you so there's absolutely no reason to be so agitated." I was not reassured by his guarantee and as I struggled to free myself, I heard a prolonged sigh from one and a murmur of impatience from another.

Eventually I realized it was useless and I asked, "What do you want from me?"

"As always, we want what's best for you. For us. Everyone."

I now saw that the man on the right was tall in comparison with his associates, but so sclerotic that his hands hung close to his knees, and that the impish person on the left was little bigger than a child. The middle man, squat and powerful-looking, his arms folded, was blinking slowly like a toad. "If you want what's best for me, why have you pinned me to my bed? I am not going to talk to you while I am all tied up."

"Pinned you?" said the imp.

"Dear fellow," began the man on the right, but he said nothing else.

The toadlike man cleared his throat and took over. "Don't be ridiculous. You are free to stride about if you choose to do so." Once more, I tried to move my feet and although I now felt the sensation of tiny ants running along my legs I still could not get up. It was then that I was sure I was in a dream. I have this memory of a state referred to as sleep paralysis, where the afflicted, forced into immobility, imagine shadow people and ghosts hovering over their beds and outside their windows. "We have only your best interest in mind, so your cooperation will be helpful to everyone concerned."

"What is it you want of me? It must be important for you to sneak into my room."

"Before we begin, can you tell us your name?" the toad asked.

I recalled all the crazy names of the actors in the carriage and I told him, "Doctor Damnation."

The imp seemed agitated by this silly name and the toad patted him like a child before he continued his interrogation. "We understand you have been wandering around."

My treatment of them as dream-figures lessened my panic somewhat. "That is true, but it is none of your concern."

"We beg to differ. How far did you get?"

"At the hill but again –"

"Did you meet anyone?"

"There was a man and a little girl."

They conferred for a while before the tall man asked, "Do you know where they went?"

"They disappeared."

"Excellent. That's a good first step."

I waited for him to continue, but it was the gloomy man who said, "They disappeared to the place all your other visions went." For a second, I wondered if I had also dreamed of the man who had jumped from the hill. It was easier to believe this of the man, but the girl's features and her voice were quite distinct in my mind.

The toad seemed to have been reading my mind because he said, "You conjured her."

"Poof!" said the imp.

I was struck by a sudden thought. "What of all the people I met in the carriages? All of them struck with some grave peculiarity."

"Peculiar, yes, but not in the manner you have framed them. Unremarkable people, but quite suggestible."

No one I had met had been unremarkable. I mentioned the loss of the ledger and the fire that had destroyed the smoker carriage. To my astonishment, the man on the right said that I had done the damage myself. "Why would I do something like this?" I asked.

This is where the dream got interesting. Speaking in a ridiculously sombre manner he delivered the most amazing tale. One worthy of the most fertile dream – even with my limited memory. In his account, I was a writer who had written a series of books that all featured the same heroes. These heroes formed a team named the Amazing Acolytes, which was able to defeat its enemies by tapping into their hidden fears and anxieties. "A group of super empaths, you might say. Very clever. Very. But, at some point, your own anxieties came to the forefront. I suppose most writers are propelled by this sort of thing, but usually it is kept under control. And for a while, this was how you operated. Your readers cheered on your heroes as they took on a variety of government agencies. Not any garden-variety hoodlums, but federal bureaus and administrative units and high-ranking officials that were somehow all involved in surveillance and control of innocent citizens."

"Can you now see how ridiculous this was?" the middle man asked.

On the contrary, I found it extremely plausible, but I said nothing. The tall man said, "At what point does an obsession darken into a psychosis?" I felt that if they had rehearsed this little event, he must have been chosen to utter all the overly dramatic statements. "Your heroes were the last defence against an encroaching world of listeners and infiltrators and provocateurs. But in time, they became something more. Only they could protect, civilize and humanize. You called it 'the superman's burden' in one of your books. Then you decided to send them on one final mission. The mother of all battles. To bring back the fire."

"The chaos," the gloomy man added.

"The slithering reptile brain," the imp said with a chuckle.

"Do you see what we are getting at?" the toad asked.

"You will have to forgive me because it's difficult to deduce who is crazier here – the writer who has created a fictional world or those who believe that this world is real?"

"Exactly!" the imp emitted.

The toad ignored him. "You ask who is crazier. Well let me tell you, it is the writer who begins to believe in the reality of his creations. I am talking about the men or women who awaken in the mornings and carry with them the fancies of the nights so that after a while the real world recedes before their fables and concoctions. Ghosts walking in the shadows, you might say. And this is precisely what happened in your case. You began to believe you were followed, spied upon, violated. Everyone was somehow connected to this great web, the only purpose of which was to ensnare or kidnap or eliminate you. You wrote threatening letters, attacked co-workers, tried to burn down the department in which you worked, barged into offices screaming your accusations and so on." He paused to offer a woeful sigh. "At some point, you began to conjure up your heroes as your personal defenders and monitors. Your guardians. And so, your presence in this place."

"Which did not turn out as we expected," the tall one intoned. "We were hoping for some improvement, but we have grown to accept that it is the very intelligent who put up the most resistance. The most accomplished."

Dream or not, I decided to put them to the test. "Why are you revealing all of this?" I asked. "Aren't you afraid your revelations about the nature of this place will add to my supposed paranoia?"

"We have nothing to hide," the toad said. "And we keep hoping for precisely the opposite elicitation. Though our experience does not grant us any optimism, we continue to hope that you will understand that your paranoiac state is far more crippling than the amnesia you claim. We keep hoping that you will become more amenable to our directions."

"And what result will this bring?"

The toad, who seemed to be the ringleader in this dream, said, "It is a common fallacy, this belief that madness involves an emptying of the mind, or, in fact, that there are different types of craziness, but every mad person has one trait in common. Voices. The mind of an afflicted person is never empty but paralyzed with these vying voices." He spread his hands. "So you see we are here only to help."

"Evacuate these voices," the imp said.

"Our happiness will be your happiness," the sombre man said. "*Paticca-samuppada.* We live, we die and we live again."

I felt like laughing at his illogic before I considered this arbitrariness was a common quality of all dreams. It is remarkable, is it not, that I should be aware of the structure of a dream while I was actually inside one? I closed my eyes and discovered that the sensation of insects running along my legs was gone. I tested my feet and found that although still numb, they could now move. However, I still felt a bit light-headed and drowsy, perhaps like the moment when one dream is transferred to another. I waited for the drowsiness to pass. I must have awakened then because I opened my eyes and, as you would expect, the room was empty.

When I tried to walk to the door, I stumbled to the floor. I waited for a short while, dragged myself to the window and saw it was close to morning. I considered the events of the night. Had I been drugged or was my residual paralysis caused by the severity of the nightmare? The rain that had begun in the night had tapered off to a drizzle. I stood watching out the window for an hour or so before I decided to visit the canteen. There was an odd ringing in my left ear and my balance was slightly off so I walked slowly, hoping the place would not be filled or at least everyone would be too distracted with something else to pay me any attention.

My wish was granted in a way. When I entered, I saw tables and chairs on the floor and Balzac and the group gathered on one side of the carriage. On the other side was a lanky man with goggles and some kind of chain-mail armour. From the state of the carriage and the manner they were glaring at the newcomer, I could tell there had been a ruckus. Now they seemed to be in a standoff. I was about to quietly leave when the stranger turned to me and said, "So you have decided to show your face. I should warn you that today Kothar means business. You are not going to escape this time." For a brief moment, I hoped he was rehearsing some line but as he stomped toward me, I knew my hope was misplaced.

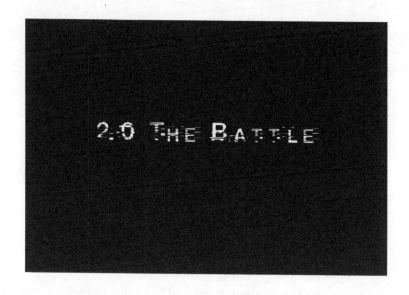

2.0 THE BATTLE

In my panic, the only thing that came to mind was, "If you do not like the role I can give you another."

He stopped so abruptly he almost toppled over. He pushed up his goggles and I saw that his frightfully red eyes were blinking slowly as if he was in pain. "Convince me."

"What would you like to be?"

"A man."

"Granted." There was a gasp from the group, but I felt Kothar was not impressed. This was confirmed by his bellowing laugh. "You were not here earlier so all the good roles were taken," I said encouragingly.

"You believe I am a random monster. A faceless monstrosity." He poured something liquid into his eyes and dispersed the liquid by poking his eyelids. "Do you know what I learned during my travels? Creatures with no faces deserve to be slaughtered. Who would take the time to rearrange the features? Have you ever looked at a pig? Poor things must be thankful just to be slaughtered. Rank ugliness. Tiny eyes. Snout. Cloven hooves. All that red flesh."

As he continued with his unnecessary description of a variety of animals, I was more taken up with his confession that he had travelled than with his clumsy self-pity. No one I had met so far had talked about the land outside the terminal. I interrupted his flow to ask, "Where did you go?"

He issued a prolonged, rickety sigh. "To wherever monsters roam? Should creatures like us saunter along merrily in the street where everyone is thinking the same thing? A single thought passed from woman to child? In Adjacentland, I was my own man."

"Where exactly is this land?" someone asked.

"Can we plot the coordinates?"

"Lolo need a cuddle."

"Will we meet our doppelgängers there?"

One by one the questions came and I saw this awkward giant who called himself Kothar losing his temper. I asked quickly, "How far away is this place? Can we get there?"

He seemed even more irritated as he shifted his scrutiny to me. "Why don't you tell me, Mr. Creator?"

"A creator who has abandoned his creation. It is most callous. It makes me hanker for gristle."

I didn't like the way the focus had suddenly shifted to me. But Kurt asked, "What colour is the sun in that place, my friend? And what is the power source?"

"Everything is powered by steam geysers. They have been using these strategically aligned vents for centuries."

Lolo began to swish and Balzac said, "Ingenious."

"Everything is ingenious to outsiders. Until it's no longer ingenious. Or they are no longer outsiders." He turned to me. "Are you one in this new rendering?"

I was not sure of his question but I told him, "I suppose I am." I noticed Fingers pointing to his head and smirking and, at another table, a group huddling and whispering.

Kothar continued, "Then you will find it intriguing that they treat epilepsy as an interruption between life and death?" I was silent for a while. I obviously didn't believe a word he had said but I briefly considered whether my own memory loss, or losses, occurred in sequences similar in nature to epilepsy. I wanted him to elaborate but he said, "This is how I live my life now. As an interruption." He grew morose and offered me his profile in a dramatic fashion, looking upward and pushing out his chin. I felt certain he was a character actor relegated to B-movie bits. He obviously carried a grudge. "I am an uncomplicated monster." He rubbed the side of his neck, twisting his head this way and that. "You made me one. Perhaps I should hog-tie you this very minute." He came rushing toward me and I moved away from the door in alarm. Outside, he slid down his goggles and gazed upward. There was a mask of suffering on his face. "I am certain this will not be the last you see of me."

"Where are you going?"

I immediately regretted the question but he answered as if he had ceaselessly rehearsed the line. "To where monsters roam. Where you have consigned me."

"You were not here when I explained my own confusion about the storyline. You must forgive me as I am trying to get a complete picture of –"

"How can any picture ever be complete until you step into the frame?" He made a circle with his thumb and forefinger and peered within as if he was watching through a camera's viewfinder. "Didn't you tell me with your own deceitful lips that nothing is complete unless it is viewed? Did you not? Be forewarned that the next view will not be pleasant." He walked away, chattering to himself and laughing.

Following his departure, everyone was silent. I felt that some of Kothar's despair had been transferred to the group because they were all staring at me sullenly. Eventually Balzac said, "Just when you think you have seen everything, a fearsome grappler returns with his bag of tricks." The Stenographer did a swift swoosh that resembled a question mark. Balzac shook his head and recited, "Atomic elbow, cobra-hold, camel-lock, clothesline, testicular claw, smoke and salt in the eyes. You name it." I had no idea what he was talking about but everyone seemed alarmed.

Sitting in the corner, his hat over his face, the man who called himself the Inquisitor and Fakir said, "Time is running out. If you say the phrase in the dappled moonlight, you can actually see the grains falling away. It's a harlequin spin."

I looked around at each of the carriage's occupants. I saw impatience, irritation, confusion and skepticism all overlaid with craziness. They seemed to be waiting for me to say something. Until I uttered the phrase, "It's time, then," I had no idea what I was going to say but my statement had the desired effect. "I don't have the ledger any longer so we will have to play it by ear. Impromptu performances." Now you may say that this was an act of stupidity, stringing along all these demented actors in a film that was a mystery to me, but I ask you: What choice did I have? In fact, I was surprised I had not thought of this before. In a sense, the loss of the ledger made no difference because I could never make sense of the storyboards and also because everyone in the carriage already seemed to have some understanding of their roles. Who knows? Perhaps the director, you and a group of pranksters might suddenly stream out from a carriage. This is the sort of unreality that has accompanied me since I found myself in the terminal.

"When will we leave?" the Inquisitor asked. "It must be soon because I can feel the turbulence a-gathering."

Why wait? "In the morning. We will gather in this carriage." The minute I left the canteen, I felt some disquiet about my decision to string along a group of actors in a film with no screenplay, director, cameramen and so on. I bolstered myself by thinking it would be better than doing nothing and witnessing the group growing more impatient each day. Maybe we would even find our way out of this abandoned terminal into some little town.

Alone in my carriage, I recalled the little girl's talk of a bus at the end of the track and my own explorations of the area and I decided that I would lead them to the field where I had seen her. Doubtless they would be angered by the fruitless trek, but I would deal with that situation when it arose. Perhaps this resolve to change my situation was overdue because that night I had the most restful sleep since I awoke in the terminal close to a month earlier.

When I got to the canteen, I saw Balzac with a broad grin, his ears high and erect. "You, my friend, are amazing," he told me almost immediately. I noticed Toeman looking over a sheet of paper and in the corner the Spiritmaster woman and the so-called countess glaring at one another. Fingers emerged from the kitchen with a great whorl of scarf and overcoat, leaped onto a table and squatted there. The countess woman seemed amused by all this but there was a trace of delectation, too, as if we were all putting on an act for her entertainment.

"What do you think of our group?" Fingers asked.

"Is everyone here?" The man who called himself the mathematician or whatever began to count, pausing several times only to begin once more. "Never mind," I told him. "It's time to leave."

"The Inquisitor is missing," Balzac said. "The erudite man wants to trust him, but it is not in the nature of the brute to trust someone who never shows his face."

Twenty minutes or so later, I stepped out of the carriage and the group followed me. I heard the Spiritmaster woman saying, "Something going to happen. Something bad. My left eye jumping."

On our way, Kurt emerged from another carriage. In his arms

was the Stenographer. He was holding him like a child. "What is our mission?" he asked.

"How many people will we have to kill? I can easily draw and quarter a dozen." Fingers said.

"Do you have a plan? Or a map?" someone asked.

"Is only spirits does talk without anybody seeing them."

They kept up their chatter as we walked down the platform and into the tunnel. Soon we were out of the terminal. I expected they would put up some protest as we headed for the forest but everyone was silent. As we approached the hill, I saw someone sitting at the brink and at first I assumed it was the man who had leaped off the other day but when we drew closer, I saw it was Kothar. He must have heard our conversation because he got up to face us and I saw leaves stuck onto his goggles and sprigs between his teeth.

"We mean you no harm, my friend." Kurt stepped forward, a hand held out, palm upraised in a stopping gesture.

Kothar took two clanking steps forward. Both men were equal in size and I felt for sure there would be a great struggle. "No harm?"

"Please step aside, sir."

"You have returned to mock me."

"I can assure you this is not our intention. Now, please step aside."

Kothar now seemed angrier. "Is it because I am a monster? A deformed replica?"

"A doppelgänger. We are nearing the other place. I knew –"

Kothar flicked aside Toeman and redirected his attention to Kurt. "And you have brought along all your friends. Yet there is no place for me. For the beast."

"You are free to join us. If your heart is pure," Kurt said placatingly.

Kothar thumped his chest. "I clean it every morning."

"Then you can join us, my friend."

I felt I should step in. "But you will have to amend your behaviour." He turned to me. "We cannot have you running around like a madman."

I expected he would be offended but he unleashed a horrible burst of laughter that ebbed into a suffocating wheeze. When he had recovered, he said, "You really don't know, do you? Not even you," he added, pointing directly to me. "The deformed man is the only normal one here. What joy!" He laughed wildly again.

"Would you mind explaining what you are talking about?" I asked.

He adjusted his goggles and spat out a piece of twig. "All of you are mad. Every single one of you. You, you, you, you, you and you."

"That is a harsh assessment," Balzac lisped.

The countess woman added, "You seem to be the only one mad here."

Then Kothar said something that was quite surprising. He said, "In a lopsided landscape, a symmetrical tree may seem crooked. Do any of you understand? Let me be more direct, then. Sanity seems like madness to a mad person."

"This could very well apply to you," I told him.

"I refuse to believe this. It's impossible. We are all gifted." This was Kurt.

"Well, here is another gift. You are all criminals. Felons and malefactors. Racketeers and arsonists. Murderers and abductors. Even you, Mr. Perfect," he told Kurt. "Scooped up from the hoosegow to have bolts of electricity shot into your brain. Only Kothar the Magnetician escaped because he is immune to electricity." He raised his head to the sky and bellowed like an overreaching performer.

"This is going too far, my friend," Kurt told him. "I will admit that Fingers and Balzac and the Inquisitor all have their dark sides, but to impugn everyone with that label is unfair. What proof do you have?"

"Proof? You want proof? Why do you think no one can remember anything? Why do you think you were sent here on this little field trip? Why do you think this terminal is deserted?" He then began to describe a compound from which he had escaped during an early round of treatment and a house he stumbled upon. "I can tell you things," he said. "Things they did to me. I hold you responsible," he added, pointing to me. "And you, too." He now gestured to Kurt and to the others. "But I escaped. And I have been free ever since. Free!" He spread his arms and his coat jangled.

I noticed he had not backed up his criminal claim but I was nevertheless struck by the fact that I was not alone in my memory loss. This was something I had not thought of before. Both Kothar and the orphan had used the pejorative *done* and I now considered they may have heard of – or been witness to – a particular proce-dure. They were the only ones not confined to the carriages and I could not help wondering what else they knew. Not that I believed Kothar, but I was beginning to wonder whether my companions were truly frustrated actors or if perhaps their psychoses ran much deeper.

While I was preoccupied with this thought, Kothar moved toward us. Fingers immediately sprung at him but reeled back, holding his hand and wailing. Most likely he had struck some steel armour or chain mail that Kothar wore underneath his jacket. Balzac rushed forward and unleashed a flurry of blows: jabs, uppercuts and a roundhouse right. Kothar staggered from the assault but suddenly he straightened his long arms and grabbed Balzac's ears and pulled upward. "That's an illegal grapple you have applied to me," Balzac screamed, unexpectedly turning erudite. "It merits an immediate disqualification."

Kurt stepped forward. "Leave, my friends," he said to us. "I will give you enough time." Both men began to strike one another, with straight blows, neither attempting to duck or evade the other's fists. As they plugged away it seemed like a battle of endurance. The blows appeared real enough but I glanced around to see if there were hidden cameras somewhere around. I saw a movement ahead of me and ducked when something landed at my feet. It was the girl's boomerang and she was gesturing from behind a thorny bush.

I picked up the boomerang and scrambled down the hill after her, but she had hurried away and I now saw her some distance ahead. I followed her once more and when I heard the crackling of bushes behind me, I turned to see the group hastening after me. I increased my pace and when I came to a sudden decline, it was too late to stop. The smooth shale was covered with some red mossy plant that made it impossible to slow my fall and once I got up, I had to step out of the way quickly because, one by one, the rest of the group rolled down. Soon the entire group, minus Kurt, was there.

"Get out of the way." Fingers brushed past us, leaped onto the hill and immediately toppled down. He tried a couple more times with the same effect. "It's too slippery," he said. The Stenographer made it halfway before he too rolled down. Fingers began to shout Kurt's name but stopped when we heard a conversation on the other side. At first, the voices were low and almost amicable, but this was soon replaced by shouting that in turn gave way to what was unmistakably a struggle. Someone was saying, "Hold him down." There was a thud and the sound of metal against rock.

"I am going up," Balzac said. As I expected, he landed right at our feet. He got up and began pounding the hill until his hands were completely red from the shale. He stopped when pieces of twigs and pebbles rolled from the top. Soon the sounds from above ceased.

"There might be another way up," Fingers said.

"Let's just go," I said tiredly.

For a while, no one said anything. Then the woman who called herself the Spiritmaster said, "It have a track there. I does see things." She pointed to a very narrow trail bordered by bristly shrubs. We made our way slowly and I felt that everyone was thinking of Kurt. Once again, I was struck at how much our little journey resembled the unrealistic plot of a cheap B movie and I desperately hoped the group was following a script that I had been unable to glean from the ledger. Still, the battle between Kurt and Kothar had been very convincing.

"A bus," the Spiritmaster shouted.

We began to run in that direction. The field was bigger than I imagined and it took a good twenty minutes before we got to the vehicle. No one seemed willing to get aboard and I wondered if, in their stifled memories, there was some anguish they associated with the vehicle. Perhaps we were all brought here, dazed and manacled. "Let me through," I told them. I stepped onto the vehicle. At first I believed it to be empty, then I saw the girl sitting on the seat at the back.

2.1 THE DELUGE

"There's only a child here."

"This is amazing."

The girl looked at us all red and ragged and smiled serenely.

"What's your name, orphan? And where is the driver?"

"My name is Dyenne," she said sweetly to the countess.

"A proper spirit name."

I made my way to the back of the bus and the girl said, "We have to leave quickly before the paladin gets here."

"Where will we go?"

"Away, but we have to hurry." She stood on the seat and shouted, "Is there anyone who can drive this bus?"

Regrettably, it was Fingers who answered. "In the nights when everyone is roosting I dream of contraptions."

"Anyone else?" I asked.

"In another universe, I –"

But Fingers was already behind the wheel and cranking the engine. He tried several times until the bus began to reek of diesel. "Hurry," the girl shouted.

"It's no use," he said. "There is no way to get this contraption to move."

"It's a harlequin spin. Should we stay on this spot and allow the turbulence to come to us or should we hasten along into the centre of the storm? Either way we shall arrive at the same spot." It was the man who called himself the Inquisitor and I wondered how he had found us here. He stepped on board, got behind the steering wheel and started the truck. "Fasten your seat belts," he said. "It's going to be a rocky ride."

Everyone sat. When I glanced back, I could not see the girl so I got up and spotted her hiding beneath the seat. "It's okay," I said, hoping to coax her to the seat but she refused to budge. I wondered whether she was frightened by the rocky driving and I was about to ask the Inquisitor to slow a bit when he stopped suddenly. The door opened and a rugged woman with khaki overalls got on board. I looked out and saw miles of abandoned fields and I wondered what the woman had been doing here.

From beneath the seat the girl asked, "Who was that?"

"A woman. I don't know where she came from."

"Does she have a cat?"

"Just a knapsack. And you should get out from there because you can knock your head in this rocky road."

"I don't want the driver to see me. Where are we now?"

We were passing through groves of spindly trees that interlocked from either side of the road to block most of the overhead light. The trees were wreathed in white and I thought of cotton balls. I described this to her and she asked why the bus was stopping once more. I turned to the front and saw the man who I had seen covered in cardboard. "Someone from the town. I don't know how he got here. He said his name was the Conductor."

"I knew this was a mistake. You got me into it. I should never have trusted you."

"Why are you so upset?" I asked her. "Would you prefer that the driver leave these people behind?"

"Everything is just like the beginning. All the same old people."

"Just be thankful we are going somewhere."

She said nothing for a while. I heard Balzac at the front asking the Conductor, "What were you doing here all alone?"

"Waiting. A man is always waiting, although if you would ask for what I will have to say it depends on the circumstances."

"Brilliant," Balzac said.

"What are they talking about?" the girl asked.

"I can't hear properly."

"Describe the view outside." When I did she said, "We are going the wrong way. I knew it."

"How do you know?" I asked her.

She eased a little from beneath the seat and glanced up. "Look at all the smoke getting out from the volcanoes."

I followed her gaze and saw steam rising from what appeared to be thermal springs. The entire area was marked with fissures and vents. I was about to relay the child's concern when I noticed that our worry was not shared by anyone; and once more I was rattled by my presence in this group. The Conductor was now leaning over Fingers' shoulder but whatever he was saying was lost in the whine of the bus. About fifteen minutes later, I observed in the distance what appeared to be a coastline and when we turned a sharp bend, I saw several pools of water covered with writhing weeds. The pools flowed into a lake and I saw now the sprouts of water flowing from nicks in the hill before us. A ridge of mountains behind the lake was so perfectly positioned they seemed to have been placed there.

"Why don't you do anything?" the girl asked me. "We are going right back to the start. I never should have trusted you."

"Why are you so afraid of the man giving directions?"

"Because he looks like a spider and he wants everything to remain the same. He can talk to animals, too. He is a spy. He pretends to be asleep, but he is like a powerful armadillo watching everything. I don't trust him. He tried to catch me, but I ran away. He was laughing and singing that he fell from heaven."

The rugged woman we had picked up glanced back and came over. "Have I seen you before?" she asked the girl. But the child returned to hiding and the woman said, "This place looks familiar."

She seemed to be awaiting some response and I told her, "I don't know. I may have seen a painting somewhere that depicted a similar scene." I did not tell her that in the painting there were blue beings and bazaars with men and women attempting impossible feats. Instead, I asked, "If it's familiar, do you know where our destination might be?"

"This is the only road, so we have no real choice," she said. "Are you a mortician, by chance?"

Her question surprised me. "I didn't know there was one in this script."

The bus seemed to be gathering speed. I got up and looked to the front and saw that we were approaching what seemed to be, from a distance, a dried-up lake. "Perhaps you should slow a bit," I shouted from the back.

Down we went. Faster and faster. Balzac and Fingers seemed excited and the Conductor was leaning over the driver. The girl now got up from beneath the seat. "There are people there. You will kill them, you crazy man."

I was about to tell her that the place was abandoned when I saw a group dragging a perfectly camouflaged sandy-coloured canopy. There were four of them, two on each end, and when they noticed the vehicle bearing down, they dropped the canopy and scattered. The basin appeared to be windy and the canvas convulsed like a dying animal before it took off, kite-like. We were heading straight toward the group. Now the girl was screaming. The vehicle lurched, seemed to hang in the air, straightened and settled on its side with a series of bangs. We were all flung to one side and the bus was enveloped in dust, much of it seeping through the windows.

By the time we had managed to climb onto the seats, the air in the bus was so hazy as to be opaque. Everyone was coughing. After a couple minutes, I heard Balzac's voice. "This is amazing. What were these men doing in this blighted place?"

My mind turned to the girl. "Hello," I called out and when there was no answer, I grew worried. I felt around and stopped only when I touched the leg of the rugged woman for whom we had stopped.

"Copping a feel?" she said. "This may not be the best –"

"I am searching for the child," I told her roughly. "Can you feel her?" I stumbled onto my knees and felt around more carefully this time. This is my fault, I thought. I had fooled myself into believing we were following a movie script, that we would find our way out of the terminal into a town, that I would once more be among rational men and women, that the child's talk of escape had been more than childish fantasy, but all I had accomplished was this disaster. Unless there were players hidden from sight, I was certain this could not be staged. I heard the front door creaking open and Balzac saying, "If Kurt was here he would have unbolted this trap in no time."

"I cannot calculate our coordinates in this dusty place."

"I think we have arrived at a portal. All the red dust…"

"Where is the driver? The Inquisitor?"

"We should be looking for the child," I fairly screamed out. "She's gone!"

"Maybe she is beneath a seat. I can lasso her with my rope and drag her out and hog-tie her."

"This is truly amazing. I feel obliged to announce that we are trapped. There is a herd of something out there blocking my path. Buffaloes and elephants."

Everyone grew silent. After a while Fingers said, "I wish Kurt was here."

There was another period of silence. The air inside the bus was now hot and rancid. I heard the Stenographer wheezing badly.

Someone said, "We have exactly twenty-five minutes before we drop dead."

Another whimpered, "A sweet-sweet mess."

"Where is the Conductor?" Balzac shouted his name but there was no reply. "He's gone, too," Balzac said. "How did they get through?"

I pushed my way past Fingers to the front and tried to step out but staggered back when I hit something that was coarse and pliant. It took a while before I realized it was the canopy, which had completely covered the bus. "It's the tent covering," I said. "We need to crawl beneath it."

One by one, we crawled out. The man who claimed to be an arithmetician counted everyone several times. I glanced around for the girl but she was nowhere. Some distance away, I noticed half a dozen sails spread on the ground and secured by pegs. The ends flapped in the wind and I walked toward the spot, hoping the child had hidden there. Someone was saying, "It looks like we interrupted something big."

"Were they building a vessel?" Toeman asked excitedly.

"I think we should try to find the girl," I pleaded.

"I don't understand where she could be hiding. This place is so flat. Do you think there might be tunnels? Maybe the men who were putting up this tent dragged her through."

"We should look for the girl before anything else," I insisted.

"It will take us precisely six hours."

"Then it will be too late."

"Maybe I should have fasted this morning."

"Can anyone see the driver and the dirty man we picked up?"

"I am a cosmic detective but I do not have my implements. I left my belt behind."

"This scenery here is amazing. Is it on the other side?"

On and on they went and I realized that Dyenne would most likely be gone for good by the time they settled on some course. I set off on my own. I expected someone would follow me, but when I glanced back I saw they were still arguing so I walked at a fast pace toward the closest laid-out canopy or whatever it was. When I got to the spot, I realized that it had not been secured with pegs but with rocks placed on the edges. I walked from one end to the other, feeling with my feet for a covered tunnel. Just to make sure I lifted the ends and peered beneath. "Hello," I shouted.

A woman was sitting in an air pocket with her hands clasped around her knees. She was so frail that, for a moment, I believed it may have been the girl but when I crawled through, I saw it was a painfully thin woman wearing some sort of blinders. "Hello. I am looking for a child."

"There is no child. She is gone."

Beneath the canopy, the woman's voice sounded like the cry of a dying bird. "Did you see her?" I asked. She said nothing and I added, "She jumped off the bus and there is no sign of her. There were men putting up some kind of tent but they, too, have disappeared. Did you see the girl or the men?"

"There is no girl, no tent, no men, no bus."

I now considered the woman was blind and had been trapped beneath the canopy. She looked sick, too, clutching her knees. I asked, "Is there something wrong with you?"

"There is no girl."

"Yes, I know that. But she was with us on the bus."

"There is no girl. Why don't you understand? I was a wet nurse once."

"A what?" She hunched herself tighter and I told her, "I am going to look for her. I think you should come, too, or you will suffocate under this canvas."

"I am safe here. The light outside will erase me. Leave me alone, please."

"Are you one of the actors? Were the men putting up the canopy creating a stage? I should have thought of this before."

"Yes."

"Did you say yes? I can barely hear you." She seemed to nod at my question. "So all of this is part of an act? All pre-arranged and staged?" She nodded once more and I didn't know whether I should feel relief that I was not trapped with a group of madmen or disappointment that my hopes of escape were now further complicated because I was caught in this mess of a film. "Do you know how it's going to end?"

"It never ends but this time it may be different. Everyone is here too soon."

"Before the set was built?"

"Yes. Too soon."

She seemed so confused that I told her, "I am going to get the child. Are you sure you want to stay here?"

"I am only here."

"Well…okay," I told her as I crept out from beneath the canopy.

"Did you see the girl?" The woman with the medallion was standing outside the canopy. "Is she hiding in there?" she asked.

The group soon came up to her side. Lolo stooped and made his way inside the canopy. "There is no one here," I heard him shouting a few minutes later. He emerged, dusting himself.

"There was a woman inside," I told him. He shook his head and I told the group, "Let us try to shift it. If we all hold an end, we

might manage. Everyone hold an end and walk toward each other."
The arithmetician began counting as we all lined up around the
canopy. It was quite heavy and because of the breeze, it took a while
before we were able to get it off the ground.

"Walk to the left."

"Walk to the right."

"We cannot do both at the same time."

"Hold it over your head."

The canvas flapped violently in the air and when some of the
group loosened their hold the rest were forced to do likewise. It took
off and flew like an airborne ship. Unexpectedly, I recalled a poem or
story of three men. Wynken, Blynken and Nod. My retrieval was
interrupted by the medallion woman who said, "There is no one here."

"Maybe she has covered herself with sand."

"Like a lizard."

"An armadillo."

"But she will suffocate."

"What should we do?"

"We should smoke her out and hog-tie her."

"There was a woman here," I insisted.

"We need to be seated now," an unfamiliar voice directed.

"Who are you?" the so-called countess asked the newcomer,
who I saw was wearing a battered hat. "Were you on the bus with
us?"

"I am the usher," the man said as he limped closer to me. "Do
you have your tickets? I can get you a group discount."

"The girl…" I tried to remind the group.

"How old is she? I can get her in half-price," the usher said.

"There is no girl," Tiffin said.

"No woman," Knife added.

"Maybe they got caught with the wind. My calculations tell me
it's eighty knots per hour."

As they continued their debate, going this way and that, asking questions in the manner of infants and offering their own tangled responses, I felt a wave of tiredness that was so sudden and leaden, it felt as solid as twin planks on my shoulders. And from this great exhaustion, I recalled awakening in the terminal with no idea how I got there and who I was. I recalled the insistence of the others that I somehow was connected to their presence there. I remembered their veneration of the ledger and its subsequent loss. I thought of the fire in the smoker and the dream of the three men who insisted I was a paranoiac who had co-opted others into my madness. I recalled the girl who claimed that I was a part of a group whose memories were stolen or transplanted and Kothar babbling about the same thing, more or less. And I thought of the woman who I had imagined just a few moments ago, vanishing. I walked away from the group before they could involve me in more of their folly.

Other recollections crowded my more recent concern; memories I could not understand and which were, therefore, useless. But for the first time I was in the picture. I saw myself, almost unrecognizable, writing phrases over and over: *Today is a new day* and *Nothing exists until we deliver our verdict* and *The past is just a place not yet visited*. Other memories, accompanied by flashes of light, flared and died so swiftly they left only the taste of the emotions to which they were tied. Neglect, shame, apprehension, anxiety, helplessness, calculation, guilt, indifference, absolute emptiness. If the girl's claims were right, we would never know who we truly were because there would be all these other influences bouncing around and jostling for prominence. Our thoughts and decisions would never be directed by our own experiences but through the urgings of strangers. Uninvited boarders and lodgers. In a way, we were strangers to ourselves.

Maybe she was right. I was – and had been for a long time – a stranger to myself.

Balzac was not a brute, Fingers not a spectral detective, and so forth. The three dream-men had suggested that I was a writer who used my imaginative talents to colour and shade the more gullible among us. They may have been half right; I was certainly not a writer who had influenced anyone into forming a team, but it was not unlikely that, in seeing all these men and women in the manner I preferred, I might have encouraged their simulations. And someone, at some point, must have encouraged mine. Kothar, the maddest of the mad, had grasped a fragment of this bitter truth.

Whether it was my confusion, or my tiredness, I cannot say but I almost stumbled to the ground. I heard voices. "Don't bother. There is no girl," I shouted.

"You, my friend, are amazing. I did not see that coming. I am flabbergasted."

"But didn't we all see her on the bus?" This was the medallion woman and I desperately hoped she would be less pliant than the others.

"Which bus?" I asked as I walked away.

I heard their voices behind me.

"He's right."

"Which bus?"

"Which of the three?"

"There's another bus."

"And another behind it."

"Which bus?"

"A tent is going up, too."

I ran away from them, falling to the ground and picking myself up once more. On the third fall, I felt blood running down my nose but I kept running with the hope that they were all wrong and there were no buses and no tent; I hoped I would turn to find I was alone in a field and I would continue walking until I reached the end, however far that may be. And at the end, I would discover that I was either dreaming or I was deranged and I would simply reawaken or accept my derangement. I would not question my current state and not wonder about what was real. I would be awake and drowsy or mad and happy. And thinking this, I felt a deep relief as if all I had held back during the last month was now solidifying and rising to the surface. For the first time, I wanted to be so truly out of my mind there would be no chance of me hoping to recover my memories.

I remembered someone telling me that there was no point in a life because all lives were repetitions of small acts decorated with beguiling significance. I remember boasting of my ability to focus and think in patterns and anticipate. But none of that was important now. It was time to close the curtains, to fall asleep, to give up. And so when I turned briefly and I saw the group running away from me and toward the canopies that were being tugged open and upward, ballooning before they were stabilized, I refused to be either alarmed or astonished.

I paused for a moment, but only for a moment to see a huge tent being formed. There seemed to be a row of buses and caravans and from each of these vehicles shuffled out passengers who appeared to be guided by men in white cloaks.

From a great distance I heard Balzac saying, "This is truly amazing." And what sounded like the tap of a finger on a microphone and a voice amplified by a speaker saying, "Prepare to be amazed. Witness the spectacle of a man driven to multiple worlds of darkness and despair."

I resumed running so I would hear nothing.

"Brought back to the beginning," the voice boomed. "Which of the six worlds will he be thrown into? Stay with us to find out."

"Can a man without wings propel himself to the heavens? Wait for it," the voice cajoled.

There was a ringing in my right ear and I felt light-headed from the heat and my exertion.

"Wait. It's coming now."

"Shut up," I mumbled. I wanted to part from this. I was simply a crazy man experiencing another hallucination. "Shut up! Leave me alone!"

"Here it comes." I was now speeding faster than I would have imagined, not stopping even when I heard a terrible thunderclap followed by the sound of expelled air. Faster now. I saw water barrelling out from the sides of the basin as if it were a giant dam coming apart. The ground grew slippery from the water and I fell several times. Soon the water was around my knees and then my chest. I flailed away and when I felt the current taking me back toward the group and the amplified voice and the caravans, I dived and swam against the flow. I did this several times and I believed I was making some progress until the undercurrent grew too strong for me. I tried to maintain my direction but the current turned me around and on my back. Something brushed past me and I saw it was the girl. I tried to shout to her and swallowed mouthfuls of sulphurous water.

I dived once more, but the water was too murky now and when I surfaced, the current spun me around. I stopped resisting and just tried to keep afloat until the flood abated. But it was surging and waves erupted from beneath and lashed me so violently I could feel the sand abrading my skin. Surprisingly, the microphone was still functioning and I intermittently heard the recorded voice saying, "I touched them and they felt pain. But they grew used to the pain and turned it against me."

My chest was burning and I realized the water had turned salty. But it was clearer now and I saw dark shapes tossed around, animals from the caravan that must have been swept away by the flood. I saw what appeared to be a boar and a bull and a giant fish with fanning scales. Then they were all gone. I was tiring and I had no idea how long I had been struggling. The others must have surely drowned as they were on lower ground. But what about Dyenne? When I surfaced, I tried to stupidly call her name and swallowed mouthfuls of salty water. I vomited and took in more water. I could no longer feel my legs either from fatigue or from dizziness. The current must lead somewhere, I thought. There is no point in struggling.

I closed my eyes and forced my body to go limp. Every now and again, I crashed against an object and I had this sensation of being simultaneously dragged down and pulled upward. And in these jolting arcs, I imagined I saw – trapped within their own trajectories – Balzac and Fingers and Kothar and the other members, and the group of tiny seniors I had seen at the terminal, and men and women I could not recognize. I saw the usher trying to hold on to his hat and another man so old and pale he was almost transparent. Everywhere, bodies seemed to be tumbling.

I saw Dyenne, too, and I thought that this moment before I drowned I might finally be granted my wish: my life would flash before me and I would see – however briefly – all that I had been trying to remember. I closed my eyes and waited. When nothing came, I deliberately swallowed mouthfuls of water. I forced my eyes open until I felt they would be pried out from my skull. Then I shut them, grew limp and allowed the water to take me.

A boy is in a park with his little sister. He is chasing after balloons while she is collecting flowers. Their parents, sitting on a bench, wave to them and the father points to the setting sun. Now, the boy is walking home from school and when he gets to his house, his parents are in the kitchen alone. Before them are scattered photographs. Now, the father is missing and the mother, trailed by her daughter, is not looking at the photographs but walking through the house with her huge spectacles. The house changes and there are many rooms. In one of these rooms is an old man looking at the floor while a younger man stands over him. The old man is in a wheelchair and he is dribbling on his knee. The younger man returns to a desk surrounded by books. He seems deeply occupied with his work, drawing diagrams and scribbling equations. Occasionally he glances at some of the framed pictures that had been in the first house. When he walks out of the building, he goes to a different house. A woman is waiting for him at the doorstep. The neighbour, a muscular man wearing a bandana, pauses his mowing and waves. Inside the house, the couple seems to be arguing. The man explains he must go on a trip and then he is in a vehicle looking out at the bridges and the hill in the distance.

What an ordinary life, I thought. But why should it have been different? What exactly was I expecting? Were these final moments expunged of everything traumatic; sanitized to provide a final restitution?

"Hurry."

Something touched my shoulder. "Hurry," came the voice again. I opened my eyes and I saw Dyenne riding on a wide plank that resembled a door. A huge wave tossed her farther away and another brought her back. I managed to grasp the end of the plank and I held on. "I told you," she said. "I told you I could fly."

The water was rising and soon I felt the undercurrents ebbing, but now the waves, though farther apart, were growing bigger. Once the plank capsized and I worried the girl was gone but I saw her climbing from the water, her hair splayed like wet grass. When I pulled her up, she pointed to another wave, and we both crouched low. And whenever we spotted a wave – spaced about half a minute apart – we crouched and grabbed the plank. We now seemed to be at the basin's top and I had this faint hope that we would be carried along the route from which we came and that the surge would dash against the sides of the hills and flood all the valleys until it filled the lake I had seen from the bus.

But close to the top, I noticed we were spinning and I suspected this vortex meant that the water was being emptied from beneath and that as the vortex's intensity increased, we would be tossed and smashed until we drowned. I pointed to the top of the basin, to a narrow outcrop, and motioned the girl to paddle toward it. But we were going against the current. I made a spinning motion with my hand to indicate we would again be reeled in the opposite direction and when she gestured frantically, I assumed she wanted some clarification so I shouted, although I was sure she would not hear. Then she released her hold on the plank and pointed to a swirling mess of cardboard from which the head of the Conductor was bobbing. I tried to reach across with one hand held out but she crept closer and began pulling my shirt. In any case, the current was carrying us farther from him.

I decided to wait until we were once more brought back to the spot, although I was sure he would be gone by then. Dyenne seemed terrified and as we made the circle, I felt she was more afraid of the Conductor than of the flood. She was frozen and I had to point to the approaching outcrop. When we were about ten yards away, I made a sudden decision and pushed her off the plank and jumped behind her; I knew she could swim because she was the only other person who seemed to have survived.

We swam madly until we managed to reach the outcrop. Just in time, too, as a huge wave was now swelling the middle of the basin. "Hold tight, child," I said as it came toward us. Something crashed against my head, and light, ragged and dazzling, swept over me.

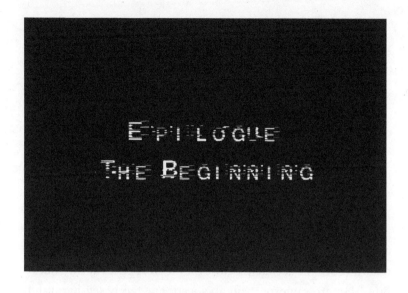

EPILOGUE
THE BEGINNING

The blue light is blinding and I cannot open my eyes for more than a couple seconds. My head feels numb and heavy and when I try to touch my forehead, I feel metal that is polished and curved. It takes a while before I realize I am wearing a helmet bolted to the bed. Earlier this morning, I felt skin instead of metal, the flesh raw and swollen where the screws had been implanted.

There are three of them peering over me and because of the light positioned directly above, I cannot see their faces. "We were waiting for you," the toadlike middle man says.

"Do you know me?" I ask tiredly.

The toad says, "Well, that depends on who you are. Would you care to help us?"

I take my time in answering. "I am not sure. How long have I been like this?"

"It's been two months and three days."

"We have been waiting."

"Do not be alarmed."

"You have been drifting in and out of consciousness."

I notice the tubes running into my arms and ask, "Where am I? Is this a hospital?"

"Don't bother yourself. You are safe now."

"We have all the amenities here."

"Although we have not used them for a very long time."

"To get back to our question…do you recall anything of the accident?"

"There was an accident?" I ask.

"Let us put that aside until you are well enough."

"Do you recall anything?"

I shake my head and they huddle in the corner of the room, away from the light. When they return, three days later, they ask once more of the accident. Before they leave, I pose my own question. They grow unexpectedly apologetic and talk of self-harm and suicide. They hint that I have indulged in this vaporization – their word – more than once and through different means. Leaping off a cliff, wandering alone until I was dehydrated, ingesting a poisonous substance, jumping into a pond. "But you are better now," the toad says to me.

I cannot tell if it's a question or a diagnosis. I say, "I don't know," and the response seems to please them.

They visit twice a week and then weekly. I believe a month has passed although I cannot be certain. The only other visitor is an attendant, a robust woman with a metallic name tag. She brings me my meals and cleans me every morning. She is rough and appears to hate her duties and when I am finally able to take a few steps to the washroom, she appears relieved. Still, she checks up on me and I believe it is mostly to chase away the men and women I see looking through the glass window as they pass by. Some of them wave to me but I turn away.

This morning I was finally transferred to a little room furnished with a bed, an escritoire with teeth marks and an iron safe. There are drawings on the walls and beneath the escritoire is a Gladstone bag with some personal effects. Next to the bag is a wicker basket with other drawings and a clutch of letters.

The three men question me about the letters and the illustrations.

"Do you know anything of the articles in your room?"

"Who might have left them there?"

"Do you know why someone would plaster their walls with useless drawings?"

I never tell them that they are not useless. Instead, I say, "Maybe the person who occupied the room before me was trying to pass time."

"Past time?"

When I understand the confusion, I spell the word. They seem satisfied. Still, they ask about the letters. Again, I cite the previous occupant.

"So there is nothing familiar about the letters?"

I shake my head. And I am convinced they do not suspect that I know the letters, deliberately vague, were all mine; written by me, to me, insisting that I create some kind of record; a timeline to guide me through the cycles of simulations. They do not suspect either that I have discovered that the drawings serve the same purpose.

The recent interviews take place in the library. They ask about the books, particularly those that deal with memory loss. I tell them that I have not stuck with any because they are just as confusing as all the others with their chapters rearranged. Once, the fat man who always takes the centre position asked me, "Why would someone take the time to sabotage perfectly good books?"

I didn't say it had been done to reflect my own prior states: the endless loops, the seizing of time, the commingling of different lives. I didn't say that I had done it myself. I told them, "I see idlers around the place. One of them must have done it."

They ask about these idlers. Do I know any of them? Have there been any contacts? What about outsiders? Sometimes, they cite passages from books or snippets of films or descriptions of fantastic places and I pretend ignorance for each. It will take a while before they are completely convinced, but I can wait. So I listen to them talk of dissociative identities and sleep paralysis and something they call "alters" and I shake my head blankly. Each day I remember something new, but because these retrievals are arbitrary, I have yet to place them in order and I know it will take a while before a chronology emerges. They ask about this, too, about my memory and I tell them that everything has been erased and with their help, I hope to slowly improve.

"It will take time. Every retrieval unspools some reconstruction."

"I am a blank slate," I said.

I try not to smile or show distress or anxiety or annoyance or even confusion.

During one of these conversations, the toad said, "This is the way of the world. The only certain outcome is the one we are most fearful of." I thought he was taking of death, but he added, "Erasure. The most primal fear is of darkness and of the night. What if the night washes away our memories and we awake as someone else? What if our souls are stolen? Are you worried by any of this?"

"I want to get better."

Sometimes, they go through a list of questions that are so unconnected I know they hope that one or more might register and I would randomly provide some information. They ask if I would leave the place if the opportunity presented itself and if I maintain a journal or a routine and whether I blame anyone for my situation, and questions about the benefits and dangers of disambiguation. During these times, I close my eyes and pretend I am sleeping. I do this often because, during these moments, they tell me in a cajoling, almost soothing manner – the tone that a mother might use in reciting a bedtime tale to her daughter – of a comic book writer who had become so close to his characters he had been unable to differentiate the events of his own life from those he had created for his characters. Once, the one who speaks in a gloomy voice used the word *breakthrough*. I prefer these stories, with their funny comic book character names like Cake and Kothar and Balzac to their lectures on procedural memories and psychoses of various kinds.

My ignorance is contrived but my tiredness, frequently, is not. I spend most of my days in my room, trying to arrange the pieces. In the late evenings, when everyone in the Compound seems to have settled in a kind of stupor, I walk through the zigzagging hedges, past the cemetery, to the back. Once I saw a brutish-looking man who seemed to be following me, but he soon disappeared. At first, I never ventured too far because I associated the tinnitus in my left ear and my bouts of dizziness with the altitude of the hill, but that has now passed and I am relaxed – as much as is possible – by the isolation and the view of the field beneath. In this setting, it is easy to reflect on the stories told by the three men. Earlier today, they related the tale of a lowly comic book writer who had created a group of heroes to take on all the established deities, the "old gods whom he blamed for the series of misfortunes in his life." Unexpectedly, the stories found an audience, prompted perhaps by the writer's decision to create heroes who were not only imperfect, but grotesque and demented. The stories were viewed as satirical and slyly subversive and darkly funny, but the writer was dead serious. He began to believe he was divinely inspired and he often referred to himself as the "last of the inspired prophets."

This writer, they say to me, had created a mythical place he called Adjacentland. Increasingly, he began to believe that his creations were real. "As the latchets of his madness tightened, it was precisely to such a place, devoid of rules and order that the writer journeyed." The sclerotic man tapped his head and continued in his sombre voice. "The chaos, you see, perfectly mirrored that of his mind."

At this point in the story, the toad had laughed, his body swelling with each chuckle. "Like all prophets, this madman was inspired only by his own hallucinations. Memory is a gift, a wound, a curse, an obligation. What do you think?" he had asked.

"I cannot say," I replied. "It may be all of those. Or none. It's confusing."

I remember another story. A comic book writer who, as they say, created a group of heroes to take on the gods. But their adversaries were not the old gods but the machines, the new gods who had determined the imagination, that primitive impulse, led only to chaos. And so the heroes were not superpowered beings but psychoneurotic men and women whose weapons were the only things feared by the machines. Emotions. Dreams. Visions. It took me my entire recuperative stay here to piece together the rest. To do this I had to fit together my scattered memories as I had done the books in the library, the notes I had left to myself, the cryptic warnings. I wonder at the effort I had taken to leave these elaborate clues that only I would understand.

I recall a paragraph from a book I had glimpsed earlier with the misleading title *A Romance Most Likely: When it was discovered that the primitives and the blighted, those who believed in spirits and sprites were the only ones still imbued with exteroception, still susceptible to visions and fancies and fevered dreams, still capable of compassion and a degree of memory consolidation, these outcasts became the focus of extended and elaborate experiments.*

But I tell the three old men, "It seems likely."

After each visit to the hill, I return with a leaf or a pebble or a pod or a piece of glass or bark or shell. I line these up in my room. They are my new markers, I suppose, a record of the days passing by.

Last night, as I was about to return, something fell at my feet. I picked it up, glanced around and pushed it in my jacket. Late in the night, I examined the ornate carving of a bird on the boomerang and because this was a special object, I hid it in the safe, next to the pills and oblong tablets I had pretended to ingest.

Acknowledgements

I would like to thank the Canada Council. And Paul Vermeersch for giving this novel a home. A chance encounter, a confession and a commitment.

About the Author

Rabindranath Maharaj is the award-winning author of three short story collections and five novels, including *The Amazing Absorbing Boy*, which won the 2010 Trillium Book Award and the 2011 Toronto Book Award, and was voted a CBC Canada Reads Top 10 for Ontario.

In 2012, Maharaj received a Lifetime Literary Award, administered by the National Library and Information System Authority as part of the commemoration of Trinidad's fiftieth independence anniversary. In 2013, he was awarded the Queen Elizabeth II Diamond Jubilee Medal, which honours significant contributions and achievements by Canadians.